The Seven Letters

Jan Harvey

Matador
9 Priory Business Park,
Wistow Road, Kibworth Beauchamp,
Leicestershire. LE8 0RX
Tel: 0116 279 2299
Email: books@troubador.co.uk
Web: www.troubador.co.uk/matador
Twitter: @matadorbooks

ISBN 978 1785899 089

British Library Cataloguing in Publication Data.
A catalogue record for this book is available from the British Library.

Printed and bound in the UK by TJ International, Padstow, Cornwall
Typeset in 11pt Minion Pro by Troubador Publishing Ltd, Leicester, UK

Matador is an imprint of Troubador Publishing Ltd

To Paul, for everything

Prologue

The old woman's shrew face tightened above mean, thin lips. She was so close I could feel her hot sour breath on my face. She held up a pair of heavy black scissors and wrapped a twist of my hair around her fingers. Then she pulled the strands towards her and the blades took hold, the softness trapped in the sharpened metal. She chopped and spliced until my hair fell in defeated heaps around me. A razor was dragged across my scalp, it nicked at the skin, slices of pain. If I raised my head even slightly I could see leering faces, four of them, so I kept my eyes fixed on the cracked tiles beneath me. When it was done I was trembling.

'Get her up, make her stand.' It was easy enough, I was thin and sapped of strength. Their eyes bulged, eager with excitement and anticipation. The words were hissed in my ear; 'Strip her!' I saw only her flat, dirty shoes. They didn't stop to undo buttons but ripped and pulled apart my dress. Then, with a single slice of a blade, my bra was cut off so that my breasts were naked.

'Go on!' It was the oldest woman, the one in the widow's weeds, her eyes glazed blue with cataracts. 'Do it.' They pulled off my knickers. The thin fabric tore away easily.

A fifth one, in the shadows behind me, grasped at my

buttocks, her dirty nails scratching the skin. The others howled with laughter. 'Give her the child. Fetch him!'

I snapped out of my trance, the whole room was suddenly loud and real and they reeked of old, rotted things.

'No! Not him.' I cried. 'Do what you will with me, but please not him.'

'Whore, whore, whore...' they chanted, ignoring my pleas. The door opened and I saw his little face grubby with the tell-tale marks of tears on his sweet cheeks.

The old man who carried him in sneered at my nudity, taking in the swell of my breasts with a lecherous grin. Yes, I thought, for all that I am a whore you too would have me right now, right here. He shoved the boy into my arms with a crude roughness, just as he might have treated a sack of kittens to be drowned. The child smelt foul, of dirt and grease and other people's sweat. He had passed the stage of crying. Spent of tears, he sought me for comfort and nestled his face into my neck, his thin arms clinging on for all he was worth. I clung to him too, covering his face with my hand, as if it were possible in some way to shield him from what was to come. What hope was there of that?

They opened the door and the noise from outside swelled. It was a dull late summer's day, the branches of the plane trees stretched towards a colourless sky. Perhaps if I kept looking up towards the sky I would not see what was coming. Perhaps, I thought, even now God would look on me and take pity, but He wasn't there for me, I knew it.

The crowd mocked as the women pushed me forward into the street, their screeching exciting more animal noises from the mob. Someone was braying like a donkey and the man, his face melted from eye to chin, spat on me - a globule of green phlegm landed on my shoulder. I felt the blow of a missile as it hit the small of my back and trickled red down the inside of my legs. The remains landed between my feet, a blackened tomato. Then something else struck me on the forehead and I saw a rotten windfall apple on the road, the brown, dead skin oozing a slash of rotten flesh.

We were both shivering with fear; I could hear a low animal moan running through him. I pressed his face to mine; his thin shirt and shorts were all that was between him and my cold flesh.

I set my eyes forward as I took cold, hesitant steps along the wet road. I had no way of protecting myself from the things they hurled at me and there were hundreds of them lining the way. They were catcalling, howling and calling me a whore over and over again, until the sound was a wall around me.

I desperately searched the crowd for his face, just one glimpse, just to know he had found out, that he had tried to do something to save me, but he was not there.

Then I saw Pollo. Her hair was gone, her body was covered in red welts so, like me, she was pathetic. A large man hauled up her limp body, her head was lolling to one side, her once beautiful face distorted. Another man, his sleeves rolled back, turned towards her holding a long piece of metal, steam rising from the end of it. There was a smell of fire, burning metal and a glow of bright red.

Someone in the crowd barged at me, making me stumble so that I lost sight of her for a moment, then the mob roared and when I saw her again I realised what they had done. The smell of burning flesh seared through the wet air.

They had branded her.

Why didn't she react? Why didn't she scream? I couldn't see. There were people crowding round her, spitting on her, but I could do nothing, except offer a prayer to God that she was already dead. I asked if he would take me too, kill me here on this cold, sodden street in Paris, but spare an innocent child who should live without blemish, despite all that I have done.

Spare him, I cried from the depths of my heart. Please God, spare him!

Chapter One

When I saw him on the bridge my first instinct was to call and attract his attention, but I was going to work, my laptop bag slung over my shoulder, the train due any minute. I sighed because talking to Freddy would have been far preferable to slogging into London on such a beautiful day. I stood and observed him fondly for a second, wondering where he was going.

He was looking across the cricket pitch towards the ragged line of houses on the escarpment. In the cloudless blue sky above, a red kite wheeled soundlessly on a thermal. It was a bright, clean summer's day, Oxfordshire at its best.

The train's horn sounded as it approached the station. By now it would be curving around the embankment, the low rumble of its wheels on the metal tracks, heading towards the bridge and the station. He was wearing his famous mustard cords and brown checked shirt, his mop of wiry hair more white than grey these days.

Then, as I watched, he raised a shaky foot onto the lower ledge of crumbling masonry. His limbs were stiff, making his movements jerky and awkward. He missed his footing but tried again, determined. Before I could take it in he was standing on the flat top stones of the parapet, swaying back and forth. The dull hum of the diesel engine

1

switched to a sharp squealing of brakes and then a hollow engulfing roar – and he was gone.

Just like that.

The sky remained high and blue. The kite was still turning lazy circles in the air and behind me two horses nibbled the balding grass in their field, as if nothing had happened, but where Freddy had been there was an empty space.

For a moment everything was suspended, unreal. Then I began to run. I dumped my bag and hurtled across the road. A horn blared and a van swerved around me, but I could only focus on the bridge. When I reached it my breath was clawing inside my lungs, I could barely breathe. A walker was there too, long hiking sticks in his hands; he was peering over the flat stones. 'Did you see that? A man, he – he just jumped off there.'

The metal-ridged roof of the train snaked back to the bend and beyond. Red doors broke the line of its blue flanks and at each one baffled faces were appearing, straining to see what had happened. Brakes hissed and there were echoes of voices from under the bridge.

It took me a few moments to register the long slash of blood on the westbound track as if a giant finger had swept red ink across the sleepers and the chippings. Then I vomited, a hot brown liquid splashed across the pavement. The walker backed away as I retched uncontrollably. He was keeping his distance, a look of revulsion on his face.

'What the hell were you playing at?' The man striding towards me was bald, a tattoo on his thick neck. He was wearing red overalls streaked with oil. His fists were balled tight and his broad shoulders blocked out the sun. I could feel the heat of his breath on my face. 'I almost killed you, you stupid woman!'

'I'm sorry,' I said weakly.

'Hold on mate!' It was the walker stepping between us. 'She's just seen something horrible, a man's just jumped.' All at once it felt like I was being pulled down to the footpath and the air was too thick and warm to breathe. A pair of strong arms hoisted me up and I felt myself being half carried, half walked on jelly legs until I felt damp grass under me and I was lying against a low stone wall.

The hand that passed me the bottle of water belonged to another man wearing a leather jacket and jeans. He placed my bag at my side, against my leg.

'Here, take a swig and then a nice deep breath,' he said gently. He had kind brown eyes. I nodded gratefully. My insides had spasmed into a hard, angular pain. I couldn't speak. He placed a reassuring hand on my shoulder. 'Take it easy, that's it …take a deep breath. I guess you knew him?'

'Yes,' I replied. I clutched my hand to my stomach, trying to stave off the pain. 'He's my friend.' Tears welled up and caught in my mascara, little black blobs of water blurring my vision.

Other commuters had gathered in huddles around us, a forest of legs. Everywhere heads were being shaken in disbelief and frustration. Watches were checked and checked again, phones were pressed to ears and they spoke in short staccato sentences. The walker was still there in my peripheral vision talking on his phone: 'Old man, yes, jumped, definitely dead, no doubt.'

In the distance I could hear sirens, then blue lights

were flashing between houses and hedges, weaving down through the town. Passing cars were slowing and curious faces peered out from them. A child in a school cap, eyes round in his freckled face, stared at me. Other people dressed smartly in suits for work were coming up the slope looking first at me and then over the parapet at the stationary train, asking each other what had happened, who had seen what?

I took another sip of water. The man with the kind brown eyes was still there crouching next to me and I noticed how worn the leather was at the end of his sleeves, it was a well-loved jacket.

'Can you stand up?' he asked as people began to loom over us, too close. I nodded and took his hand. My trousers were wet with dew and I felt them peeling away from my skin as I struggled to my feet. He led me to an old black Discovery parked on the verge across the road. Its tailgate was open and inside I could see camera bags, lights and tripods.

He took a tin foil blanket out of a First Aid kit and unwrapped it; 'Here, put this around your shoulders, you've had a bloody awful shock, you need to keep warm.' He placed my bag next to me on the sill of the boot. I could see my folder of meeting notes was crushed under my MacBook. I didn't care.

'I was coming down the hill,' he told me. 'I saw you screaming. You ran into the road and that man over there nearly hit you.'

I began to shiver and pulled the thin foil around me. I couldn't remember screaming. I felt numb, nothing seemed to make sense and suddenly I felt overwhelmingly grateful to him for being there.

4

'I'm Connie,' I told him as my teeth began to chatter. 'Thank you for stopping to help me, I don't know how I...'

'Matt,' he said. 'It's no problem, anyone would have done the same.'

At that moment a police car pulled up beside us. A young, fresh-faced officer climbed out, placing his cap over spiky hair.

'Are you all right, madam?' he asked.

'This lady saw it,' Matt told him. 'She's called Connie and she's a friend...of...'

The policeman nodded, seasoned to it all. 'Are you hurt at all, Connie?' I shook my head. 'Shocked, eh, looks like you've been a bit faint?' He put a hand on my arm. 'Does the gentleman concerned have any relatives?'

I felt a great sob heave through my body, it was a moment before I could speak. 'He has a housekeeper, Harriet, Hat. They are very close.' I gave him the number.

'Thank you, Connie. You take it easy and we'll be back to sort you out in a few minutes.' His colleague walked past us with a large roll of incident tape in his hand and the two of them talked together, organizing a cordon.

Things had begun, the separating of Freddy's existence from our own, a thin spit of formality that would become a solid, impenetrable wall.

Matt sat down beside me and we watched in silence as people were herded away. 'For one horrible moment, when I saw you running, I thought you were his daughter,' he said.

'No, he was my friend. I met him the day I moved here. He insisted I called in for afternoon tea the next Sunday, and I did. He was eccentric and complex and sometimes hard to know, but none of that mattered...'

My voice trailed away, everything suddenly felt so bleak and hollow. How could I describe the relationship I had with Freddy? How do you relate the long conversations and the hilarious laughter when he was on form?

Matt and I sat side-by-side in a deep empty silence; the reality was becoming relentlessly awful. In front of us the blue and white incident tape was quivering in the breeze, making a soft burring noise. When eventually he spoke, I knew he was trying to be kind, to keep my mind off it all.

'It is beautiful here. I love the river and the way the town is built up the hill. I've only lived here a few months, but I already feel at home.'

I followed his gaze. The town fanned up from behind the station, its reassuring honey-stoned cottages and tall, colourful Georgian buildings set cheek by jowl. There was such a long history in this one place and so many lives lived. At the top of the hill, crowning it, was a row of tall red-bricked chimneys, Freddy's house clearly visible in the morning sun.

I was suddenly overcome with the reality of it all. His house was still there but he was below us on the track surrounded by complete strangers. Officials and medics and people who were angry about late trains and inconvenience. They were people who didn't know him, who would think he was just another anonymous dead person, and there was nothing I could do to explain that he was special.

I even tried to tell myself that despite what I'd seen with my own eyes it couldn't be Freddy, not Freddy, not after all this time.

Chapter Two

The train had screeched to a sliding halt, its wheels locked. A long trail of sparks sprayed into the inky blackness of the darkened fields. It was a starless night and the binoculars were useless. It wasn't supposed to stop! It should have gone up; it should have gone up; it had all gone wrong. The words raced through Claudette's head. She could feel her heart hammering in her chest as she searched the darkness for a sign of Yves. He had been only feet away from her when the train skirted the slope of the hill and drew parallel with their position.

An arc of torchlight swept the bank behind her and instinctively she threw her body flat against the ridge. Her lips brushed the cold blades of grass on the bank. There were men's voices shouting and, in the distance, a dog barked. As she rolled over, her hair tugged on a bramble and the pain made her flinch but she suppressed any noise. There was another sweep of light, illuminating the twisted briars and wild grasses in front of her. Claudette ducked lower, pressing her cheek down into the damp earth.

A hand grasped her ankle, hard. A man's hand. 'Keep down – move – now.'

She was on her back and, half sliding and scrabbling for a foothold, she slithered down to the lower part of the bank. At the bottom Yves pushed her forward and they ran headlong through the cover of pine trees and down the needle-strewn path to the firebreak.

'You go that way, use the stream. Get to the safe-house and I'll draw them away.' His voice was barely a whisper and one look at his face, even in the darkness, showed clearly that he was scared. Yves was never scared.

Claudette followed the line of the firebreak and then over the gate where she cut across the field of cows, breaking the herd into startled bucking shadows. She slid on cow shit, but that at least was good, it would disguise her scent. On the far side of the field she waded down the length of the brook, picking her way over the loose stones and cursing as her ankles buckled beneath her. The ice-cold water filled her shoes. She could feel the soles ridging up inside them.

There were sirens, more dogs barking, shouts that were clearly audible then drifted off again into the distance: 'Holen sie die Hunde. Schnell! Hier entlang!' Stumbling up the muddy driveway, she reached half way and scrambled through the wire fence with the ragged hole cut for the purpose. She bent the wire away from her but her coat still caught on it; she heard it tear. When eventually she had made it through, she turned back, pulling the two halves roughly together. The wire was cold in her shaking fingers. She was finding it difficult to catch her breath as she scaled the incline, but she made it to the back of the house and under cover of the dense laurel bushes, she clicked on her flashlight. She opened the cellar door taking hold of the rope attached to the underside. Jumping from the ledge she pulled the rope so that it slammed the door shut above her, then she slotted the heavy wooden bar into the

8

metal struts to secure it. Dark and damp, the cellar had a heavy loamy smell. She shone the torch into the far corner at a stack of logs. Moving four or five to the back of the trapdoor she pulled it up and slid inside. The logs shifted as she pulled the trapdoor down and hopefully covered it, if only a little, enough.

Claudette shone the torch around the small, musty space. In front of her were a thermos flask and a tin box. She knew it would have some fruit in it and maybe some biscuits. In a small alcove to her right there was a pot covered with a muslin cloth, her toilet. Only four feet by four, the space was tiny and not deep enough to stand up in. She pulled her arms around her knees as a shiver of cold ran through her. Her wet feet began to needle. There was silence, a deep pervading stillness and no sound of the dogs. Yves had drawn them away. She let go the deep breath that she had held onto since the moment the train had stopped. Only then, when she was totally sure she was hidden, did Claudette Bourvil let herself cry.

Chapter Three

Harriet was walking towards me accompanied by a policewoman. Her face was drained of colour and her eyes swollen and sore. She grasped my arm so hard I thought her nails would tear through the skin.

'I knew it,' she said. 'I knew it, it's all my fault, Connie.' She was shaking her head. 'I should have been up earlier this morning.' She was holding a balled up tissue in her hand. 'I might have heard the door, I cannot believe I overslept.'

'I'm sure it's not your fault Hat,' I tried to sound reassuring. 'When did you last see him?' She looked bewildered, as if it were the hardest question in the world.

'Last night, he went to bed early with a tummy ache. Oh my God, what have I done? If only I'd woken up earlier.' She was holding my fingers in a white-knuckle clasp, her whole body quaking.

As I clung to her I could feel her fading, becoming smaller in my arms. The policewoman caught my eye and I understood the message.

'Come back with me, Hat, the police will want to talk to us both. We'll go to my house. You shouldn't be alone.' She nodded miserably.

'I'll drive you up there if you like,' Matt offered. The

policewoman nodded in agreement and told us she would follow behind.

My cottage felt cold and unwelcoming when I let us in. Hat pushed open the lounge door and slumped down heavily onto the sofa, hands over her face. Matt stood at the threshold of my front door, uncertain of what to do.

'Would you like a coffee?' I asked.

'I won't, but thank you, I'd better get off to my shoot.'

I knew I must have looked a sight. I had black Panda eyes and my cheeks felt swollen with tears. 'Thank you so much for looking after me, I would have gone to pieces if you hadn't been there.'

'It's no problem, I'm glad I could help. It's all so sad. I hope it…I mean…please tell Hat I wish her well through what's to come. And you.'

I gave him a hug, an involuntary one that signified the enormity of what we had shared, something entirely dreadful. Then I passed him the silver blanket that I had folded back into a small square even though it was crinkled and would never be used again.

As I closed the front door my mobile rang. It was my boss, Will. He was very angry: 'Connie, where in God's name are you?'

'Will, I'm sorry there's been an –'

'Do you realise how important today is? Jesus, we have this one chance!' Will had always lived on his nerves, but the recession was making things ten times harder. I could imagine him pacing up and down on the mock teak floor of his office. 'They are here in twenty minutes and I have no revisions to show them.'

'There's been an accident Will,' I told him flatly, not

11

paying any interest to anything he was saying, I was thinking only of Hat.

'Well, it better be serious, I can tell you, if I find –'

'A friend of mine has – has been killed…by a train. All the trains are at a standstill. I'm sorry, I won't be in for the rest of the week.'

'Is this a relative?'

I hesitated. How dare he? Freddy was as close as a relative to me, and what did that matter anyway? Where was the man's compassion? Then it struck me that he had none, no empathy, never had.

'You need to email me the designs now, send whatever you've got!' he barked, 'and thanks for ringing me to let me know what was happening, by the way. This account might not seem much to you but right now it's our bread and butter.'

I hit the red button without responding to him. He was an arse. I picked up my laptop bag and then dropped it again. He could wait, put the meeting back, Hat was more important.

'I don't believe it, Connie, I just cannot believe it.' She was leaning on the arm of the sofa, another tissue rolled into a small white cone in her hand. My cat, Mr. C, rubbed himself against her legs trying to attract her attention, but she was ignoring him. I sat down next to her, reaching for his long stripy back. 'All those times I've talked to him,' she sobbed, 'everything I did, all those experts I made him see. If only he would have talked to me, not bottled it up inside for all those years.'

'You did your best, Hat, no one could say any different.' It was true she had been selfless. I pulled a fresh tissue from the box at my side and she dabbed her eyes with it. Her shoulders were shaking. This was not the Harriet James I knew, because my Harriet never needed help or advice. She handled everything her way, with uncompromising humour and good spirits, but Freddy in his latest bout of dejection, finally, was her breaking point. Not the trouble he caused her, the episodes, the threats, the long silences, but the sudden and absolute finality of his death.

Chapter Four

'We have a weak link, a threat.' Yves was looking at them, regarding each face one by one. When his eyes fell on Claudette it was not because she was a suspect, she knew that, but because she was new and lacked confidence.

The tack room was inside a barn at the back of another safe house in the hamlet of Cassel, fifty minutes by train from Paris. A single gas lamp lit up the dark space, giving a ghostly edge to the faces around it. There was a smell of leather and linseed oil. Outside, rain was sheeting down and steam was rising from woollen jumpers and jackets. Pascal Canet threw down his cigarette stub and stood up.

'It's not me,' he said grimly. 'I have too much of a grudge against the bastards, so no-one can label me a traitor, right?'

'No one is saying that,' sighed Yves. Canet was the one he could rely on without question.

'The man protests too much.' Vincent Gabin, the student doctor, sneered from the corner where he was leaning against a pile of dirty canvas rugs. He was the one who had come close to capture recently, he was wary of everyone. Canet threw him a dark look, there was no love lost between them.

Yves held up his hand. 'The someone doesn't have to be one of us. It could be one of our links, the safe house

14

in Fréon we no longer use or Stéphen Lhuy's widow, she's terrified after what happened to him. Whoever it is, it's a major problem for us. The train last week should have gone up. Instead they had information and they disabled the device. It's handed them a major advantage, even more than ever.'

'And more ammunition for retribution killings,' added Gabin. 'How many more this time, eh?'

'We'll need to deploy away from here and hit them when and where they least expect it. We need to go further, into the city.'

'But it is heaving with them. It's mad. You are making it countless times more dangerous.' Maurice Joubert said as he drew deeply on a roll up. It smelt sweet.

'I'm certain it's not one of us, the person who's doing this doesn't know us by name. It's in the line. If he knew who we are we'd all be dead by now.' The men nodded in agreement.

'We will change everything, every aspect of what we do and recruit new people if needs be, I have two men in mind in Paris.' As he spoke Yves looked weary.

'We need women now,' Joubert was looking at Claudette. 'They move with more ease in the city, especially if they have children in tow.' Claudette realised the space in the conversation was hers to fill.

'I can suggest some names in this area,' she said at length. 'But I don't know anyone in Paris.'

'We'll set up a new line. I'm telling no more than three of you the details,' said Yves. 'And if that backfires I'll kill the traitor myself, with my bare hands.' Claudette looked from face to face, only Joubert failed to respond. Canet and Gabin grunted in agreement, but Joubert was staring straight at her, his eyes under heavy black brows dark against his white, pock-marked skin.

'Me too,' he said grimly, his eyes set fiercely on Claudette. 'Me too.'

'Ignore Joubert,' Yves told her the following week. They were sitting at a table in the back room of the Café J. Phillipe. It was early and the café was closed, the normal chatter replaced by the muted sounds of life out in the street. Yves had made them both a coffee, it was not the real thing of course, it was an acrid tasting toasted barley mixed with chicory. He apologised as he placed it in front of her. Even this mediocre mix was becoming scarce, along with just about everything else. 'He's angry. If I told you his story, and what they did to him in the last war, your heart would bleed.' He absentmindedly rubbed his hand back and forth across his forehead. 'But that's the thing, I can't tell you, you can't know anything.'

He was businesslike, being efficient. Claudette listened, watching him with her usual fascination. Yves was earnest and possessed of a belief that nothing was going to stop him until France was free. She knew that he carried out all this, the fighting and this secret business, in spite of himself, because at heart he had always been a gentle soul. She'd known him right through school, from the first day when he smiled as she stood lost and bewildered. Since that day he had always looked out for her and not only her, either. He was the first to pull apart a fight, calm arguments down, listen to both sides of the story. She and Yves had been the two most promising pupils but neither of them could afford to go further, even if they had been able to try for a scholarship. Before the war, times had already been hard and they both needed to earn money for their families and so they had left school as early as possible to work in their family trades.

Since she was thirteen Claudette's father had been too ill to work and she and her mother took in endless piles of sewing and darning. Yves was two years older, almost twenty-four and to her far wiser, more worldly. He had an independent spirit, due, in no small part, to losing both parents in a road accident when he was nine. His mother's sister had brought him up, she and her huge bear of a husband. No one ever mentioned his parents and she had watched the steely expression on his face when the schoolteacher talked about their fathers. Yves would write about his uncle instead. He was still hurting.

'The thing is,' he was speaking slowly, his fingers resting on the rim of the coffee bowl, 'it's got to be you, I can see no other way.' She was used to his round about approach, the way he never gave her a directive. Sometimes he would mull things over, his jaw flexing and relaxing as he ran new ideas through his head. Whatever the decision, even though she had guessed the nature of it, she would give him time to explain and hear him out.

This time there was something about the hesitation on his lips and she realised he was struggling to say the words.

'What are you talking about, Yves?' she leaned forward, eyes probing his face for an answer. 'Just tell me.' There was a small knot of apprehension tightening inside her.

'We must get to the heart of it, to the decision makers,

find out what they will do next, instead of being purely reactive.' As he spoke he kept his eyes fixed firmly on the bowl in front of him. Her heart sank a little and she felt the apprehension turning into a sense of foreboding. 'We need someone in Paris.' At first she thought he was about to discuss it all with her because she had become, for want of a better word, his confidante. He had always involved her in his plans and schemes, it was something she knew bonded them, made them essential to each other but, instead, he took a deep breath and said, 'I think you could do it.'

'Me! Not me, surely, what could I do to help?'

He looked at her from under the strands of dark hair that fell across his eyes and immediately it seemed he had regretted asking her. She was suddenly aware of how tired and careworn he looked. Fine red thread veins dulled the whites of his eyes and beneath them were dark circles, but the eyebrows knotted together above them left no trace of doubt, he was serious.

'I can't go to Paris,' she told him. She could feel her heart quicken, her voice was unnatural, fearful. 'I've never even been there.'

'It's just a town, just like Vacily, but a big one.' He half smiled and for a few seconds the brightness of his youth appeared, but it was fleeting.

'I don't have the clothes, the accent, the style, I can't carry off being a Parisian woman. I sew for them occasionally, that's all, it's the closest I've ever been, you need to think of someone else.'

Yves stood up and walked over to the heavy velvet curtain he'd drawn between them and the front of the café.

He pulled it back a little and scanned the street for anyone who might be in the vicinity before sitting back down.

'Jean will be back soon to open up and I've promised I'll be gone by then. You will be fully briefed, you won't need accents or fancy clothes or whatever. You will be a girl up from the country who has found work in the city. A maid, or something of that nature. The final pieces are being put into place and you will have the full picture the next time we meet.'

'Will I have contacts?'

'Of course, yes,'

'A place to live?'

'Yes, with your work.'

'What is the work?'

He refused to be drawn further. 'Claudette, you don't need to worry, I will be there with you.'

'In Paris?'

'Of course in Paris, what did you think I meant, in spirit or something?'

She felt a blessed sense of relief run through her and she allowed herself a small, imperceptible sigh. He would be there. It would be all right if he was there. It could so easily have been Joubert or the ghastly Pascal Canet who, for some reason, Yves seemed to hero worship.

'Really?'

'Yes, I will be in the city working somewhere. It's not yet confirmed.' Her shoulders relaxed, with him in Paris she would feel capable of doing anything.

'And Giselle?'

'What of her?'

'Will you leave her here?'

19

'Of course, I can't risk her safety.'

'No, of course not.' Claudette looked down at her hands. A quiver of disappointment ran through her, something he must never be allowed to see. Giselle's baby was due at Easter. Naturally he would protect his wife at all costs, and their little boy, Louis.

Chapter Five

When I arrived at work the following week Will called me into his goldfish bowl office and straightaway, without any reference to what I'd been through, told me I'd let him down. He and his partner Rod had had a long talk and unfortunately things were going from bad to worse. I knew he had been furious about the meeting and I understood, but I was also filled with inertia. A deep, cavernous emptiness now existed where Freddy once was.

Eventually, when he'd calmed down and the dust had settled, he asked me if I would go freelance. He was all promises and "we'll feed you lots of work" and "think of the opportunities." With that, no ceremony at all, I was given garden leave for a month. They made me sign documents saying I wouldn't work within a twenty-mile radius of their firm, or for any of their clients "wheresoever" they might be based. At first I was shocked. I hadn't really seen it happening to me in spite of the grumbling of my colleagues. I was creative and expedient in my work and I put the hours in.

I made some calls and the signs were that some of my contacts in Oxfordshire needed holiday cover in August and September, it could have been far worse.

A week later, still in a sort of trance, I was sitting perched precariously on a stile and staring out across the meadow to the railway, watching the horses cropping fresh grass. Previously the field had been sectioned off with a white electric tape, but now their tails swished rhythmically as, heads down, they worked their way steadily towards me up the slope.

'Hi, Connie!' It was Matt striding down the hill towards me. I was so surprised to see him that as I turned I nearly fell off the stile. 'Sorry, did I make you jump?'

'Yes, no, it's just I thought I was on my own.'

'I saw you from the top of the hill, when I came out of the pub, I was having a swift half. I wondered how it's all been going.'

I bit on my lip to stop myself getting emotional. 'It's not good,' I told him truthfully.

'Really? I am sorry.'

'I lost my job.'

He looked genuinely upset. 'Oh, I'm sorry, that really isn't good timing for you.'

I jumped down into the field and turned to face him over the wooden fence. 'I'm pretty low about it all, it means I'll be self-employed at the end of July.'

'I wouldn't wish that on my worst enemy. It's not easy, especially now we're all being so austere and all that crap.'

'I know, I might have to chat to you about it, what I should do next. Would you mind?'

'No, not at all, any time. What do you do exactly?'

'Graphic Design, illustration and stuff.'

'As a photographer I see some synergy here.' He looked genuinely pleased. 'I'd be happy to help in any way I can.' He nodded towards the railway. 'What about all that other stuff, the Freddy thing?'

'It's horrible, Matt. I'm finding it hard to sleep. I can't stop myself going over and over it. I see him there climbing over the wall all the time, and Hat – well, she's a real mess. The family's solicitor has been in touch and told her she can stay put in the house until it's sold, but then she has to go. Not that she's the sort to mind, but it's hit her hard about Freddy.'

'Poor Hat. It's a dreadful thing to happen to anyone, but at least she has you.'

I nodded. I was doing my best but I felt like crumbling too. 'And everyone else here, they've all been really supportive. They all loved having a playwright in the town, even if it was a long time ago.' I sighed more heavily than I expected to.

'A playwright?'

'Yes, he's Fredrik March, was, he wrote that one called 'Documentation' and the one about the Resistance in France, I can't remember what it was called.'

'Sortie Par la Mort.'

'That's it, Exit by Death,' I replied. 'I can never remember the title, but then I don't speak French – well hardly at all. I did a bit of German at school, for all the good it will ever do me.'

'I saw it in Paris and Bath,' Matt told me. 'My mother was a French teacher and I was dragged along to anything that might improve my language skills and make me a more cultured person.'

'And did it work?'

'Well, I'm fluent in French, but I wouldn't say I was all that cultured.' He smiled and I thought about just how nice he was in a solid and reassuring way. He had eyes

23

that understood. Then I found my thoughts running on to Hat and felt the deep pang of guilt about being so useless. I had talked to her, listened, held her hand, made tea and then more tea, brought her chocolates and little treats from the deli to keep her going, but she was still drained of colour and as shocked as she was that first day. 'So, I presume you're fairly free right now?' Matt interrupted my thoughts.

'I'm helping with the house. Hat's told them, the family that is, that she'll oversee the clearance but she's so low with it all and it's a mountain of work. The solicitor says they want any scripts or photographs she finds from his writing days, but nothing else. I'm going to give her a hand now that I have nothing better to do.'

I suddenly felt a wave of emotion rising up inside me, something to do with losing my job and Freddy's death happening all at once, I expect. Quite without warning the foundations of my life that had been there for so long had been uprooted and changed before I had time to think about the ramifications. To make matters worse, Hat told me the day before that she would be going to live on the coast, with her sister Annette. It was one thing after another and now I was about to lose my closest friend too.

I must have looked a bit shattered because Matt reached forward and put a hand over mine. I caught his eyes for the briefest second then looked away. He removed his hand and then there was a space, an awkward moment, I should have said something, but I didn't.

'Why don't I take you out for lunch?' He sounded uncertain as if he were treading on eggshells, but he persisted. 'A friend of mine has bought a pub in Elwell, we could go over there and have a talk about it all. You'll need feeding up if you are going to be a freelance artist type; the next thing you'll need is a poorly furnished garret and a cat.'

'I've got a cat.' I told him.

'Right, then you're on your way.' His dark brown hair was catching the sun so that there was a thin crescent of gold on the very top of his head. 'What?'

'Nothing,' I replied.'

'What's up, have I got something in my teeth?'

'No,' I told him. 'But thank you, you've just made me smile for the first time in over a week.'

Chapter Six

As Claudette cycled along the road through the fields of young crops she saw the unending flatlands of Normandy under a wide blue sky. She cycled past the lake where the familiar pair of white swans drifted, their heads bobbing to alert their young to her presence. The field edges changed from one to another with no strip of land or hedge between them. In these verdant pastures Marc Albert, one of the many farmers who produced food for the Nazis, grew his crops. He wore his arrogance like a badge, head held high whilst the people of Vacily fixed him with venomous stares or ignored him in the most obvious ways. Many of the other farmers had left huge tracts of dusty land abandoned because the price of supplying the invaders was too high.

It was such a beautiful day and with the sun on her face Claudette could, in other circumstances, have forgotten that there was a war on at all. She cycled up to the junction and stopped, leaning on one leg. The road to her left took her back to the village, but her attention was drawn to the right and the rumbling, throaty roar of the lorry heading towards town. She saw it before its passengers had seen her and her natural instinct was to turn back, but she knew full well that attracting any attention was the worst thing she could do. Instead she began peddling the bike, even though her nerves took her over so that she had to steady herself with one foot on the road as she took off. She started off again and cycled on towards the lorry.

The soldiers were sitting with rigid backs in the truck, sharp grey uniforms making them look identical under their helmets, their rifles pointing skywards. Claudette cycled on, fixing her gaze on the horizon and the far off forest at Durcy where she was heading. None of them looked at her, not even the driver. As she drew level with the lorry, immediately before the small humped back bridge over the brook, she forced herself to look ahead and not over her shoulder. She wanted to follow and see them arrive in town, worrying about what they were doing there, but her focus had to be on the line of trees half a mile away.

She finally looked over her shoulder as she reached the mottled purple shadows beneath overhanging trees. The ribbon of road stretched away from her in each direction, empty. The bike bobbled across the mud and became stuck in the ruts of baked earth. She cursed and lifted it over the bumps and folds in the ground. It was an old bicycle, heavy and angular. She pressed on; leaving it leaning against a tree was not an option. In the woods light streamed down onto the snaking trails to each side. The ferns and wild garlic blended into the sweet scent of spring.

Claudette took a path that quickly narrowed. Undergrowth scratched her legs and her skirt caught on a long spur of bramble. She winced as a stinging nettle spiked her calf and she angrily swept up a dock leaf to press on to it. Eventually, she reached the familiar fallen tree that blocked the path. She turned left and waited in an open glade. The sun was at its hottest and the forest was yielding layer upon layer of greens. A drift of scent from bluebells was caught on a breeze; she drew it in, loving the familiar reassurance of it. Laying the bike down in the undergrowth she sat with her back against the solidity of a birch tree, her knees drawn up against her chest. She was far too early.

They had agreed to meet in the woods where they had played as children, where every corridor of trees and sunlit glade was familiar even now. In those days the fallen tree had been a pirate ship or a bridge to another world, the haze of a distant memory drifted through her mind. It seemed so very long ago that the children in the village had been able to play without fear anywhere around Vacily. It had been a long time since all of them had been free from the burden of the occupation.

The war had barely scarred the town because the residents had given in so easily, being led, as they were, by the Mayor, who had appeased the Germans with his wine, cheese and a promise of his loyalty. The townsfolk had watched, dejected, as he led the Nazi invaders around the streets, his tired suit looking worn against the fine cut of their Hugo Boss uniforms. They did not take Monsieur Bonnier seriously, they stood beside him, towering over his rotundity and shining baldpate, but he worked hard at impressing them and pledged his allegiance. In no time at all graffiti appeared on walls and posters were pinned to trees; the image was always the same, him in bed with Hitler. He was marginalised and undermined at every turn.

When they arrested him, two months later, they had found evidence in the cellars of the town hall that he had been harbouring people. No one knew who it was, possibly a Jewish couple, they whispered, maybe insurgents. The soldiers ransacked his extensive wine cellar, his pride and joy, the very moment he was dragged away. They shot him at six o'clock one Tuesday evening behind the church. His trousers were round his ankles.

Monsieur Bonnier. Claudette had known him all her life. He had passed sweets to her in Mass; he always had them in his pockets ready to hand them out to all the children. 'For when it gets boring,' he would say. He had the gentlest smile and the kindest, most caring heart.

'Are you all right?' It was Yves. 'For a moment there I thought you'd died on me.' She looked up; he was towering above her with the light behind him so that he was a silhouette. He gave her his hand and pulled her up. In the green of the glade he looked like the boy she remembered, hair ruffled, eyes looking for adventure, clothes dirty and dishevelled. He was looking around, scanning the trees and scrub, listening intently. A scrabbling in the bushes made them both start, but the female pheasant soon dived for cover soundlessly, as if she knew she must make no more noise.

'I was remembering Monsieur Bonnier,' she told him.

'A very good man,' he said. 'We underestimated him and we did him wrong but then we've probably got a lot wrong, there are no rules any more.' He was still holding her hand as he led her across the glade and said; 'Come this way.'

'The bicycle.'

'It'll be fine, but we haven't got long.' Yves ducked under a low branch, his grip tightening on hers. There was a hollow in the ground, a large semicircle of leaves and tangled bushes, a bomb crater from the first war. He guided her round it then let go of her hand. 'Through there.' He pointed to a place where two thickets parted and the floor of the forest became loamy and dark.

They arrived at an enormous fallen oak, its thick roots splaying out above their heads. Yves glanced around and then stooped down. Pulling away some black earth, he retrieved a small hessian bag, the strings tied loosely together at the neck. He felt inside and produced a leather wallet. There were three documents; the outer one folded around the other two. 'These are your papers and these two are most important,' He tapped his finger on them. 'Your Identity Card and Work Permit. Look after them, they are not easily come by and they cannot be replaced.'

'When am I going?'

'Saturday. Tell no one except your parents, and only tell them that you are working elsewhere, do not mention Paris.' She nodded. 'You will be working as a maid; your name is Françoise Favelle. The maid who you will be replacing there is leaving; you are the sister of the handyman, Jacques. He's with us. You will be met at the Gare du Nord by him and he will take you to an address where you will be briefed.'

'How will I know him?'

'He will stand by the tobacco kiosk looking at a newspaper or magazine. Once he sees you, walk behind him and he'll lead the way. There will be Germans everywhere, try not to make eye contact with anyone. Remember what I have taught you, remember everything.'

'They were on the road, a truck full of them.' Claudette

indicated with her head in the direction of the town. Yves, looked down for a moment, his shoulders rounded like they were heavy with a burden.

'I know,' he said, 'they are looking for me.'

Claudette felt her eyes watering, yet her mouth was suddenly dry. 'What's happened?'

'I've been called to work for them, they are rounding us all up. That's why we're in the forest, but we'll soon be on the move. Any day now.'

Claudette felt the rise of breath in her chest being suppressed by the sudden grip of trepidation. 'You won't be with me in Paris?'

'No, I'm afraid not.' He looked frustrated and he chewed on his bottom lip, she knew he was upset because he was going to let her down.

'Who then?'

'You'll be looked after, I promise.'

'Giselle has gone, hasn't she? I haven't seen her for weeks, no one has.'

'She's safe, they both are.'

Claudette saw the adoration in his eyes as always when he talked about his wife. Giselle was from the Auvergne and there was little doubt in the village that he'd moved her back there to be with her parents and the safety of their house up in the hills. Claudette pictured her small face surrounded by her long fair hair and the gentleness that made her so popular. Then there was the baby boy, Louis, a carbon copy of his father, whose christening had been held in the church with the doors locked and only a handful of chosen guests, Claudette had been there. They had shared the few remaining pitchers of cider and a

31

small amount of the tasteless rice bread topped with goat's cheese that was donated by a local farmer. There was no gateaux or fine clothes and now there was another baby on the way.

'I promise you'll be fine, Claudette, trust me.' He took her hand and kissed the back of it, as if that would seal his vow, but inside her was a tremor of nerves that already made her start to regret ever getting involved with the Resistance. She took a deep breath and renewed her determination to help, to make a difference. She rolled the documents in readiness for hiding them in her handlebars and, as Yves kissed her on both cheeks, she turned and began to find her way back to the bike. She could feel the mark of his lips on her hand. She touched the place gently with the tips of her fingers then she wiped it on her skirt because from now on she knew she was on her own.

Chapter Seven

'I can't do this.' Hat was resting on her haunches and leaning back against a row of old encyclopaedias, russet red with gold lettering, twenty four of them lined up from A to Z on two low shelves. She looked drained and absolutely exhausted.

'You can,' I said gently. 'In your own time, it doesn't have to be done now.' I had been helping her sort through everything including the vast collection of books in the library. Old and musty, they reminded me of my childhood. The mottled pages contained secrets, memories and the traces of other people. A smudge here, a blot of yellow there, a smear of dried blood and sometimes a scribbled note, a postcard or a tired bookmark. I find books totally absorbing and so my days of sorting them out had been unhurried and a pile of the unwanted was being transplanted to my cottage each evening. Hat had told me I could have anything I wanted and she paid me at the end of the week. I was at the same time both elated and deeply troubled. Pleased because it was money to live on, upset because it was from her and I would have done this for free.

At first we'd imagined that a house clearance man would come and ship it all out but it soon became clear that Freddy, a natural hoarder, had kept everything. We were both very concerned that we might let something go, something important and we would never know.

We were both still heavy with sadness, but having something to occupy our minds was helping enormously. I was at least hitting my bed exhausted at the end of the day and I suspected the same of Hat.

We had taken a tidal wave approach, working from one end of the four storey rambling Georgian terrace to the other. The kitchen was easy enough, we boxed everything up and the dining room, full of long unused china in cabinets, was soon empty. None of the china was a complete set, there were three or five of everything. The vases and jugs were cracked, the pictures old and faded.

We were in the library when Hat finally broke down, in her hands a black and white photograph of Freddy as a young man. It was a picture taken for a billposter. The poster had yet to emerge but Hat remembered it, years ago, framed in the downstairs loo. I shuffled across on my knees and gave her a hug. She felt very slight like a bird. She had lost weight over the three weeks.

She had travelled to the funeral in Ledbury with our friend Jon and I had been worried sick about her from the very second she left. Jon told me later that she was inconsolable and the family had seemed unconcerned, absorbed only in their own problems. The "family", it transpired, comprised two distant cousins, an ancient aunt and a scattering of hangers on. They had paid no heed to Freddy when he was alive, probably, we supposed, because of his illness but all of them were picking up the scent of the house and what it might be worth, let alone the rest of his estate. They had asked that the funeral be attended only by family and closest friends, because they were worried the press would turn up incognito. Hat and Jon represented us, the town he made his home.

Hat wiped away a tear. She traced the line of Freddy's cheek with her little finger as if it might re-connect her to him. 'I did love him,' she said, 'even when he was a beast and believe me, he could be.' She sniffed.

'I know you did and he'd have been lost without you.'

'He really was the best friend I ever had,' she told me. There was a wobble in her voice as she said, 'I'll miss him like hell.'

'We should do something for him, acknowledge him here where he lived –'

'And died,' she added. 'And died.' Her voice cracked and I rubbed her forearm as reassuringly as I could trying to show her my support.

'Come on, now,' I said, sitting back on my haunches. 'Let's get this finished today and then we've only the bedrooms to do, oh, and the bathroom.'

'And his room.'

'We've done his bedroom and the guest room.'

'He has – had – another room,' replied Hat. 'A fourth bedroom, a box room really, he wrote in there and listened to music. It looks out across the garden, he loved being in that room.'

'Whenever I saw him he was coming out of here, or the kitchen,' I told her.

'That is strange because he spent all his time up there unless he was in the garden, of course,' she replied. Then at length she said: 'I really don't think I can face his room as well.'

'Hat, don't worry, I'll do it. I'll go through everything and anything I think you would want, whatever it is, I'll box up for you to go through later.'

'Would you?'

'Of course.'

'But I feel awful because we've sorted everything out together so far.'

'Hat, it'll be my pleasure, honestly.'

'I'm going to go and see my sister in Brighton this weekend, I'll give you the key, would you do it when I'm not here?'

'Of course.'

'Does that make me sound stupid?'

'No.' The relief on her face was palpable. She was clearly grateful.

'Someday I'll do you a favour like this,' she promised.

'Hat, I hope you never have to, it'll be no trouble at all.'

At that moment I really believed I was right.

Chapter Eight

The main street of the town was empty as she cycled in. Vacily was a linear settlement huddled along each side of a treeless road and from this end she could see right through to the other, and the small church hunkered down behind a low cedar hedge. There was not a person in sight. Shutters to each side of her were closed and locked. The properties of those who had evacuated in the Exodus were always still and quiet, but now the other houses were silent too. She jumped off the bike and left it against a whitewashed wall at the side of the bakery. Cautiously she crossed the passageway to the café. It was a place that was open morning until late at night on most days, but the door was wide open, no one inside. A chair lay on its side blocking the aisle to the bar. Her heart was thumping like a hammer. Biting her lip, she went back outside, scanning the street both right and left; save for an old car and a rusting Citroën van, it was completely empty. At that moment a large, yellow dog wandered across the road further up and as she cycled up to it outside the pharmacy, it regarded her with indifference and carried on sniffing at a pile of horse dung.

Claudette stopped and listened carefully. She could hear a throb of voices from the market square directly opposite the church. As she drew closer, the hum of conversation was more distinct. The next right hand turn led down to the old well. She parked her bike in the dim shade of the laundry, hiding it from sight. The murmur of conversation was rising, an excitement of voices and the sound of women crying. She walked along the path that skirted the brook; the noisy trickle of water running over the stones was blocking out sounds. She craned her neck to hear. Was she right? Were the voices dying away? Edging round the back of the garage, she trod silently on the sandy forecourt between parked cars and vans. As she drew level with the church, she stayed close to the low hedge until she could see the crowd across the road gathered around the old fountain. There were no Germans to be seen.

There was a woman kneeling on the floor, Antoinette Gabin. She was grabbing at the dust and gravel, throwing it down in big handfuls in front of her, wailing uncontrollably. There was bright red blood all over her clothes and the features on the right of her face were blurred into a ghastly mess of torn flesh and bruising. Her friends were trying to get her to her feet, attempting to calm her, but she was hysterical. Two old men were talking and arguing angrily, they shoved and pushed at one another.

As the crowd started to break up, the faces turning towards her were vacant, pale as phantoms, each one in shock. Others covered their faces with their hands, heads shaking, sobbing. At the edge of the crowd, towards the back and talking to bemused friends and neighbours, were her parents. On seeing her, Claudette's mother's face brightened visibly and she ran over, arms open wide.

'Claudette, oh Claudette, we had no idea where you

were!' As Francine Bourvil wrapped her arms around her daughter, tears began to flow down her cheeks. 'Oh, thank the Holy Mother that you are here, thank you, thank you.' She raised her eyes skywards, hands clasped together in prayer. Claudette looked over her mother's shoulder at her father; he was shaking violently, stress made his condition far worse.

'Papa?'

Her father's expression was a grave warning to her, he held up his hands as a barrier. Without words, he was telling her to go no further, but she let go of her mother's hand and kept walking. The fountain was blocked and there was no sound of running water. In the middle of it was the pillar of stone topped with a rusty cross that had been bent out of shape over the years. On the side facing Claudette was blood, a spray of it, with rivulets running down and pooling into the still water.

Behind it, lying on his back with his head turned to her, his clothes wet and body broken, was Vincent Gabin. The front of his blue shirt was deepening into a large circle of ruby red. She looked at the young face, the black curly hair, the elegant line of his jaw and she saw in him the hopes of his parents, the pride of the people of Vacily. Claudette felt a claustrophobic grip of horror inside her, this was what she had been warned about. She looked at Vincent's face, but the young, honest features were transposed into the face of another man, one who could so easily have been there instead.

'Claudette, child, come away.' Her father rested his hand on her arm. She turned and buried her head in his jacket. It felt rough against her cheek but deeply comforting. She didn't cry, tears would not come. She held her father's jacket, bunching the material in her hand as tightly as she could.

'What happened, Papa?'

'It was terrible, Claudette. They arrived an hour ago, a truck full of them. The whole town, everyone, ran inside. But they knew who they wanted and where they would find him. They went straight to his parent's house and ransacked it. His mother was screaming, then she stopped, silent, just like that. They grabbed his father and took him into the street. Poor Hubert, he was terrified. Antoinette followed after him, her face bloody. She had blood pouring from her eye and she was holding her hand like this.' He covered his own eye. He faltered as he carried on and Claudette rubbed his arm, understanding his pain. 'She tried to run towards him, but a soldier pulled her back. We all watched from behind our shutters because we were shameful, as always, cowards. But what could we do?' He rubbed his hand across his perspiring brow, shaking his head. 'They made Hubert march down the street hands behind his head until he was in the middle of town, then they used a loudspeaker and called for him, for Vincent. There was no response. I thought he wasn't even here, maybe not even in town, I prayed, Claudette, I prayed but... I felt absolutely powerless. They were level with our house, your mother and I were watching from the attic window. We'd locked ourselves in there like you told us to.

'The loud haler started up again telling Gabin to come out, yet still nothing happened. Then one of the soldiers walked towards Hubert and held his rifle up. He was pointing it at his back, pushing the poor man forward into

40

the middle of the road. It was horrendous, like watching one of your own nightmares. I wanted to open the window and shoot him, the soldier, but I don't have a gun. I don't have anything. How could I have helped? What use am I?'

'What happened, Papa?'

'They counted to ten, in English, it was bizarre, but now I realise Vincent had English for his medicine. A really clever boy… I can't believe it.'

'What happened?' Claudette was becoming impatient, her father's reliving everything was making him talk more and more slowly.

'I'll tell you girl,' said a voice behind her. 'The boy came out of the café.' Claudette turned round to see Esther Bonnier, the widow of the Mayor, her long face drawn and old, brown bags under her eyes, a wretched, bitter woman wearing black from head to foot. 'They pushed Hubert out of the way and when he tried to come back they slammed a rifle butt in his face. Broke his cheekbone, like Antoinette's. I wouldn't be surprised if they've done that to her as well. Then they marched that lovely boy down here and did that. They have no shame, no mercy. That is what they did to my man too. In cold blood, cold blood.' There was a mumble through the crowd. 'And let that be a lesson to us all!' she shouted to everyone, a bony finger in the air. Some of the townsfolk were walking away, others stopped and regarded her with pity. 'We know why they came for him, don't we, eh? We know it's what he's been up to and he's put us all at risk. All of us! And just for living in the same town. My husband knew all about it, look what happened to him.'

Martine Cornillion gently led Esther Bonnier away.

Other hands reached out to calm her down and reassure her. Claudette could tell that many would have echoed her sentiments, but they said nothing.

That night, as Claudette stared at the thin vegetable soup and black bread for which her father offered up thanks, she felt something inside her had snapped and was broken beyond repair. It was the knowledge that they could come to her town and commit such a heinous act in cold blood. She knew now that the Nazis were after Yves too. They had found Vincent Gabin and it would not be long before they were back and combing the forest with dogs. Then who next – Joubert or Canet or even herself? She cared nothing for herself, but she feared for the fight, for the Resistance. France was holding on by a thin thread to its very existence, the time had come.

'Mama, Papa, I have something to tell you.' Claudette straightened her back and took a deep breath. Her mother's face was wan, she was expecting the worst. Her father mopped his mouth with his napkin, his hands were trembling and his rheumy eyes were sad and lost. 'I can't tell you any details, but I am going away. I may be gone for some time.' Her parents listened in silence. 'I am leaving on Saturday.'

'Oh, Claudette,' was all her mother could say. She bit into the back of a white knuckle to stifle a cry, but she made no fuss. Her father had closed his eyes, eyelids creased into thin lines. In the dim light of the tallow candles on the table, he looked very tired and old.

'I'm sorry, Papa, Mama, but it's what I have to do.'

Her father leaned across the table, his fingers trembling as they settled on hers.

'We know,' was all he said, 'we know.'

Chapter Nine

Matt picked me up from my cottage. The Cotswolds sparkled, iridescent greens and ripe yellows stretched across the valleys. In dips between rolling hills and on the ridges around them, ochre stonewalls and Stonesfield slate tiles of hamlets and snug villages nestled into the landscape.

'I'm so glad I suggested this,' said Matt. 'I have been cooped up for weeks decorating and working and working and decorating, I must smell like a Dulux dog.'

I laughed. 'No, but you do look like one!' His hair was dishevelled and a heavy fringe tumbled over his forehead, 'Haven't you found our barber yet?'

'We have a barber?'

'Yes, along the main street and turn left at the paint shop.'

'We have a paint shop?'

I laughed again.

'You mean I've been driving to the DIY superstore for paint that I could have got in town?'

'Town's a bit of an exaggeration, if you don't mind me saying, we're an extended village really.'

He grinned. 'An extended village with a barber and paint shop I don't know anything about.'

'You do know we have three pubs, don't you?'

'Oh yes, found those on day one. "Sawdust", "Posh" and "Posher." Done all three of them and more than once.'

I looked at him over my sunglasses.

'We decorators have to eat,' he replied in his defence.

We were in his old Discovery and high up in the passenger seat I could see everything, like when I used to ride. The things you can see from a horse open up a new world of private back gardens, swimming pools and old vintage cars under wraps in car ports. I missed those days, but since my break up it was a hobby that was too expensive for me.

'How's it going with Hat?'

'She's a bit better, she's gone to Brighton to stay with her sister for a few days and I've promised to do Freddy's house when she's away.'

'Do it?' he asked, raising a quizzical eyebrow.

'Sort it out, we're going through everything. She's fairly paranoid about throwing something away without knowing. Like birth certificates or old scripts and things like that.'

'Is it going well?'

'It's going very slowly,' I replied. 'He kept everything, a real hoarder. I'm starting on his room today.'

'Room?' He extended the word into a question. 'Sounds sinister.'

'Hat wouldn't even open the door to show me, she says it's "too him," where he spent all his time, full of his stuff.' We turned onto the A361, the remnants of Cow Parsley and newly flowering Rosebay Willow Herb flashed by and a skein of Canada Geese honked alongside, then peeled away. It made us both smile, it really was a beautiful day.

Lunch was easy and relaxed, we chose the same things

44

from the menu. Matt was funny, he had a relaxed manner that reminded me of my father. 'Why are you staring?' he asked. 'Spinach?'

'What?'

'I have spinach in my teeth?' he said.

'No, we haven't even had spinach, you're paranoid about that, aren't you?'

'A person only stares like that at someone who has something green in their gum line,' he said.

I shook my head. 'I promise you, your teeth are fine, I'll let you know if…. when, you know.'

'What then?'

'I was just thinking how much you remind me of my father,' I said.

'Uh oh.'

'No, he's lovely. He's very quiet, but when he says something it's worth hearing and he's funny. He's one of those people who simply enjoys life, he doesn't let anything get him down.'

'You are very lucky,' he replied. 'My father was completely different. My family is very religious, manically so when I was young. No singing, no music except in church and Sunday School from the age of three, all fire and brimstone and getting through this dreadful life, surviving the misery, to get to heaven. It was madness.'

'Wow, and yet you're so normal.'

'Thank you,' he replied. 'That's reassuring.'

'Was it hard on you being brought up by people like that?'

'Well, we didn't celebrate Christmas because of its Pagan origins, Sundays were for church and it was three

45

times a day. All that lost time grieves me. At the end of the day, I know now that I was being brainwashed and that I find it hard to forgive.'

'So do you resent your parents for it?'

His face clouded over, suddenly serious. 'Yes, I do, I was completely trapped. Now, looking back, I realise that all I wanted was freedom to do things, find myself, if that doesn't sound clichéd. I suppose I wanted Freddy's life instead, being allowed to be creative; writing or painting, just being allowed to think.'

'How did you free yourself from it?'

'Read the Bible,' he replied, 'that sorted it out.'

'You read the Bible to free yourself from it?'

'Yep, really read it and I realised I was not compatible with religion. My parents and other relatives made it very hard for me and for a while it screwed me up and I used to drink away the pain.'

'That's so sad, poor you.' I looked at him, tilting my head to one side. 'And now?'

'I don't have much to do with them, they do faith healing and speak in tongues and are way too woo woo for me and it's embarrassing now.' He went quiet for a moment. 'But I'm fine, really I am. I've worked at it and I don't drink to the same extent now, honestly.'

'I've never been clear on any of it,' I told him, 'it always seemed an opportunity to start wars and not tolerate other people to me.' I really did feel for him, there was a little tug on my heart as I thought of him growing up and being so trapped. My parents never railroaded me into anything and I've always been free to make up my own mind.

'You're right, it's behind most wars,' he continued as

we stood up, the chairs scraping on the uneven flagstones of the pub floor. 'But enough of war and religion, we have work to do.' He had a broad grin on his face.

'Do we?' I asked, a little excitedly. 'Where?'

'At Freddy's house, I'd like to give you a hand with "the room".'

'Really?'

'Yep, as long as I can have any old photos we come across for my collection. That's the deal.'

'What are you collecting?' I asked.

'Old photos, I just said that.'

'I meant what for?'

'I scan them and put them on the 'net', it's a resource for artists, authors, historians. It helps if I can post info about them too, but the images alone are fascinating for people all over the world,' he said.

'I'm not sure I can let you have any of Freddy or his plays or the actors and so on.'

'I'm not after them, it's more street scenes and countryside or events I can use, if we find any.'

'Do you know, I think Freddy would love to think some of his things had a use now he's gone, like a legacy? We must check with Hat, of course, but I'm sure she'll be fine about it.'

'Good,' He put three twenties on the table to cover the bill and then, standing up, he said; 'Let's do it.' At that moment I couldn't think of anything I'd rather do than spend my afternoon with Matt in Freddy's "room".

The door opened half way, teetering piles of papers and books leaned dangerously towards toppling over onto the floor if we pushed it any further. Matt moved them to enable us to enter the room together. It was a real, traditional, old-fashioned mess. The only visible furniture was an old armchair, its sponge stuffing springing out through tattered holes in the tweed fabric. The blotter on his desk, although completely covered in doodles, was clear of paper. Everywhere else, each surface and square foot of floor was covered in newspaper cuttings, coupons, magazines, typed letters and books – everywhere books. There were stacks of them, shelves of them, and furniture made of them. Two piles of large books made a makeshift coffee table, with a plank of wood on top. An empty cup, stained brown at the rim and a dinner plate ingrained with dried food were on top of it.

'Wow.' Matt scratched his forehead.

'Bet you're wondering why you volunteered now?' I said brightly, though in all honesty I was thinking the same, it was a huge task.

'I think we'll need a lot of tea,' was all he said, and with that he began to pick up anything on the floor that was preventing us from moving forward.

We agreed on four piles on the landing. One for the family, one for the charity shop and a pile to throw out. The fourth pile, divided in three, was for Matt, Hat or me. Matt and I each had a bin bag and it was easy once we got our system going, and being able to talk to each other helped. We found a file with all of Freddy's' important papers including the mortgage saying that he owned the house officially, mortgage free, in 1968. Matt opened a book on warships and found a thin piece of paper, flimsy and fragile, a receipt for a pair of boys shorts dated 1952.

'F.T.Bernheim and Sons, Farthing Road, London,

E2. The sum of one shilling and sixpence. Received with thanks.'

I read another out loud: 'Locke and Mead Publishers, London SW3, For short story two hundred pounds. Payment in full.' It was made out to Freddy. The paper was crinkled, as if it had been screwed up and flattened out again. I wondered when he'd done that, possibly on one of his bad days when, no doubt, he locked himself in this room alone. Poor sad Freddy.

I made tea and commented on how quickly the stacks had grown, except the one for the family. It was still little more than a pile of documents and bills, most of which would be of no interest to them. Mine, of course, was made up of books, including two copies of The Barchester Chronicles and a well-preserved first edition of The Lion, The Witch and The Wardrobe, exactly as C.S. Lewis would have seen it.

'I hope I don't do this to my family when I'm gone,' said Matt as he took a break to sip his second cup of tea. 'I'd get rid of everything in my own way long before someone else had to do it.'

'Me too,' I replied, blowing across the hot tea in my cup. 'Though, when I go, there will be a hell of a lot of books to sort out, that's for sure.'

'I do like that about you, Connie,' he said. 'You deal with technology in your work, but go back to books in your own time. No Kindle?'

'No, I love the feel and smell of books and the cover, it's a package for me, a 3D thing.'

'That's why I love old photographs, it's only one step on from the truth.'

We had made headway and we both came to the decision that three hours was long enough. My knees ached from kneeling and I felt bad that I'd kept Matt so long, even if he really didn't seem to mind. He stood up, stretched out and then looked around. 'Well, we've made headway,' he said and I laughed, because in actual fact the irony was it was hard to tell we'd even been in there. The floor was cleared and underneath a mountain of papers and cuttings on the desk we found his Imperial Typewriter, two of the keys stuck together, 'A' and 'S', but we were still surrounded at every level by Freddy's papers, books and possessions.

'Tomorrow?' he suggested. 'I've got a couple of hours to spare in the morning.'

'Really, you don't mind?'

'Not at all, I still haven't found a single photograph for my resource project, I guess I'm still looking.' He took my mug from me and carried both, and a handful of books he had selected for himself, downstairs. In the hallway the house felt empty with neither Hat nor Freddy in it, and all of a sudden I felt like we were trespassing. Matt must have noticed my pensive expression; he squeezed my elbow as he passed by, his touch like electricity forking through my body. 'Come on, you,' was all he said as I turned to look at him. 'Home James and a hot bath for us both, I ache.'

'Me too, but I'll just have a check around to make sure nothing's open.' I pulled back. 'See you tomorrow.'

'Okay,' he said aware, I'm sure, that I was putting distance between us. I shouted thanks to him, but the front door banged as it closed after him.

We were back at ten the next day, I left the door open for him and I heard it close and then the heartening sound of his feet on the stairwell. 'Hi, Connie,' he said brightly as he entered the room. He had such a warm, friendly face, I immediately felt uplifted seeing him again.

'Shall we get on?'

'Yes, but before we do, look at this, I found it yesterday in the "Boys Book of Adventure" I took home.' He handed me a piece of paper, yellowed and old, it had a child's writing in faded pencil. The date at the top was 19 September 1957, the letter was signed Fredrik. I read it and then over again and again.

'Stanford House'
Barnes
London
19 September, 1957

Dear Father,

I am WRiting to let you know that I am doing well. I would like to meeT you and hear all about the army.

Yours Truly
Fredrik March

'I don't understand, Freddy's mum was single, Hat told me he'd never known his father.'

Matt shook his head; 'Well, it looks like Hat was wrong.'

Chapter Ten

There was a crush of people at the station, all of them avoiding eye contact with each other. Joubert clicked his tongue and his old horse moved forward as people moved out of its way to let the creaking cart through. A soldier on duty monitored the queue, looking at documents and then up and down at those who were standing in front of him. His face was inflexible, cold. Two other soldiers were watching passengers on the platform and a small group of officers were standing in a cluster, laughing and joking with each other.

'Whatever you do, don't attract attention. If any of them become over interested, look like you've seen someone you know and use it as a chance to get away.' Joubert was irritating her. She knew all this, Yves had trained her carefully for weeks. She couldn't understand why this obnoxious man always thought her such an amateur.

'I'll be fine,' she said. 'Thank you for the lift.' The old man grunted. He waited for her to climb down and retrieve her small leather suitcase from the cart. 'Got your papers?' he asked, grating on her nerves once again.

'Yes, of course,' she said curtly.

'Good, take good care.' He sounded suddenly forced and too loud. 'And say hello to that brother of yours for me.'

Claudette watched as he flicked the reins across the horse's rump and turned the cart away from her. She watched him go, his back hunched over the reins, the horse plodding up the road. He was an awful man and he made no attempt to disguise the fact that he didn't trust her. She turned and joined the queue of passengers. There was a woman with a taut face and loose jowls right in front of her and a nervy old couple with their granddaughter behind her.

'Papieren.' The soldier held out his hand towards her as she edged forward. He was hot and there was a thick line of black on the rim of his shirt collar. He looked at her documents, then up at her. He waited a second then waved her on. They thrived on their domination.

The little girl behind her broke free of her grandfather's hand and made for a friend on the platform. Her grandfather called urgently for her to come back, but she ignored him. The Nazi looked over at her and for a moment time froze. To everyone's astonishment he smiled. Relief clearly flooded through the grandparents, their faces softened. 'Kinder,' he said with a shake of his head and a smile, as if he knew all about children. Claudette watched as the grandfather nodded, a look of suspended belief on his face as he handed his papers over.

The small crowd of passengers surged forward once the train, its brakes screeching, pulled into the station. Smoke and steam descended onto the platform increasing the heat and intensity; travellers picked up bags, scooped up little children and pressed towards the carriages. The officers looked superior as people stepped on to the train, they were going off duty and were excited as they headed for the city. In stark contrast the French on board were nervous. Their eyes darted from one soldier to another, or maintained an empty stare straight ahead.

Claudette found the nerves and overt fear amongst the other passengers a camouflage. No one was interested in her, an unmarried country girl in her early twenties with dull, mousy hair and a worn, summer dress. She soon became accustomed to her anonymity, for it made invisibility easier.

From where she was in the carriage she had only a partial view of the outskirts of Paris. The countryside changed from a checkerboard of sage green and bright yellow to black turned earth, long straights of overgrown grass, grey clay spreading across broken roads. Every so often a village or small town would appear, some of the houses wrecked and burned into black skeletons.

The train stopped, thick black smoke descended, darkening the carriage. There was a new tighter tension amongst the passengers until, with a hiss of brakes and a clunk of couplings, it began to move forward again. No French was being spoken, instead the laughter and uproar from the German officers at the end of the carriage brought into sharp focus the drained faces and silence of the other passengers. The man opposite Claudette was fidgeting nervously with his pocket, his hand dipping into it as if he were checking something over and over again. Even the children on board were quiet and withdrawn. A young boy watched the soldiers from under his mother's arm, his large brown eyes fixated by them.

Finally, the sway of the train changed into a long braking halt, steam hissing up into the high roof of the

Gare du Nord, blocking out the sunlight. The station tasted of smoke and engine oil. It was hot and clammy and Claudette felt as if her legs were heavy, even her small leather valise seemed to have doubled in weight.

At the gate a line of blue-uniformed policemen stood watching each and every individual as they walked past. Every traveller maintained a steady gait, eyes forward, papers in hand. Some of the hands were shaking.

The police officer who blocked Claudette's path had grey teeth and greasy hair; beads of sweat ran down his temples from under his cap, she moved towards him slowly. In front of her a young woman, who was holding the hand of a small boy, frantically rifled through her handbag.

To Claudette's left was a soldier with an Alsatian dog. Its haughty eyes settled on her and she realised his handler, in turn, was looking her up and down too. There was no sign of the newspaper stand. The soldier looked away, his attention drawn by the man who had been checking his pockets, who was now mopping his head with a dirty handkerchief. The dog scratched himself and was reprimanded with a sharp pull on the choke chain. Finally, the woman found her identity card and had it gripped in her hand to show the policeman who simply nodded and let her pass.

Women with children are invisible, Joubert had said. He was right.

'Documents,' said the policeman. Claudette handed them over. 'Name.'

'Françoise Favelle.'

'Why have you come to Paris?'

The queue behind her was strained and quiet. Amongst the noise, heat and bustle of the station, there was a pool of silence so that the only sound was the thundering of blood in her ears.

'I have a job as a maid.'

'Where?'

'I don't know yet. My brother has organised it for me.'

'Brother?'

'Yes,'

'Where is he?'

'He's meeting me here.'

'His name?'

'Jacques Favelle.'

'And you don't know where you are working?' he raised an eyebrow.

'No,' replied Claudette as calmly as she was able.

'Wait there.' He pointed to his right and she moved over obediently, placing her suitcase on the floor by her feet. The dog handler was looking her up and down again. She pretended not to notice, but for the first time she felt visible and exposed. There was nowhere to go; the passengers joined by others from a second train surged forward. The grandparents and their charge ignored her, the woman with the jowls too. No one wanted to register her existence. When, after a long wait, the people had passed her by, the policeman closed his gate and turned to her.

'Come here,' he commanded. 'Where are you from?' Claudette looked past his shoulder and saw a man by the paper stand. He was wearing a flatcap and a scruffy jacket. 'I'm from a small farm near Vacily,' she said evenly. She looked up at him and then again at the man by the paper stand.

He had gone.

Claudette was eye to eye with the policeman who was weighing her up.

'What do you do there?'

'I am a seam-'

'Is anything wrong here?' The man in the flatcap was standing right in front of them, on the opposite side of the gate.

'Who are you?'

'Jacques Favelle, sir, I am this lady's brother.'

The policeman looked from Claudette to the man in the cap and back again. A black line of sweat ran from his forehead into his eye and he grimaced.

'Where is she working?'

'In Twelve Rue Ercol,' replied Jacques. 'Where I work.'

The policeman's raised his eyebrows and his lips parted into a smile.

'I see.'

'She will be a maid, I am the caretaker there.'

'I would have been very surprised if you'd told me different,' said the policeman as he ran his eyes over Claudette's dress and scuffed shoes. 'You're definitely not a resident.' He opened the barrier and waved Claudette through. 'You look too old to be her brother,' he said to Favelle over her head.

'One of my father's mistakes!' Favelle winked as he hugged Claudette and made great play of it. 'My lovely Françoise, I never thought you would come to Paris, what a pity your first time has to be now. She is not so beautiful,

57

but she still has her heart.' He stank of beer and his eyes, close up, were bloodshot. There was dandruff in his beard. She tried not to take in the heavy stale sweat smell of his clothes as he drew her to him.

The policeman had strutted away, bloated with his own self-importance. He nodded at the German soldier and offered him a cigarette. 'Arsehole,' growled Jacques under his breath as he took her case from her and then looped his arm into hers, leading her through the milling crowd. 'Bastard.'

'I thought he'd spotted something about me,' said Claudette, allowing herself a breath of relief.

'No, he does it at random, picks on someone, sometimes he pushes them around. The Boches think he's a prick, but they like how he keeps the poor sods on edge. Helps them to spot the ones who have something to hide.'

He took Claudette's arm and pulled her through the milieu of people outside the station. Everyone coming or going made way for the Nazis whose imperious presence was ubiquitous and in stark contrast to the dejected and jaded expressions of the Parisians.

'Keep walking,' said Jacques. 'This way.' There was a beggar kneeling on the pavement, his eyes hidden beneath wild grey brows. When he caught hold of Claudette's dress, she thought it would tear and pulled it sharply out of his grasp. Jacques swore at him and pulled her along the road. 'I told you, keep walking,' he snapped.

There was no time to take anything in, but the dirt and squalor outside the station blocked their path so that they had to walk around debris and discarded rubbish. They headed along a broad main street. Soldiers sat outside the cafés, boots resting on the chairs in front of them, laughing with one another as people hurried quickly by. Jacques took a left turn and headed across the road. She tripped after him, her feet pinching in her shoes. There was no room on the pavement because people were standing four deep across it. They were listless in the heat of the sun, bunching up towards a butcher's shop, their faces weary. Another queue was forming on the opposite side of the road.

'What are they queuing for?' she asked as they passed a woman holding a crying baby. She was pressing it against her shoulder patting its back, her eyes watering. People were gesticulating at her, telling her to leave the queue and take it home.

'Meat,' he replied stiffly. 'A slice of horse if they are very lucky and a few crumbs of cheese; there is no food.'

'No food?'

'Not for the poor and the lowly, it's been getting worse; the Boches take everything. Bastards.'

Paris was busy, its citizens moving about at a pace. Women in high heels walked by in twos and threes, handbags hanging from their arms, white gloves in hand, but as they passed Claudette she saw the gloves were dirty, the bags scuffed, the heels chipped.

There were queues at every corner, some of the people patient, others breaking out into scuffles as they neared the shop. The heat of the city was almost unbearable and Claudette felt as if she was melting. Perspiration ran between her breasts, her dress was sticking to her skin.

At the end of the road they passed a small café in a back street with a couple of Frenchmen sitting outside. They were smoking so that the rough edged odour of cigarette smoke mingled with the heat haze. They turned down a narrow street, Favelle taking a sharp right turn and then left. His brisk pace was unrelenting.

'You can be stopped anywhere,' he told her, 'and questioned.'

She ran after him, trying to avoid the clusters of rubbish on the pavement. 'In here, now.' He pushed her inside a pair of doors, half-glazed, a filigree of decorative wrought iron in front of the dirty glass. The building was refreshingly cool.

'Upstairs, quickly,' he whispered urgently. 'Right to the top, no noise.' She took the marble stairs two at a time on her toes. It curved around four floors, on each level passing anonymous, unnumbered doors, the paint peeling off them. All the nameplates were empty, the names removed.

The room at the top was small and airless. There was a single round window through which the sun streamed onto a bare, wooden floor. 'It's awful in here,' she said breathlessly, 'can I open the window?'

'What? Yes, it needs a push, do it quietly though.' Once open, the fresh air was a relief, the sound of the city below a distant hum and only the occasional car horn could be heard. Claudette took in deep gulps of air and pulled her dress away from her sticky skin. When she turned around Favelle was watching her, one of his eyelids drooping, his face red with heat. He ran an eye over her as if she was a horse he was buying.

'He's right,' he said, 'that policeman, you're not what I expected. There is an idea of what a woman of the Resistance looks like and you're not it.'

'How many have you met?'

'Just you,' he said with a curt nod of the head. 'As I said, it's not what I expected.'

'Well, I'm all you've got,' she said with defiance, she was tired of being treated this way by older men.

'That's what worries me,' he replied.

'If I'm not what is expected it will surely give me an advantage?' she countered, but he wasn't interested. She looked around the room. There was a stack of boxes, a mattress, a small stove and a table, but no traces of anyone living there. No blankets, food, crockery.

'What is this place?'

'Shelter from the storm,' he replied. 'A pot to piss in.' She leant against the window ledge, the soft breeze cooling her back a little.

'Is this where I'm working?'

'God no, this is were I brief you and it's for you to know about if you need it. Though if you ever do need it you might find you have a room-mate or two. It's essential that no one sees you coming in or going out and that you never make a noise. If we're lucky, it'll never come to that; I'll show you where the key is hidden.'

'Is there anything to drink?'

He produced a flask from his pocket, unscrewed it and poured water into the lid. She took it and sipped only a little, exactly as Yves had taught her. 'I see they've taught you something' said Favelle with a smirk. She ignored him, he was too much like Joubert.

'So are you briefing me?'

He swigged from the flask and wiped his hand across his mouth. Claudette watched him, he was unrefined and brutish. Had her real brother lived past his second birthday and not died of tuberculosis, she imagined he would have been a better man, a good man, like Yves.

'You will be working at twelve Rue Ercol, as a maid. It's frequented by Boches, all the time. You will be watching, listening, being discreet, always discreet and you will act as if you are deaf and blind to what goes on.'

'Is it a hotel?'

'No, I'll come to that, just wait. You will cook and clean, I'm told you can sew, is it true?'

'Yes, my mother and I sew and mend for people, since the invasion we've had a lot of work to do.'

'You'll have a lot more of it to do here.'

'Am I starting tonight?' All at once she had the uncomfortable feeling that she and Favelle were spending the night together in this cramped oven of a room.

'Yes, I'm taking you there at six. I have told Madam Odile that you are my sister and she is happy enough. She trusts me, I do errands for her.'

'What does your job involve?'

'For her? I drive the car, when we can get any petrol, I do maintenance and I am security when I'm needed. For us,' he paused. 'I do what you will be doing, but I can't get close enough, that's why you're here.'

'What am I listening for?'

'Anything. You pass on to me absolutely anything you hear that can help us, these Germans get sloppy when their boots are off.' As if to prove the point he took out a packet of German cigarettes and lit one. 'They are very careless with whisky inside them too. You want one?' It was obvious, as he held the open pack towards her that he was hoping she'd refuse. She did.

'Do I have a day off?' Claudette changed tack.

'No, you get fed instead. Don't worry, there is nothing to have a day off for, the Germans have seen to that. They're in every street, every hotel, every café. You'll hear gunfire and find you'll have to walk the long way home to avoid it.' He took a drag on the cigarette. 'For us it's safer to stay inside.'

'And this guest house?'

'What guest house?'

'Where I'm working.'

His laugh was mostly a sneer.

'It's not a guest house, it's a brothel, a whore house.' Her gasp was audible and he continued to scoff. 'Plain little Catholic country girl finds works in brothel, your mother would cry no doubt.'

Claudette rose to the challenge. 'Actually, I think she'd expect me to do anything I could for a free France, to free us.'

'Noble talk,' he said, dropping the stub of his cigarette on the floor and grinding it into the wooden floorboard with his shoe. 'I don't think we'll ever be free again, we have conceded, we've caved in without a fight. It's humiliating, but we'll have to live with it now.'

Claudette studied him, the open pores of his nose, dark eyes, the yellowing teeth and the coarse black beard. He was repulsive. He stood up abruptly and looked out of the window, leaning out over the wide ledge to look down on the street.

'I'm going out, I'll be back at six. Do not move,' he ordered.

She nodded.

'Practise everything you've learned about Françoise Favelle, go over it again and again. What's her favourite colour? What food does she miss? Recite your birth date, you've been doing this already, yes?'

'Yes,' she replied.

'Good.' He was about to turn the doorknob when he looked back at her.

'Do you have a sister?' she asked.

'No, I don't, I have no siblings.'

'So you've had to learn all about me, too.'

'Yes, everything.'

'Won't they check, at some point, if not now?'

'They'll find everything is in place, we're from a farm near Vacily. Our parents left in the Exodus and are missing.'

She nodded. 'But won't they find out you never had a sister, in some way?'

'No, Jacques Favelle did have a sister, Françoise, and they lived on a farm. It wasn't near Vacily, but that's been sorted out.'

'Your name isn't Jacques Favelle?'

'Of course my name isn't Jacques Favelle. We're both working under assumed names, forget that and you're dead. Worse than that, I'm dead, and when they kill you they take their time, they like to make us suffer.' With that he opened the door a crack and peered out. As he prepared to leave he turned back once again to Claudette and whispered, 'If I don't come back, go to twelve Rue Ercol, they know you are coming.'

Chapter Eleven

I was sitting in the garden, nursing a mug of tea and missing Freddy. He and I had tea together on a Sunday afternoon from time to time. We used to sit side by side on the ancient garden swing, the rusted chains just about holding up the grey slatted seat. The garden was overgrown, the lawn patchy and the shrubs that had valiantly flowered amongst the weeds and grasses were dying back in the heat. There was a thin path of crazy paving through the parched turf and at the end of it a stone shed. When I heard the scrambling sound from behind it I knew what to expect. Sid, next door's dog, appeared with the familiar look of surprise on his face, as if he'd never broken in before. He was a rescue Beagle who often popped in to eat anything he could find and wee on everything else.

'Sid,' I clicked my tongue and, on seeing me, he made a beeline for my lap, landing with a heavy thump and licking my face with great earnest. He was panting and was soon off again looking under the chair for crumbs from the chocolate biscuit I'd eaten. He sniffed around, keeping one eye on the back door at all times, I knew he was waiting for Freddy to appear.

'He's not here, Sid,' I said with a sigh. 'He's gone.' As soon as I said it I felt a deep crushing pain inside me, I really was going to miss my old friend very much. He was a lovely man, quiet at times and thoughtful, or loud and often risqué, a really old luvvie. Of course most of the time he'd been ill and more often than not I'd call round for tea on a Sunday and he'd be in bed; when he was on form, though, no one could deny he was an absolute joy to know.

I wondered what Matt was doing. I had been thinking of him whilst I sorted through the boxes of programmes and scripts I'd found. Freddy had worked with them all – Gielgud, Olivier, Richardson, their faces on gloss paper of programmes going back to the fifties. The last was dated nineteen seventy nine when Freddy had had his first severe bi-polar episode. After that, he told me, he could never function properly and he had to give up writing. Hat told me it was depression, not anxiety, a remnant of the grief of his mother dying, of losing his only tie to the world.

Sid's tail was wagging like a metronome as he zigzagged around the garden, nose to the ground. He did another fly-past, his wet nose touching the tips of my fingers and then he was gone, back through the gap in the fence. It was deliberately left for him to come and go as he pleased.

Once again it was quiet and I sat long after I had finished my drink, knowing I had to go back indoors and carry on in Freddy's room, but wanting instead to sit in the sun letting it warm my face. Eventually, as I stood up, a grey watery cloud pushed across the blue of the sky and it began to spot with rain.

The room felt empty without Matt, but it allowed me to be lost in my own thoughts and I took it slowly, picking up books and getting immersed in the odd chapter, or reading a cutting that Freddy had jammed between the pages in a reference book.

A bluebottle buzzed against the window and when the noise began to irritate me, I stood up and leaned across to open it. There was a pile of books in the way and I knocked one, a copy of David Copperfield bound in black leather with gold type, to the floor. It fell with a thud, disturbing dust that puffed up into a miniature cloud. It caught, splayed open on the crossbar of the chair, and a letter fell out. I picked it up, turning it round to read it; it was another one written by Freddy.

St. Patricks School for BOys
Lymstead
13th July 1955

Dear Papa,

I have not heard from you but I know that you must think of me often, Mama is dead. I thought you shold know. I have been very sad indeed and I think you would be if you knew. Mama said you were a very nice man and that I am quite like you because I am a gentleman.

I hope you will soon come and take me away from boarding school as I don't like it at all, specilly sports. I like doing English and drama.

Kind regards

Fredrik

I turned it over, there was nothing on the reverse, the paper was folded neatly in three, the writing was in ink and not pencil as before. There was no envelope and no hint of the address of the person who was to receive it.

I slid it into a brown A4 envelope with the other one to show Hat when she came home, and carried on. The rain was pattering against the window. I clicked on the radio and listened to Radio Two whilst I sifted through the scripts of a BBC Play for Today, pink or pale blue paper bound with a yellow or green cover. They were all typed and the actors had made their own notes in pencil with lots of crossings out. Only one or two had put their names on the cover, and I didn't recognise them, so I didn't know if I was looking at scripts once held by a big star, a supporting role or a producer. I found myself wondering what it would have been like to rub shoulders with that sort of talent. Those famous names familiar still; Freddy must have been very special.

I found a photograph of a young bright-faced Freddy with a group of actors. They had uncorked a bottle of champagne and the shutter had clicked the very second the cork had been fired. All of them were laughing, all eyes focussed on the spray of liquid bursting from the bottle. I recognised some of the faces, but the names were lost to me – well before my time.

The next photograph was of The Wyndam Theatre's blue stage door, then a picture of a Windmill Girl covering herself demurely in ostrich feather fans. It was signed 'With all my love, Jilly.' There were some nondescript theatre shots of plays, and then, rising to the surface, appeared a black and white photo of Marlene Dietrich.

I looked at the handwriting to see if it was a printed or an authentic autograph. The ink sat on the surface of the glossy paper, definitely signed as I thought, an original signature in dark blue ink. She was beautiful, thin eyebrows, thick lashes, long slender nose and absolutely perfect lips. Her nails, resting against her face, were long and neatly painted. I looked at my own nail varnished fingers as I held the photo, they were all chipped and cracked. The blouse she was wearing was sheer with clusters of sequins, looking as if they'd been sprayed on her. The handwriting, in contrast, was surprisingly scruffy, in fact more what I would describe as a scrawl. It said simply; 'Fredrik, Best wishes. Marlene. X'

I knew it was worth money, a genuine, autographed photo, and I suspected the family would probably sell it. I stared at her face, wondering what would happen if I slipped it into my own pile, between the copy of The Merchant of Venice and Star of the Sea and then I corrected myself for even thinking that way. I was never dishonest, something my father was very clear about. "Have nothing in your past that can catch up with you later."

I put the picture in the envelope with Freddy's letters because I wanted to show Matt before it went and, of course, Hat. She was late, she'd aimed to be back for five and it was nearly six fifteen. I carried on, there were letters from friends, tales of holidays and far away places. 'Capri is beautiful, you must come out;' 'Biarritz is crowded but Faye and Ronnie are here, great value as always;' 'Bunny was a hoot and says to wish you best for the final curtain;' 'Jack is working on getting the play to The Garrick, he's sure as am I that it will run and run.' There were bills and calling cards and the trivia of theatre land. I found myself envying his life, the life before he was drowning in sadness. I was looking at an album of random photos when Hat appeared at the door, making me jump with fright.

'Sorry, Connie, I thought you'd heard me, I did shout,' she said. 'I've just got back, the traffic was awful. Did me good, though. How are you getting on?' She was on the threshold looking at the half-tidied room. 'Wow, you've been busy, I'll never be able to thank you enough.'

I explained about the piles on the landing, though others had also emerged "The Review Again" and "Possibly Valuable" stacks were becoming taller as time went by.

'We've checked everything.'

'We?' she said, head cocked to one side like Sid when he's trying to comprehend humans.

'Matt helped me yesterday, and this morning for a few hours.' She arched a questioning eyebrow, but I ignored her and carried on. 'He asked if he could have any photos that aren't of a personal nature.'

'Yes, that's fine, it would be nice to think there were some of Freddy's things in the village.' Her face dropped a little, her eyes wistful. 'Cup of tea?' she asked shaking off the sadness. 'Or better still, wine, white and cold, straight from the fridge?'

'Ooh, lovely.' As I stood up my eye caught the brown envelope with Freddy's letters inside.

'Hat, before you go, what do you make of these?'

I handed her the two letters. She looked completely dumbfounded and read them both twice. 'Father?' she said, quite obviously completely puzzled. She scratched her head. 'Now that is very confusing. Maybe he was making it up, like a game, using his imagination?' I offered the explanation Matt and I had discussed.

'That must be it, or perhaps he simply had no address, just wanted to pretend he was sending them.' She nodded in agreement, her hand touching her cheek the same way Marlene Dietrich was doing in her pose for that photo. That reminded me.

'And this,' I said, passing it to her. 'Fancy him knowing her too.'

'Wow, he's never spoken about that, lots of other big names, but not her.' She touched the surface of the photo gently as if she had once known the actress herself. 'That really is something.' Then she turned it over and went very quiet.

'What's wrong?' I asked. She stared down at the reverse of the picture then handed it to me. On the back, at the bottom was the same handwriting, it said, 'Von einem traurigen deutschen zu einem anderen.' I knew enough German to translate it. 'From one sad German to another.'

Chapter Twelve

When Claudette opened her eyes the first thing she saw was a pair of black shoes and grey trousers. She sat up with a start, blinking into the light. It was Jacques Favelle. 'They didn't train you to sleep lightly, then,' he said, shaking his head. She pushed herself up, her head heavy and groggy; a line of pain was splitting her skull. It was still furiously hot.

'Is there any more water?' she asked. Jacques passed her the flask.

'We need to go now,' he said as he picked up her valise. Struggling to her feet, she slipped on her shoes and straightened out her dress. He nodded towards the window. 'You need to close that.' They left as silently as possible, he gently clicked the front door closed behind them.

'Take my arm and smile at me,' he ordered. 'Act like you love me.' Like that they made their way through the back streets, Jacques telling her to memorise each twist and turn. On the corner of one street he stopped and looked around.

'Look like you have something in your shoe, take it off.' She leaned on him and did as she was bid. 'See that loose stone in the wall, just below your eye level? You pull that out and the key is behind it, I have one too. I'll show you where I keep mine later.'

The house was tall, six storeys at least, some windows were open. From somewhere up above she could hear music, the soft lilting strains of Mozart mixed with café jazz. Jacques put a large key in the lock and opened the door. The smell inside was of polish and the heavy intense scent of the lilies on the reception table. He clicked on the desk lamp and looked around. There was a large room to the right, a bar and sofas, the soft light from behind the bar spilling across the highly polished floor. To the left was a large red leather Chesterfield with a cushion placed in the middle of it. The female figure embroidered on the cushion was naked, holding up a chalice, and the words sewn beneath said: 'Drink From Me.' To the side of it was a glass door with 'Salon' etched into the frosted glass. It was closed.

'This is the main door to the house. There is a back door but we have had it blocked off, and Madame Odile has the only key. It means we are less prone to attack. Even deliveries come through here now.'

'Attack? From the Germans? But I thought –'

'Not from the Nazis, I'm talking about the French. We are not exactly popular, though most people seem to think that this is a gentlemen's club, what they hate is that we all work for the Hun.'

Claudette took a deep breath and tried to focus. In front of her was a narrow metal lift shaft, the ornate metal cage inside ready to ascend. 'You must never use the lift, it's for clients and ladies only,' said Jacques. 'The likes of us must walk.' He led the way up the stairs. The carpet was a rich deep pile, a dark purple, the walls a pale grey. It took them to lobby after lobby, double doors leading to the rooms on each floor. At each level were stained-glass windows letting in shafts of coloured light that danced on the plain walls.

'What a beautiful place, and this carpet,' she said, stopping briefly to look at it.

'You won't think that when you're cleaning it every Sunday morning,' grunted Jacques. 'It will soon become the bane of your life.'

'And there are no back stairs?' Claudette asked.

'They've been blocked off too.'

On each landing was an oil painting of a nude woman; sensuous, alluring or mischievous, each one of them beautiful and looking down at Claudette, their eyes following her as she climbed the next staircase. The final floor, the sixth, had a single shabby door. Jacques led her through into a narrow corridor with a linoleum floor.

'In here,' he said, 'this is your room. The other maid, Marie, sleeps next door. She is not to be trusted, no-one is.' He pushed open the door. It was small, similar to the room in the other place, but there was a ewer and basin on a table under the small window and a rickety chair with a basket weave seat. A woven mat concealed the worn floorboards. The bed was narrow, the striped mattress thin, sheets and blankets were folded on top ready for the bed to be made. 'Unpack, then wash, smarten yourself up and put on the uniform, here on the back of the door.' Behind the door was a black dress and white apron, a small frilled cap hanging on top of them both on the hook. 'When you are ready, come down, and beneath the staircase on the ground floor is a door. I will be down in the kitchen, meet me there.'

With that he was gone. Claudette looked out of the window, across the street was another building of the same type, a mirror image of her window, but dirty and covered in moss. The street below was not visible.

She washed her face and arms, then unpacked her coat, her thick woollen skirt and jumper for winter, and her best dress. She wished she had a picture of her mother and father, but it was strictly forbidden. Instead, on the only nail in the wall she hung an embroidered picture of a garden made by her mother.

She had brought her rosary, her Bible and a copy of Madame Bovary with a pressed flower in it, a Marguerite. It reminded her of Vacily and the wild swans on the lake, and of her parents and Yves. A tear brimmed in her eye. Already she did not like Paris, it smelt worn and tired, the rubbish everywhere reeked and there was obviously no food. She wiped it away, took a deep breath and put on the slightly too large uniform.

When she stepped out of her room there was total silence. The landing was narrow and the paint peeled off the walls. Her feet echoed on the lino as she walked. She opened the door at the end and was once again treading on the purple carpet, her rough, worn shoes making no sound.

As she arrived at the first floor she saw someone coming up the stairs on the other side of the lift shaft. It was too late to turn away, she had been seen. The woman looked up at Claudette, her eyes large and brown. Her skin was like porcelain, the soft milk white of her face framed by a roll of glossy dark hair. She was naked save for a sheer negligee that was completely unfastened. Claudette could not look away, she had never seen anything quite so dazzling, except in paintings and only then in books.

'You are staring,' said the woman, she was making no effort to cover herself. As she drew level with Claudette, she added, 'You know it's rude to stare don't you?' The voice was lazy, warm, like melting caramel.

'I'm sorry,' said Claudette, looking down at her shoes and in front of them the slim bare feet and red painted toes of the woman: 'I didn't expect to see anyone.'

'Don't worry yourself.' She reached out and touched Claudette's cheek with the back of her finger. 'You have come from the country, I can tell, those cheeks are aflame with sun and fresh air.' Claudette flushed red as a sting of embarrassment ran through her. She didn't dare raise her eyes to the woman's face. 'I am Lilia. And you are?'

'Cla-Françoise,' said Claudette, inwardly cursing herself for such a basic error.

'Ah, she has made you change your name,' said the woman, nodding sagely. Relief flooded through Claudette as she realised the woman was probably one of them, the Resistance. Then she said, 'They even make the maids sound glamorous here to impress our clients.' She pulled the wrap around her, it tightened over her breasts, the hardened nipples showing clearly through it. 'Have you just arrived?'

'Yes,' replied Claudette, she was now more guarded before speaking.

'Come and see me when you're settled in, I am in the Indian room. If you knock twice and I answer, I am available. You'll soon learn the routine.'

With that the woman carried on upstairs, her feet silent

on the carpet, hand dragging languidly behind her on the banister. The flesh beneath the negligee was creamy white, flawless. Claudette hurried down to the door beneath the stairs, her shoes beating a retreat on the shiny tiles.

Jacques was in the kitchen. He was cleaning a rifle, poking a cleaning rod into the barrel then looking down into it to see if it was clear.

'Ah,' he said, almost verging on a friendly welcome. 'There you are. There is an apple and some Brie there on the table for you, and a glass of wine.' He also had a glass beside him on a small table at his elbow.

'Brie and an apple? Wine?' Claudette couldn't believe her eyes. The fruit was large and yellow and the Brie was starting to ooze across the plate. She fell on it, she had not seen food like this since before Christmas. The juice of the apple ran down the sides of her mouth, she caught it with the end of her index finger and sucked on it so as to waste nothing. Jacques Favelle was watching her, his eyelid drooping. She ignored him and turned away to look around the kitchen. It was the best she'd ever seen, a big range, a wealth of cupboards and working surfaces. Shining copper pans hung on the walls and a big pine table in the middle was scrubbed to within an inch of its life. The windows were barred so that the light fell in slats from the street above. There was a lazy, far away, clip clop of horses' hooves when she listened, but no other sound was detectable.

'It's like a sanctuary down here,' said Jacques. He had returned to servicing his gun. 'But I don't ever kid myself there is not someone listening somewhere.' He nodded towards a pipe. 'People have been known to hear on the floor above through that sort of thing.'

Claudette carved a slice of Brie and forked it into her mouth. Its rind felt like velvet. 'How on earth do you get this?'

'The Boches, they make sure we get anything we need, on condition it never leaves the house.' He indicated above with his eyes. 'Though I'm certain it does. The girls will often go without to send food to their families.'

'I met one, Lilia,' said Claudette. 'She caught me unawares, on the stairs.'

'Naked?'

'Almost.'

'She's probably high too,' said Jacques. 'That's something else they get easily enough, though Lilia is the worst, she's hooked.' There was a moment of silence, as she studied him. 'No, I don't,' he said out of the blue. 'If that's what you're thinking, I need a clear head to do what needs doing here.'

Claudette was wondering why he was so quick to protest his innocence. 'How did you manage to keep your rifle? I thought they had all been banned?' she asked.

'I have it for our protection, they gave us a special license. Nothing is too much trouble for us.'

'Who cooks?' she asked at length, finishing the cheese and wishing there was more.

'Madame Farine!' He finally smiled. 'At least that's what we called her. She is always covered in flour, has an arse the size of Luxembourg and never stops talking. Her name is Clarice, but we called her Madame F. Marie helps her down here whilst you and the daily maid, Perrine, do upstairs. When Madame F gets back from visiting her sister, who's unwell, at any time now she will tell you all about your job and then Madame Odile wants to see you at eight. At nine the meal is served and then you make yourself scarce. Sometimes the ladies need errands run for them. Sometimes they ask for a bath to be drawn for their clients, others might need you to clean up before their next client arrives, but the staff all finish at ten thirty.'

Claudette felt a stretch in her stomach, the nerves twisting inside. 'You mean I go in, when they are in there… together?' There was a catch of nerves in her voice.

'Yes, of course you do, and that's when you observe and watch and listen. Hang up a jacket for the gentlemen, making sure nothing falls out of their pockets.' He gave her an exaggerated wink of the eye. 'It's essential they are comfortable because Madame Odile accepts nothing less.'

'And will they leave me alone, I mean, if I go in?'

'I should hope so, I can't have a maid who's breeding or squirming with the clap and needs replacing. Simply show yourself to be willing and helpful, but silent, always silent unless it's to say yes sir, or no sir.'

Claudette considered his words for a second, but she couldn't imagine herself calling any German "sir". In her mind's eye she saw Gabin's face, the blood drenching his shirt and his poor mother on the ground clutching gravel in her hands. She vowed to herself that she would never call them "sir", ever.

'Here.' Jacques pointed at the hearth. 'See that crack under there?'

'Yes,' nodded Claudette leaning forward to look at it.

'That is a little hole where I keep the second key I told you about.'

There was a bang of a door and a large woman came hurriedly down the steps, arrived in a flurry of skirts and a waft of lavender water. She was big, with powerful forearms and a shot silk jacket that winced across her ample bosom. 'Is this her?' she asked as she looked at Claudette, her nose in the air and her hands on her wide hips.

'Yes Madame F, it's Françoise, my baby sister.'

'Very baby.' Her eyebrow raised in Jacque's direction. 'Other side of the blanket?'

'Not that we know of, eh, Françoise?'

Claudette nodded, looking suitably shy.

Madame F was unfazed. 'What's the age difference then?'

'Almost twenty years,' Jacques replied. 'A big surprise for my mother.'

'Scrawny,' Madame F said over her shoulder to him as she stood squarely in front of Claudette. 'Are you certain she can do this job?'

'I work very hard,' said Claudette. She was tired of being talked about and quite felt indignant. 'And I sew too.'

'You sew! Professionally?'

'Yes.'

'Then thank all that is holy, we have a mountain of sewing since the – '

There was a moment of awkwardness until Jacques spoke. 'Our seamstress was a Jewess.' Her eyes fleetingly caught those of Jacques, they obviously had a mutual affection for the girl.

It was Madame F who said: 'Lovely girl,' with a regretful sigh. 'They just took her away, and her whole family with her, in the middle of the night. It was a terrible shock for

80

us all.' There was a silence as Madame F stared into space, deep in thought.

'What do you need me to do tonight?' Claudette asked, changing the subject.

'Marie is back late tonight, she is waiting for a package of goods at the station from Berlin, so I need potatoes peeling and then apples and then I need the table set.'

'And she is seeing Madame at eight, don't forget,' added Jacques, pointing his rifle at the dresser as if he might shoot a plate. He rubbed a soft cloth over the sight and tried again.

'Marie will be back by then, she can take over.' With that Madame F began to collect pots and pans together and asked Jacques to bring in the sack of potatoes. Claudette turned an apple round in her hand, it was blushed red, its skin perfect, unblemished. She ran her finger across one, the skin didn't wrinkle or break.

'Come on now, hurry up, don't just stand there staring,' said Madame F. 'Have you never seen an apple before?'

'Not for a long time,' said Claudette. 'Not for a very long time.'

Chapter Thirteen

I met Matt in the Posh Pub. He had been meeting with a client, an earnest young man with a round boyish face and smiling eyes. He was leaving as I arrived. 'He's all yours,' he said, holding the door open for me.

I thanked him and sat down opposite Matt, no kiss hello, I wasn't ready for anything like that, not yet. I moved the empty pint glass to one side.

'Hi there,' said Matt as he put his ipad away in his bag. 'Drink?'

'Half a cider please,' I replied. The bar was old-fashioned with Old Hooky on tap, but the rest of the room was sage green and cream, unmatched chairs around assorted half wood, half painted pine tables.

'There you go,' he said, as he sat down and placed my drink in front of me.

'Thanks.'

'How's it going?'

'I'm about half way through.' I told him. 'Found something weird.'

'Really. What?'

'Well, would you believe we found a photo of Marlene Dietrich, signed in ink and with a personal message to Freddy on the back.'

'Wow, really? That's quite something.'

'Yes it is, but this is the weird bit, it said: "To one sad German from another".'

'German?'

'Yes, and written by her in German.'

'Maybe he was born there and he nationalised himself.'

'But, the weird thing is he didn't speak German and Hat says he has never been there nor talked about it.'

'Well, perhaps he came here as a youngster, or maybe his Mum was married to one,' he suggested.

'No, she was never married.'

'Strange.'

'And there was another letter to his father, like the last one, but when he was at boarding school.'

'Did you Google him?'

'Yep, and it says he was the son of a single mother, born in London.'

'Citations?'

'Yes, after the word London, but no others,' I told him

'Well, you can't trust wiki, we all know that.'

'I know, but it said that elsewhere too, on other websites.' I had drawn a blank.

'That is strange then, Freddy's a bit of a mystery, are you going to do the "room" tonight?'

'Yep, Hat's going to WI. Would you like to come?'

'If you want me to.' He looked a bit anxious and suddenly I felt I'd been too distant, I never mean to, it just happens.

'Of course, let's do it.'

At six thirty I made us both a steaming mug of tea and we sat, cross-legged, like children on the floor. Matt had pointed out that we could now see all the carpet and half of the daybed. When we'd started we didn't even know it was there.

'Here's a picture of the Windmill Theatre. Look at all that totty with no vests on.' Matt passed me the photos of the girls posing as Greek statues, covered from the waist down in diaphanous, almost transparent fabric. 'Apparently, they were allowed to be naked if they didn't move,' he said, finding another. 'Wow, nice one, am I allowed to keep these?'

'I don't see why not, they're not personalised, are they?'

'No, nothing front or back.'

He placed them on the floor next to him.

'Old schoolbook here.' He lifted it up and passed it to me. It was a maths book, one of those with fine grids in pale blue on the pages. Freddy's maths was awful, lots of red slashed through the untidy numbers with "see me!" on most pages.

'Poor Freddy, he must have been discalculate,' I said with sympathy. 'I'm no mathematician myself. In those days no-one knew all those labels we use today.' I pressed my hand on the cover of the book as if it might connect me to him in some magical way. 'He kept everything, didn't he?'

'Including loads of cigarette cards in an old Meccano box, it seems,' said Matt, rummaging through the tin box and finding Laurence Olivier, Olivia de Havilland, David Niven and Montgomery Clift.

'They might be worth something,' I told him. 'We'll give them to Hat; she might be able to sell them on-line or something. She does a lot of fund-raising for animal charities.'

'And here's his Atlas.' Matt passed the large book to me, the glossy cover caught the light as he did so. 'We all had one of these, didn't we?'

'Ooh, I haven't seen an Atlas for years.' I took it from him and flipped open the cover. An illustration of the whole globe was in front of me, spinning in a shroud of swirling clouds, the green and blue of land and sea a blur. The next pages were flat maps of the world, the British imperial pink dominating all those countries that have since been declared independent. The Atlas was over sixty years old, the spine was missing and the binding in tatters. It smelt of old paper, cigarettes and mothballs.

I opened the Europe page, it all looked so unfamiliar. Someone, perhaps Freddy, had drawn a ring around Interlaken and Paris. I turned the page and there, on thin, blue airmail paper was another letter, the writing harder to decipher, the pale ink blurred and difficult to read.

'Roseberry House'
Ledbury
Herefordshire

3rd August, 1959

Dear Father,

I wish you would write to me, I have long wanted to meet you and tell you about Mama. She said you were a good man, that you fought in the war and that you loved her. I should very much want to know about all that.

Perhaps you could telephone? My number is Ledbury 252.

I leave for school in September in the interim I shall await your reply with great anticipation.

Yours in hope
Freddy.

'Wow! This is really strange, Matt. He's writing to a father no-one knew about and he's obviously overseas because he's used airmail paper.' I turned the paper over, it was the sort you folded and it created its own envelope, very light weight and therefore cheap to send. There was no address.

'My mother used to send her sister in Africa letters on that paper,' Matt offered. 'Very see through and light.'

'And no address, it was never sent.' We both stared at it for a moment.

'Or,' Matt suggested thoughtfully, 'He did a copy for himself? He wouldn't have had any way of copying it for his own records.'

'Brilliant!' I sat up on my haunches, 'And that's why he didn't address it.'

'I bet he used an address book,' said Matt brightly, 'And, what's the bet we find it somewhere in this mess?'

Chapter Fourteen

Claudette knocked on the door and straightened her hat. Her hair was too soft to stay beneath her lace cap so it was falling around her face in wisps. It was eight o'clock and still warm, the house was suffocatingly hot.

'Enter.' The door was wide and heavy, making it hard to push open. Madame Odile was standing with her back to the door. She was gazing out of the tall open window, a cigarette between her fingers, long nails elegantly scarlet. Claudette closed the door behind her and stood waiting for the woman to speak to her. When she turned round she took a very long, measured look at her new maid and let out a disappointed sigh.

'You have not done this before, I hear?'

'No, Madame,' Claudette replied.

'But your brother says you are a hard worker and you learn quickly.'

'I am, Madame. I do.'

Madame Odile took a few steps towards her and drew on her cigarette, arms still folded. She was much younger than Claudette had imagined, no more than mid-thirties. She had high cheekbones and smooth skin, but there was hardness behind her eyes, as if she had seen everything and nothing would ever shock her. Her blouse was done up to its top button, a fine silk scarf knotted over a sharp and immaculate petrol blue suit. She was a businesswoman through and through, hard and impervious. To look at her was to understand that the war, and the damage that it wrought on her city, were playing to her strengths. She was cashing in on it. She pointed down at Claudette's tired shoes.

'Our last maid had the same size feet as you, I'm almost certain, see if hers fit. I refuse to buy new if what we have will be of service. If not, tell Jacques you may have a pair. And your hair, it is not in good condition and it must look tidier.'

Claudette nodded, 'Yes, Madame.'

'Perrine knows what she is doing, get her to teach you, or ask her to do it, it would be quicker all round.' She sighed deeply as if she was frustrated. 'If it weren't for this, this – situation – maids would be ten a penny but all of them are working at the big hotels. You are to be the soul of discretion, did your brother make that clear?' She waited for Claudette to respond. 'Anything you see or hear within these walls is to go no further. He says you are unshockable, he promised me that.'

'Yes, Madame.'

'Work hard and we will get along. Cause me any problems and, brother or no, I will let you go.'

'Yes, Madame.'

'Well, that is everything, as long as we are clear.'

Claudette turned to go.

'One more thing.'

'Yes, Madame?'

'You are a seamstress?'

'Yes.'

'Yes…'

'Yes, Madame.'

'Please take in that uniform, it is too big for you.' She was expressionless as she spoke.

'Yes, Madame.' Claudette turned and opened the door, its heaviness almost overpowering her. She padded quietly back downstairs, her knees feeling suddenly weaker.

'How did you get on?' asked Madame F. 'She's quite formidable, is she not?'

'She is,' replied Claudette as she returned to her task of rolling out the pastry. Jacques was sitting by the fireplace looking through a newspaper.

'The ladies will be ready at nine,' said Madame F. 'This all needs taking upstairs and placing on the warmers. Marie, Marie girl, where are you?' A plain young girl, no more than seventeen, appeared from another part of the kitchen. Her face was flushed and her frizzy hair was bursting loose from her cap. 'This is Marie,' she helps me down here; not up there.' Madam F looked upwards to the ceiling.

'Hello,' said the girl. She was thin with a hooked nose and her small beady eyes darted up and down Claudette, assessing her.

'Hello,' replied Claudette. 'It's good to meet you.'

'Enough, enough, come on, this all needs taking upstairs,' said the cook, her hands flapping.

'Now, where is Perrine? She should have been here ten minutes ago, honestly, I do struggle with all this.'

At that moment Perrine arrived, her feet tripping lightly down the stairs. She was tall and pretty, her dark hair rolled above her forehead. She was wearing a scarf over the rest. 'So sorry.' She was breathless. 'There was a shooting in the Rue Berger. A man, young, came flying past me, he slid across the road and then two SS came round the corner. I ran the opposite away, then I heard the shot.' She was visibly shaken.

'Sit down, my dear Perrine,' cried Madame F and she took the girl in her arms. 'Jacques get her some brandy. My poor, poor girl.' Perrine was guided to a chair where Madame F untied her scarf. Her brown hair was pulled back into a neat chignon.

'Here,' said Jacques, handing her a small glass. He glanced at Claudette. 'This is what I warned you about, Sister, you must take real care if you have to go outside for any reason.'

'Thank goodness you didn't actually see it, Perrine,' added Marie. 'Poor man, I wonder who he was?'

'Poor man!' exclaimed Madam F. 'Poor man, what's all this? It is no good, they should accept what has happened, for God's sake. Life has changed and what is done is done. Is it so bad? When this settles down we can all adjust, get used to it. It will become as normal as the life we had before.'

'Madame F, you do not know what you are saying,' growled Jacques. 'You cannot speak like that, it is talk for defeatists and I won't have it.'

'Say what you will,' she waved a dismissive hand at him. 'It's all collapsed around us, everything we knew, and now we have to face the facts.'

'And the Jews, like Anna, our Seamstress? What about them?'

The girls looked from one to the other. Marie stepped

back nervously against the wall. There was an escalation of voices.

'Well, it's part of the new way of things, isn't it? There had to be some losses, there always is in war.'

'Some losses?' Jacques turned to face her full square on. 'Some losses!' He was puce with anger as he reinforced what he was saying. 'How can you describe the thousands of people who have been taken from Paris as some losses? You are incredible, woman!'

'They have been taken to work camps, I am sure they are being used to make useful things for when the war is over. They have taken them away to re-educate them and find somewhere to live where they can all be together. It actually makes sense.'

'My mother says they are being loaded into cattle trucks,' said Perrine. 'Hundreds at a time.'

'No, they're not, it's just hearsay and gossip. You shouldn't believe what you hear, Perrine,' Madame F turned to her preparations, shaking her head.

Claudette did not know what to make of it. She saw Jacques pulling on his jacket, he was still angry. He pushed past the cook and went upstairs, then they heard the distant bang of the front door as he left.

'Well, he won't get far in the curfew,' said Madame F. 'Silly man. I hope you are not like him, Françoise, I can't be doing with that sort of thing in my kitchen.'

'No,' said Claudette. 'My brother is much more passionate than me.' Her eyes followed the direction of the stairs and she wondered if Jacques Favelle was not too passionate, and dangerously so.

91

Chapter Fifteen

Freddy's room was almost empty, I had found no more letters. The desk was cleared, the pen pots were filled with the multitude of pencils that we found everywhere. The daybed was uncovered and stood proudly against the wall under a picture of Paris, The Luxembourg Gardens, with people promenading, cantering by with their horses on the bit, and children in the distance playing with the toy boats. I suddenly wanted to be there, right in the middle sitting at the café, watching people go by. I'd been to Paris once as a teenager and had fallen in love with it as, it seems, everyone does but my father had worked there for three years in his twenties and felt he had seen enough of it for a lifetime. Our family holidays were spent in The Dordogne, or on the Amalfi Coast. All at once something inside me longed to be right there in the Luxembourg Gardens in the café under the shade of the trees.

'Thank you, Connie,' said Harriet as she put her arm round my shoulders and squeezed. 'I could never have done all that. You've been amazing.'

'Honestly, Hat, I was glad to do it. I actually do love sorting things out, and the books I found, well, I'm thrilled. Are you sure I can have them? Two or three have his signature in them.'

'All the more important that you do have them; the

thought of you looking after them and treasuring them makes me feel so much better.'

I heaved a big sigh of relief. The job was done, the furniture could go and now we only had to move the bags and stacks of papers and books on to their final destinations. I looked at the pile for the family and suddenly found myself asking Hat if I could deliver those items myself.

'Really?' said Hat, surprised.

'Do you mind?'

'No, not at all, but…you know they're a bit strange, don't you?'

'I'd love to do it, I'll take a drive up there,'

'Why not take Matt?' She threw me her famous look, the one that eggs you on to do things.

'Oh, I don't know.'

'He'd give you some moral support and I get the feeling that there's something between you, something nice?'

I had to smile because Hat is very intuitive and rarely wrong. 'He is really nice, Hat. I like him but, you know me, I'm not really ready, not after what I went through.'

She put a finger under my chin and forced me to look her straight in the eyes. 'That was then, this is now. Live for the day, my darling. What's done is done.'

I knew she was right, it was time to put the past behind me, hurt as I was. It had been a ten-year relationship that buckled and collapsed in the end under the weight of his lies and deceit. I never wanted to go there again. I was certain I would never be able to trust anyone a second time. 'Hat, with all this wisdom you possess have you ever thought of becoming a Buddhist Monk?' I asked.

'I wouldn't suit being bald, and red is not my colour, anyway,' she said ruefully. 'And I'm too busy, I have the WI one Thursday a month for a start.'

Matt was sitting next to me in my Mini. 'I had one of these, a real old Mini, in 1988. I got it when I passed my test. Drove it to Le Mans for a holiday with a girlfriend and it broke down miles from anywhere. We were towed by a Shire horse to the garage in the next village.'

'Percheron, more like.'

'What's one of those?'

'French heavy horse.'

'Ah, horsey, are you?'

'I was, used to ride a lot but life got in the way, too expensive. And you?'

'No, in spite of my rugged good looks, lantern jaw and Popeye muscles, I'm not very outdoorsy.' I laughed, as he pulled a cartoon face on me.

'So, Popeye, what do you like to do?'

'I like visiting places and getting up at silly o'clock to photograph views and wildlife and things and, don't get me wrong, I love a walk. I had a dog, Dave. He died last year. We did a lot of walking but nothing rugged, not like the three summits in twenty four hours brigade. I like taking the time to enjoy everything around me.'

I could feel that he was looking at me, even with my eyes fixed on the road. 'Me too,' I agreed. 'I've done fast living. I'm becoming more Jamie Oliver about life now.'

'That's one thing I do love, Slow Food. And there's a superb little place in Ledbury called Chez Bruno, we should have lunch there before the big reveal.'

'Big reveal?'

'Freddy's family, they sound a right bunch.'

'I know, but I'm hoping they'll fill in the gaps. Freddy's been intriguing me. Hat told me that the remaining members of his family live in the almshouses of a big estate, and then there's someone called Daniel who lives in France. There's two cousins and an ancient aunt in Ledbury.'

'Not close enough to come and help with the house then?' asked Matt.

'No, the aunt is very frail and the cousins have an illness, that's all I know.'

He pulled out a map book and traced a finger across to Ledbury.

'Well, they are here.' He tapped the map with his index finger. 'About fifteen minutes out of Ledbury. What do you say we have lunch in town and go there for two?'

The Cotswolds gave way to open, green fields and cattle grazing. The turned earth was terracotta and red brick farms were dotted along the route. The journey was straightforward and the weather beautiful.

Bruno was a tall man, his skin was nut-brown and the teeth in his broad grin looked whiter for it. He took Matt's hand and gave him a hearty handshake. I was kissed on the hand and we were shown to our seats in the little garden under a broad pagoda. When Bruno returned with the menus he spoke in French with Matt.

'Been here a lot, then?' I asked after Bruno went. I had felt a bit left out.

'I have, actually. I work a lot with Bruno's PR man, James. He helps French people who want to set up in

England. To be honest, I think he'd be better off doing it the other way round, more English people going to start businesses in France and all that, but he makes a good income. He and I both speak the lingo, so it's a good fit.'

I perused the menu. Running across the top was a beautiful fisheye lens photo of the restaurant's interior and, at the bottom, another one, a white fish and fresh samphire on a blue plate, crusty bread in a basket and a glass of white wine.

'Did you do these pics?'

'I did.'

'They are really lovely.'

'Thank you.'

"But…'

'There's always a but, isn't there?' he said, winking.

'I was going to say that the layout and type are a bit hit and miss.'

'I know, that is the downside. James' daughter does it, two years at Art College, now a hairdresser, so she's supremely well-qualified.'

'Will you tell him about me?'

'Of course, he does need to re-think that side of his business. Send me some samples of your work and a CV. I'll put a good word in for you.'

'So, what slow food are you having today, Popeye?'

Lunch was superb. Matt was telling me about his life. I told him more about me and I can honestly say I loved being with him. He was kind, generous and thoughtful and so different from my ex. I couldn't imagine him ever hurting me. We left for the Almshouses at two, with a quick stop off at the chocolate shop before we reached the car.

The road snaked out of the town and passed through pretty villages and hamlets, the countryside more and more expansive as we travelled on. The Malverns appeared on the right and fell away again as we turned left into a small village hidden in a dip in the valley. The church was on a bright triangle of green, with sheep-nibbled turf around it. Behind was an arc of cottages and a large manor house, three storeys high. The house was overlooking a wide expanse of moor and a couple of sheep, with lambs grazing around the gate. I parked the car and we stepped out on the green.

Matt was so impressed, he whistled. 'Wow, what a place, photo opp or what? Look at the light over there.' There was a deep, hyacinth blue sky with dark clouds tearing across it and below it a slash of emerald green pasture.

'Looks like rain,' I said, just as the sun broke through the cloud and beamed on the moor; it was changing by the second. 'Or, maybe not!'

'So where are the Almshouses?'

'Those?' I pointed towards the crescent of thatched cottages.

'No, look, next to the big house there's a sign.'

It was an old metal road sign painted black with white type on it, most of it scratched away. The words "Alms Cottages," were still visible, but barely legible. The small houses were hidden behind some oak trees a hundred yards along an unadopted lane. As we walked towards them, Matt whispered out of the corner of his mouth; 'Spookier and spookier, Scooby.'

97

There were four, all identical. The wooden frames of leaded windows were covered in layers of thick red gloss and the arched doors were heavy, studded wood. We rang the doorbell of number two where the cousins lived. The bell was a long piece of metal that I pulled downwards with some effort and was rewarded with a solitary clang. After a long pause there was the sound of an inner door opening and then the front door was being unlocked. There were at least three bolts, if not four, barring our way. Matt raised an eyebrow and I had to stop myself laughing.

The face that greeted us was that of a very thin woman with pale blonde hair, a white face and blue veined hands.

'Hello, I'm Connie Webber,' I said.

The woman merely stared at me without acknowledgement. I wondered if she'd heard me at all. 'And this is my friend, Matt Verney.' Still there was no reply, her face was blank. 'Harriet phoned to say we were bringing over your cousin Freddy's things.' There was another pause.

'Ah, yes,' she said at last. 'Do come in, I am Merioneth.' She had a soft, barely perceptible voice. We stepped over the threshold and then into the tiny lounge. It was very simply furnished with a two-seater sofa, an armchair and a dresser. Through the door I could see an equally spartan kitchen with a small fold down table, two chairs and an original Butler sink.

'I will fetch my sister,' Merioneth said quietly and with that she went into the kitchen and turned sharp right. I could hear the trace of her tread on the stairs, but only just.

'I think she may be a ghost.' Matt's whisper was so

loud, it sounded as though he were performing on stage.

'Sssh.' I nudged him.

He whispered again, but lower: 'We won't be able to tell when she's coming back.' I glanced around, something about the house was making me nervous, it felt strange, unsettling.

The sisters appeared together, one with her hair loose and down her back, the other, Merioneth, had hers drawn neatly up behind her head. Other than that they were identical. They both wore pale green Laura Ashley dresses, thick flesh coloured tights that bunched around their thin ankles and flat, black lace-up shoes.

'I am Aeronwen,' said the second twin, extending a white hand. It was icy cold. At that moment I realised that except for the fireplace, which was empty and swept clean, there was no other form of heating. The place felt damp and cold as if it was never properly warmed.

'Can we get you something to drink?' asked Merioneth.

'Tea, please.' I said, and glanced across at Matt who nodded his agreement. Merioneth sloped off to the kitchen, feet dragging on the floor like a very old lady. I tried to guess their age, they looked like relics from the thirties.

'We don't have a lot of visitors,' explained Aeronwen. 'We both have M.E. you see and tire very easily.' She rubbed the back of her hand, her fingers travelling over thin, blue-veined skin. 'I'm afraid my sister and I have become quite reclusive, but we've always enjoyed each other's company.'

I felt sorry for them. Where were the books, the magazines, television? The things to do? There wasn't so much as a jigsaw puzzle.

'We are Plymouth Brethren,' she said as if she was reading my mind. 'We read nothing but the word of the Lord.' She indicated to the other window behind us. Once we had turned round we could see the large leather bound Bible on a lectern.

Matt's eyes bulged when I caught sight of him, he was manfully forcing back the desire to laugh. I turned my attention back to Merioneth.

'I see,' was all I could say. I waited for Matt to tell them he was of Puritan stock himself, but he wasn't going there. Aeronwen arrived with a wooden tray, the sort you use in cafeterias, and a plain, brown teapot. The cups were white Pyrex decorated with little red flowers, of the sort I haven't seen since my childhood in the seventies.

'Thank you,' I said, as she placed everything on a low side table and handed us our drinks. 'We've brought two boxes of Freddy's things with us.'

'What sort of things?'

'Scripts, photographs.' My heart skipped a beat when I thought of all the pictures of nude women we had on board. 'There are some posters, books, bills, theatre memorabilia mainly, and stuff like that.'

'I hardly think that sort of thing would be of interest to us,' said Aeronwen, recoiling as if we were sent from the devil himself. 'With all due respect, and thank you very much, I think they would be best delivered to number four.'

'Number four is?'

'Our Aunt Alberta and her housekeeper, she is the one who is more likely to want such things. She knew Freddy very well, more so than us.'

I tried to imagine the Freddy I knew in the same room as these two women. He used to belch when he was drinking and tell saucy jokes and say 'up your Aunt Fanny', as he swallowed back a slug of whisky making his eyes go wild and his voice hoarse. He was a reprobate, there was no mistaking that.

Was a reprobate I thought, was. 'We'll drop them there, then', I said. 'But, I wonder, are you able to help me with a few questions about Freddy?'

'Well, we'll try...' said Merioneth without any conviction.

'We found a picture, it's in the car, of Marlene Dietrich?'

'Who?'

'The Hollywood film star, nineteen forties?'

They shook their heads, looking mutually blank.

'Anyway, on it she's written something about Freddy and her both being German; it's written to Freddy, in German.'

'Really?'

'Are you aware that he was German?'

'Certainly not, that is not possible, he was British as you or I', said Aeronwen. She was obviously the more forceful of the twins. 'But you see, we didn't know him as a young man. We were born when he was twenty or so –'

'Twenty one, in fact', said Merioneth thoughtfully. 'We were born the very year he was twenty one.'

'Oh, I see', I said flatly. 'So you knew him as he became a playwright, really?'

'Yes, but we only knew of him, really, you see we would never be involved in any of that, because...' Merioneth drifted off again, not completing the sentence.

'I see,' I said once more, not sure of where to go next.

'What did you know of him?' asked Matt, taking up the baton.

'Well, he was very funny and, of course, famous. Our Uncle Elwyn adored him, and the two of them – he and his wife – followed him everywhere. They were very proud, you see.'

'Yes, I can imagine, what parents aren't?' There was a moment of silence.

'Oh, no, no, not parents, they were his guardians.'

'Oh, yes of course, his mother wasn't married.'

The two ladies looked at each other disdainfully. 'Well, naturally, we don't like to talk about all that, I'm sure you understand. We can, however, vouch for the fact that he was most happy with our Uncle Elwyn and Aunt Catherine. They gave him everything a boy could wish for, including a fabulous education, albeit High Church.' Aeronwen exchanged a look of disapproval with her sister. 'The two brothers, our father and our uncle, were chalk and cheese religiously, but as brothers –'

'As brothers they were very close indeed,' Merioneth said softly.

'Oh yes, they were,' Aeronwen agreed.

'Do you know anything about Freddy's mother, anything at all?'

'No, nothing, except that our father was very upset that Uncle Elwyn took her under his wing, as you might say. One minute she was working for him, the next he had her son living at his house; obviously people talked.'

'So, she actually worked for him, they weren't related at all?' Matt cut in.

'Exactly so, and of course he made Freddy his ward and then he left him all that money, financed his plays and bought him a house.'

'How generous,' I said. I couldn't imagine what it must have been like to receive such unsolicited kindness. I caught Matt's eye and he raised his eyebrows. 'What did he do for a living, Elwyn?'

'He was an investor, properties and railways and that sort of thing. He lived here in the mansion and that's why we're left behind here in the old almshouses. He bought them for us. You see, our father had no money at all. He was a lay preacher, he didn't believe in wealth of any kind. He always told us 'The Lord will provide' and he was right because He has.' The thought occurred to me that in fact Uncle Elwyn with his good business head and his sound investments and great kindness had actually provided, but I carried on, regardless.

'Would your aunt be able to tell us more about Freddy?' I asked.

'I'm sure she will,' said Aeronwen. She glanced surreptitiously at her sister. 'But we need to hope it's one of her lucid days.'

Chapter Sixteen

Claudette laid out lamb cutlets, sprinkled with mint, each one a mouthful of heaven. She tried as hard as possible not to crave just one bite. There were timbales of potato Dauphinoise, little round stacks of layered cream and potato. She breathed in the aroma deeply and let the smell of it settle deep inside her. The smell of Apple Tarte Tatin wafted by as Perrine passed her holding the pudding aloft and placed it on the end warmer. She too inhaled the smell.

'What I wouldn't give to have that sort of dessert every night and not to have cooked it.' She giggled then, checking herself, added, 'only I wouldn't give what they give.' She had a wicked smile.

At that precise second the double doors were flung open and a blast of colour and noise entered. There were five women, hair shimmering in the light from the chandeliers. The floor echoed with the clicking of finely pointed stiletto shoes. The smiles and laughter were infectious. It was as if the dreary streets outside had brought in a troupe of goddesses who had lost their way. The clock chimed nine as if in celebration. Claudette stood gazing at them whilst Perrine slipped out of the door.

'I am so hungry I could eat a horse,' said the tallest one, a platinum blonde. She was wearing a long silk dressing gown in peacock blue. Under it a thin chemise made of the same, and lace-edged panties to match.

'All that work this afternoon,' laughed another, her bright red hair falling in waves around her head. 'We should name you Voracious Venus – Freya doesn't do anything for you.'

'At least mine are one after the other and not at the same time,' Freya retorted. 'I have some self-respect.'

The other three laughed. 'Double the money, double the fun, eh, Apollonia?' said one. They poured themselves a glass of wine and clinked glasses.

'Hey, what are you staring at?'

It was the smallest one, she had dark, almost black, bobbed hair and around her head was a diamante band with a black feather in it. She wore a red and black basque and short black negligee. Claudette froze as she realised they were all looking at her.

'I'm sorry,' she said, 'I'm new, Cl…Françoise.' She bit her lip, she had done it again.

'Clançoise. Interesting name.' A woman entering the room stopped and looked straight at Claudette. She was very tall, helped by her hair braided and wrapped around her head which gave her extra height. A sheer dress clung to her full, round figure and highlighted her broad hips. She loomed over Claudette as she drew close.

'Where are you from?'

'Vacily, it's–'

'Why are you here?' The eyes were icy, searching.

'Leave her alone, Bella,' Lilia had arrived, her eyes heavily made up, her face languid, she was barefoot and wearing a gold and red kimono.

'We've met, she's very sweet. Madame always changes everyone's names.' She was slurring. 'You have no right to interfere.'

Bella searched Claudette's eyes again. 'That true?' she asked.

'No, my name is Françoise, I'm sorry I was going to say Clarice sent me up here,' Claudette lied. This was treated with peels of laughter. 'Clarice, Clarice,' they mocked her voice.

'That's Madame F! No one calls the old bird Clarice,' said Freya, helping herself to the lamb and half a portion of potato.

'I suspect you're a bit scared of her, are you?' said Lilia, pouring herself a glass of wine. 'We all are truly. You come to me if she's hard on you. I'll get my attack dog Bella onto her.'

Bella sneered.' Madame Odile should inform us if we have a new maid,' she said, 'she could be anybody.'

'I am Jacques' sister,' Claudette told her.

'Oh, well, why didn't you say?' Bella's face lit up. 'Why, Jacques is our friend, he runs our errands for us and he looks after us.' She threw a look at the other ladies, a curl in her lip. 'Doesn't he, girls?'

'A bit too much looking,' said Apollonia. They all laughed again.

'As long as he doesn't touch us, Pollo, that's when you have to worry about catching his dandruff!' Lilia said, giggling.

'Amongst other things,' Bella added as another peel of laughter ran around the room. With that they sat down to eat, fussing and talking amongst themselves. They ribbed each other and talked about their hair and make-up. They were all fresh and ready for their night's work. As Claudette went to leave, Bella turned round in her chair and snapped hold of her wrist. 'I hope we didn't upset you back then with that little bit of a joke about your brother,' she said. 'Only, you didn't seem to mind too much, I was watching your face.' Close up she had oval eyes, green like a cat. Her throat was long, ice white.

'No, I didn't mind,' said Claudette.

'Good.' said Bella, releasing her grip.

As she left Claudette caught sight of Lilia, she was watching through her black, heavily lined eyes. Her false eyelashes were coming unstuck on one eye, she had lit a cigarette and wasn't eating. Claudette carried on walking out of the room just as two more women entered it. They mouthed 'who's that?' to the others. She could see the reflection of them in the mirror as they pointed at her.

'That's Françoise, our new mysterious, mousey maid,' said Bella loudly. There was a shout of laughter as Claudette headed downstairs; at the bottom Perrine was waiting.

'They are all bitches, but they are harmless bitches. They pick on everybody and each other all the time. Lilia and Nannette are the nicest, but Bella is trouble, it's in her nature. And she's the one they all want.'

'Who?'

'The Boches, of course, they all try to book her, she does anything, if you see what I mean?' Perrine raised her eyebrows. 'They're all lost souls, though, I feel a bit sorry for them at times. My mother can't believe I work here, but she doesn't object to the money I bring in.'

'What happens after dinner?'

'The Boches arrive and mayhem ensues,' said Perrine. 'Keep out of the way, we're not expected to be around. They have lackeys outside, you'll see them sitting in cars in all weathers waiting to drive their captains and generals home.'

Claudette looked at Perrine and asked, 'Is your name made up by Madame Odile?'

'No, it's very strange but they all think we're working under assumed names, because they are, they think it will protect them. When this is all over and we've won France back I reckon they'll disappear like ghosts in the night clinging to their real identities.'

'Why do they do it?' Claudette asked. 'It's demeaning.'

'You tell me how demeaning it is on payday when you and I get our wages and they get theirs,' Perrine said with a smile. 'If I had their looks I'd do it. Have you ever seen a group of more beautiful women?'

'No,' Claudette replied, still reeling from the experience, 'they are incredible.'

'And they have brains, all of them. They're playing the long game,' added Perrine. 'They are the survivors.' The doorbell rang giving Claudette a start. 'Don't worry it's only Agnès, she's always here by 9.15pm.'

Agnès was a tiny woman dressed in a simple black dress and heavy flat shoes, also black. She bowed her head slightly at Claudette as they were introduced, but there was no eye contact and she said nothing. She reminded Claudette a little of her mother and her heart pinched a little.

'Agnès helps,' said Perrine, and with that the old lady bowed again and began to take the stairs slowly, her progress desperately laboured and difficult.

'Why doesn't she take the lift?'

'No one but the girls, the Boches and Madame Odile, it's the rule.' They made their way down to the kitchen. Madame F was sitting down wafting herself with a fan, the room was sticky hot and airless. Jacques was in a suit looking stiff and uncomfortable. Marie was clattering pots and pans in the sink, soapy pots piling up on the draining board.

The smell of garlic and herbs and cooked apples lay heavy in the room. Claudette's stomach growled as Perrine sat down heavily beside her, brushing the loose hair off her forehead. It was a stiflingly hot night and in spite of the open windows, no air was circulating.

Perrine and Claudette returned to the dining room just before ten. Half the food was left and most of the pudding, but the carafes of wine were empty. They carried everything downstairs again, Claudette looking at the remains of the food and wishing she could eat the leftovers.

'We can have anything we like when it's returned to the kitchen. It's a shame your parents aren't nearby, I take dessert home for my mother,' Perrine explained. 'Make the most of it, this is Saturday night's dinner, it's not like this every day!'

When the kitchen was cleared up and Madame F had retired to bed in her small room off the kitchen passageway, Perrine left.

'What about the curfew?' Claudette had asked.

'If they stop you, say "Ercol" and it's no problem, but I only live at the end of the street and everyone knows me here.'

Claudette and Marie climbed the stairs to the attic at

ten thirty in exhausted silence. Claudette wanted to see what was behind those double doors on each landing, but there was silence. As they reached their rooms Marie turned to Claudette, her skin sallow under the dull light. 'Sleep well; I'll wake you up at six thirty. Madame F says I must talk you through everything you have to do, so it's going to be a long day.'

Claudette felt the ache of tiredness in her body and the overpowering need for sleep. 'One other thing,' Marie added, 'whatever you hear in the night, don't get up; ignore it. Even if it sounds really bad.'

Chapter Seventeen

'Kill me now,' said Matt as we lifted the boxes out of the boot. 'What the –?'

'Puritans?' I replied. 'Is that what your house was like growing up then?'

'They make my family home look like a bordello. "We only read the word of the Lord!" how sixteen sixty-three is that? That gave me the creeps. And those stockings –'

'Tights,' I corrected him.

'Those tights, heavens to Betsy, talk about thick, and it's so sticky hot today. What do they wear in the winter, for God's sake? They were like the maiden aunts in my family. Horrid.'

We walked back along the small lane, the clouds brooding and black above us, a fresh breeze was blowing in on the back of them. Merioneth was standing by the open front door of number four.

'I'm dreading this next one,' Matt whispered from the side of his mouth. 'I'm seeing the woman from Blackadder who liked sitting on spikes.'

The room couldn't have been more different. It was packed with furniture, books, two very old stand alone radios, well past their useful days, and a green sofa with wooden hand rests straight from the seventies. It was covered with a tatty crocheted blanket in bright green and yellow with scalloped pink edges. In the middle of the overcrowded and quite gloomy living room was an old woman, her white hair so coiffured it could only be a wig. Her eyes were heavily pencilled and her thin face was heavy with thick powder.

'Do come in,' she said more brightly than we expected. 'Take a pew.' Her voice was kind and stronger than she looked. Matt put the box down by the front door. 'Lucy!' she shouted. 'It's three o'clock, dear.' She turned to us. We were both sitting on the seventies sofa, Matt next to a very fat, white cat who was fast asleep. 'Or, as I like to call it "Gin O'clock".' She chuckled and gave us a wink in such an endearing way that I took to her immediately. 'Lucy dear, do come!' she called again.

Lucy appeared at the door wearing a walking coat spotted with rain. She smiled at us and acknowledged Merioneth who was, I suddenly realised, still standing at the threshold rather nervously.

'Do go away dear,' said the old lady dismissively. 'Lest we infect you with our debauchery.' She waved the back of her hand at the cousin who left without a murmur. 'Oh, thank goodness for that,' she said with great annoyance. 'It's like having a wet weekend arrive if either of those two come round.'

'Bertie,' said Lucy, taking off her coat, 'be nice.' Lucy was much younger, late sixties or early seventies perhaps, her complexion clear and healthy, someone who spent a lot of time outside. 'Would you like a G and T?' she asked.

'Yes please,' said Matt. 'I'd love one.'

'I'm driving.' I added, looking sideways at Matt,

astonished he would drink a cocktail so early in the day, but he ignored me.

'I'll make yours more T than G,' said Lucy warmly as she withdrew back into the kitchen. We could hear the bottles clinking and the fizz of the tonic being opened.

'Now, my dears, what can I do for you?' said Bertie, her eyes twinkling through heavy black lashes.

'We've brought Freddy's things with us for you to do with what you like,' I explained.

'Such as what, my dear?'

'Photographs, programmes, bill posters, theatrical stuff and some legal documents.'

'Oh, dear poor old Freddy. Such a loss.'

We both nodded. 'I adored him,' I told her with all honesty.

'We all did,' she replied, her face clouding over. 'We all did. But life must go on, do you see? It must go on.' She had formed a fist with her bony hand and she thumped on the arm of her chair.

Matt stroked the cat's head and down the length of its body and as he ran the back of his finger over the fur, its ears twitched with appreciation. We neither of us knew what to say next. I felt like we were intruding in the life of another family where another world existed.

After a short pause I ventured a question. 'Were you very close?'

'Oh yes, my dear, yes indeed, I adored him, you see.'

'Did you go to see all his plays?'

'Oh yes, London, Bristol, I saw them two or three times. He was a genius and not recognised, that's the problem, not as recognised as he should have been.' She heaved a great sigh, her mouth pursing. 'So sad about what happened. I would have thought one could buck oneself up, such a great loss, don't you think?'

'I do,' I said. 'But he was bipolar, he had no control over it.'

'My dear, we had no time to be depressed, we had the war, do you see? I'm ninety-four, I didn't reach this grand old age by being upset about every little thing.' She was getting a little testy and I could tell she didn't take prisoners.

'Do you know if Freddy was German born?' Matt asked, changing the subject for which I was grateful.

'Oh no, dear, if anything he was French by birth,' Bertie replied. 'What an odd thing to say, that doesn't make any sense to me at all.' Lucy brought a tray of drinks and a bowl of ice with bright silver pinchers sticking out of it. The cat looked up, stretched out a small pink paw, yawned and went back to sleep. Matt accepted his drink and said thank you to Lucy. There was a somnolent atmosphere in the room, the gentle tick of a clock, the feeling that time stretched out more in this room than elsewhere in the world. Lucy pulled up a tapestry-backed chair and joined us.

'Why do you ask?' she enquired.

'Oh, it's just that we found a signed photograph of Marlene Dietrich and on the back it said: "To Fredrik, from one sad German to another." It's written in German.' Matt stood up, went over to the box and produced the envelope with the photograph and the letters in it. He slid out the picture and passed it to Lucy who then handed it on to Bertie. The old girl's thin, pencilled eyebrows knotted together as she considered it and stroked her powdered chin with thin fingers.

'You see, Freddy knew everyone, the Oliviers, the Richardsons, his address book really does take some reading,' she said.

'Do you have it?' asked Matt, beating me to it.

'Oh no, no, it would be with his things in his house,' Bertie replied adamantly. 'No, no, I'm absolutely sure of that.'

'We didn't find it,' I told her.

'What were you doing looking?' asked Bertie, a little too sharply, I thought.

'We've been helping to sort out everything for Harriet. She couldn't have managed to go through his things in such a big house on her own. There was a lot to do.'

'I see,' said Bertie. Her eyes darted from me to Matt and back. She took a huge gulp of gin. 'And, tell me, what else did you find?' Her face, and I could have been wrong, took on a rather accusatory expression. It was fleeting, but disconcerting.

'These,' I said, emptying the letters out of the envelope and handing them to her.

Her hands were very old, withered in fact, with purple veins. Her yellowed nails bore a single stripe of bright pink polish. I was struck by the fact she read the letters without the need for glasses.

'Now that is what I describe as a mystery,' she said, taking another sip from her glass. 'It's very strange indeed. Lucy, my dear, go and fetch me the big box.' Lucy returned with a large hatbox, sepia in colour with pictures of Victorian women wearing bonnets around it. It was held together by the paper wrapped around it, the cardboard was crumbling and left a dusty deposit in Lucy's wake.

'Open that up, young man,' she directed Matt. 'You will find in there a folder, it has pictures of fruit all over it.' Matt began looking. The box contained all manner of certificates and bills, invoices, a copy of her will, hand-written letters and finally the folder.

'That's it, open it up, dear,' she instructed. Matt did as she told him and pulled out two or three papers. One of them had been screwed up and then folded out flat again, the top half torn off.

'That's the one,' Bertie said, pointing with a bony finger.

It was a Xerox of a letter. Matt read it and passed it to me.

I have written so many times, I know that you must have received my letters because they were never returned. Please do write to me, or call I am at Oxford University, Christchurch.

Yours, in hope,
Fredrik.

I turned it over – the reverse was blank.

'How strange is that?' asked Matt. 'I mean, that you should have one of Freddy's letters too.'

'But you see, I thought it was to a girlfriend or such, I never imagined it was his father,' said Bertie. 'I mean it still could be a girlfriend, there's no date, no addressee. I kept it because it's the only bit of handwriting of his that I have.

You see, I think you can learn so much about a person by their writing. Don't you?'

'So what do you know about Freddy?' I asked. My curiosity was piqued.

'Well, his mother adored him, I do know that, yes, she adored the boy. She worked in London as a translator.' Bertie took a large swig of her drink, with the ice cubes barely defrosted it rattled. She held it out for a refill. Lucy obliged immediately. She asked us too, but we had hardly touched our drinks.

'What did they do?'

'Who?'

'The people who gave her a job, was it the civil service, a shop perhaps or a private company?'

'Oh yes, private I think, investment bank and what not. I really don't know. I am nearly ninety-five you know.' Lucy passed her a glass and she sipped it again as if she'd been waiting for it for a while.

'Was Freddy's father German?'

'Who was?'

'Freddy's father. German?'

'Oh no, he was one of us, British through and through.'

'Do you think he might have known Marlene Dietrich, by any chance?'

'Oh, my dear,' Bertie replied. 'He knew everyone.'

'What was Freddy's mum's name?'

'Who?'

'Freddy's mum.'

'His mother?'

'Yes.'

'It was… her name, now let me think.' She took

another sip, her mouth puckered around the glass. I saw the fine hairs above her lip, the heavy foundation plastered over her face to conceal her age. 'I'll have to come back to her,' she said. 'I don't remember, you see she died before I knew her, I was in South Africa with my husband.'

'Oh, I see,' I replied. 'So your brother employed her eventually?'

'Yes, yes, she did work for him, for Elwyn not Dafydd, that is, never get them confused. Perfect French, you see, and she learned English very quickly.'

'And the boy Freddy?'

'They paid for his childcare; she must have been very much appreciated. Now, what was her name?'

'And they came to live in the big house?'

'Oh, no, no, she was gone by then, he lived at the big house with Elwyn and Catherine, after she died. The mother, now what was her damned name?' She took a sip, ice-cubes chinking. 'They made him a ward, they were his guardians.'

'What did she die of?'

'What?'

'What did she die of? Was she ill?'

'Who?'

'Freddy's mother.'

'Oh no, my dear, that's the thing, she was murdered.'

Chapter Eighteen

Perrine and Claudette were sweeping down the stairs with stiff brushes. Claudette blew a strand of hair out of her eyes and spoke in a low voice. 'I don't like this carpet at all now, it's a nightmare to clean.' They were talking in low voices because the house was full of sleeping people. The Sunday morning stair cleaning was a ritual, Perrine had explained to her, because everyone was asleep.

'It's the only place I know in Paris that has a stair carpet,' she said. 'Except for the big hotels, of course. And the stupid thing is no one except us uses it.' The door above them opened with a rush of air and the elevator was called. They both watched as a German descended, his back to them. He was straightening his tie and pulling the cuffs of his jacket into place. He had the red and gold insignia of a Bereichsleiter on his shoulders. His cap was under his arm, and the reddish brown hair that was thinning on top covered a freckled scalp, but that was all they could see of him. He left the lift on the ground floor and they listened to the creak of his boots as he strode across the marble lobby.

'Boches,' said Perrine. 'I hate them. They scare the life out of me. I have no idea why Madame F thinks that way, they have ruined France.' She rubbed the back of her hand across her forehead, leaving a dusty mark.

'What is he doing here, are they staying all night?'

'Yes, some of them pay Madame for "exclusivity". I can assure you it costs a lot of money. That one pays for Eva – you haven't met her yet. She tends not to eat with the others; in fact, if you ask me, she doesn't seem to eat at all. Perhaps he brings her food, that's what Bella thinks. He's called Rechstein. It's best if you give him a wide berth, a really nasty piece of work. He's very high up, organises retribution killings. He just gives the order and they round men up off the street. One minute they are delivering food to a café or coming out of the office for lunch and the next they are in a lorry on the way to Drancy if they turn out to be Jewish, or God knows where if they are French.'

'Drancy?' Claudette was still brushing as she spoke.

'They have a holding centre in offices that they commandeered. The police ran it when it first opened, but then the SS took it over completely and the prisoners are being evacuated more quickly. I only know because my brother told me he saw some people being rounded up in the Marais. They weren't allowed to take so much as a rucksack with them. They seal the houses up after they've helped themselves to all the valuables, that is.'

'Only Jews?' asked Claudette. There was a hollow in the pit of her stomach, up until now she had only heard the rumours of the evacuations.

'No, they've started exporting Poles, Communists, The Resistance.'

Claudette sat back on her haunches, her heart was pulsing under her ribs. 'What happens to them?'

'That's the thing, nobody knows, no one has ever come back. I don't even think the Boches here know, how could they? Wherever it is it will be hellish. I can't think that they are going to be re-educated as Madame F. thinks they are, but we really don't know.'

'Surely Jacques has told you this? Didn't he write to you?'

'No, not about that, anyway, perhaps he was sparing me the details.' Perrine looked at Claudette, her head tilted a little, but before she could say any more there were the sounds of various movements in the household. It was eleven o'clock.

'We need to finish this and go to fetch breakfast. It'll be ready.' They quickly finished the carpet and hurried downstairs. They both washed their hands and faces and put on white aprons, then Claudette took the baskets of freshly baked bread and croissants up to the dining room. Perrine followed, carrying a silver tray of jams served in delicate crystal bowls.

Bella was there on her own, her head in her hands. 'Do be dears,' she said, without raising her head, 'don't make such a lot of noise.'

Perrine smiled and raised an eyebrow at Claudette. 'A good night, Bella?' she asked wryly.

'Long night,' Bella replied, looking up under heavy lashes. Her hair was down around her face, her make-up smudged and black around her eyes, but the skin was still white and smooth as marble. 'Make me some coffee, Perrine, I can't stand up, my gown is too loud.' Perrine poured a cup and handed it to her. 'I'm going back to bed, I can assure you it'll be nothing short of a miracle if you see anyone else. They had us in the Salon playing their dreadfully dull, childish games. Thank God for Courvoisier, is all I can say.'

121

Perrine and Claudette watched her go, then Perrine grabbed a croissant from the basket and tore it in half. She handed one end to Claudette and they both stuffed their mouths. Even though they were bolting it down, the soft doughy bread felt like heaven.

'Bella would have wanted us to,' laughed Perrine. 'I just know it.'

'I saw that, you two!' They spun round, eyes wide. It was Freya. She was entering the room with her face cleansed and clear of make-up, looking nowhere near as beautiful as she had done the night before. She had a broad grin on her face. 'Have mine too, if you like, I'm still full from last night.' Neither of them moved. 'Oh, come on, I'm not telling anyone,' she said with a yawn. She stretched her arms above her head, linking the fingers. 'I need only a coffee... and a bidet.' Perrine handed her a coffee; snatching a glance at Claudette, she pulled a disgusted face. 'It's all right for you two,' she yawned again. 'You only clean up after them, we have to do it with them, it makes my skin crawl. I hate them. Bastards.' She poured cream in her coffee and stirred the spoon around and around. 'I'd give up tomorrow,' she said, her voice laced with melancholy, the spoon still stirring. 'I would, I'd give it up tomorrow.' Claudette moved towards the door. 'They're moving Jürgen, anyway, he's going to Belgium again. He's the only one I enjoy, the others are just Boches to me, dirty, filthy, stinking Boches.'

Claudette walked back. 'Is there anything I can get you?'

'Is it true you mend things?'

'I do.'

122

'What can you do for hearts?'

Claudette looked down on her with pity, Freya was miserable. 'Nothing, I'm afraid.'

'Then you can't help me.'

Jacques was in the kitchen when Claudette returned downstairs. She looked down the corridor to see if Madame F was around, or Marie. 'Someone called Jürgen is moving back to Belgium.' She told him, sotto voce. 'Freya knows him, she seemed to be very fond of him.'

'I doubt it, she's only trying to make herself feel less bad,' replied Jacques and then surprising her, he said. 'Well done, I have other information on Jürgen Wahl, I'll pass it on.' Claudette checked again to see if anyone was around. 'They're at Mass,' he told her, lighting a cigarette. Pollo's bell rang at that moment, the tinkle of it light and old-fashioned in the dullness of the kitchen. 'She's in number seven, floor four.' He drew deeply on his cigarette, lazy eye almost closed.

Claudette made her way up the stairs to the fourth floor, wishing Perrine was around to help her. A shaft of sunlight caught the filigree of brass on the lift shaft and diffused into a myriad of curling patterns on the pale grey walls.

Room seven had the same door as everyone else, including Madame Odile's, just as heavy to open too. Pollo was inside lying on her bed, reading a magazine. She was nude and terribly beautiful.

'Draw me a bath,' she ordered without looking up. She flicked the page of the magazine over, a cigarette between her fingers, the plume of smoke rising towards the ceiling. Claudette averted her eyes and looked for the bathroom door. 'Through there,' Pollo nodded towards the bedroom wall where Claudette caught sight of a small door handle. She realised that the door was disguised as part of the wall. Inside was a Lion's Claw Bath with two big taps at the centre. Whilst the water was running Claudette turned to look back at Apollonia's room from the threshold of the bathroom doorway; it was extraordinary. The walls were papered in a leopard skin print, the floor black as ebony. The chairs and sofa were covered in animal skin fabrics, a tiger and something like leopard, but it was smaller, more densely spotted. On the floor was a massive Polar Bear skin, its big open mouth containing yellowed teeth. The head was disfigured with flecks of black in the white fur, it reminded her of Joubert. The room smelt of musk and warm fur, the windows were all closed, claustrophobic and cloying.

'I have salts in my bath,' said Pollo and as she spoke she had moved like a cat so quickly that she was suddenly standing in front of Claudette, looking into her eyes. Her breasts were firm and round, her mouth sensuous, hair the colour of topaz falling away from her face.

Claudette was speechless and rooted to the spot, unable to move.

'I'm guessing it's all a bit much for you?' said Pollo, almost kindly. 'We're quite a tribe, aren't we, we girls? A bit too much for a good Catholic girl, are we?' She stepped closer and examined Claudette's face intimately with something akin to childlike fascination, then she blew softly on her cheek. 'Why,' she mocked, 'you are a startled rabbit, aren't you?'

Claudette didn't know what to do. The water was

thundering into the bath behind her, echoing around the bathroom; she was aware it must be fairly full by now. Apollonia had a lazy smile on her face under a magnetic, hypnotic stare. She reached up and ran a finger down Claudette's cheek, the touch light as a butterfly wing, it travelled down her neck and on to the buttons of Claudette's blouse. Pollo watched her face intently as she placed the finger into the loop of fabric between the buttons. Claudette was suddenly aware that it was stroking the inside of her breast, inside the cup of her bra. She wanted to gasp as Pollo's lips came closer until her breath was right there, soft against Claudette's ear. Her breath was warm and sweet and the smell of her perfume close up was exotic, intense and rich.

The laugh was harsh, suddenly cruel and the finger that had been inside Claudette's blouse was being snapped before her eyes. 'Virgin!' she barked. 'I knew it!' Her laugh was haughty; she reminded Claudette of the Alsatian dog at the Gare du Nord. 'You won't even know yet if it's men or women that excite you,' she carried on, her voice derisive. 'My advice is not to care, do as you please! Maybe I could fix you up with one of the little grunts that sit outside all night in the cars freezing their balls off. There they are waiting until Herr Käpitan comes out with a self-satisfied grin on his face. Why, you could warm up the pasty-faced youths for us.' She threw her head back and laughed again.

Claudette turned away without a word and went back to the bath. She stopped the flow and dipped a finger into the steaming bathwater, it was boiling hot, the cold tap had barely been running. She unwrapped and dropped a cube of lilac bath salts into it and returned to the bedroom.

'Your bath is ready for you.' She said the words without so much as a glance at Pollo, and with that she left the room.

Chapter Nineteen

'It's just a hunch, but I think when the Puritans said lucid, they meant sober,' said Matt as we walked across the green to the car. It had tickled us both to watch Bertie down another gin and tonic and become quite merry.

'She's a game old girl,' I said as we clipped on our seatbelts. 'I'm going to be exactly like her when I'm old, no wonder she got on so well with Freddy.'

'What a very false looking wig, though, and the make-up is applied with a trowel, isn't it?' Matt added. 'I've never met anyone like that before.'

As we left and Bertie had finally slumped into an alcoholic fug, I thanked Lucy and asked her to call me if Bertie ever did remember Freddy's mother's name. When I'd given her one of my newly printed business cards, she picked up the three letters and the photo and slid them back into the envelope handing them to me at the door.

'Keep these,' she said. 'They'll only be put in that hatbox and forgotten more likely than not. Someone else should have that photo for certain.'

'Thank you,' I said, I appreciated her kindness. She gave us both a hug and told us we'd made a dull afternoon far more enjoyable for Bertie who seldom had visitors.

'Well, talk about two sides of a coin,' said Matt as we drove past the big house and the lane leading to the Almshouses.

'You're telling me,' I replied. The rest of the village was sporadic and only bits of a roof here and a gable end there could be seen in gaps between the tall roadside hedges. Taking the turn for Tewkesbury at the next junction, the rain was now falling and splashing onto the road. I continued; 'You know I'm half tempted to ring Channel Four right now.'

'Me too, what an experience,' Matt was fishing for his phone from his jacket pocket. 'So, we've got Elwyn, Dafydd and Alberta, a strangely un-Welsh name, and only two offspring, the Puritan Sisters, and Freddy who's a ward of court. What exactly is a ward?' He was trying to get a reception on his phone, holding it in the air then squinting at the screen.

'Well, it's like a guardian, I think.'

'In loco parentis, you mean.'

'That's it.'

'I can't Google, there's no reception.'

'So poor Freddy's mum dies and the boss man takes him on and gives him all the money, whilst Uncle Dafydd and Alberta are in the Almshouses.'

'Well, it's not uncommon that son number one inherits the lot.' I was running it all through my mind.

'Except he wasn't son number one.' Matt pointed out. 'He was ward number one. That must have smarted a bit, no wonder they're asking their solicitor to sell Freddy's house. They want out of the poor house. I wonder who lives in the big house now, we should have asked.'

'I can't see the puritans and the game old girl wanting any money, unless they have to pay rent now or something.'

Then we both remembered Daniel in Paris, we said it at the same time.

'Daniel!'

'Where does Daniel fit in?' asked Matt

I could tell he was dying to Google, all this had to be on the Net somewhere.

'And why are we so interested?' I asked as we passed the large army base with two tanks on show either side of the gates.

'Because we watched Scooby Doo when we were kids?'

'You mean we are Those Meddling Kids?'

''Sactly,' Matt was laughing. 'It's just fascinating, isn't it?'

'Daniel is.'

'Well, I'm googling now and that name is not coming up in association with Freddy, March or Elwyn. In fact there is nothing about an Elwyn March at all.'

'I'll ask Hat,' I told him and pressed on to Tewkesbury.

Hat was none the wiser. She didn't know Freddy's mother's name, he referred to her as Mama and nothing else and Daniel was "just a member of the family".

'Tell you what,' she said, 'I'll ask the family solicitor, he'll know.' She and I were sitting in the garden, there was rich, full sun beginning to drop behind the trees and the insects were threading triangular paths in the last of the light. 'So, they were weird, eh?' She passed me a plate of nibbles.

'It was a strange old afternoon, but actually a lot of fun, Aunt Bertie is a scream, she certainly likes her gin.'

'She came to the funeral propped up by her housekeeper, you know.'

'You told me she was there.'

'The housekeeper, Lucy, is lovely.'

'Yes, we talked for quite a while. She's very fond of Alberta,' I agreed, then I said; 'I do wish I'd gone to see Freddy off, but I didn't want to intrude.'

'I know, we'll do something here to remember him. For all of us, I mean, instead.' Hat spoke with a renewed resolution. 'I promise.'

'And who was there?' I asked.

'At the funeral?'

I nodded. 'The vicar, of course, the local doctor, lovely man, Bertie, Aeronwen, Merioneth, a couple from the village who knew Freddy very well, they often came here to see him in the sixties. That actress who was in the comedy about the old people's home, with the posh voice, looks like Annette Bening –'

'Oh God, Hat, you've lost me.'

'– and her husband, oh, and one of the Windmill Girls; she was eighty odd and quite beautiful even now.'

'Daniel?'

'Well, I don't know.' She was trying to recall, her lips pressed firmly together. 'There were a few people I didn't connect with. Jon and I had a quick cup of tea and then we came away, I was finding it pretty tough. Come to think of it there was another man at the end of the aisle, one back, behind us and along, if you see what I mean.'

'Old? Young?'

'Freddy's age I would say, very white hair.'

'French looking?'

'No, I wouldn't say that, old English, tweedy.'

I sighed, what was I asking all this for? I felt less fired up without Matt and not for the first time Hat appeared to be a mind reader.

'How are things with you and Matt, any developments?'
She said "developments" in a silly voice.

'He nearly kissed me tonight when we got home.'

'Really?' She shifted in her seat. 'Do tell.'

'I dropped him outside his house and we did that thing where you talk trying to put off the kissing goodbye thing.'

'And?'

'I put it off.'

'Oh, Connie.'

'I know, he would have kissed me, but I just can't.'

'Some day you have to let all that go, you know, and consign the bad times to history.'

'I know and I will some day.' I said. 'But it's still too soon.'

Chapter Twenty

Madame Odile looked Claudette up and down as she walked around her in a slow circle. 'Do you have anything to say?' her words were clipped, economical.

'No, Madame,' Claudette replied.

'So you are saying it was simply a mistake?'

'Yes, Madame.'

'Apollonia is a very valuable asset to this house, do you understand?'

'Yes, Madame.'

'If this or anything like it happens again I shall dismiss you without question, do you hear?'

'Yes, Madame.' Claudette's cheeks were stinging, her stomach churning.

'And another thing, that uniform. You know what I am going to say, don't you?'

'Yes, Madame, I haven't had time yet to take it in.'

'Well, get it done, and your hair, it's awful. Ask Nanette to run a colour through it for you, tell her I said so.' Madame Odile walked back to her desk. 'I want the private room cleaned from top to bottom and I want it done by five o'clock.'

Claudette nodded and turned away, biting her lip. Perrine was waiting for her at the bottom of the stairs, by the kitchen door. 'How was it?' she whispered.

'I thought she was going to sack me, she said Pollo is a "valuable asset".'

'The foot will heal, silly bitch, she should have checked the water before she got in,' said Perrine defiantly. 'They're not that helpless.'

'I've got to clean the Private Room by five this afternoon. Top to bottom.'

'Oh, you poor thing,' Perrine screwed up her face. 'If you like I'll help you, follow me.'

Perrine led the way up to the first floor, through the double doors and into a dark corridor. To the left were Madam Odile's private apartments, in front of them her office and, round the corner to the left, were two doors. Perrine walked to the furthest room and knocked gently. There was no reply. 'It can't be booked, otherwise she wouldn't have let you in,' she told Claudette. The heavy door eased open to reveal a dark, ruby red room about sixteen feet square. There were two sofas against the walls and a double bed piled up with red satin cushions. Draped over the backs of the sofas were heavy brown furs, and velvet cushions in a deep violet. When Perrine opened the door that was tucked away in the corner, a slash of light cut across the interior, highlighting the spinning dust motes. 'Bathroom,' she said, shutting it again. With the door closed it became invisible once more. The only light was the dim glow of red shaded wall lights, making the room dark and furtive again. 'Madame Odile allows clients to book it for their own entertainment,' said Perrine. 'Look here.' She moved forward and clicked on a projector that was hidden in a nook in the woodwork of the back wall.

Claudette watched it spring to life. The flickering

images filled most of the opposite wall. The machine whirred and guttered, she had only seen projectors at the cinema, but this was much smaller and she had never seen pictures like these. The man on the film was in a dinner suit with tails, he twirled his moustache like a silent movie rake and held out his hand, his forefinger beckoning two women to come towards him. They walked on screen both coquettish and demur but, at his command, began slowly to remove their clothes. The music was slow, enticing. The man lay down on a chaise longue and watched as they performed a striptease. At his command they kissed and began to fondle each other.

'Look at your face!' said Perrine, drawing Claudette's eyes from the screen. 'You are such an innocent, Françoise. If you think this is shocking, I can tell you it's nothing compared to what goes on upstairs! You wait.'

Claudette turned back to the screen, the women were undressing the man. The music heightened as they aroused him, waves of sound emanated around the room. Perrine clicked the machine off and rewound it back to the start, then she flicked the main light on and the room lost its lustful aura. It was a dreary room with heavy wooden walls, ruby drapes and rugs, and worn animal furs that smelt heavy and old.

'It's all done with lighting, it makes every room work in the same way. This one is the only one the clients can lock themselves in so that they can relax, as it were,' she winked. 'I'd hate to think what goes on in here at times.' She screwed her nose up. 'It always smells the same, sort of seedy.'

For the first time Claudette felt absolutely lost, entirely

bemused and out of her depth. 'So, are all the rooms between here and my floor occupied by the ladies?'

'Yes, except floor five. Next floor up is Eva, Nannette, Sophie; then three has Freya, Monique and Babette, then Pollo, Lilia and Bella.'

'So why is floor five empty?'

Perrine hesitated, as if she was going to say something, but instead she shrugged her shoulders. 'I suppose Madame Odile couldn't afford to do them all up, the rooms have probably been left until she has more money.'

Claudette knew this, she had taken a look at the dark empty corridor, still and silent, the doors all locked.

'After all, she has spent a fortune on the boudoirs, each one is themed; The Roman, Orient, Hindu, Versailles, Luxury. You name it, she's thought of it.' She opened a panel in the wall with a soft click and pulled out a mop and bucket, cleaning cloths and polish.

'All the rooms have these. We clean them at the ladies' request. They have to keep the room smart themselves, but they need help with the beds. There's a lot of clean linen required, and mending,' she giggled, 'A lot of ripping goes on!'

Claudette was still feeling dazed. 'Are all the clients Boches?'

'Now they are, but before the war there were film stars and government officials and the like. They tipped very well for "anonymity." That's why we never saw them come and go and the girls could only hint at who they'd had, otherwise it would have been the chop for them.' She drew a finger across her throat dramatically.

'Are you frightened, Perrine?'

'Of what?'

'Of what the Boches are doing in here, of this house entertaining these people, our enemies?'

Perrine pursed her lips, thinking. 'I try to focus on the benefits to us and the girls, there is so much hardship outside it feels like a sanctuary in here.'

'That's what Jacques said in the kitchen.'

'It is, but it's also a prison.'

'Because we can't have days off?'

'That, yes, although we have free time on Sunday and sometimes Saturday afternoons too for as long as we're not needed, and we are allowed out on errands if it's urgent. The ladies aren't allowed out at all.'

'Not at all?'

'Haven't you noticed how white they all are? They look bleached! Madame Odile won't let them go outside, she's concerned that they might run away with their clients or do favours elsewhere, or worse, get shot by Parisians. She keeps all their papers in the safe in her room. They are seen as collaborators, well, to be honest, we all are. Madame Odile depends heavily on the Germans supporting us against those who would like to burn the place down.'

Perrine left to fetch the vacuum cleaner, leaving Claudette alone in the silence of the room. She picked up the cushions and the furs and made piles of them so that she could clean the sofas. As she worked her way along she saw a wallet jammed down the back of a cushion. She opened it and two bright-eyed fair-haired children were staring up at her, their innocent smiling faces at odds with her surroundings. It made her shiver. She pulled the contents out, it had fifty marks in it and an identity card.

She flipped it open and revealed a picture of a young man in an SS uniform, his hair short under the black cap. The signature underneath read Karl Rumitt. His face looked so young and innocent, she couldn't equate it with what she heard about the SS. She snapped it shut and dropped it into her apron pocket.

After half an hour, she had the carpet edges swept and was beginning to polish the wood. There was a knock at the door, it was Jacques, he had brought the vacuum cleaner up for her.

'Perrine's busy, she asked me to bring this up.' He was obviously irritated at the interruption to his Sunday afternoon off. 'She told me about Madame, you were very lucky; surely running a bath isn't beyond you?'

'No, the bitch deserved it, she's a nasty piece of work,' Claudette told him.

'I suspect they all are, it's what they do and no sweet little virgin's going to last long in a whore house.' He cast a meaningful glance at her but she ignored his barbed comments just as she ignored Joubert's, they were both as awful as each other.

'Look at this.' She handed him the wallet. He smiled and it was such a big grin it nearly split his face in two.

'Excellent,' he said, opening it up and taking out the identity card. 'Excellent. Where did this come from?'

'In here.' Claudette pointed at the sofa.

'Keep looking, dig deep,' he said, pushing the wallet into his trouser pocket. 'If you were my real sister I'd give you a hug, this is exactly what we need.' With that, he left.

At five o'clock the door opened, it was Nannette. She had a kimono on, a luxurious silk print. Claudette felt intensely dull and dirty every time she came across one of the ladies and Nannette was no exception. She had round amber eyes, her hair was in a roll high above her face, the jet black of it outlined a chalk white face and slash of blood red lips. She had an ethereal, oriental quality about her.

'Madame O says I must colour your hair,' she said with a kind smile. 'And what Madame O wants Madame O gets.' Claudette wiped the back of her hand against her forehead. She felt the filaments of fur that she had disturbed when she was cleaning sticking to the back of her throat. 'My room in half an hour,' said Nannette. Her eyes were bewitching.

Claudette ached when she'd finished the room. She carried the vacuum cleaner back downstairs, her back wincing with the pain of lifting it.

'Oh Françoise, I'm so sorry,' Perrine was contrite as she entered the kitchen. 'Madame Odile caught me coming out of the room and she told me I wasn't to help you. I will make you some lemon tea.'

'Which room is Nannette's?' Claudette asked, flopping into Jacque's fireside chair.

'Second floor, room two.'

As Claudette climbed the stairs again her legs felt like lead. Nannette's door was open, waiting for her so she knocked lightly and stepped inside. It was as if she had walked into China. There were tall ginger pots almost the same height as her with exquisite designs of dragons chasing each other around them, the double bed had four golden pillars at each corner, the walls decorated with fabric. The lacquered floor was deepest black, the cushions on the armchairs were made of watery silks. Claudette reached out and touched the counterpane on the bed. Her rough fingers snagged in the delicate weave of it. The room looked like a Hollywood film set, but in full colour, vibrant and astonishing.

Nanette was in the bathroom humming a nameless tune; she was laying out what she needed to colour and cut hair. 'Come in, Françoise,' she called. Her voice was light, almost fragile. She had drawn a bath and the steam rose above it, misting over the mirror so that they both looked like apparitions. Nannette drew up a chair for Claudette to sit down.

'I used to work as a hairdresser in my past life,' Nannette said as she began to brush through the tangles of Claudette's hair. 'And let me tell you, this hair needs dressing.' Claudette felt the gentle touch of the fingers through her hair, the coaxing of it and teasing of the brush, her neck relaxing, a stupor coming over her. The effect was soporific and her head became heavy, until she felt like she would fall asleep under Nannette's nimble fingers.

'Right, into the bath with you.'

'Pardon?' Claudette sat upright.

'While the colour takes, jump in the bath.'

'But, am I allowed?'

'No, but that's never stopped me, I can tell you're exhausted. I'll watch the door, but I saw Madame O going out about half an hour ago so she'll never know and what the cat doesn't see…'

Claudette let her clothes fall to the floor, she had never been undressed in front of anyone, but unlike Apollonia, Nanette took no notice of her. The water was hot and steamy as she slipped down into it. Her eyes were level with the low window, she could see the building opposite – it looked to be unoccupied. She closed her eyes, the bath salts were lavender, she felt her muscles relax and her rough hands soften as she sank deeper into it.

When Nannette rubbed away the condensation on the mirror Claudette could not believe her own eyes. Instead of the careworn, plain face of Claudette Bourvil, there was an elegant woman with pink lips, neat eyebrows and lustrous brown hair slicked into a Pompadour. The hair lifted high above her face, and her skin was lightly dusted with powder.

'Oh, bless the Holy Mother,' she exclaimed. 'That can't be me, is it me?'

'I dare say Madame O will be pleased.'

Claudette gaped into the mirror, her mouth wide open. 'I can't believe it, I just can't –'

'Any time,' said Nannette. 'The Boches bring us all the things we need.'

'Oh, Nannette, how can I thank you?'

'It's my pleasure.'

Claudette stood up, her neck felt completely different with her hair pinned up. She hugged Nannette, who felt thin and bony under the kimono.

'Thank you so much.'

'There you go,' she replied, an impish smile playing on her lips. 'Now you're one of us.'

Chapter Twenty One

It had been a fortnight since Ledbury, during which time I had received a card from Lucy. It was a watercolour of pink peonies in a glass vase, very delicate. She told me it had been very nice to meet us and that she had found out that Freddy's mother was called Madeléine. She also sent Bertie's best wishes. I looked at the small, neat handwriting. I'd liked Lucy very much and perhaps because it had been such a nice day, because I was with Matt and the sun had shone so brightly in Ledbury, the memory was sharp and clear.

It had been raining heavily all day and Mr C was curled up on my lap safe and warm inside. I had been reading, but I'd put the book down and was considering making a cup of hot chocolate when my mobile buzzed. 'Hi Connie, it's me.' It was Matt. I noticed the absence of the usual levity in his voice.

'Oh, hi Matt,' I replied, 'Are you OK?'

'Yes, fine. You?'

'Yes, I've had some work from Will, a website design, so that's been good.'

'It's work I wanted to talk to you about,' he said, his voice flat and unnatural.

'Really?'

'Yes, but first how are things with Freddy's house?'

'It's on the market, but no-one's been round yet. The agent's told Hat there's a lot of work to do on it, we all knew that.'

'Someone will want it but the market's very slow right now.'

'I know, she can drop the price easily enough if needs must.' I paused, then asked, 'What's the work thing?'

'Do you remember the guy I work for sometimes who does PR for French companies?'

'Yep.'

'Well, he wants me to do a shoot in Paris at the end of the month, but Cherry, my assistant, is on holiday. Would you consider coming with me to style the shots?'

I felt like a balloon was being expanded inside me. Then, of course, the negative voices in my head were shrill and telling me no, but I said yes in spite of them. As I put the phone down a thrill of real joy welled up in me at the thought of seeing him again. I typed the dates into ical on my ipad and stared at it, waiting to see if anything would come up to stop me going. There was nothing.

Half an hour later the rain stopped, leaving a soggy wetness everywhere. The black clouds had broken into a bright Magritte sky. I took a walk down to the woods and then up through the meadows. They were brimming over with Marsh Marigold and Mayweed. This particular Sunday afternoon was very quiet, the usual distant sounds of leather on willow and cheering were noticeably absent because of the rain.

As I walked along the High Street I decided to visit Hat, I hadn't seen her for two weeks because I'd been working. The house rose imperiously from the street, it's symmetrical façade and faded beauty at odds with the bright white For Sale sign attached to the frame of the front door. The bell made the familiar whirring sound and I saw Hat's silhouette in the frosted glass long before she knew it was me.

'Hello, stranger.' She hugged me hello. 'You must be psychic, I've just switched the kettle on and I wanted to show you something.'

The house felt completely different, very cold and empty. The hall, cleared of the old macs and umbrellas, seemed much bigger. There was no nineteen seventies telephone table with a stack of worn directories. All that was left was a French mirror with a curlesque frame and freckled glass that I had barely noticed until then. The rest of the space was bare.

We walked through to the kitchen where the kettle was boiling triumphantly. Hat made us a cup of tea and, as we sat down together at the kitchen table, she asked about Matt.

'How do you actually do that?'

'What?'

'Read my mind! Do you think you might have been a witch in a past life?'

'No, magician. I can never look at a rabbit without getting the urge.'

'You're feeling better,' I said, noticing the pink in her cheeks and the lines of sadness around her eyes were just that little bit less stark.

'I still miss the old rogue,' she said. 'The inquest is next week, Jon's going with me. Do you think there will journalists and such like?'

'Oh I doubt it.' I might have said the words, but I didn't believe them entirely. Even though Freddy's death had not been much more than a sentence on the local television, an inquest always had possibilities for salacious gossip.

'Jon says the Coroner only wants to say how Freddy died, not any whys or wherefores.' Hat pulled the biscuit barrel towards us. It was full of Hobnobs, chocolate; I was doomed.

'So? Matt?'

'He phoned about an hour ago, he wants me to go to Paris with him.' Hat's eyes bulged over the rim of her cup.

'Really? Wow,' she said.

'Work.' I replied. Her eyes were still bulging.

'Work with benefits maybe?' she partnered the intonation of her voice with a wink. It made me smile.

'We'll see, I'm not sure about anything where he's concerned. You know me I do this to myself, I give off all the right signals, convince myself I'm ready and then I sabotage everything.'

'You can't go through all that heartbreak and move straight on to someone new. I doubt anyone could. If you'll take my advice you'll take it slowly, give it a chance, no pre-supposing.' Hat was right, of course she was right, she's like a big sister to me. I looked around at the kitchen, all but the essentials had gone. No dresser with its jumble of pots, plates and postcards. No pair of green wellies by the back door or rattan chair, its pile of newspapers waiting to be made into spills for the winter fire. The house was soulless and desperately empty of Freddy's belongings.

'Come with me,' Hat stood up and reached for the keys from the kitchen counter. We went through the wide back door and stepped outside into the garden. The grass was still glistening with rain. She picked her way down the narrow path to the shed as I followed behind.

'Do you know, I completely forgot about the shed until today. Isn't that ridiculous? I've gone through all the rooms and blitzed them. Jon has taken carload after carload to the tip. Then, just today I was looking out at the rain and wondering what I should do next when Sid burst in and began doing laps of the garden, nose to the floor as usual. I suddenly focussed on the shed and realised I hadn't been in there.'

She put the key into the lock of the old blistered door and pulled it towards her. It creaked on its hinges and a heavy scent of wet wood, tar and mildew wafted out. There were assorted tools; a very old, unused workbench and a kitchen chair with a red plastic seat. Cobwebs hung from the pitched roof and covered a row of rusted Castrol GTX oil cans. There were the signs that a rat was not too far away, large droppings were scattered everywhere.

'No wonder Sid is sniffing around all the time, it's a rat he's after.'

'Well, it will all have to go, I'll have to set about it this week,' said Hat with a sigh. 'But look here, this is what I wanted to show you.' She pulled a small metal chest out from under the workbench where it had been balanced on an old coffee table. It was either the colour of rust or it was completely rusted. As it turned out it was a bit of both. It was also quite heavy. The padlock on it had been broken and was swinging loose. Hat lifted it on to the workspace with my help. It was about sixteen by twelve inches in size.

We eased open the lid and the smell of damp paper

filled the air. I reached in and pulled out the top document, it was a passport. It was a faded black with a trace of the lion and unicorn on it. Inside, the pages were mouldering. There was a black and white picture of a woman, the image almost spoiled by a ring of damp. She was very pretty and her face was framed by a nineteen forties hairstyle. The name on the cover was Madeléine March.

'That's Freddy's mother.' I handed it to Hat so that she would see it. 'Funnily enough I got a card in the post from Lucy, Bertie's housekeeper, giving me that name.'

The rest of the passport was water damaged, the patterned leaves stuck together. 'What a shame,' I said, trying to turn the page but realising that it was falling apart in my hands. There was the faint imprint of a stamp, France to England on fifth September 1944, and another, June 1952 back again. The rest of the pages were blank and so water damaged it was impossible to see anything else.

'Is there a passport for Freddy?' I asked.

'No, there's some other stuff, though.'

I pulled out the next item. It was a small pink booklet almost completely damp. The front cover said Rose in big decorative type, but everything else was water damaged. From the odd words I could see it was in French. As I lifted it over to the dusty surface of the workbench it started to fall apart.

There was a thin book of English grammar, a checked cream and grey cover, its cream pages listing all the nouns and verbs, then adjectives and so on. Possibly from Freddy's school days. Wrapped in a black cloth I found a beautiful tortoiseshell comb, the sort women wore in their hair in the twenties and thirties. There were non descript items; a pencil; a cheap white brooch shaped like a shield with alpine flowers on it; various leaflets and an old A to Z with a map of the London Underground on the inside cover. Someone had drawn a ring around Marylebone and Covent Garden stations. There was a small printed piece of paper, like the bottom of a newsletter, with a phone number scrawled on it. Finally, at the very bottom I found a brown manila envelope; it contained two letters, the paper aged and flimsy. The writing was in French.

'Take them into the house, let's make another brew,' Hat suggested. It was unseasonably cold in the shed given that it was mid-July.

'Can I take these bits and bobs?' I asked.

'Yes, of course, I'm sure the family wouldn't be interested. I'll check with them about the passport, though.'

We laid everything out on the kitchen table and I carefully opened up the frail letters. They were so old the paper had absorbed the ink right through and made the blurred writing a pale lilac. Hat put a fresh cup of tea in front of me. 'How's your French?' I asked her.

'Schoolgirl.' She held the first letter up to the kitchen light. 'The address is smudged completely, it says a house name, I think, but the word isn't one I know. The date is 21 March, 1946. The writing is so typically French, those were the days when everyone learnt to write the same way.

'Dear Madeléine, Something the town five years ago, this letter something, something. I am so sorry I can give you no further help.'

She turned the letter first this way then the other.

'I can't read the next sentence, something about 'un

147

tragédie terrible et un grande douleur' it's signed Annalise.'

'A terrible tragedy and a what?' I asked.

'A sorrow, a great sorrow.' I unfolded the second letter, the paper was the same, from the same pad.

'This one's worse.'

The top of the letter was completely illegible, I sighed with the frustration of it. It was like having a jigsaw puzzle with the pieces either damaged or missing, and no lid.

'I presume it's Dear Madeléine, I can see the I, N and E. 'I write to tell you that he came back and I was able to tell him you were looking for him. He is very changed, I doubt you would recognise something, something.' Hat puffed out her cheeks, 'This is so frustrating!' 'If you come in June you can stay with me but I will understand if it's too difficult. You have a young – that must say boy – young boy and coming back would be trés difficile. You know that since that terrible day everyone has changed, I am so glad you were able to do what you did. I think of you all the time. It would have been so different for us all if –' Hat stopped reading and flipped over the paper, 'It's got a second page, this is just the first one. Damn and blast, that's all there is.'

I sat staring at the things in front of me. It gave us no clues whatsoever about Freddy's mother, except that she had an English passport. I sat opposite Hat looking hard at the letters as if I might find something else hidden amongst the blurred words. There was no chance, I'd have to ask Matt.

'If I take these anywhere they will simply fall apart.' I was thinking aloud.

'Photocopy them, I've still got the photocopier in the library.'

When I left I had the two photocopies, not very clear ones, given the raw material, in a plastic ring binder insert. Hat lent me a canvas bag and I stowed the other things. The day was fading into a pink twilight as I walked up the hill to my cottage. I let myself in and Mr C immediately began his campaign for his supper, tail upright, eyes squinting, declaring his undying love for me. I emptied his food into his little fish-shaped bowl and watched as he took careful, gourmet chunks of it and savoured them.

I unplugged my ipad from where it was charging and checked my emails. The usual job opportunities in the arts were waiting for me, all of them London-based and most of them unpaid. Then there was the latest offer from Amazon Local, several charities begging for money, and a printing firm was having yet another grand sale.

Then there was one from Matt.

Hi Connie,

Glad you can help me out, I'll send details later of the job. You'll find it very straightforward, I'm sure. Attached are the hotel's details. I've done the bookings at a hotel near the shoot, very handy, in fact.

See you on 27th July, if not before.

Matt

No kiss, or sign off, just his name. The thought crossed my mind, of course, that this was a work email and bound to be more formal. His company logo and contact numbers were beneath it. I clicked on the attachment, it was a confirmation, all very straightforward. Two rooms, four nights, the dates were okay. I scrolled down until I got to the 'special requests' box:

'Must be on separate floors.'

Matt, it transpired, had decided I was a no go, and who could blame him?

Chapter Twenty Two

Claudette had been working for Madame Odile for two weeks, settling into the strange routine of the place. German officers would enter during the day, often a small group with excitement writ large in their eyes, but it was in the evenings after ten that the house was full. Perrine always went home then, Marie went to bed and it fell to Claudette to sit by the row of bells, a throwback from when the house was privately owned and decent, when servants kept the place elegant and traditional.

The women were self-contained in their rooms. They had all kinds of drinks in a multitude of colours, fresh fruit cut into exquisite shapes and plates piled with fresh cream and tiny quenelles of meringue. Macaron, in subtle shades of browns and purples were stored in big glass jars next to nougat and marshmallows. Claudette filled these and dreamt of being allowed to eat them. She had never seen such sweet fancies before. The rooms were all exotic and rich, the drapes and bed coverings the highest quality and the art exquisite. By mutual agreement Perrine cleaned Apollonia's room and Claudette avoided her as much as possible.

The bell rang and Claudette felt her heart lurch. She hated being called upstairs, and worse, it was Apollonia. She looked across at Jacques who was reading a newspaper.

'Well, don't look at me, I'm not going,' he said. Claudette stood up and brushed down her apron. She had been reading a magazine on Paris couture that had been thrown away in the Salon.

'I hate going up when the Boches are here,' she told him.

'Just go,' Madame F said as she came out of her bedroom. 'Stop dithering, girl, and get on with it.'

Claudette began to climb the stairs from the kitchen, her legs were heavy and tired. She turned and over her shoulder said: 'I'll go up to bed after this, if you don't mind?'

'Yes, that's fine, they know we're all finished down here.'

Claudette half opened the door into the lobby and listened. There was jazz on the gramophone and men speaking German, punctuated by the sound of women laughing. She stole out, trying her best to be unobserved, but as she rounded the corner to go up the stairs she saw that Sophie, Fifi and Bella were in the bar with six officers. The men's uniforms were undone, their collars open. They were drinking steins of frothing beer. The three girls were naked and sitting astride the soldiers' knees. The stark white of their bodies against the grey green uniforms made the scene look like a marble tableau with the male figures covered in mould. All six were raucous and rowdy, shouting and yelling to one another above the music. Bella and her client stood up and then she bent over, rubbing her bottom into a German's groin as he slapped her buttocks, his face stupidly drunk. The officer in front held her dangling breasts, large and pendulous, in his hands, his face wildly excited. Claudette was transfixed, willing herself to move, but she had never seen anything like it nor felt anything like it. Her stomach clenched as her whole body seemed to be taken over with a feeling she couldn't fathom.

'There's our little virgin,' shouted Bella above the music. 'Unsere kleine Jungfrau!' She was speaking German, her voice condescending and cruel.

'Ein Jungfrau!' One of the officers pushed past Bella and strode towards Claudette, his boots hard against the marble floor. 'Virgin,' he said in French. Claudette felt her insides turn inside out, the man was walking around her as if he was inspecting a horse. 'So, this is what a virgin looks like in France, nice.' He lifted Claudette's chin, his arrogant features cold above the gold and red braid on his lapels.

'Gehen sie auf ihr ein gute zeit, Herbert,' one of the soldiers shouted over Sophie's head. He had his hands cupped over her breasts and she was licking his ear.

The man ran his finger up to Claudette's ear and tugged on it. 'Give her a good time, yes, I think I will. All Frenchwomen need to be taught a lesson in how to become good whores now that we are here.' There was a shout of laughter from the bar. Claudette saw that Bella was leaning against the doorjamb her face cold and impassive.

'Maybe a good fuck would do you good, Françoise, eh? Loosen you up a bit?' she said.

Claudette felt unable to breathe and stood perfectly still, her skin prickling with perspiration, not knowing what to do next. 'Excuse me, sir,' she said, cursing herself for finally using the word. 'I have to go to Miss Apollonia, she has sent for me.' His face broke into a smile, he had yellow teeth, there were fragments of food on his lips.

'Then why didn't you say, Virgin Girl? I would not dream of Miss Apollonia being let down, I have a date with her myself tonight.'

Claudette turned and fled, her embarrassment garnering another peal of laughter from the officers. She was shaking, her head down, eyes fixed on the purple carpet, the humiliation and fear hurting deep inside her. Not only had the whores done nothing to help her, their drunken eyes had been uncaring and their slurring voices had egged him on. Her heart was hammering against her rib cage, how was she supposed to handle all that?

She rounded the corner and was standing in front of Apollonia's room. She felt breathless, a shiver inching down her. Knocking lightly she hoped she would be told to go away, but she was called in. Apollonia was in bed, her head against the silk pillow, her naked body on top of one of her furs. The German Officer was wearing his jacket, nothing else. He was having sex with her, biting at her throat, sucking on her breasts, his tongue licking all over. Apollonia's hair spilled out behind her, dark and red cascading in waves, its sheen soft in the dull light. Her eyes were fixed hard on Claudette, deep green penetrating shards of spite. The soldier urged himself into her like a mongrel in the street, groaning and gasping. Claudette saw Pollo's foot was bandaged and, though she refused to give anything away, she was glad, glad that Pollo had suffered, but certain that this new humiliation was her revenge.

'Yes, miss?' she said as calmly as she could, even though her heart was racing.

'Ah, Françoise.' Pollo's eyes widened with amusement at her maid's compromised situation. 'Can you pass me that glass of wine?' It was less than eight inches away from her, on the bedside table. Claudette picked up the glass and passed it to Pollo who put it straight back down without drinking from it.

'You can go now,' she said with satisfaction written all over her face. Claudette left the room before anything else was asked of her. As he pulled the door closed she heard the German moan and cry out; 'Ja, Ja, Ja!'

She hurried up the stairs, her heart hammering, tears brimming in her eyes. She wanted the solitude of her bedroom and an escape from everything. As she rounded the corner to floor five, her head was heavy and she was still looking down. She walked headlong into a German officer who was standing by the lift. He grabbed her arms, preventing her from falling backwards down the stairs.

'Hey, watch where you're going!' Unlike most of his compatriots his French accent was impeccable. His jacket hung beautifully from his tall frame, his blonde hair was cut short and lay smoothly against his head. She looked up at him, her face flushed and her breathing ragged.

'I'm sorry,' she said immediately, dropping her eyes back to the floor. His boots were highly polished, the spurs on them silver.

'No matter.' She looked at his face. It was lean with a high bridge to his nose. He was clean-shaven, so different from Yves, Joubert, Jacques. She held his gaze, the eyes were clear grey, the colour of the lake at Vacily in the winter.

'Are you all right? You seem to be shaking.'

'Yes, I'm fine, I'm very tired; I'm sorry.' She found herself drawn to look at him again and she could see there was a softness in his face. He was nothing like the Nazi downstairs in the lobby, his teeth were clean and white for a start. 'Excuse me,' she stepped sideways around him. As she glimpsed at him from the stairs he was looking at her, his eyes meeting hers. He was young, mid-twenties no more, a little older than her. She hurried to her bedroom, closed the door and leant against it, her head spinning. She had never seen a man like that before.

Claudette was up early the next day, her sleep had been fitful. As she arrived in the kitchen she asked Jacques, 'Why was there a German coming out of the fifth floor?' Jacques looked at Madame F and then down at the shoes he was cleaning. Neither of them replied. 'I don't understand.' She looked at them both, waiting for an answer.

'He was probably lost.' Madame F said, concentrating on the dough for the croissants, her arms were up to the elbows in flour. 'There is coffee on the stove, pour yourself a cup and sit down, you'll be upset after last night.'

'You heard, then?'

'About that evil man, yes. Madame Odile found out when she came home last night, she is dealing with it,' said the cook. Her expression was matter of fact. 'Perrine's in the Salon cleaning, when you've had your coffee go and see her.'

'If any one of those Boches gives you trouble tell them I'm your brother,' said Jacques. 'I won't take that kind of shit from them.' His cheeks were an angry red.

'And what exactly can you do, Jacques?' Claudette

156

retorted. 'Stop them, tell them not to bother me, ask them to please not boss us around? I'm sure they'll listen to you! Maybe you've been too long in your sanctuary down here, but they are in charge now. They do exactly what they like and if you give them any reason to, they shoot you.'

Claudette felt her resolve hardening. She had spent the night tossing and turning thinking about Vacily and her parents, going over and over again in her mind the ramifications of her failure for the Resistance. She would not let Yves down. She drank her coffee watching Jacques over the rim of the bowl.

Perrine was cleaning the great mirrors in the Salon with vinegar and newspaper, she stopped when Claudette came in. 'Oh Françoise, I can't believe it, poor you, Madame F. told me, it's just awful.'

'With the exception of Nannette and Lilia they all treat me like I'm a piece of dirt.' Claudette shook her head and sat down on one of the plush red salon chairs. 'Just because of Pollo and her stupid foot.'

'And it was a mistake, anyway,' added Perrine. She put the paper and vinegar down and gave Claudette a hug. Holding her at arms length, her hands on her friend's shoulders, she said: 'We work in a whorehouse, with whores, it was never going to be easy. When it gets too much think of the Tarte Tatin on a Saturday night, and fresh croissant and real coffee.'

'And the hair-dye,' added Claudette, but her smile felt weak. 'Perrine, why would a German Officer be on floor five? Isn't it empty?' Perrine looked away and picked up her cleaning where she left it.

'He will have gone up too far in the lift, that's all, a

simple mistake. He will have realised and be wanting to come down again.' There was something about Perrine that wasn't quite right, she was turning away, concentrating a bit too hard as she drew the folded paper down the glass.

Claudette picked up the duster and a tin of polish. She began to wipe the soft cloth across the top of a walnut cabinet. It was inlaid with ivory and mother of pearl, the finish exquisite. Watching Perrine from the corner of her eye Claudette knew she was keeping something to herself. Her hair was the deep dyed brown like her own, also done by Nannette, her slim figure and round, pretty face reflected in the looking glass. For the first time Claudette felt there was something between them, something Perrine knew, but was not going to discuss.

Jacques opened the door, the sweep of it let in a damp breeze meaning that the front door was also open. 'Sister,' he said grimly. 'May I have a word?' Claudette looked over her shoulder at Perrine who was not paying any attention, and stepped out of the room. Jacques took her across the hall and past the front door where Madame Odile was talking to a woman whilst she opened her umbrella. She paid Jacques and Claudette no heed as she pulled the door closed behind her.

'She's going out with her Madam friends,' said Jacques. 'Comparing prices and the latest cure for crabs.' Claudette didn't know what he was talking about. He took her into the bar and then round the end of it, into the quiet corner where the chairs formed an almost perfect circle round a glass table. 'I'm sorry about last night,' he said, hanging his head. 'I feel bad I wasn't there to protect you.'

'Thank you, Jacques. I was fine in the end, though the

whores wouldn't have stopped him, they were egging him on.'

'It's a long time since those bitches had any scruples,' he said forlornly. 'We're all the same now, it's been a long time since any of us could afford to have them.'

'Don't count me in with that lot. I never thought I'd be here, doing this. Perrine says we should focus on the Tarte Tatin,' Claudette said dully. 'That says it all.'

'I have news for you,' Jacques reached out and put his hand over hers. Instead of reassuring her it felt disturbing. she pulled her hands away and tucked them under her thighs.

'Am I that repulsive?' he asked, his eyes searching hers for an answer.

'I'm sorry but, honestly, after last night I've got a completely different view of things and especially men. And I also think you are keeping something from me.' There was a pause, she waited for him to speak, he said nothing. 'Floor five?'

'I have no idea why there was a Boche up there, forget it, we have real work to do here.' He was agitated. She changed the subject, she would get nowhere with him and she knew it.

'What did you want to tell me?'

'On Wednesday I am sending you to an address in the Marais. You are to go there and you will be collecting some sewing materials. The person in the shop upstairs will be Yves.'

Chapter Twenty Three

I was on the concourse at Ebbsfleet. A group of businessmen in tight suits all looking like variations on Jack Whitehouse were walking towards me, none of them was Matt. I took a seat and checked my ticket for the twelfth time that morning. The sun was high, and I was looking at puffball clouds, imagining I was illustrating them in a children's book, when Matt touched me lightly on the shoulder. He said hello and immediately began fumbling in his bag. It was the same tactic I use when I don't want to greet someone with a kiss. We had driven separately because Matt hadn't suggested anything different and it seemed ridiculous now. What had I done? Broken up a friendship before it really had a chance, that's what.

'We can go through now.' Matt nodded towards the group of men who were bunching through the ticket check. I followed him, holding out my ticket to a very smiley lady wearing a lanyard, and running through ideas in my mind about how to talk to him about me, and my stupidity. In the waiting room he went into WH Smith and flicked through magazines and books, idling his time away, away from me.

On the train we sat side by side, his knee touching mine, awkwardly. The train picked up speed and it occurred to me then that this was how we met six weeks before, it had all been about a train, the train that killed Freddy.

We talked very little. He was reading a Dan Brown and I lost myself in my book too. It was a convenient escape. He was friendly when he spoke, but the flirtation was gone, the sense of fun over. I felt awful, the engineer of the whole downfall, and here I was with him for four days on separate floors, by request.

The countryside of Normandy has always intrigued me, an endless patchwork of fields without hedges, ochre and burnt umber flashing past the window. Water towers, steepled churches in pink and grey, pylons very different from ours, linking farmhouses to hamlets to towns. I tried to picture it during the war, the trenches of 1914, the skeleton buildings and dreary greys of the Second World War, but I couldn't see it. Everything looked so neat and ordered, the ravages of war lost in time.

At the Gare du Nord a thrill of excitement ran through me; Paris. They were offering sweets at the gate enticing us to think nice thoughts about our journey. The concourse was full of people looking up at departure boards for platform numbers, groups of bemused tourists with irritated locals skirting around them. A beggar, with greasy auburn hair and a face almost the same colour, asked me for money. I caught his eye, but I had to pass him by as I hastily followed Matt who was threading his way at a pace towards the taxi rank. We waited behind two women, one with a poodle under her arm, its woolly coat the same auburn colour as the beggar.

It was a good ten minutes wait, during which Matt pointed out quirky things he saw, avoiding real conversation. There was a huge American man trying to squeeze into the seat of a taxi-bus and complaining that the seat belts weren't made for real people in France. There was a couple arguing loudly, her face indignant and his the colour of a blood orange. A Japanese family had just walked out of the concourse and into the taxi at the front of the queue, paying no heed to the line of hot, tired people behind them. The man who was organising us into line, under the long gazebo, raised his eyebrows but ignored them because he'd seen it all before.

Our cab pulled up and the driver got out. He had very black skin, black sunglasses, a black shirt and black jeans. On his wrist was a huge silver watch with a thick chain-link strap that glinted in the sun when he waved us over.

As we battled to leave the station our driver said something in French that ended in 'idiot!' and which made Matt laugh. I didn't understand and Matt didn't translate. The driver had the scars of tribal initiation on his face, deep ridges in his cheeks. I couldn't help but wonder how he had been able to stand the pain of it.

We were held up by the taxi with the Japanese in it. There were lots of gesticulations as our taxi driver shouted and punched his horn at a cyclist who, for no apparent reason, had stopped in front of him. It was chaos.

My eyes fell on the sign on the wall next to me. "Andre Dubois, the heart of the Resistance in Paris." I found myself wondering about him as the car horns started and the cyclist continued to argue with the taxi driver. I Googled Dubois' name on my phone but there was very little, only random facts about his life and his time as a radio operator in Tours working for the Resistance, but nothing of his time in Paris. He died in Gross-Rosen, Poland, having been arrested and shot multiple times. I Googled his image. He looked more like an accountant than a resistance fighter.

'What's that?' Matt had caught sight of Dubois' photo on my phone.

'That plaque back there, to Andre Dubois, that's him. Looks like an accountant.' Matt took the phone from me and looked closer.

'The Resistance were just normal people forced to do extreme things,' he said. 'In the main they were average Joes combining their small efforts to greater affect.' Then he added; 'It's so sad, all those lives lost under the Nazis, round every corner there is some sort of plaque or memorial to the war. There's a heartbreaking one in the Temple area to the children who were taken from local schools to be transported to death camps.'

'All that misery and loss, it's so evil.' I felt a tinge of sadness as I recalled the films I'd watched; The Pianist; Schindler's List; The Boy in the Striped Pyjamas, and when I was at college, Nacht und Nebel, which affected me deeply for years.

The driver unloaded our bags outside our hotel and we went inside to check in. Did I imagine it, or did the woman in her Hermes scarf at reception smirk when she read 'separate floors'? It's a weird request at the best of times.

My room was on the second floor overlooking the street at the front of the hotel. There was a magnificent building opposite with decorative ironwork in front of the tall windows. A man on the floor level with mine was

163

walking backwards and forwards talking on his mobile, wearing only his boxers; on the floor below a woman was watering the geraniums hanging from her balcony. The water dripped down onto the people passing underneath, some even held out their hands checking for rain.

Matt and I were starting work that afternoon. It was a furniture shop, an expensive Swedish designer and they had delivered a mountain of tables, chairs, sofas and lighting to a studio in the 14th Arrondissement. Matt was in work mode, focussed and busy. I was introduced to Clemence and Yan who were in charge of marketing. They spoke broken English and smiled a lot. I had to make sure everything was set out artistically, that there were no nicks or cracks on anything and that the props were used to their best advantage.

At eight we had three sets ready for the next morning. The studio they had hired was large and the technician friendly, even though he and I couldn't communicate. I do a good line in hand-signals and drawings.

'Why have they used you and not a French photographer?' I asked Matt as we returned to our hotel at eight thirty. My stomach was growling for food.

'James' decision, it means he can control the images and we can manipulate them together. He's very hands on is our James.'

I was about to suggest an evening meal at a little café I'd spotted just around the corner, when Matt spoke. 'I'm bushed,' he said. 'Long day tomorrow, I'm going to do room service and have an early night.'

'Right,' I said, a little wrong-footed. 'Okay, then, I'll do the same.'

He turned to go.

'Matt.'

'Yes?' I thought he looked rather sad, even dejected.

'Can I ask a favour?'

'Of course, yes.'

'Could you phone Daniel for me?'

'Daniel?'

'Yes. You know Daniel, the Daniel. He gave permission to the solicitor for me to contact him.' I felt disappointed that I had to remind Matt who I was talking about.

'Oh right, can I do it tomorrow? It's just I really want an early night.'

I felt uncomfortable because I thought he'd do it. For me. 'Yes, sure,' I said, trying to sound as if it didn't matter. 'That's fine.'

He left the hotel lobby and suddenly I was standing in his wake wondering what to do next. When I turned round the receptionist was giving me a pitiful glance and I felt like an idiot.

Chapter Twenty Four

Claudette was cleaning Nannette's room. She was pulling the counterpane into place when she saw something underneath the bed, half hidden by a discarded chemise. She pulled both things out. The chemise was silk, smooth and cool in her hands, the other was a folded piece of paper. It had notes, in German, written in pencil and a small map with arrows drawn on it.

'What have you got there?' Nannette had entered the room carrying a parcel. It was so big she could barely peep over the top. Claudette spun around hiding the piece of paper in the folds of the chemise.

'This,' she said. 'Such a beautiful piece of lingerie and it was in the dust and dirt under the bed.'

'Oh, that, you have it, wash it and enjoy it.'

'Really?'

'Yes, of course. Look, I bet there's at least one in here.' Nannette placed the parcel on the bed and cut the string with a Swiss Army knife that she produced from her pocket.

'You have a knife in your pocket?' Claudette asked, whilst slipping the note into hers.

'I carry it everywhere and have it tucked into the bed head when I'm bedding a Boche, because you never know.' She said it matter-of-factly as she opened the brown paper and a pile of silk underwear slid out, covering the bed in a pool of dusty pink, pearly ivory and duck egg blue.

'Oh, how absolutely beautiful!' exclaimed Claudette.

'Look at this.' Nannette held up a long mauve nightdress with coffee coloured lace at the bottom and an open seam from hip to toe.

'And this,' said Claudette, rubbing her cheek against a red silk scarf.

'You have that, too,' said Nannette. 'We're not allowed to go outside and we never use scarves, too much temptation for the psychopaths.'

'Oh Nannette, you are kind, I can't thank you enough.'

'You know, you are really pretty when you smile.' Nanette told her. 'You could easily be one of us with your new hair, and you have beautiful eyes. You need only to lose some rough edges.'

'Like what?'

'Nails, they're awful and body hair. The Boches like everything clean shaven.'

Claudette's eyes widened. 'I don't stand a chance with the nails, not with the work I do here as –

'Shaving is easy enough, I'll sort you out what you need.' Nannette began folding the garments she'd received and putting them into a black lacquer chest with drawings of Chinese men and women wrapped around each other all over the doors.

'Where did they come from?' asked Claudette. 'Who sent them?'

'One of my clients, Heinrich, was posted to Russia. He sends me gifts like this all the time, he's in love with me, or so he thinks.'

'Do you ever wonder how he gets them?' asked Claudette.

'Probably killed some poor unfortunate person,' said Nannette with an exaggerated sigh. 'But that's not the fault of the lingerie, is it?' She opened her wardrobe unveiling a rainbow of coloured garments and sighed. 'All of these come with a price one way or another.' She pulled out a pretty blue day dress and a pair of matching kitten heel shoes.

'Here, have these, and this bag to match.' Claudette couldn't believe what was happening. She took the clothes from Nannette, her heart lifted by the joy of being given things so beautiful. Nannette laughed as she watched Claudette hold them up against her. 'You see,' she said brightly, 'We all have a price, Françoise.'

'I'm going out this afternoon, on an errand. Do you want anything brought back?' asked Claudette, 'I'd like to repay you in some way for these things.'

'There's nothing I need,' Nanette said with a small sigh. 'We have everything we need here – except our freedom.'

When Claudette stepped out of the house she was wearing the blue dress and the matching shoes. She looked left and right and saw that the street was empty and quiet. A shiver of nerves was rising up inside her and suddenly the world seemed huge. The street widened then narrowed in front of her. She closed her eyes tightly and opened them again and when she did she found she couldn't focus. For a minute, the street felt like it was closing in on her, it was spinning around and the road looked molten, as if it were moving. She pulled the door shut leaning on the handle as a wave of dizziness overwhelmed her. Making her way down the three wide steps and along the narrow road she felt uncertain and quite weak. There was a crossroads and on each side of it a German soldier. She realised they were stationed there to protect the house. As she passed by, one of them turned and leered at her from under his helmet, the other looked at her as if she was worthless. Or did she imagine it?

She crossed over to the other side of the street, but the spinning began again and the road was coming up to meet her. The sky, a tepid brown-grey, the same colour as the buildings seemed to press down on her. She leant against the railings of a house, her eyes focussing in and out on a pile of rubbish banked up against the low wall below.

'Are you all right?' It was his voice, the same perfect French.

Claudette took a deep breath, trying to look at his face, but it was swimming before her eyes.

'Come in here, take a seat.' She was led into a bar, the rough wooden chair under her so different from those in the house. There was a heavy smell of cheap cigars and wine mingling with the odour from the toilet.

'You, boy, brandy!' The German flicked his fingers imperiously at the barman. The brown liquid came in a cheap opaque glass. The officer held it out so that she could sip it, it tasted warm and sharp at the same time.

'Thank you,' she said, pushing it away. 'I'm fine, it was just a dizzy spell. Please, there's no need for you to – I don't know what happened.'

'Are you pregnant?' he asked. She was taken aback by his audacity.

'No,' she shook her head. He smiled, he knew he'd shocked her. When, eventually, she stood up straight and was looking up at him, he said: 'I am very remiss. Let me introduce myself, I am Fritz Keber.'

'I am Françoise Favelle.' He was looking at her so intensely she had to dip her eyes. 'I'd better go now,' she said. 'I mustn't be out too long.'

'Where are you going?'

'To the Marais, I have some sewing materials to collect, I'm a seamstress.'

'Ah, I see, well maybe I should walk you there.'

'Oh no, honestly, I'll be fine.' Thoughts rushed around her head, this was not as things should be. This was a Boche, the enemy.

'I insist. Come, take my arm and I'll walk you. The fresh air will do you good. You probably have mild agoraphobia, they don't let you out of there very often, do they?'

'No, that is, I'm not–'

'Not what?'

'I'm not as confined as the others.'

'Because you're a maid?'

'Yes,' she said. 'I clean and sew and follow orders.'

'Well, we all have to follow orders from someone.' He offered her his arm, and she took it, not least because she still felt so strange. As she started to walk she realised his car was following slowly behind, the driver watching them impassively from behind the wheel. 'So tell me, what is it like working for Madame Odile? I suspect she is strict, yes?'

'Yes, she is, very, she actually makes me shake with nerves.'

'She's a pussy cat really,' said Keber. 'I've known her for quite a long time.'

'Really? Before the war?'

'Yes, I was a student in Paris. Just before the war, I renewed our acquaintance after we arrived here.'

'She's a real businesswoman,' said Claudette. She was feeling a reassurance by being on his arm and the strength of him so close to her. A man in a suit walked towards them and averted his eyes, but as he passed by, his arm clashed with Claudette's. It was hard enough to bump into her, but not enough to stop her; Keber didn't notice.

'Which shop are you going to?' he asked as they stopped to let a woman pushing a baby in a pram go past. Claudette hesitated, not wanting to get anything wrong.

'I don't know the name, it's on the Rue Trésor.'

'I know the one, a tailor's shop, it was run by a Jewish family.' He seemed to wait for her to speak, but she didn't. 'We sent the family away last year, it's now owned by a woman called Cécile Flaubert who was very grateful for the new premises to work from. You see, we are already making the lives of the French better.'

Claudette kept her eyes fixed on the street ahead. She was hoping for signs to tell her where she was and how far she would have to walk with Keber. On the other side of the road two Frenchmen were cleaning a wall of graffiti with two German soldiers standing behind them, rifles over their shoulders. Claudette tensed.

'The Parisian is a strange creature,' said Keber. 'They fight not with guns but chalk and paint. We've lately arrested a most famous graffiti artist and he's in prison with seven of his friends.'

'What will happen to him?'

'Some very bad things,' replied Keber. 'But let's not talk about them, let's talk about Madame Odile again, she has always fascinated me. Do you know what she used to do for a living?'

'No. I have no idea.'

'She was a prostitute, exactly like her ladies, she worked in the Chabanais. Do you know it?'

Claudette shook her head.

'That's how she got all the ideas for her rooms. I've never seen anything like the Chabanais, the rooms are spectacular, the women utterly exotic. Your house runs a close second, though, but it is so slick and ordered by comparison. And, of course, it is all German and no French, which is by far more preferable, even if the French are film stars and notables.'

Claudette looked at his face, it was beautiful. His jaw and chin were strong, defined, and his bearing upright, well bred, gentlemanly, but he spoke exactly as she knew he would; he was a Nazi first and foremost.

'What about you?' he turned the conversation in on her so swiftly she had no time to prepare herself. 'Tell me about you.'

'There's nothing to tell, my brother Jacques and I were brought up on a farm. Our parents left in the Exodus and have not come back.'

'And, do you know where they are?'

'No,'

'Do you want me to make enquiries?'

'No, there really is no need,' Claudette replied a little too quickly.

'Really? You don't know where they are and you don't care?' He looked down on her, his eyes immediately trying to fathom her out. He had stopped walking. After a moment he took out a leather bound notebook from his jacket. 'Here, write their names in here, I'll find out for you.' He handed her a pencil and the book.

She hesitated.

'Go on, I can trace them for you.'

'I'm not sure, I –'

'You're worried I'll have them shot or something?'

'No, I, it's just.' Claudette realised that she couldn't remember Françoise's father's name. He was studying her, looking intently at her face. She raised her head, remembering Yves words, "Remain silent while you think, give nothing away." At the same time she was trying to remember the name, Jérôme, Jeannot, it began with a J, but it was gone from her mind. Jean, was it Jean? This is why Jacques told her to say it all over again and again. And, what if he made enquiries and found out they didn't exist? Keber was working her out already. He lifted her chin, cupping it in the space between his thumb and fingers and stroked her cheek softly with his index finger. Then, slowly, he put his other arm around her back and pulled her to him. She let the hand holding the notebook drop down, dangling away from her body and lifted herself to meet his kiss. He pressed his lips against hers, the pressure hard. She felt a need to give in to him, to feel the strength of him holding her. When he let her go, he took the notebook from her and closed it. His eyes fixed on her as he slipped it into his pocket.

'I wanted to do that the other day when I saw you on

the stairs,' he said. Claudette stared at him in disbelief. 'There,' he said, still looking into her eyes whilst pointing along the road. 'That is the shop you are looking for.' Claudette stepped back from him but she was transfixed, he was still staring at her too.

'Thank you,' her voice faltered, she felt unable to think straight.

He waved to the driver of his car and, as it rolled forward and stopped alongside him, he climbed in. The driver was staring straight ahead. It pulled away and she stood perfectly still watching it disappear, not believing what had just taken place.

A globule of phlegm hit her cheek at that precise moment. She put her hand up and wiped off the green-yellow slime. The man was walking hurriedly away from her head down and hands in his jacket pockets. She pulled out her handkerchief and mopped it up, her stomach churning.

'Whore,' said a woman under her breath as she walked past, her eyes fierce.

Claudette walked quickly along the Rue Trésor, the pavements were narrow. Peeling, torn posters and police warning notices plastered every spare inch of wall. Some of the people who scuttled by were wearing yellow stars. There were women walking boldly on the arms of Nazi soldiers, men turning to eye her up, all of them could see her clothing was clean, new, expensive.

The shop had dark blue peeling paint and grimy glass. The materials in the window, bales of floral cotton and fine intricate lace looked wrong, too bright. The bell rang as she entered and a woman came from the rear of the shop.

'Good day,' she said, with an unconvincing smile. There was tension in her jaw, it was as if she felt guilty for being there. Claudette could understand why. 'I am here to collect an order for twelve Rue Ercol.'

'Ah, yes,' the woman replied calmly. 'You need to go upstairs.' She pointed towards a narrow door at the back of the shop. 'It is through there, and up.'

Claudette felt her heart beating fast. She reached the top of the stairs and entered a small room – it smelt stale and musty. Yves was sitting at a square table surrounded by unpacked boxes and skeins of material wrapped in brown paper. He stood up immediately and threw his arms around her, pressing her so tightly to him she didn't think she would be able to breathe.

'Oh Claudette,' he said, almost sounding like he might weep. 'I'm so glad you're safe and it's so good to see you. I can't tell you how good it is, truly.'

'It is good to see you too, Yves, how is everything?' They both sat down at the table opposite each other. He was staring at her as if they had been apart for years and not weeks. She saw that he had lines on his forehead and under his eyes dark circles, his lips were cracked and his chin rough with stubble. 'Are you all right?'

'No, not really, it's hard at the moment,' he said starkly. 'I'm on the run. We took down a communications line and things were left behind, by mistake. I think they know who I am. I've got false papers and accommodation is being found for me, but I have to stay here until I'm able to move on.' He looked at her, as if he were taking her in for the first time. 'You look amazing.' The words gave her a thrill. He cast his eyes over her, taking in the hair and nails, the dress, the shoes. 'I didn't expect you to look like this. Your hair –' He reached up and touched the side of her head, her skin felt sensitive under his fingers. She wanted to take his hand in hers but she thought of Giselle and how she must never give anything away.

'I'm surrounded by the most glamorous women you can imagine,' she told him brightly. 'It rubs off!'

'Well you look wonderful.' He was gazing at her as if he didn't believe she was real.

'Did you know that I was going to work in a whore house when you sent me here?'

'Yes. Yes, I did.'

'Well, I have to tell you, it gave me a real shock.' She tried to look indignant but it was impossible, because being with Yves always made her feel so much better.

'I know, I understand,' he said. 'But it's vital, we must do anything it takes. Count yourself lucky you're not sleeping in the forests, the prettiest thing I've seen for weeks was a boar.' She sniggered. 'I've missed that laugh,' he said. 'You know you're my oldest friend, don't you, especially now that Vincent…?' The thought warmed her heart, the fact he said it meant that their relationship was solid and real.

'How is Giselle doing?'

His face darkened. He looked down at his hands, balling them together in a white knuckled fist. 'I don't know,' he replied. 'We can't find her or Louis, there has been no word.'

'Oh, I'm sorry. I truly hope she's all right, Yves.' She meant it, she knew what family meant to him. 'Have you any idea at all?'

'None. They say the south is more dangerous than here

and God knows it's bad enough here.' Claudette leaned across and placed her hands on top of his. He unclenched the fists and took her fingers in his.

'I only hope the Allied Forces can act quickly now. It feels like the whole of France has capitulated, no-one is fighting except us and we're too few and far between. I was hoping for better.'

'How are Mr and Mrs Gabin?'

'Broken, hearts and minds. She has had a nervous breakdown. He is devastated.'

'Did you find out who it was?'

'No, whoever gave us away is still active.'

'And my parents?' Claudette felt a lilt in her voice, her pulse quickening.

'They are fine, some people wanted to know why you'd gone so suddenly, especially after Vincent, but mostly people don't want to know anything in case they have the Boches come knocking. If you don't know, you can't tell.'

Claudette felt suddenly homesick, for her parents, for Vacily and the lake and the flat, uncomplicated countryside, but not, it was suddenly clear to her, for her former life. She pictured the piles of mending dropped off at the door, the dresses and skirts she made from rough, course materials, cheap linens and cambric. She had seen so much more here in Paris already. 'Will I see you again?'

'I think perhaps not,' he said flatly. 'One way or another, because they're looking for me I will have to disappear for a while, assume a new identity. I'm going to head south to see where Giselle is.' He gulped, Claudette saw his Adam's apple moving, he was holding back his emotions. One day, she hoped, one day she might find someone who loved her as much as Yves loved Giselle.

'Look after yourself, Yves, please. And find Giselle, you were made for each other.' He looked suddenly weary and quite miserable.

'I hope I can,' he said, 'I hope I can.'

'You will, and when you do send me a message.'

'Yes,' he said, nodding. 'I'll be sure to. Oh, I forgot, another thing you should know, Joubert is in Paris. He's been forced into working as a labourer for the Boches. I don't know where, but you never know, your paths might cross.'

Chapter Twenty Five

Clemence and Yan took two hours for lunch but Matt and I kept working. We made a good team. He knew exactly what he wanted and was a real perfectionist. I watched him working on the close details of the furniture to show how well it had been made, asking me to move this prop or that light to create the perfect shot.

In coffee breaks I thought we might talk, but he worked through. The day was long and we finished after seven. I was exhausted and was thinking of a hot shower and an evening watching rubbish TV in my room with a bottle of wine from the local Super U. 'Fancy dinner at that café we walked past?' he asked.

'I'd love to,' I said a bit too quickly. 'Shall I meet you in reception at eight?'

'Great.'

The waiter pulled a chair out for me, the café was heaving, we had the last table. The waiters were rushing from the restaurant to serve a covered seating area on the opposite side of the pavement. They swept past us taking orders on winks and nods. Menus were placed in front of us with a practised flourish.

'It's going well,' said Matt, allowing himself a long breath. 'We'll be finished by tomorrow afternoon at this rate. How do you fancy a touristy day on Thursday?'

I was really pleased, it cheered me up immediately; Matt was back.

'No strings, yes?'

He wasn't coming back.

'Right, yes, of course,' I was hiding my face in the menu.

We ordered the fish of the day, sole and fondant potatoes and a bottle of Sancerre. There was cigarette smoke all around us, the raw smell of tobacco mixing with exhaust fumes and the hot musky scent of the city. 'Could we ring Daniel, do you think? It would be good if we could go and see him together, if you don't mind helping me, I'm not sure if he speaks any English.'

'Got the number?' he asked.

A fire engine sliced through the traffic, red with yellow lines along the side. It edged its way through a sea of green lights on top of taxis. I felt in my bag for my notebook and flicked it open, holding out the page where I'd written Daniel's number for him.

'I'll go over to that street, where it's quieter,' Matt told me. 'Back soon.'

I watched him as he dialled and stood talking, the sheen on his black leather jacket catching the lights around him. His hair fell down over his face. I liked that about him and the way he talked and frowned, then his face would light up and his smile was radiant. I really liked that about him too.

He came back, slid into his seat and looked apologetic. 'He's just leaving for the airport.'

'No!' I couldn't believe it.

'He's going to be in Prague until Friday.'

'Friday morning?'

'Evening. Connie, I'm sorry, I should have called him last night when you asked me to, I was just –'

'What?'

'Peeved.'

'About what?' I asked as the waiter placed our sole down in front of us. Of course I knew why he was peeved.

'It's just I thought you and I, well I thought there was a spark between us. Then you cooled right off and didn't get in touch.' He sipped a glass of wine, and reached for the pepper mill, but put it back unused. I had to put him out of his misery.

'When I met you, I really thought you were lovely, in spite of the circumstances and everything. The problem is –'

I then reached for the pepper, used it a tiny bit and put it back. 'I had… that is, the last relationship I was in ended really badly.'

'Was he a shit?' Matt asked.

'He dumped me and really hurt me. He had always been controlling but in an insidious way, you know drip, drip. When he left me he made sure I was reduced to nothing emotionally and I realised he had drained me of feeling.'

'Ah, I see,' said Matt. 'And I've come over the same way?'

I couldn't believe he could think that, not for a second. 'No, absolutely not.'

'Well, thank goodness for that,' he said, taking another, longer sip of wine. 'Just for a minute there –'

'No Matt, don't be daft, you're lovely. I'm the one with

the problem here, not you. I took so long to get over that relationship, I didn't feel like I could have another one for ages.'

He leaned across the table. 'I do understand, I had a clingy girlfriend once and Dave was quite controlling too.' I could imagine the girlfriend, but the one called Dave? 'My dog, remember my dog?' he said, pulling a face.

'Your dog was controlling?'

'Oh yes, it was all "it's food time; it's walk time; it's food time." Great licker, though.' He smirked. That was when I burst out laughing. How could I think Matt was anything like my ex? They were chalk and cheese. 'What would happen if I promised not to control you in any way?' he said earnestly and with a smile.

'That might work. It means letting me eat chocolate on my terms and not telling me what to wear or telling me that I'm not intelligent enough to participate in conversations at business dinners.'

'Right, understood,' he said. 'Should I be making notes or something?' We both laughed and from that moment, I felt a weight lift off me, the burden of worrying.

'Can we take things slowly?' I asked.

'Yes,' he said, a simple yes, and then he reached over and touched my hand. I felt the solid weight of it over mine and I felt everything was going to be all right.

Chapter Twenty Six

The men were dead.

They lay flat against the pavement, eyes glassy and wide open, faces grey. The buckets of water were turned over and the brushes they had been using were lying across the road. They had been shot in the back and the blood that had seeped across the backs of their shirts formed ragged wet patterns in the cloth. Claudette tried to avert her eyes but she was drawn to the scene, to the dead men and the fact that people were passing by and not looking, not wanting to see, avoiding all involvement.

She hurried on, remembering the way she had walked with Keber. There was a café with green painted woodwork, a German eating onion soup with a sophisticated French woman. A grey horse, its head hung low, stood in the shafts of a cart piled high with wooden cases of wine. Two men were unloading and taking the cases into the café. They weren't talking, their faces looked strained and uneasy.

Claudette watched them just a bit too long as she walked by. The German saw her and looked around, his eyes questioning. She hurried away and reached the house at five o'clock, she could never have believed she would be so happy to get back safely. She put her parcels of fabric by the kitchen door and ran straight upstairs to change.

When she came back down to the kitchen, Jacques was lighting the stove with great difficulty.

'I hate this bastard and it hates me, bastard,' he was saying as he struck another match and began a long diatribe of offensive words about chores and hard work. Finally it lit and he stepped back. Claudette took the folded paper out of her handbag and handed it to him. He took it to the corner of the kitchen and held it up to the light.

'Where did you find it?' he whispered.

'Nannette's room.'

'Very good, I'll pass it on.' He stuffed it into the pocket of his gilet. Perrine arrived and, pulling her headscarf off, she placed a basket on the table.

'I got the medicine, the doctor said he's due for the monthly check tomorrow. anyway.'

'Are you ill?' asked Claudette.

'No, Eva is, she has a fever and earache.'

'Shall I take it up?' Claudette offered.

'Oh, would you, that would be lovely, my feet are aching. I've walked miles. I'll make you a lemon tea and then I can get the vegetables done for tonight.'

Claudette took the brown bottle and a spoon up to Eva's room on the second floor. She knocked, but the reply was muffled. Eva was in bed, the covers pulled tight around her. Her teeth were chattering and she was wet with perspiration. Claudette made her sit up, plumping up her pillows. She was tiny; her face, without make-up, was childlike, the skin soft and clear of blemishes.

'Here Eva, I have medicine for you.' Claudette spoke softly as she poured it onto the spoon and lifted the girl up to sip it. 'You poor thing, you are really unwell, aren't you?'

Eva nodded. 'I have to be better, Madame Odile says I will lose her valuable income if I don't get well.'

'Forget Madame Odile,' Claudette put a hand onto Eva's forehead. 'You are nowhere near well enough to work. Perrine says the doctor's coming tomorrow for the monthly check. What's that?'

'He examines us all for the clap and crabs,' Eva told her. 'He's very nice, the only French man allowed to see us at all. Don't tell anyone, but he takes messages for us and sometimes he asks about the clients. We all think he's with the Resistance.' She sipped the water Claudette had poured for her, her large, grateful eyes dominated her face.

Claudette looked around the room, it was decorated in pale pink. There was a day bed against the window set with pink satin cushions, a bookcase full of children's books and a large white rug. Under the window was a box of untouched toys. She stood up and went into the bathroom where she ran a pink facecloth under the cold tap and brought it back to place on the girl's head. Eva was perspiring, her nightdress was wringing wet. 'Let's get this off,' said Claudette. She pulled it over Eva's head, the cotton was thin and sodden. Claudette pulled a new one out of the armoire. She turned back to the girl who looked even smaller and utterly vulnerable naked. She was flat chested, her body was scrawny, the bones of her back prominent through the pallid skin. As Claudette dropped the new nightdress over her head it was like handling a small bird.

'How old are you, Eva?'

'Sixteen.'

'How old really?'

'I told you, sixteen.'

Claudette waited.

'Fourteen. But you mustn't tell anyone, promise me. Only the doctor knows, and he says he won't say anything.'

'Do your parents know where you are?'

'They're dead. They were sent away, first to Drancy and then somewhere else.'

'Are you Jewish?'

'Please don't ask.'

'Oh Eva, is that why you don't eat with the others?'

The girl nodded. 'I go down and take the leftovers before you clear it all away, if I can. Sometimes Nannette brings me something.'

'Does your exclusive know?'

'No, and if Madame Odile knew she'd...'

'Eva, you're playing a very dangerous game.'

The girl closed her eyes, a silvery tear brimmed on her lower eyelid. 'I've lost everyone, every single person I knew was taken in the first round up. I don't care any more.'

'Don't they ask for papers?' Claudette was astonished.

'No, they ask for your body and what you can make it do for them. I was very popular and now my exclusive pays a lot of money for me.' Claudette put the lid on the bottle and filled the glass with fresh water. She mopped Eva's brow and ran a finger over her cheek. 'If you need anything, just ring, Perrine or I will come.'

'Thank you, Françoise.' Eva's voice was as thin as her tiny body. She was exhausted. Claudette left the door ajar and went downstairs.

'Eva is really ill, and she's very thin,' she told everyone

in the kitchen. Madame F, can you do a broth for her?'

'Yes, of course, poor child.'

'That's all she is, a child,' Claudette said with an accusatory look at them all, 'A poor child.'

'We're all of us caught up in this,' said Jacques. 'At least she's safe and warm and she gets fed in here.'

Claudette felt unconvinced. 'Which one is her exclusive?'

'Rechtstein, I told you, remember?' Perrine said over her shoulder as she peeled potatoes over the sink.

'The one who organises the exportations?'

'Yes, evil bastard.' Jacques was making sure he spoke loud enough that Madame F. could hear him. He shook his head. 'Bastards, all of them.'

Claudette picked up her mending, her eyes focussed on the needle going into the fine lace of a pair of knickers. They were intensely beautiful, a true duck egg blue, torn along one seam.

Chapter Twenty Seven

Matt and I were walking along the banks of the Seine, the Alma tunnel on our left its Flame of Liberty catching the car headlights in the gathering dusk. 'I really do think that's the only true memorial to her, you know,' I said as we crossed over and looked down at the tributes and photographs in Spanish, French, Polish and three undecipherable languages. There were tatty, faded pictures of her; dead flowers; a once pink, now grubby grey teddy bear, and graffiti scratched into the stone. Everywhere the name: Diana, Diana, Diana.

'Have you seen the fountain in London?' asked Matt.

'Yes, I saw it when it was new, for me it has nothing of her about it. Trust the French to come up with a ready made one that still catches the mood so well.' We watched as a man, wiping back tears, placed a note down on the base of the statue and backed away with reverence. We left him to his thoughts and walked through the city, its purring nightlife a blend of cigarette smoke, hot pavements and the excitement of chatter.

'I love Paris,' said Matt as we stopped to gaze out across the Seine. 'I could live here.'

'So could I,' I agreed, and the sharing of this small fact felt, all at once, significant. Paris, the most romantic city of them all and I knew why. Even I could leave the countryside for Paris.

A Bateau Mouche was floating serenely down the middle of the river, the reflections of her lights glittered in the dark water and a singer's fine operatic voice drifted towards us on the breeze. 'I'll take you on that on Thursday,' said Matt. 'My way of saying thank you for your help this week.'

'There's no need, I've really enjoyed myself, and I'm being paid.' I said this in spite of the fact there was nothing I would have liked more.

'There's every need,' said Matt. He turned to face me, his eyes catching the twinkling city lights, as if Paris was inside his soul. He kissed me, his lips brushing softly against mine. I felt the whole world spin around me, cascading colours, bright stars, everything.

'Oh Matt,' I whispered. I kissed him back and never wanted it to cease. His hand was on my neck, stroking his fingers through the hair at the base of my head.

'Let's go back to the hotel,' he whispered in my ear. We walked, hand in hand and suddenly the world felt right, everything seemed have fallen into place.

'What a shame,' I said. 'After finally getting to Paris we've missed Daniel, I knew I should have called ahead.'

'We don't have to miss him, we could stay on until Saturday, or even Sunday, it's no problem.'

'Really?'

'I'll leave a message on his answer phone,' Matt said and he squeezed my hand.

Outside my hotel bedroom I stopped. Matt, I could tell, was guarded, expecting me to turn cold on him. 'I'll go if you're not ready,' he said. I kissed him and opened the door, leading him inside with my hand. He pushed me against the wall, his kisses falling on my neck. I felt the weight of him against me. He took off his jacket and we both fell back onto the bed. I was so hungry for him and he for me, his mouth was finding mine, his hands undoing my blouse. I felt the recurring fear rising, but it was distant and I knew I could keep it at bay. I willed it to keep away and he must have sensed it because he whispered: 'I will look after you.'

I knew he would.

Chapter Twenty Eight

Lilia's face was pressed against the tiled floor of the bathroom, dark rings of smudged mascara around her eyes. She was unconscious.

'Help me lift her,' said Jacques, as he strained under the dead weight of her. Claudette caught hold of the limp legs and they laid her on the bed.

'What is it? Is she ill?' she asked.

'No, she's drugged up to the eyeballs, this happens all the time.' Lilia had her chemise and knickers on, the ones Claudette had repaired weeks before. The duck egg blue was almost the same tone as her skin.

'I'll get Madame,' said Claudette.

'No, don't, she doesn't need to see this.' Jacques said sharply. Lilia's eyes opened at the sound of his voice. They were glassy, staring like a dead fish.

'Get the doctor,' Claudette told him. 'She's going to die.'

Jacques looked at the girl lying as still as a statue on the silk bedspread and then hurried out of the room. Suddenly the body arched and sharp smelling saffron yellow liquid was vomited all over the silk spread. Claudette rolled Lilia over onto her side so that she would not choke. Then she remembered her little brother all those years ago and the way her mother had dealt with his sickness. She had loved him so much whilst Claudette found the stench of sickness made her retch. She had been unable to cope; perhaps she hadn't loved him enough, not as much as her mother loved him.

'Lilia, Lilia, you are all right, Lilia.' She tried rubbing the girl's hands. 'Lilia, you're going to be all right, just stay with me.' She went into the bathroom and ran cold water on a flannel, placing it over the damp forehead. Then she retrieved a cloth from the cleaning cupboard and mopped up the vomit.

Lilia was groaning. Her words came but they were sporadic and unintelligible, until she said very faintly; 'Save him.'

'Who, Lilia?'

'Save him.' The words were barely formed.

'I'll take over here, Françoise.' It was Madam Odile, cool, unflappable. 'Well done, Françoise, you've turned her over, it's important that she doesn't choke.'

She leant forward and placed one hand on Lilia's brow, taking her pulse with the other. Then she cupped her fingers around the lean chin, looking hard into the unseeing eyes.

Claudette stepped back as Madame Odile took Lilia's hand in hers. She was praying, eyes shut, the words on her lips soundless. There was a loud stillness in the room, no sound in the house. Somewhere very far away the strain of a classical refrain could be heard, a piano being played, but it was from another building in the street. Claudette hesitated at the threshold of the open door. She heard the faintest whisper, it was so quiet it vied against the soft sound of the faraway music.

'Don't die, don't die my little one, don't die, my beautiful sister.'

Claudette didn't dare breathe, or move. Madame Odile was whispering softly, then she began to hum a gentle lullaby. Time in the room was suspended, unreal.

After what seemed an eternity the doctor arrived. He was an old man with pince-nez glasses and a round face. He carried a leather medicine bag and he was wearing his stethoscope over his three-piece suit, as if he'd been interrupted during the examination of a patient. Claudette mutely pointed into the bedroom as first the doctor, then Jacques, rushed through the door. Nannette arrived and Claudette saw her exchange a look with Jacques, covert and with only the slightest of nods between them. She carried on upstairs to floor five.

Perrine arrived, running headlong up the stairs to say that an ambulance was on the way. Suddenly the room was all activity and orders, but Claudette was staring at Madame Odile, her face drained of colour, standing by the bed. She was crossing herself.

That evening Claudette was sewing in the kitchen. One of her own woollen stockings was stretched tightly over the darning mushroom as she mended worn patches. The nights were drawing in.

Madame F was sitting by the fire, her head nodding towards her ample bosom. Jacques was sitting opposite on his old armchair, staring into the fire. Marie was finishing scrubbing pots in the scullery and Perrine was reading. Sunday, and the few precious hours after lunch when they were free of chores, had come to mean a great deal. Claudette was imagining her kitchen at home, her father reading at the table, her mother would be making greengage compote at this time of year. She missed them very much, but there was no way to make contact, she knew that. Then she thought of Yves and whether or not he had found Giselle and Louis.

The door at the top of the stairs opened, groaning on its hinges. Then there were footsteps on the stairs, the rhythmic clicking of heels on stone steps. They all turned to look and Jacques scrambled to his feet. It was Madame Odile. She looked older, her face always aloof and unreadable, was edged with strain.

'I simply wanted to say thank you for your help with Lilia. Because you acted so promptly, all of you, she will be fine.' She coughed. The words that followed were masking her emotions, her self-discipline was walking a tightrope. 'Thank you all.' She paused again. 'I would like you all to take Wednesday afternoon off and I will pay you all double your wages this week.' She nodded and withdrew, backing away. Then she added: 'Naturally, this is all absolutely confidential. That, I hope, does not need saying twice.' With that she was gone.

'Well,' said an astonished Madame F. 'when was the last time Madame came down here, what a turn up for the books.'

'Wednesday off and double wages, she must think very highly of Lilia.' said Perrine. 'Mind you, she's always been a favourite.' Claudette looked from one to another, waiting for someone to point out that Lilia and Madame Odile were sisters.

'Lilia was the first one, the first she recruited,' said Jacques. She started before I was taken on.'

'Is it true Madame Odile was one too?' Claudette asked.

'One what?'

'One of the ladies.'

'Oh yes, she worked at La Chabanais, it gave her all her ideas for this place,' replied Madame F.

'And the money to buy it and do it up?' asked Claudette.

'She inherited it, I think you'll find, some say she's a widow.'

'You don't know that.' Jacques interjected.

'Well, she isn't short of money, that's for certain.' Madame F. huffed.

'And she chose to open a bordello of her own?' Claudette asked.

'She saw the Germans invading and a whole new opportunity arising. She is as sharp as they come, a real head for business.' Jacques was sitting back in his chair, eyes settling on the fire once more.

'In every way,' said Claudette. 'I'm squeezed into the previous maid's shoes as proof.'

'Just ask for new shoes if you need them,' said Jacques, irritated by the interruption of his quiet afternoon. 'She knows that a maid with bad feet is a bad maid.'

'I'm going to buy a pair with my extra wages,' said Claudette, picking up her darning mushroom again. 'I am going out on Wednesday to buy them. Would you like to come with me, Perrine?' Perrine glanced across at Jacques and Madame F.

'Oh, why not?' said Madame F. 'I'm going out too.'

'And me,' Marie added as she entered the kitchen wiping her hands.

Jacques grunted.' It's for your own safety that you're not allowed out, you all know that,' he said. He looked from one woman to another, knowing that opposing them wasn't going to work. 'Just take care, all of you.'

Paris was autumnal and somehow even more beautiful as the plane trees turned russet on the streets and the mulberry bushes in the Tuilleries were bright as new gold. Perrine walked alongside Claudette swinging her handbag. The day was mellow, round, expectant with possibilities. Claudette hugged the parcel containing her new shoes to her chest.

'I'm in love,' said Perrine brightly, she span around. 'I have a beau.'

'What? Who? When? Tell me.'

'He's one of our soldiers, we met before the invasion. They've sent him to a work camp, but we have been writing to each other. He writes beautiful letters, Françoise, just beautiful. It's strange because I love him more each time he writes, yet I can't hear his voice or see him. I love the way he thinks, how he writes about everything, what he confides in me.'

Claudette found herself thinking, not of Yves, but of Keber. His eyes, his kiss. Two Nazis walked past, their grey uniforms severe and out of place in a park full of melodious colours. 'I'm glad for you,' she told Perrine with honesty. 'I hope he comes back to you and you are married and have six beautiful children.'

'Seven,' said Perrine. 'At least seven!' and she laughed. Claudette giggled. She had an almost overwhelming desire to tell Perrine about Keber, to share him, to tell her friend how she had never met anyone like him, what he did to her soul. She was about to ask the name of Perrine's beau when she saw her expression cloud over.

'Well, who would have thought it?' It was Keber. He was standing in front of Claudette, his eyes focussed on her and completely ignoring Perrine. Claudette could not speak. 'What a beautiful day.' He kept his gaze fixed on her and she found herself silenced by his presence.

'Yes.' It was all she could say. Claudette knew that Perrine was stunned to see her talk to a German. Her friend was staring with eyes wide, and her jaw dropped open. She looked from Keber to Claudette and back again.

'Please leave us, I need to talk to this lady,' he said, without giving her even a glance. His irritation at her presence was very clear. Perrine didn't know what to do, she looked to Claudette for guidance.

'It's all right, Perrine, I'll be fine.' Keber turned and walked towards the stippled shade of the mulberry bushes. 'I'll be back soon,' said Claudette.

'Are you sure? Will you be all right? Should I fetch Jacques?'

'No, it's fine, but don't tell anyone, please,' said Claudette urgently. 'And please would you take my parcel back for me?' Perrine left, casting a very obvious glance over her shoulder, as Claudette turned and walked away towards the trees.

He was waiting, his back against a tree, foot resting against it. She stood in front of him feeling a power in herself that she had never yet felt, the power that comes with being wanted, desired.

'Hello,' he said.

'Hello,' she replied.

'You do know that if I weren't a decent man I would tell you to take your clothes off here and I would have sex with you on the grass?' Claudette flushed. 'What? You work in a whorehouse and have never heard anyone speak like that? I find it hard to believe.'

'I've heard worse than that,' she replied evenly. 'But I've never had such a thing said to me.'

'And not by a German?'

'No.'

'I could if I had a mind to, make you do it. We are, after all, an occupying force.' She did not rise to the bait, she despised him speaking like that. Instead she moved forward and kissed him, taking the advantage. He did not move, did not give any quarter. She stepped back, looking up at his face.

'Hussy,' he said with a smile that made his face light up.

'Hun,' she replied

He took hold of her and placed his mouth over hers, his tongue urgent and strong. He turned her round, pinning her against the tree and then his hands were cupping her breasts. She had no means of escape, but she possessed no desire to try. He kissed down her neck, running his hands over her hips. Claudette could see the railings of the park over his shoulder, the dim shadows of people passing by unseeing, unknowing that she was here with this man in the Tuilleries Gardens, in the heart of Paris. He pressed his hand into her groin and the feeling exploded within her, the release of everything, fear, pressure, worry, loneliness, Yves. The blood in her ears roared.

'I want you,' he said, his French edged with Germanic hardness. 'And, I will have you.' He bit her ear lobe, sucking on it. Her head became light, dizzy, then he turned and without a word, left her. She was breathing short ragged breaths, her body feeling as though it was drowning in its own passion. He was walking through the park, away from her, as if absolutely nothing had happened.

Chapter Twenty Nine

Matt lent over me, head resting on one hand, the fingers of the other tracing a line between my breasts. I was gazing at him, the beauty of his face and the depth of colour in those brown eyes. I lifted my head and kissed him slowly, and for a long time.

'Time for work,' he said as he pulled away at last. 'Work first, play later.'

The day wore on slowly, me carrying out my role, he being the consummate professional as ever, but sometimes in between shots or when I passed by him, he would smile and it was infectious. At one point during the afternoon, Clemence nudged Yan and I felt stupidly shy, and at the same time, immensely proud of myself for having such an amazing man in my life. Hat would have been over the moon for me and, whilst I could have texted or mailed her, it meant so much to me I wanted to tell her in person.

The next day, Thursday, we walked through Paris. Along the Rue de Rivoli, through Les Halles, with people sunbathing and children playing on the bald grass. We saw a Modernist exhibition in the Pompidou, having queued in the sun for an insane length of time. Matt nipped off and bought us both freezing cold, expensive bottles of water. All I cared about was being with him and nothing else.

We visited Delacroix's house and stared intently at the beauty of his stone etchings and I kissed Matt on the bench in the garden outside his atelier. We watched a Japanese mother and daughter take pictures of each other. They wore sun hats and neat, designer clothes, which looked freshly pressed. Behind us was a high wall and there was a peacock in the garden, mewing and listening for a reply, but nothing came. He was alone.

Out of the blue my mind conjured up a memory of Freddy. We were sitting in the gardens of the big house in the village (they were open for charity), sharing a bench and waiting for Hat to return with ice cream. There were two peacocks strutting about, a male and female, with the self-importance common to all of them. Freddy turned to me and said: 'They really think they're it, don't they? I wonder what they taste like?' He had folded his arms across his old tweed jacket and licked his lips with a gleam in his wicked eye. The sense of grief from this long forgotten reminiscence was almost overwhelming and I found myself welling up.

'Are you okay?'

'Yes, sorry, I just remembered Freddy. It's so easy to forget he's no longer here when you're in a completely different place.'

Matt brushed the back of my hand with his forefinger.

'You thought the world of him, didn't you?'

'I did, as did Hat and Jon, we all did.'

'And, lest we forget, the Puritans and the old soak in Ledbury!'

I laughed and ran my finger along his. 'We need to have questions ready for Daniel. I need to know what happened, I feel that I owe him for all the precious times we spent together. I want to find out why Freddy's past is so muddy and sort it out for him. I don't know, I feel as if it is my last gift to him.'

'And the murder,' said Matt, he said 'murder' in a Scottish accent.

'And the murder,' I mimicked like a minor bird. 'It won't be anything worth writing home about. I bet it was an accident and she was just unlucky.'

'Madeléine March.' He said running the name over his tongue. 'Have you Googled?'

'Nothing.'

'Library?'

'Who goes to a library any more?'

'Well, we ought to,' Matt replied firmly. 'It's next door-but-one to the barber's shop, did you know?'

'I do, I have lived there considerably longer than you.'

His smirk was boyish. 'Let's think about Daniel and know what we're going to ask him,' he said, brushing a stray hair away from my cheek. 'It would appear that Bertie was a great one for lighting the fires of burning questions, but she had no answers.'

'I know, she actually seemed to know nothing but the headlines. I think we –'

''Cuse me.' It was the Japanese mother. 'You take picture?' She was nodding and pointing towards her daughter who sat expectantly on the curved bench in the middle of the garden. She held the camera out to me with both hands. I took it from her and, while the lady sat next to her daughter I took the photograph. Matt, the pro, was watching me with a smile on his face. They both nodded several times to say thank you as I handed back their camera.

We left Delacroix's walled garden in peace and quiet with only the occasional lonesome call from the peacock on the other side of the wall, to break the silence.

Chapter Thirty

Perrine was not talking to Claudette. She used only perfunctory sentences and relayed orders. Nothing more than that passed her lips. When Claudette had returned from the park that Wednesday evening a month ago, Perrine had pushed her against the wall, jamming the parcel of shoes into her chest.

'It's one thing having the whores do it with the Boches, but you! They're the ones who have my boyfriend locked up. They took Anna away and they cleared whole streets of her people. I would have thought you had higher standards.' Claudette knew she could not defend herself.

'What have you done to upset Perrine?' asked Jacques days later.

'Nothing,' she replied as she checked that the damsons for her jam were not boiling too quickly.

'Well, whatever it is, make it up to her, you never know when she might be useful, I mean with what she knows. And we need information on the one called Keber. He comes three times a week, afternoons or late evenings. You know who I'm talking about, the tall blond officer, silver epaulettes?'

'I know, I've seen him,' replied Claudette. She had no idea Keber came in during the afternoon as well as evenings.

'Well, he's a rising star for the Boches, he knows a hell of a lot. By the way, that scribbled map you found,' Claudette nodded, 'really useful. I asked why and my contact wouldn't tell me, but the message I was to pass on was to say well done.' Claudette felt something akin to pride that at last this whole thing, which she still felt very uncertain about, had borne fruit.

It was Saturday and November was chilly, seeping its dank wetness into the house. Claudette was bone-tired. It had been a long day. Once the Germans arrived at ten thirty the house became alive. There was singing, jazz in the bar, the Salon humming with laughter and conversation. As she climbed the stairs with stiff legs she reached floor four where she could hear sounds from different levels; sharp shouts, moaning, giggling, the sounds of sex. She was about to start on the next step when she saw leather riding boots standing in front of the lift shaft on floor five. She crept up, treading a little further, knowing exactly who it was. There was a rush inside her, a dissolving of rational thought. The boots turned and went back through the double doors.

She half ran up the stairs, adrenaline coursing through her, past the doors and began to mount the stairs to the attic, slowing down with each step. As she reached half way she heard the doors open. She took a sharp intake of breath and waited, willing him to sense her presence. Opening the door to the corridor, she listened again; it was silent, Marie had gone to bed half and hour before her.

As she walked along the worn lino it squeaked under her flat shoes. She laid a hand on the door handle but didn't turn it. She stopped as she heard his boots echoing along the corridor behind her. She turned and saw him coming towards her.

'Go inside,' he said, his voice flat, unremarkable. She opened the door and he followed her in, calmly with no secrecy. He looked around the room, the small single bed, the framed tapestry, her rosary over the back of the old chair. His lip almost formed a sneer. He stood against the door and finally levelled his eyes on her.

'Take off your hat, let your hair down,' he ordered. He spoke at normal pitch, unafraid of being heard by Marie or anyone else. She unpinned her hair and let it fall, placing the lace hat on her chair. 'And the blouse, take it off.' Claudette felt the tremulous sense of desire clutch at the very base of her stomach.

'And the skirt,' he nodded at it. 'Slowly.' She undid it and it fell to the floor. She was wearing Nannette's bra.

'Take it off.' His blue eyes were impassive until they fell on her breasts. There was a lust in them, the like of which she could never have dreamed. 'Come here.' He said the words in German, as if he had forgotten to speak French. She walked towards him and he encircled her with his arms. Her bare chest was smooth against the roughness of his jacket. It felt good, her nipples hardened. She searched for his mouth, nuzzling his chin. He kissed her deeply, passionately.

'Tomorrow, I will be in Madame Odile's Private Room. You will be there. I don't make love in a room like this, not for anyone.' His voice was toneless, expressionless, at odds with his eyes. She could feel the strength of him under his jacket. The power of his presence engulfed her.

'But I'm not sure if…'

'Be there at three.'

Chapter Thirty One

Matt was watching me dress. I was fastening my bra and he was watching with wide, excited eyes. 'You have beautiful boobs,' he said.

'Thank you, kind sir.' I replied. 'I bet you're thinking to yourself "why did I order separate rooms let alone separate floors?"'

He cocked his head to one side. 'What you on about?'

'Well, if we'd had next door rooms you could have nipped next door for your stuff more easily.'

'That would have been rather presumptuous of me, don't you think?' he said as he threw back the covers, revealing his lovely body. He was heading for the bathroom.

'Well, different rooms is one thing, but different floors?'

He stopped and turned towards me. 'Oh that! Christ no. That's for Cherry. She's sixteen. She has one hell of an over protective father and he's a big bloke. I always make sure I'm on separate floors so that he can't ever complain I'm after her.'

I had to laugh. 'Wimp!'

'No, I mean like really big, huge, with big, no, massive muscles.'

'That's rich coming from you, Popeye.'

Matt came over to me and grabbed my face playfully.

'Do as you're told, Olive, or I'll…'

'What, get Cherry's dad on to me?'

'Yeah, so watch it.'

He wrapped himself in the towelling robe and headed once more for the bathroom. 'I'm going to have a shower and if you're not in there with me in two seconds, I'll force feed you spinach.'

Chapter Thirty Two

The next day Claudette faked period pain. She told Madame F. that she wasn't well and would have to lie down. 'Poor you,' said the cook with sympathy. 'I used to get it badly, couldn't stand up sometimes. You go and have a nice lie down.'

It was three o'clock when she entered the Private Room. It was dark, womb-like, the lights on the lowest setting. The door opened and he was inside. He locked it behind him and sat down on the nearest sofa. Claudette, who hadn't slept all night for thinking of him, stood in the corner of the room. He stared at her, watching her intently.

'Take off your clothes,' he ordered as he leaned back to watch, hands behind his head. With great clarity she saw him sitting behind a desk or out in the streets barking orders at soldiers or terrified civilians. She felt a shiver of apprehension and took a deep breath.

'No,' she said squarely meeting his eye, 'you can take them off me.'

His lips had a wicked curl to them. 'Fine then, you seem to be in charge, come to me and tell me how you want it done.' He grabbed her wrist and pulled her down on top of him. Putting his arm around her he kissed her face eagerly. His lips pressed into hers, his tongue exploring the soft folds of her mouth. Then he led her to the day bed and laid her down on it, undoing her blouse deftly with quick, experienced fingers.

He ran a finger over her left breast and, as it grazed her nipple, it hardened responsively. He kissed her neck and her earlobes, sucking on them, sending a wave of desire through her. He undid the small pearl buttons on the bra and it fell away. 'You are beautiful,' he said. His eyes were drinking in her nakedness. 'Very beautiful.' He parted her legs with his hand and felt her hot wetness. Then he was entering her, him in full uniform, her half-undressed. He pushed and thrust himself at her, biting her neck and arms. His mouth moved over her skin. She wished it would go on forever, never coming to an end, always him here with her. When at last he released himself into her he collapsed on to her, his face contorted with pleasure.

'I'm your first, it's true isn't it?' She nodded. The back of her head pressed against the pillow, as if it might anchor her in time so that she could never forget what had just happened. She was gazing up at him. 'And you don't care about protection?' he asked.

'I am Catholic,' Claudette replied. 'It is against our beliefs.'

'I'm a Catholic too,' he said, rolling off her. 'And I know we are not to have sex before marriage.' He covered himself, buttoning his flies. 'Looks like we have committed a sin…but, it must be said, a very enjoyable sin.'

'I don't care about any of that,' she told him. 'I don't think we stand much chance of seeing this war out.' Keber patted his breast pocket and then pulled out a silver cigarette case. He flicked it open and offered her one. She shook her head.

'I don't,' she said.

'Everyone should smoke, it's what gets you through this shitty war.'

'I can't afford to have a habit,' she told him. 'Not on my wages.'

'You seem very intelligent for someone who cleans other people's houses.' He leaned back against the pillow, watching her, taking in her body. He took a deep drag on his cigarette, then he turned onto his side and looked into her eyes.

'Where would you be now if you hadn't ended up here?'

'At home, on a farm, in a small town with a big lake,' Claudette was lying flat on the bed, her dark hair spread out behind her, her body naked, liberated by him. Her mind wandered back to Vacily. How she wished they were there lying together on the side of the lake. 'We have a pair of swans on there, always. Sometimes I sit on the bank and watch them. If they are startled they flap their wings and rise out of the water. It's so majestic. Once I was there at nightfall and I stood on a twig that snapped I saw them rise up and fly in front of the moon. I have never seen a sight like it. That's when I tell myself that there isn't a more beautiful place in the world.'

'And, you spend a lot of time, at night, observing these birds?' He was watching her intently as she spoke his words almost mocking her, but gently.

'No, only occasionally, and nowhere near as often now that your colleagues can arrive at a moment's notice.'

'You're with the Resistance, aren't you?' he said without expression.

She froze, still staring up at the ceiling. She couldn't bring herself to move a muscle. Suddenly she was vulnerable, naked, someone who had given herself to the enemy with no mental struggle, who lusted after him more with each passing moment.

'I thought so,' he said plainly. 'I'm not stupid. I knew this when you hesitated about your parents' names. It is always the hesitation that gives you people away.'

'What are you going to do to me?' she asked, the fear creeping through her as she realised she was completely at his mercy. He took a long drag on his cigarette, expanding the agonising period of silence.

'Nothing,' he said eventually. 'Firstly, because I want you, no matter who you were or what you were, I would want you.' She let out a small gasp of relief. 'And secondly, because I'm sick of it all. A friend of mine, a man I went to school with, was killed the other day outside a café. The Resistance carried arms in wine boxes into the shit hole and then came out, guns blazing. They mowed Alaric and his lady friend down.' He was silent for a moment as if he needed to dwell on it. 'You know what? Most times you'd sense something was wrong and demand to have the crates opened, but Alaric was stupid, he let it go. He's... he'd become too relaxed, got the Paris bug. I can't forgive him for that.' He shifted position on the bed. 'And now look at me.' Claudette was still feeling tense, what did she know of this man? Nothing. 'I'm just sick of it all. I was forced into this by my father and his military friends, he told me I had to do my duty by Austria. It was like a magnet, like being pulled into something you can't stop and being given no choice because of words such as family pride and dishonour.'

'But you're known as a rising star,' she told him. 'You must believe in it.'

He shook his head. 'I'm very intelligent, that's all. They use me to work out strategies and if I'm honest, truly honest, I don't care who wins, I only want life to get back to normal, whatever normal means at the end of all this.' She shuffled across to him supporting herself on her arm and she kissed his lips as tenderly as she could.

'If I can get messages to the Allies, give them the information they need, the war will end in the right way,' she said.

'And, if I'm found out I get shot, and no doubt tortured before I'm shot. No, I'm not inclined to help anyone anymore, I'm finished.' She saw the vague threat of a tear in his eye, his arrogance had all but evaporated. 'I've done things I'm not proud of. I've done things I hate myself for and always will, but Alaric was the tipping point for me.'

Claudette reached up and teased her fingers through his hair. 'There's no exit strategy for people like us,' she said. 'We're absolutely stuck here, in the here and now.'

'There is always exit through death,' he told her. 'I see it written all the time on paperwork they are sending to the camps, ordering one death or another on a whim. Now, because of paperwork and my involvement I'm nailed down more than I ever thought possible.' He was suddenly distant, as if his mind was elsewhere. Then his expression changed again. 'I sometimes think exit through death is my best option, my own death, by my own hand.' The sense of alarm in her was all consuming, she couldn't bear him talking like that. She put a finger over his lips.

'Don't talk like that, nothing's worth that.' He rolled on top of her and began kissing her face as if to distract himself from his thoughts.

Chapter Thirty Three

Daniel's hair was still light brown, only a smattering of salt and pepper greys in it and he didn't have a beard. He had deep brown eyes, an aquiline nose and he was about Freddy's height, but slimmer. He was sitting in a blue salon chair, the evening light highlighting areas of the room in warm gold. The room was blue, a blend of different hues and shades, but with a shock of red here and there, an artistic touche de rouge.

Matt and I were sitting on a hard sofa, the same salon style as Daniel's chair, the fabric a most stunning ice blue. We were each holding a large glass of chilled Pineau and on the low table before us were olives and cubed Mancheeta cheese.

'It is lovely to meet you, yes, yes, quite lovely,' said Daniel. 'How nice to have a visit from people who knew Freddy.'

'Well, to be honest, sir,' Matt replied, 'I came on the scene after Freddy passed away, but Connie knew him very well indeed.' I signalled agreement with what he said. I was so relieved that Daniel spoke English that I hadn't said very much at all. Matt had started in French until it was revealed that our new friend was fluent in English and, as it happened, German too. And friend he was. He had given us a warm welcome, supplied us with a very large glass of vino and asked us all about our work even before we sat down.

'Of course, the person who thought the world of him was Harriet, his housekeeper, they were inseparable,' I ventured. 'She's been hit very hard by all this.'

Daniel looked down at his chest and mumbled something about it being a bad business. Then, he seemed to gather his thoughts and said, 'And you are here because you discovered me amid all the fall out? I understand you need some of the gaps filled in?'

'We do,' I nodded hopefully. 'If you can help us, that is.'

'And where, if I may ask, is all of this leading?' He reached forward for some cheese. 'Are either of you writing about him, some sort of article?'

'No, no, far from it, we're not journalists or anything, we simply find that Freddy's story is a mystery, particularly his mother.' I hoped I sounded completely honest because I found Daniel's tone of voice a little accusatory. He reminded me suddenly of Bertie. The windows were open and there was the sound of chatter in the square below. A cyclist was ringing his bell. It was a warm and very pleasant evening. Perhaps the backdrop just made his voice seem a bit more tart.

Matt picked up the conversation for me, sensing I was losing focus. 'From what we know his mother was French, her name was Madeléine March and she brought Freddy over to England after the war.' Daniel raised an eyebrow as he listened. 'She found a job as a translator, seemingly learning English very quickly, and one of her employers thought she was so wonderful he made Freddy a ward of court.'

'Well, you know more than me,' said Daniel. I must have looked at him askance because he added quickly; 'About the English side of things, anyway.' For a moment I think Matt and I thought we'd squandered the fare home on Eurostar for nothing.

'You see, Freddy was very private,' Daniel continued. 'He had a public persona and a private one. I bet you've tried to Google to no avail, haven't you?'

'Yes, as a matter of fact we have,' I told him.

'He always kept everything about his private life very close to his chest. You see, people didn't know it, but he was gay. When he and I were young men that was a sin. Do you remember Alan Turing?' We both nodded. 'They killed him, drove him to do what he did. In those days you could be prosecuted for homosexuality. They gave Turing oestrogen injections and the like in an attempt to cure him. Freddy grew up in the shadow of all that, it scared the life out of him.'

'But he was amongst creatives and people with far more liberal approaches to such things.' I offered. 'I mean people on the stage.'

'Yes, Connie, but that cut no ice, you had to be very strong-minded to stand up for yourself. This was a time when people beat other people up for being different and the law backed them up, you must understand this.' He steepled his fingers over his stomach, Freddy used to do that too. 'Freddy was never that strong and his mother was a Catholic. In truth, I believe it was the lack of a father in his life that he railed against, that I suspect more than anything else. He'd built up a picture of his father as being quite a someone. His hero, in fact, though of course he had

217

nothing to go on. But you see, that's what we do, all of us. If it isn't there we invent it for ourselves. Imagination can be a way of escape, but it can also be our prison.'

'I see.' I said thoughtfully. 'And because he was gay he never married, never found anyone to spend his life with?'

'Precisely,' replied Daniel. There was a moment of silence. It was I who broke into it.

'There was a photograph in his things of Marlene Dietrich,' I told him, 'From one sad German to another, it said on the back.'

'Yes.'

'Do you know anything about that?'

'Yes,' Daniel replied. 'It was my father's.'

Chapter Thirty Four

For some reason Claudette thought Christmas would be special in the house, but it was quite the opposite. A huge Christmas tree arrived and was erected in the entrance hall. The note said it had been sent from Bavaria by train. Perrine, who was now speaking to Claudette again, albeit in a more guarded way, was helping to decorate the tree with silvery baubles that contained miniature depictions of the nativity. The presence of anything religious felt at odds with the house. Claudette even found her rosary was out of place and she had kept it hidden in her valise under the bed.

Presents piled up under the tree over the next few days, the labels scrawled with German names, and far worse, pet names: 'Herr Licky;' 'Ihre verzauberten ein;' 'Sex-sklavin.' The ladies pulled the present wrappings apart on Christmas Eve with no ceremony. Half the contents were discarded, there was no cherishing of anything and no gratitude. Claudette wondered if the German officers imagined the opposite, but in truth she didn't care one way or the other. As for her, Keber had not been in touch for six weeks. She was crestfallen, which is why she suspected Perrine had started being kind to her again.

At one in the morning on Christmas Day they were clearing up the discarded wrappings and separating out the presents left behind. The ladies had gone to bed, Christmas Eve was the one night they had free of clients.

There were beautiful things in the pile of presents, a diamante bracelet, a compact inlaid with turquoise flowers and pearl leaves. Claudette held up a scarf made of purple silk, the edges scalloped in gold.

'Find homes for all of those.' It was Madame Odile, she had been walking quietly down the stairs. 'Keep them yourselves if you want, but obviously don't wear anything in sight of the Boches.'

'Really, Madam?' said Claudette, she had never owned anything nearly as beautiful as the compact.

'Yes, why not? The ladies won't want reminding of their clients all year long. It's bad enough that they have to do it on an almost daily basis, anyway.' Perrine threw Claudette a look of total surprise and Claudette mirrored it. Madame Odile sat on one of the salon chairs in the lounge, her legs, elegant and long, crossed over at the knees and slanted sideways. Since Lilia, they had seen a change in Madame Odile, she looked more lost and lonely than anything else.

'I hate Christmas,' she said, almost as if she were thinking to herself. 'What is Christmas in a war with people being killed all around us? It's the same as every other despicable day.' Neither maid knew what to say, so they sat on their haunches awkwardly, each with a look of astonishment on her face.

'Where is your family, Madame?' asked Perrine after an interval of silence. Madame Odile looked as though she had been woken from a trance.

'Mine?' she asked. 'Here,' she said, but then checking

herself, she quickly said: 'Reims.' She stood up and looked down on the girls. 'Come now, let's all get to bed. No men in the house, it's time for some rest.' Claudette saw a vague smile cross the lips of her boss, but it was gone in a trice.

'Look,' Perrine pointed to the lower branches of the tree after Madame Odile had gone. 'There's a little box with your name on it, look just there.' Claudette reached out and pulled it towards her. She traced a finger over the writing. 'Well, open it!' exclaimed Perrine. Claudette pulled the ribbon and the box fell open. It was a silver pendant of a swan flying in front of a crescent of the moon. There was a note saying he would meet her in the Luxemburg Gardens on the first Wednesday of January at three o'clock. Her hands were shaking.

Claudette took the note to Jacques, she had no choice.

'Fritz Keber wants to see me on Wednesday next week, I have no idea why,' she lied.

'No, too dangerous,' said Jacques, his eyes huge with disbelief and alarm. 'I won't let you do it.'

'You have no choice, you need to tell them here that I have an errand to run. Just like the sewing materials.' Claudette was determined.

'No, that is the headquarters of the Luftwaffe, the security is tight, I won't have you go anywhere near it.'

'Jacques, if we need to gather information on Keber and he wants to see me, then we really have no choice.'

'Why would Keber want to see you, for heaven's sake?' Jacques was rubbing his beard, flakes of skin and leftover food started falling from it.

'I have no idea, he asked me some questions before,

maybe he wants to ask me more about the house, or our Madam, or something. It's probably something completely insignificant and workaday.'

Jacques stood up, and on doing so clasped her hand in his. 'I would regret it very much if you got hurt,' he said. He leaned into her. 'I feel we have become good friends, eh?'

Claudette stared at him, her eyes regarding his face. There was a look in his eyes she had not seen before; 'I'll tell you if there is anything worth knowing.' She broke free, making for the stairs and a breath of less stale air.

Paris had disintegrated since she had last been out. There had been Allied bombing, and talk was of violent attacks on Germans. There were Resistance leaflets pasted over Nazi declarations. Everywhere there was a feeling that something had cracked, a fissure had begun in the Nazi war engine. On the streets the soldiers Claudette saw were less bold. Jacques had told her that since the assassination in September of Julius Ritter, the SS Colonel, they had, as individuals, felt less sure of themselves. Nazi newspapers had described the shooting as an abominable act, as if their hideous exploits were dimmed by it.

He was standing by the boat pond watching some young boys prod their galleons with long sticks. The boats swept serenely across the flat water carrying imaginings and secret stories. Keber looked lost in his thoughts.

'Hello,' she said, standing beside him with a broad smile across her face.

'Hello,' he replied, taking her face in his hands and kissing her. He looked terribly drawn and grey and he had lost weight.

222

'Are you all right?' she asked. 'You look awful.'

'I've had flu,' he told her. 'In the end they sent me home. I haven't been well at all, it was on my chest, and yet normally I'm fine.'

'Are you better now?'

'Getting there, it's been weeks, lots of us have had it, but I seemed to get the worst dose of all.' He looked at a little boy pushing his boat away from the edge of the pond, where it had become stuck. 'Maybe I deserved it more than other people.'

'What do you mean?' A chill shuddered through her, his voice was wrong, not normal.

'Nothing,' he replied. He took in a deep breath. 'Walk with me.'

'I've been dreaming of this,' said Claudette as they made their way along the avenue of trees to the west of the gardens. 'Of being with you.' She slipped her arm into his.

'Enjoy it, my sweet, because it's all going to end.'

'Are the Germans losing heart?'

'We're losing the fight to your friends, the Resistance,' he told her. 'Hitler is losing his mind and we are on the back foot.'

'What will happen?'

'I have no idea. I have offered one strategy and that is to move out to the edges of Paris and protect the centre, but to go no further. Others have different ideas. We cannot support further losses, because every soldier worth his salt was sent to Russia. We're dealing with what is left, whilst the French, who have laid down and played dead for four years, have suddenly found they have something worth fighting for, Paris.'

'You can't blame us, we've been through an ordeal.'

He placed his hand over her arm. 'All I can think is how much I want to make love to you,' he said quietly. Maybe it was the illness, maybe the end of what was happening here, but he had lost any air of the authority or superiority about him.

'You're wasted as a maid picking up titbits of information for them, they should have you on sabotage or underground newspapers. You're very bright for a country girl. Do something after this mess that counts, promise me.'

'Maybe I'm a country girl, but I've grown up fast.'

'It strikes me you must have been class star at school?'

'There were the three of us, one wanted to become a doctor, one was going to become a scientist and I wanted to be a historian.'

'What happened?'

'Well, a squad of your men shot the student doctor last year, the scientist is scouring France for his wife and the historian is here thinking she would give up everything if she could find a very predictable life.'

'I'm going to book the Private Room for this week. I'll leave a note for you under the base of the lamp in reception when I want to see you. I need you.' He looked incredibly forlorn.

She was about to turn and kiss him when her attention was drawn to the sound of marching feet, not neat and rhythmic like the Nazi's but odd and irregular. It was a ramshackle group of French workers, shovels over their shoulders, humiliation about being marched by their own police written clearly on their faces. All eyes fell upon her as they passed by, she was wearing Nannette's red scarf and a grey coat. On her head was a hat that Sophie had thrown away and an expensive handbag, a gift from under the tree. Her hair was the colour of burnished conker, thanks to Nannette.

She was looking at the men, willing them to do something rather than capitulate, to have some pride in themselves, but they were tired, stooped and slovenly, and some of them had bruised faces and dried blood on their lips.

Keber looked towards them, his back straightened, the ingrained power in him just below the surface. He drew their attention and then with their eyes on him he leaned down and kissed her very forcefully and at odds with his behaviour until then.

She struggled and pulled away, but they had all seen it and she was furious. 'You only did that to show off, it was horrible.' She was panting and pushing against his chest. She tried to turn away, but he was too strong.

'I know, that was bad of me, but it's in our training,' he said. 'Suppress the Frenchman by screwing his woman. We can't help it.'

She stared at him, wondering how she could possibly be with a man like this. What he had just said left her feeling cold and she knew all at once that this affair must end now. She looked at the red ribbon tucked into his jacket, at the silver decorations on his shoulders and then up to his eyes. They were fired up, searing into her. He pulled her to him and held her so tightly she felt she might never breath again. Her line of sight fell on the ragged platoon of men.

At the last second one of them turned round and delivered a look so venomous it made her heart clutch behind her ribs. The eyes were intense under dark brows, the anger in them so hot it could have burned her. The eyes belonged to Maurice Joubert.

Chapter Thirty Five

'Your father?'

'Yes,' replied Daniel. 'He was a man called Fredrik, or as everyone knew him, Fritz Keber. He was a reluctant Nazi from Austria, but, trust me, I make no excuses for what he did. His actions were, as with all Nazi war crimes, deplorable.' A very impolite part of me wanted to ask what he'd done but Matt was shooting me a cautionary look. 'It is important that we never, never forget what they did.' He shook his head, I even thought a tear might follow because he looked so sad.

'And your mother?' Matt asked gently. 'What about her?'

'She died when I was almost two. Her life was in turmoil and she couldn't bear it and so I was brought up by my aunt in Interlaken. That is where I lived until she died, when I was nineteen. Then I returned to Paris and took my degree in modern history. I made it my job to study the war and its causes and to dedicate the rest of my life to preventing war from happening again in Europe. I still advise the EU on security, but at a very boring level, no James Bond activity, not even an expense account.' A ghost of a smile touched his lips.

'When did your father pass away?' asked Matt, putting his empty glass down on the table and leaning forward to take some cheese.

'Three years ago, in the summer.'

'Only three years ago?'

'Yes,' said Daniel. He stood up and reached for the bottle of Pineau, topping up first my glass and then replenishing Matt's.

'He had a very long life.'

'Were you in touch with him?'

'From time to time, but not for some years now, I'm afraid. He became very ill, mentally ill, as well as decrepit in the end, like any nonagenarian person. He still walked on the hills around Interlaken until he was into his late seventies. A very fit man, although following a bout of pneumonia during the war, he did have weak lungs, which brought him low at times. Still, it didn't hold him back.'

'So you stopped having contact?'

'We were never a father and son in the traditional sense. Our personalities clashed, for one thing. He could never talk to me, he always preferred to keep me at a distance. I blame the fact that I reminded him of my mother. It must have been so hard for him, he obviously adored her. Then, twenty years ago there was a serious argument between us, I don't want to go into it. As I say, he suffered ill health and put up a barrier. Sometimes it's best to leave things where they are.'

'Was he bi-polar?' I asked.

'Possibly, but of course that was before we all became so understanding. Mental health has always been so very difficult for people to comprehend.' I imagined that was where Freddy had got it from and wondered about Daniel too, but it was a question too far.

'Wasn't he tried? Lots of the German officers were

executed if they didn't….' I paused, wondering what the right word to use might be.

'Top themselves?' He sat back down, his glass refreshed too.

'Yes, that's what I was going to say, I mean was he ever brought to trial?'

'No, the Allies lost heart for taking it out on officers who had simply done as they had been directed, after they had paraded the major criminals at Nuremburg, that is. The mess they got themselves into trying to bring those evil monsters to account had to be seen to be believed. Also, in my father's case, it is thought that the Resistance spoke up for him in France, they even say he betrayed the High Command in Paris. Well, that was the rumour, he would never be drawn on the subject.'

'And he never married?'

'No, as I said, I believe he was very much in love with my mother and there could be no equal in his eyes. I am pretty certain it was the root of his mental health problems.'

'So I am very confused,' I admitted.

'Was Freddy's father German?'

'I really don't know, if he was,I suspect there is a strong possibility it was my father. You see, the strange thing is, our mothers shared the same name, Madeléine March, and Freddy and I share the name March. That's why I gave him the Dietrich photograph, I thought if we did have the same father he should have something of him. I'm very sorry, but I've never got to the bottom of this, without a birth certificate you can't get very far. I had to pull a lot of strings to be recognised as it is.'

'So you don't know if you are related to Freddy by blood?'

'Neither my aunt nor my father would ever talk about it, or the war. That's why I was so intrigued when you two turned up with a special interest in it all.'

'Your mothers had the same name?' I asked incredulously.

'Both March?' said Matt, with a hand stroking his chin. 'But not relatives? Neither sisters nor cousins?'

'I don't think so, and I can tell you that Freddy had no idea if they were related either. He knew his mother was in Paris during the war, as was mine, of course, but it's all confusing. They can't have been the same person and yet they had the same name.'

'But how did you make contact with him?' I asked.

'I attended the opening night of one of his plays in Paris, the one called 'Documentation'. It was extraordinary and I made a beeline for him at the final curtain. With our surnames being the same, him English, me French, it was a great way of introducing myself. The play had made me think, little things in it, the kind of references he made to the Resistance and the Occupation. I had to know why he was so obviously hung up on it all. He told me his mother never recovered from losing his father, that he wrote everything as a tribute to her.'

'And did you keep in touch?'

'Yes, I wrote to him. I visited from time to time and we would have a meal together. We often talked it through, whether my father was his or not, but we simply had no idea. Freddy asked to see him, but my father always said no. I asked my father once, tried to clear it up, but he simply refused to speak. He told me I should never mention the war, that it was unforgivable to speak of it.'

I felt annoyed that Daniel had given up so easily, it could have been so simple to have found the answers we needed from him.

'Freddy was such a lovely, lovely man,' he said, 'I was so pleased he remembered me in his will, after all this time.'

'What did you get?' I asked, without thinking how direct I sounded.

After a short pause, Daniel said: 'He left me a watch and a pair of cufflinks that were kept in a safe deposit box in London. Nothing remarkable in value, but obviously he had treasured them and that was enough for me. I believe they were Elwyn's.'

'Did you ever do a DNA sample?' asked Matt.

'No, no, we were acquaintances a long time before such things. I thought the coincidence of our names, and our mother's names, was just that.'

'He was writing to your father.' I told him.

'Really?' He was surprised.

'Yes, letters imploring him to get in touch.'

'I never knew.' Daniel looked crest fallen. 'I had no idea, he never said a word.'

'It would appear that he never received a reply, either,' I said.

'Something obviously led him to believe your father and his were one and the same.' said Matt, puzzled. 'I wonder what it was?'

'I did wonder, at one time, if our mothers had worked in a hotel in the Latin Quarter, but I don't know if it's true,' Daniel said thoughtfully. 'I found a wage slip in my mother's belongings, I tend to suspect they were both maids there. It is quite possible they took the name of the hotel proprietor, they may have been illegal immigrants or perhaps Jews in hiding. It was a very disturbed and brutal city in the war. My aunt would never tell me, she said the past should stay in the past. I'm certain she knew everything, but she was never one to look back.'

'Was she Jewish?'

'No, but I also wonder now if she was an aunt by marriage, or if she just took me in. She told me that my mother would have loved me very much.' He looked down at his shirtsleeve and picked up a piece of lint, flicking it away between thumb and finger. He was stalling for time, this was obviously difficult for him.

'What was the address?' I asked, interrupting his thoughts.

It was in the Rue Ercol, but I have no idea where, it's a long street and certainly has no traces of any hotels that I can see and yes, I've Googled.' Daniel said.

'And the Marlene Dietrich connection?' I asked, coming back to where we started.

'Ah yes, my father spent a year in Paris before the war. He was from very wealthy Austrian stock, hence I own this apartment and my little place in Antibes, and I am lucky enough to have no money worries.' He continued after a short pause. 'Well, during that time, being a teenager, what I think you English call "ooray 'enrys", my father visited a very famous restaurant called Le Beouf à la Ficelle, where the waitresses served wearing only an apron and a pair of high heels, if you understand.' For a moment I thought he was going to wink, but he seemed to change his mind.

'Who knows what went on there? They probably got up to all sorts, him and his loud, excited friends. In your country they become Prime Ministers and Mayors, am I right? In the war we sent our young men to fight for us, only to end up in work camps in darkest Germany.'

'And that's were he met Marlene Dietrich?' ask Matt.

'Yes, exactly so. He told me that one night she walked in and eventually he introduced himself, probably as a bet with all his friends watching. I should imagine he was totally bewitched by her, I know I was when I saw her in concert myself in the sixties. It would seem they talked for quite some time. He told me she was very sad about the war and she had been one of the first Germans of note to openly oppose Hitler and what he was doing. Everyone in Germany at that time had committed to Hitler's plan because they were all caught up in the propaganda. Did you know the most convinced of them were, in the most part, women and young boys? They saw him as a god and they hero-worshipped him. If not that, then they experienced the pure fear of a wicked regime. My father told me she gave him a fresh perspective on everything, it made him question. Anybody who makes you question your beliefs and values has done good work.' He paused. 'It's what you choose to do next. Fight for them, examine them or continue to follow them blindly.'

'Like religion,' said Matt.

'Exactly so, Matt. So many of us stick with what we are told is true, we never ask ourselves if it is really true. People give away their minds so easily to a belief or a doctrine. It diminishes a person's ability to make well-informed decisions. Like the church that gets its claws into you before the age of five, or the regime that indoctrinates you at school and makes you wear a brown shirt. Only the very strong kick against the system.'

'And your father?'

'He wasn't strong, I'm afraid. His conscience was overpowered like so many others. I think the nagging doubts tore him apart and that was thanks to a famous film star, but the Nazi machine and its terrible desires was the real winner.'

'Unless, as you say, he betrayed them at the end.' I suggested.

'Precisely, someone must have got to him if that was the case. I can only think it was my mother.'

'Do you have a picture of her?'

'Yes, one from her passport.' He stood up, fetched the ancient French passport and handed it to me. I opened it with great care; it was on its last legs and I had seen the English version of it before, back in Freddy's shed. Matt leaned over.

The picture was of Freddy's mother.

Chapter Thirty Six

The shot rang out clearly in the night. The short sharp sound had no echo, it was inside the house. There was silence, an awful, grating silence. Claudette sat up in bed, listening as hard as she could for another sound, anything that might orientate her to where it had come from. Was it best to stay where she was? She remembered Marie's warning. Was it some sort of raid? Surely there would have been more shots? Could she barricade herself in on this floor? She scrambled around for an idea. The door clicked open and she held her breath; they were already here, it was too late.

It was Marie. She looked like a ghost in the pool of moonlight that lit up the room. 'Did you hear that?' she whispered. 'It was a gun shot.' Claudette crawled out of bed and pulled on her grey coat and shoes. Marie stood shivering in her white cotton nightdress and an old shawl.

'Stay behind me,' she told Marie. 'Stay absolutely silent.' They tiptoed along the corridor, beneath them floor five was quiet, deserted as usual. They crept downstairs to the fourth floor. Bella, Lilia and Pollo were standing on the stairs, peering down into the lift shaft, quietly listening.

'Is it a raid?' Claudette spoke as quietly as possible.

'No, there's only one car outside, and one driver,' Bella whispered back.

'Rechtstein's driver,' whispered Pollo. 'He's still here.'

They stalked carefully down the stairs where the other women were standing on their landings. They were a cascade of colour tumbling down the stairs, the colours of their gowns and negligées like a bank of extraordinary wild flowers.

Outside Eva's landing Jacques was standing with his back to the double doors, his hands clenched around a pistol. Madame Odile was standing adjacent to him, her back against the wall on the opposite side of the door. She was wearing a thick cotton nightdress, her hair in a single, long plait. He used his head to indicate to them all to back away and then he turned and slipped through the double doors.

The silence was draining, the women looked from one to the other helplessly. Then there was the sound of Jacques entering the room, Eva's room, and the low rumble of men's voices.

A sweep of cold air entered the house, Madame F was speaking. It seemed she had opened the front door because suddenly half a dozen soldiers were storming up the stairs, rifles at the ready. The women, including Claudette, fled upwards, hurtling into Sophie's bedroom. Pollo opened the windows leaning out to see if they could hear anything.

It was a cold March night, there was a frost clinging to every surface, sparkling white in a road grey with dreary buildings. Claudette crouched between Pollo and Bella, her hands leaning on the freezing cold window ledge.

There were muffled sounds at first, then slightly clearer noises and sounds of furniture scraping. Jacques shouted, it was unintelligible, but they could tell he was pleading. Then they saw Eva's small body on the next window ledge down, her naked skin being scraped across the frosty stone. A green-grey sleeved arm pushed her and she fell over the edge and down on to the street, hitting the road between two black cars. There was a splattering of blood as she hit the floor. Her body had fallen limply, she was already dead. She lay against the strip of frosted road, her naked body white as her platinum blonde hair. There was a black hole, from a single gunshot under her ribs, the only blemish.

'Oh Jesus!' said Bella. 'No!' She covered her face with her hands.

Pollo leaned out of the window as far as she was able to and shouted. 'Bastards!'

The front door opened, a light cascaded across the street, it glanced off the two cars and highlighted Eva's body. She looked even more beautiful, like a fragile sculpture. Rechtstein walked down the three steps, his Walther in his hand. He shot her three times. Her body flexed each time and red spattered across the frosted road surface. He yelled "Juden" and kicked her.

'Bastard!' Pollo shouted again. Rechstein looked upwards as he holstered his gun. 'Jew lovers!' he yelled at them as he wrenched open the car door. His driver took the direct route straight over Eva's body. Claudette felt so numb she thought she would never be able to move again.

Jacques was sitting in the lobby, head bent over his knees, eyes closed. Madame F was standing by him, her wide hips barring his exit through the front door as if she thought he might do something stupid. 'Bastards,' he growled, 'Bastards, bastards, bastards,' over and over.

'I know, my love, they are, but there is nothing we can do. We can't help her now, poor little mite.' Madame F had been crying, her eyes were red, her face blotchy and swollen. Claudette was standing amongst the women, some were weeping on each other's shoulders, the remainder were sitting on the stairs rocking themselves. Lilia's face was hollow and haunted, her eyes half closed.

'What happened?' asked Babette, a lone voice in the silence once Jacques had stopped talking to himself.

'The bastard had shot her. When I burst in he was standing over her, he had a face like a devil. I nearly shot him, the bastard. His men came up, took my gun off me and then they just threw her out of the window, like some sort of rag doll. She was so small, like a little girl. I tried to stop them and one of them punched me.' He pointed to his ribs and then clutched them as if he remembered the pain anew. 'There was nothing I could do, nothing, I let her down.' No one replied, two of the ladies were weeping.

'We all let her down,' said Bella. 'All of us.'

There was a hollow knocking on the door. Everyone started. It was Claudette who stood up and opened it. Perrine rushed inside and closed the door behind her. 'Oh my God! What on this earth has happened? Eva's out there on the road, have they run her over? Oh my God!'

'How did you get through at this time of night?' Claudette asked, astonished to see her.

'You should see it out there, there are people coming out to look, like it's the most gruesome spectacle. They've left her uncovered.' Perrine's teeth were chattering.

'Oh, they have, have they? Bastards!' Bella stood up and disappeared into the salon. She re-emerged with a brocade coverlet in red and gold. She was wearing a fine satin negligee, cut on the bias, which clung to her every curve. They watched as she opened the great front door – more cold air filled the lobby – and proceeded down the steps. She walked over to what was left of Eva, the blood congealing in the freezing night air, her hair still beautiful, silver, untouched.

A soldier stepped out and barred her way with his rifle. She looked at him, levelling a stare straight into his eyes and said starkly. 'Geh mir aus dem weg, du Abschaum.' He ran his eyes over her curves, mentally frisking her body. 'Mir aus dem weg.'

Whether it was the spoken German, the ice-cold stare she fixed on him or the sheer beauty of her, none of them knew, but he gave way, and Bella placed the throw over Eva's body. In the shadows shapes moved, people backed away into their houses and rapid footsteps were heard on the cold pavements. Bella turned and walked back into the house, her head held high.

'It would have been better for him, and for all of us, if he'd kept that quiet,' said Jacques after the door was closed. 'He's in charge of deportations, it'll be humiliating for him. We'll all pay a high price for this, you mark my words.'

Madame F stood back, her mouth opened and closed like a goldfish. 'Who here knew that about the girl?' she demanded, but no one answered. 'Who here knew?' she shouted. 'Someone must have known, Nannette – you did her hair, didn't you?' Nannette looked alarmed, and as Sophie gripped her forearm for support, she shook her head.

'What's the use of asking us now?' said Sophie. 'It's over, isn't it?'

'And how do we know? Any of you could be Jewish, with your hair dye and your tarty make-up. Who knows who you're related to?' Madame F. was sneering.

'Jews have been in Paris a thousand years, we're probably all Jewish, if you're asking, Madame F, take your pick.' Pollo was dragging on a cigarette, which she had passed around to the others. 'Have you looked at yourself in the mirror? You have very dark eyes.' Madame F had no time to answer, there was a flash of lights and the ceiling above them lit up, highlighting the patterns and scrolling in the plasterwork.

'What now?' cried Marie. 'Are they going to take us all?' She fled to Madame F's skirts, seeking comfort there like a child. There was banging on the door. Bella, who was nearest, opened it. When Jacques stood up, his legs almost buckled. Perrine grabbed his arm to support him and Claudette saw that a dribble of blood was running down his neck. Soldiers came in first, they formed a ring around the hallway. A vase on the side-table wobbled precariously, then smashed to the floor in pieces. The tall figure who came in next had his head erect, his shoulders back, he assumed an air of authority. He was wearing an army great coat, which made him look broader, indomitable.

It was Keber.

'Now,' he said, looking at them all slowly and deliberately. 'I make it nine prostitutes as recorded by Madame Odile and five servants in total, excluding the one Agnès Guilles. What does she do?'

'The bookkeeping,' said Madame F 'and other administration. But she only works in the evening, she works for other people during the day.'

Keber looked at her for a moment, causing her to step back. He had his back to Claudette. His eyes searched around the hallway like a torchlight, taking in one character after another. Never had Claudette seen everyone all together in one place, they were surreal, like phantoms who might vanish before her eyes.

'So, you are all here?'

'Yes,' replied Bella, her voice hard. 'Except, of course, the one you have murdered tonight. Eva.'

'Yes, Eva also known as Hélène Resnik, a Jewess.' There was an angry silence, he thrived on it, Claudette could see it in his body language. 'And where, may I ask, is Madame Odile?' They all ducked and bobbed looking around for her.

'I am here.' The disembodied voice came from the stairs and everyone turned to look at her as she proceeded to walk steadily down them one by one. She had put on her brown suit with a fox fur slung over one shoulder. Her make-up was full, lips the colours of rubies and her hair was scraped back against her head with two tortoiseshell combs. On her arm was a Chanel handbag with matching tortoiseshell handles. 'I will answer all your questions about Eva. I insist that you let everyone else get back to bed.'

'Are you harbouring any other Jews in this house, Madame?'

'No.'

'Resistance?'

Claudette gripped her nails into her palms tightly.

'No.'

'Any others that we would consider undesirable in Paris?'

241

She held firm her gaze as she drew level with him. 'No. Apart from the woman Madame Guilles, who does my accounts, there is no one else. Everyone is here.' She stood before him absolutely still, her chin held high.

'Then we shall take only you for questioning.'

Jacques wavered and fell back into his chair with a groan. Perrine put her arm around his shoulders. Keber turned on his heel so that he was facing Claudette. As he left through the door, there was only the briefest glimpse from him, the softness of eye he saved for her, as he passed by. Then he strode down the steps and climbed into his waiting car.

Chapter Thirty Seven

The Rue Ercol stretched out before us, a long plain looking street with houses on each side that opened straight onto the pavement. We walked up and down it looking for anything that might be evidence of a hotel. Two or three larger houses had a flight of steps up to the door, and all of them seemed to have long forgotten basement rooms hidden beneath chicken wire that collected all sorts of rubbish. There was a small supermarket and one house had been removed with a new frontage created, and a half-hearted attempt at a little precinct of shops, all of them "A Louer," for rent, with signs that had been put up a long time ago.

We walked round the corner and sat under the shade of a café awning.

'Well, that's got us bloody nowhere,' Matt exclaimed, as he came back from the loo. You know those two Dan Brown characters in "The Davinci Code", Thingy and the French woman?' I wondered where he was going with this. 'I feel like their alter-egos Hopeless and 'opelesser!' I smiled. Admittedly I felt the same, done in and nowhere to go next.

Daniel had scanned his mother's passport and printed a copy for us. I was studying it carefully, but it was identical to the one we had. I took a long sip of my iced tea and took out my ipad. I'd made a list of all the things we had in our possession and I had scanned and emailed to myself the five letters. Matt had given the two from the shed his best attempt, but even I could see it was a non-starter. If the originals were bad, the copies were twice as bad.

'That note there, the Rose leaflet, what was that?' he asked.

'A little guidebook of some sort, tearooms?' It was all in French with price lists in tiny type.

'Google Little Book Rosé, Paris,' Matt leaned forward to watch as the results came up. It offered pink macaroni, patisseries, hotels called The Little Pink in villages across France. 'Try Little Guide Rosé instead.' I re-typed it. There were lists taking us off in all directions including a guide who would show you all the pink-themed places in the city, quite bizarre. 'Go to images,' he suggested, I tapped on the screen.

It was covered in small thumbnails of naked women and in one case a whole room of naked women, all sitting sedately and looking like they were taking tea at Claridges. I scrolled down and there it was; for sale in America for three hundred dollars, a Petit Guide Rosé exactly like the one I'd seen with Hat. 'That's it,' I said, turning the screen round for Matt. He read the description. "The 1930s guide to Maison Closes in Paris. Only a very few remain, this one is in excellent condition."

He turned to look at me. 'I have the unsettling feeling that Daniel's mum and Freddy's mum were working for "Ladies of the Night."' He scratched his chin. 'That would explain the name, maybe it was the House of March, Maison du March, or something. Or, oh my goodness –'

'Or they were the said ladies of the night,' I chipped in as the thought dawned on us both at precisely the same time.

'For the Germans, being hospitable to the occupying forces and all that,' Matt was pursing his lips. 'I didn't see that one coming.'

'Shit. That's why his dad was German.'

We stared at each other without saying another word, because this was one hornet's nest that probably should remain unkicked.

Chapter Thirty Eight

Everything had changed at the house in Rue Ercol.

Claudette had opened the door to Madame Odile the following day; she had walked all the way back from the Avenue Foch. There was a blue bruise on her cheekbone and a long scratch on her neck. Her hair hung around her face, the tortoiseshell combs sliding out. She was dangling the fox fur, letting it drag behind her, and her handbag was scuffed as if someone had kicked it around the floor.

She half collapsed into the chair that Jacques had been sitting in the night before. Claudette went to the bar and poured her a large Cognac. Madame Odile's hands shook as she curved them around the glass.

'Did they hurt you badly?'

'Mostly it was my pride,' she said, shaking her head. 'I'll get over it.'

'Will they close us down?' asked Claudette, feeling for the first time a surge of anxiety for the women who now shared her life.

'What do you think, Françoise?' Madame Odile snorted, her lips curling into a sneer. 'A place were they can fuck beautiful women who do anything they are told to do?' Claudette dropped her eye contact, feeling a stirring of shame. 'And women who are bewitched by these Aryan monsters with their blue eyes, golden hair and supreme intelligence. Did you know they speak three languages, virtually all of them? They are a world away from what these girls have known.' Claudette nodded, thinking of her own German officer. 'A woman working here can earn three times the wages of the average Frenchwoman by sleeping with just one German. So no, they are not closing us down, they are demanding what they had before, but free of charge. And, they will be all but running it themselves. I'm only a front now, all of us will have our income cut to the quick and who knows how long we can last? I will have to go cap in hand to that man every time I need something from rubbers to eggs.'

'Rechstein?'

'No, Keber,' she said flatly. 'They have put him in charge, he reports now to the Gestapo.'

The knock on the door at noon was done with a stick, hard and hollow, a sound of foreboding in itself. Claudette answered it, hoping it was Keber. It was the Gestapo doctor. He was a small man in a long leather coat who wore thick bottle-bottom glasses making his weasel eyes huge. He introduced himself as Herr Doktor Diess and handed her an exquisitely carved silver-topped cane and his ornate peaked cap.

'I am here to examine all the women.' His voice was clipped, efficient.

'I will show you to Madame Odile's office,' she replied as calmly as possible.

That evening the women all gathered for dinner, even Lilia who often took a tray of food away with her. Their heads were low, shoulders rounded, make up in some cases forgotten. They had chosen blacks and greys to wear, gone was the vibrancy and the steely arrogance.

'He hurt me,' said Sophie, sipping her wine as if it might comfort her. 'Really hurt me.' She looked forlorn.

'And me,' said Freya. She looked as if she had been crying all day, her eyes were red and raw.

'Odious little creep, it's part of their plan,' said Bella. 'They will grind us down. Any other business harbouring a Jew would have been razed to the ground and the people in it would be hanging from lamp posts. They have other plans for us, you watch.'

They were silent as they ate. None of them mentioned Eva who was still lying under the brocade rug outside, guarded by a single soldier morning, noon and night. A trail of Parisians had walked past to stare at the remains and to see what was now confirmed as a Bordello and not a gentleman's club for German Officers. Some of the people passing by spat on the small shape of a body under the ornate cloth. Whether it was because she was Jewish, a prostitute, or because she was a collaborator, Claudette couldn't tell. Maybe they did it to impress the soldiers to show whose side they were on.

The next morning Keber arrived. She heard his voice as she came up the kitchen steps. No one was around, everyone had slept in or they were staying in their bedrooms avoiding contact with others. Perrine had let him in and he stood talking to her in the entrance hall, his great coat making him look powerful, untouchable. Claudette stood watching him, before he saw her.

'I have some questions for Françoise Favelle,' he told Perrine. Claudette stepped forward from behind the turn of the staircase. 'Take me to the Private Room,' he ordered.

She led him away and up the stairs. Perrine was staring in revulsion at them both, her feet rooted to the spot. Once inside, he locked the door and then stood with his back to it. He took a deep breath and shrugged off his coat, letting it fall carelessly to the floor. Claudette watched, not moving as she stood opposite him.

'That was the hardest night of my life,' he said, sinking down onto the nearest chair. 'Why in God's name employ a Jew? I cannot believe her abject stupidity.'

'She had no idea,' said Claudette, 'No idea at all.'

'Truthfully?'

'Only I knew, and I wasn't going to tell anyone.'

He looked at her, deadpan, his face barely processing the thought. 'I had to strike her, had to hit her,' he said. He shook his head. 'Of all the stupid…' his voice drifted away. Eventually he looked up at her, beckoning her to come towards him, but she stood absolutely still, though her knees felt weak as if they might collapse under her.

'Come to me,' he pleaded. 'I have done my best for you.'

'Your best? For me? What have you done, Fritz? Only beaten her up a little? Only sent a doctor to hurt every woman here? Only killed a beautiful young girl? She was fourteen, Fritz!' He shook his head once more, his skin was slick with perspiration.

'I have done everything in my power. I had to convince Rechtstein to leave this to me. I told him his job was to manage his own reputation. He had eight Frenchmen shot this morning, one for each prostitute left alive in here. Then I said I would interrogate Madame Odile. Trust me, if he'd done it she would have been suspended by her hands from a beam and her body would have been covered in whiplashes. So yes, I only beat her up a bit. As for the new regime, and that shit of a doctor, I have to look like I am taking a strong action. What else would you have me do? Do you think I was given the job of overseer in this house? I had to play the game, make myself available.'

Claudette stood opposite him, taking it all in.

'Is it my turn now?' she asked. 'Am I a pawn in your game?'

'No, my love, you are not. Everything I did, I did to protect you.' He stood up and took her face in his hands. 'Nothing matters to me more, nothing. I have fallen in love with you and I care about one thing, and one thing only, and it is you.'

He reached over and pulled her down into his lap, kissing her softly and tenderly. Then he hugged her tightly and she felt a new urgency about him, a need she had not experienced before and an escalation of her own power. He had done all that for her because he loved her. She arched her body into him, returning his kisses with great intensity, giving herself to him, knowing that as she did she was loving him more deeply than she could ever have imagined.

When they parted he held her hand in the entrance hall, as if he were scared to let her go. The house felt completely empty, as if there had been no-one living in it for months. No music, no shouts of laughter, no hum of distant sounds. He kissed her beside the reception desk, risking everything. It was as if he needed to taste her right up until the last second, to keep him going.

'I love you, Françoise,' he whispered softly in her ear and then he turned, opened the door and was gone.

'You little fool!'

Claudette spun round, her heart completely missing a beat. It was Madame Odile standing at the foot of the stairs. 'You stupid little fool.'

Chapter Thirty Nine

Matt called the waiter over. In French he said, 'Excuse me, do you have any idea where there might have been a Maison Close on the Rue Ercol?' The waiter's eyes widened and he said "no" with some disdain, but ever the professional, he would ask inside. 'Oh, my goodness,' said Matt, 'He probably thinks I need one.'

'Don't worry, they've been closed down in Paris for years, it says here.' I was scrolling through an article in an English newspaper. 'Seems the French are a bit more prudey these days.' The waiter came back, placing Matt's bill on a little black tray. He told Matt that no one had ever heard of such a thing in this part of the city, even going back some way in time. Matt thanked him, noticing that the waiter was watching them both as he wiped the glasses behind the bar.

'Here,' I said, 'listen to this. "Alcohol-fuelled orgies dominated the Maison Closes at a time when the majority of the population had to abide by a curfew. The debauchery carried on as Allied bombs rained down on suburban factories and people in the city were being sent to camps in Germany.

The Nazis revived the fortunes of the many Brothels that had been threatened with closure before the war, in fact it became a golden age for the Maison Closes.

There were twenty-two well-known brothels

commandeered by The Wermacht and SS units who transformed them into establishments for the exclusive use of military staff and some compliant French officials. The German invaders were insatiable customers."

'This is interesting,' I said, reading down further.

"Their outer appearance had to be discreet and they were all operated by a woman, typically a former prostitute-turned-madam. The Nazis published an official guide to the brothels and guards were posted outside the major ones when senior Nazis were visiting. With single visits often costing the equivalent of a senior officer's weekly pay, fees paid to the madams in charge were some of the highest in the history of the sex industry. All visitors were expected to bring champagne, clothes, chocolates and cigarettes for the residents and to tip well. To maintain a sense of decorum the Maison Closes projected the image of a gentlemen's club, which deceived the locals."

'Wow,' said Matt. 'I didn't know any of that.'
'Amazing.'
'Tell you what, Google that place Daniel mentioned.' He suggested.
'I can't remember what it was called.'
'Le Beouf....' He was puffing out his cheeks, 'Le Beouf.... à la Ficelle, à la Ficelle, that's it.'
I discovered on my first search that Beef on a String is a favourite dish of France and England, even though I'd never heard of it. I searched again, inputting Le Beouf à la Ficelle, Paris 1940s.

"Le Boeuf à la Ficelle was a famous Paris restaurant. Waitresses would serve diners like Cary Grant and Edith Piaf wearing nothing but an apron and high heels. During the Nazi occupation, this x-rated establishment was highly popular among the German officers."

I read on and added '…and Miss Marlene Dietrich, I think you'll find.'

'God, that Cary Grant was cool,' said Matt. 'Not sure I could have pulled that off, all those boobs swinging freestyle above my meat and two veg.'

That made me roar with laughter and the people who had been sitting down around us looked at us as if we were the loud Brits they all dread. Inside, the waiter polishing his glasses peered out again like a nervous bird.

'Try March, Paris 1940s Bordellos.'

There was nothing.

'Try Ercol, Paris, WW2.'

'Nothing.'

'Try Madame, German Officers, Ercol, WW2, bordello?'

'I'm offered a haunted American house or some antiques including an early Ercol rocking chair.'

'Damn.' Matt had a look of defeat about him. He took out his phone and began tapping in words.

'Excuse me.' The man was tall and very elegant; he had white hair that fell long over his collar. He was wearing a pale lemon jacket and a light blue open necked shirt. He was about ten years older than us, in his mid to late fifties. 'I couldn't help but overhear the waiter inside asking about a bordello in the Rue Ercol, was it you who wanted to know?'

'Er, yes, we were asking because a friend used to know of it,' Matt replied a little sheepishly.

'A much older friend, I suspect,' he said with a smile in his eyes. 'It's been gone a long, long time.' He spoke English slowly in a measured way, conjuring each word up from his memory. He had a gentle voice, rich and warm.

'It was number twelve, but it will do you no good to know this. It was a block of offices for a long time and then, for some reason just – how do you say it – left behind?'

'Abandoned?' I offered.

'Abandoned, yes. It used to be very grand with beautiful scrolling.'

'Do you remember it?' I asked.

'No, no, I have a picture of it in about 1930 in a frame in my apartment. My wife collected art and it was one of her purchases in a brocante. Would you like to see it?'

Matt threw me a look of 'why not?' and we stood up to shake hands, introducing ourselves properly, which we knew was expected. He was called Theo Arnold and he was an architect. He had a very kind face, handsome too. He walked us to the site of the Bordello, but it was a sad and forlorn place with a flat, faceless glass front door and nineteen seventies metal window frames around dirty panes. Theo pointed upwards. 'The whole facade has completely changed. I suspect in England you might have stopped the developers, but here in France I'm sad to say that anything goes.' He walked on past a big shop with a huge pink ammonite hanging outside. I liked the Latin Quarter, it was arty, I could see myself living there.

Theo's apartment overlooked Delacroix's house, which was quite bizarre given that we'd been there so recently. The small square had four tall trees, one at each corner and one or two exclusive shops with dark secretive interiors. Theo waved us through the front door of his apartment. Inside, it was dark, heavily panelled and very old, very similar to the artist's house across the way. We carried on up some warped wooden stairs and Theo opened the door at the top with a key from his pocket. 'Come, come inside, I will make something to eat.' He spoke with gentle, unhurried words.

'Lunch?' he asked when we were in his dining area. 'I have bread and cheese and some fruit.'

It sounded lovely. We sat at a table in the open window of the apartment, which was full of polished uneven floors, and bookcases made to fit the strangest of spaces under beams and between doorjambs.

'I am an avid book collector,' Theo told us. 'I always have been, it's my downfall. Without my library I'd be a very rich man.' He nodded sagely, then added, 'and also very bored.'

'I know exactly what you mean,' I told him, 'Me too. Freddy had some brand new editions of the classics. Treasure Island was one and The Lion, The Witch and The Wardrobe.'

'And Freddy is?' he asked.

'My friend, that is, he died recently. I've been clearing out his house with Matt's help and we have been sort of drawn into something of a mystery.'

Because Theo was the type of person who listened without interruption, we found ourselves telling him the whole story. Even recounting the list of things I had found in the shed and Freddy's letters.

Theo raised his eyebrows when I mentioned the little pink book. 'Le Guide Rose is a collector's item,' he told us. 'You will occasionally see one on the Internet, but less and less now. When I was a child I remember them being about here and there, always in bookshops scattered about, but when they closed down the Maison Closes they purged the city of all the ephemera of the seedy Parisian lifestyles.'

'And what do you know of the Bordello in Rue Ercol?'

'I'm afraid all I can offer is the picture I have. He disappeared into a sunlit salon next door and came back with a small painting of the street, a very fine water-colour. The dominant house was an elegant mansion with tall windows, a large front door and ornate railings.

'Can you see how they have desecrated her?' asked Theo; he looked quite forlorn. 'She was once home to a musician, a man known for his great knowledge of Berlioz. I can imagine the sound ringing out of the windows.' He sighed. 'Now everywhere has changed so much. You say you are leaving this weekend?'

'Well, that's the plan,' said Matt, 'Though it's the big French Getaway Weekend, so we're going to struggle to get tickets.'

'It's just that I might be able to make a phone call, an acquaintance of mine who knows about The Maison Closes in Paris. Let me phone him. I have an idea, the faintest recollection that he knew someone who worked at Ercol a very long time ago.'

Chapter Forty

Madame Odile's face was burning with anger. 'How long has that been going on?' she asked. 'No, don't tell me, all the times he's booked the Private Room, the errands you've supposedly been on, the rumours amongst the girls that he had someone...' She stood leaning heavily against her office desk. 'And all along it was my maid, my stupid, fucking maid.'

'It's not my fault, I –'

'No, of course it's not your stupid, fucking fault. It's him, he's charmed you, you have been completely won over by him. I've heard it all before.'

'I didn't mean to fall in love with him.' Claudette spoke up for herself, but Madame Odile was having none of it.

'Fall in love? You don't know the meaning of the word. You're a stripling, a fool. You know nothing of men, especially evil men and that man is one of them.' Claudette hung her head, she had nothing to say, except she knew in her heart Keber was not evil. She could not love a man who was that bad.

'When you came here they called you The Virgin. I remember that I had to pull Pollo up for making fun of you. It's ironic, isn't it, the virgin in the whore house has been bedded by one of the evil monsters who now, in effect, runs the place?' She leaned forward and pulled a cigarette from the enamel box on her desk. She lit it with a large alabaster lighter and threaded the fingers from her other hand through her hair. "I simply cannot believe this, anyone else, even Perrine, I would have found it believable, but not you.'

'He's not evil.' Claudette sunk her head into her chest; her head felt heavy on her shoulders as if someone was pressing a weight on top of it.

'Oh really.' Madame Odile stepped around to the front of her desk, 'Really?' She stubbed the cigarette into an ashtray and taking her blouse in both hands tore it open. The tiny silk buttons popped one after the other in rapid succession and scattered across the floor, bouncing everywhere. Her chest was slashed with red lines, the colour clashing against the whiteness of her bra. The welts were angry, weeping. She had pushed cotton wadding on top of the injuries and there was a smell of antiseptic as it fell away. 'This is Fritz Keber. You know nothing of him.'

'He said he had to, Rechtstein would have done far worse to you.'

Madame Odile lurched forward, her hair spooling out of its combs and pins. She was looking more manic by the minute. She grabbed Claudette's wrist in her left hand and dragged her to the door. Claudette tried to fight her off, but the clasp she had, with her now ragged scarlet nails, was too tight.

Madame Odile called the lift and within seconds it clunked and clattered up from the ground floor. She pulled back the gate and threw Claudette in, shielding the exit with her body. The lift began to chug and Madam Odile closed the brass filigree gate across to seal them in.

Claudette counted third, fourth, fifth floor, it stopped. Madame Odile pushed her out and through the double doors. Within seconds they were in the corridor. 'Go on, go to the door at the end. Go!' Madame Odile pushed her in the back until they reached a door, then she opened it with a key from her pocket and shoved her maid inside.

The smell was foul, it made Claudette's eyes water. It was a small room ten feet square, if that. There was a rocking chair, a threadbare rug and a pail with what looked like soiled white rags submerged in water. Opposite, there was small door. Madame Odile stepped forward and opened it, the key rattled in the lock, but it was not locked. The room ran the entire depth of the house, long and thin. There was a bed and a figure lying on it, unmoving; beyond that, a baby's crib. There were no windows, no light from outside at all, only the glow of embers in a dying fire and a lamp dangling into the gloom from a sloping beam.

Claudette stepped forward as Madame Odile moved out of her way. On the bed was Lilia, her eyes almost glazed over, her hair straggled behind her, her skin ghostly. Claudette was horrified. The room was in turmoil, a tray of food on the floor, a child's toys strewn across the dirty mat.

The child was a little boy. He sat in his playpen sucking on a red rubber ball, his eyes brown, hair blond. He was thin, a small, skinny face atop a grubby playsuit. He looked at Claudette, but made no attempt to be lifted up or even to draw her attention.

Lilia groaned and moved her legs. 'She's always up here like this these days,' said Madame Odile. 'You see she can't cope any more.' Lilia didn't respond to the sound of voices.

'She's got you, her sister,' said Claudette, sounding more assertive than she felt. Madame Odile's eyes narrowed, her hair looked as though she'd been ravaged.

'How do you know that?' she asked.

'I heard you say it the day she was overdosing.'

'And can you guess who the father is?' Her words were scornful. Claudette felt her heart hammering against her ribcage. 'Yes, that's right, Fredrik Keber, your lover. This is the kind of debris he leaves in his wake.' Claudette stood looking around the room at the mess, the squalor and the child with his sandy hair and lost eyes.

'What's his name?'

'Daniel.' Madame Odile replied. For a moment she looked at the toddler with pity then she took a sharp intake of breath. 'So from now on this is your problem. I have looked after this child, I have tried endlessly to stop my sister's habit and now she is useless, a complete waste of my time and effort.'

'My problem, how?'

'You'll look after the boy as well as your normal duties. She,' Madame Odile looked at Lilia, 'is incapable.'

'What about Agnès?'

'How do you mean?'

'Well, I'm guessing she comes in to sit with the child when Lilia is working, doesn't she? She always arrives in the evening.'

'Yes.' There was a pause. 'Yes, and I will make her come earlier while you serve dinner, but from the morning until five o'clock you will be here when the child is awake, unless Lilia is feeling better.'

'So I'm a nanny?'

'Exactly, I can't afford anyone extra now, Keber will see to that.'

'And he visits?'

'Yes, whenever he has the time or the inclination.'

'So he knows what Agnes does, he knows she doesn't do your accounts?'

'Yes, of course he knows, but that is neither here nor there. Except that it shows you what a good liar and actor he is.'

'And if I'm here when he visits?'

'The chances are you will be, but I don't care. If he can screw you he'll maybe make life easier for us, I really don't know how his mind works.'

'Why don't you give the boy to him?' asked Claudette.

'Because he would win, and it is my meal ticket, the reason I have been able to run this place and not lose my sister or my nephew.' There was a catch in her voice, emotion being swallowed back. 'Only Keber outside this house knows about this, no one else. The boy has never been out of doors, he would not be safe if anyone knew he was a German's bastard. It is for his sake you must tell no-one.'

'And everyone else in the house?' asked Claudette. 'Do they all know?'

'Yes,' she replied. Claudette suddenly realized it all made sense.

'Here is the key to the door, it must stay locked at all times, I have another,' Madame Odile dropped the key into Claudette's hand. She raised her eyes, her gaze was steely, uncompromising. 'I don't like you, Françoise, I never have, but I have few options these days.' She turned on her heel and Claudette was left in the stench and half darkness.

She cast her eyes over everything, the shapes of furniture and old cardboard boxes in the recesses of darkness and the ridges of filthy coal dust that lay on the old rug in front of the fire. There was nothing for it but to sort out the room and see if the boy needed changing. There was a smell that suggested he did. As Claudette lifted Daniel from his cot Lilia stirred but went back to her strange half awake doze. The boy felt thin, underweight. His eyes were too big for his head.

As she held him he sank his little body into her and buried his head in her neck. She pressed his head to her and hummed a tune that came to her from a distant memory of her own childhood.

There was a small bathroom at the end of the eaved room where Claudette changed and cleaned the boy. A heap of dirty nappies were piled into a bucket. She carried them out and placed them outside the room, the smell made her eyes water.

In the Armoire she found bedlinen for the cot and some clothes for Daniel. She changed him and gave him a bottle of milk that had been standing next to Lilia's bed. He lay back in his cot and suckled, his eyes staring through the bars of his little prison.

Claudette woke Lilia. Slapping her face, she said roughly, 'Come on, up you get!' as she hauled her out of bed and towards the door. She half walked, half dragged the woman down the corridor and into the lift. Eventually, she had her back in her own bed and away from the sad little room where her son lived. Lilia fell onto the bed and into a deep unconsciousness.

Claudette took all the cleaning equipment from Lilia's

cupboard and put it in the lift. She rolled up the Indian bedside rug and took spare linen out of the drawers. Then she took everything upstairs. Two hours later Daniel's room was clean, the bed aired and remade. The rug gave her somewhere to play with the boy and she was ready for Agnès who arrived at five.

'I will bring a tray of food for you and Daniel,' she explained. 'I am now in charge of the boy and this sorry excuse for a room and I will organize everything from now on.' Agnès nodded, saying nothing, and took a seat on the rough wooden chair where she sat with a vacant expression, staring at the child in his cot

'Play with him,' Claudette ordered. 'Amuse him, the poor little mite is desperate for attention.' Claudette took up the bin of nappies and the tray of leftovers from the last meal. As she walked downstairs anger rose up inside her, and she felt nothing but loathing for Fritz Keber and his ghastly secrets.

Chapter Forty One

Gaél Henri spoke no English so our conversation had to be translated by Matt. We had met in a café close to the Padlock Bridge. The sun was beating down on us and we'd both asked for mineral water with plenty of ice. Theo had very kindly walked with us telling us about the architecture and the history of the Île de la Cité as we went.

He was a lovely man. As we talked he asked us about Oxfordshire and Freddy. I described my cottage and the village and he listened graciously, asking me to expound on it. In turn he showed us the secret places of Paris, the bar where Hemingway and James Joyce ate and the site of the garage where Gertrude Stein first heard the words "Lost Generation" spoken by the owner.

Gaél, his friend, although much more busy and fast-talking, turned out to be just as helpful. He was a small rotund man with a Gaelic face and slick black hair. His skin was heavily tanned as if he worked outside a lot, but he carried a briefcase with a Paris crest embossed on it. He told us he was a civil servant.

'I will leave you in the trust of my good friend Gaél,' said Theo, shaking our hands. 'I go to the theatre tonight, I must not stay longer.' I felt the prickling of a tear in the corner of my eye. I would have liked to spend more time with him, possibly meet again for dinner. He was such a gentle soul. All at once I was feeling emotional about everything, perhaps because we'd talked so much about Freddy.

I watched him walk away, his tall body standing out above a group of Japanese tourists who were milling around studying guidebooks. As I turned back to talk to Gaël, Theo turned to look at me a final time, his smile accompanied by a brief wave of the hand.

'Gaël says Theo is a very good man and a fine architect, but he's never been the same since his wife died, very sad. He says they were made for each other.' Matt gave me that knowing look that reinforced us as a couple.

'What did she die of?' I asked.

Matt asked and Gaël said: 'Ancer u sein,' then in English he said, 'Breast Cancer.' He sat down with us and unpacked his briefcase telling Matt that he'd brought some books that might be of interest to us. Matt picked up a small hardback called 'The Bordellos of Paris' and thumbed through it. I saw him check the index but Rue Ercol was obviously not there.

'Listen to this, it's about our King Edward the Seventh: "Edward who was morbidy obese had a love seat or Siege D'Amour made for him. It was manufactured by Louis Soubrier, Cabinet Maker of the Rue de Faubourg Saint-Antoine. It allowed easy access for oral, and other forms of sex, with several participants."

Gaël was grinning and he said: 'Oui, Oui, le Roi he was bad no!' That made me laugh. I told him in English that our King Edward the Seventh had been a very bad man. He understood and smiled. The waiter arrived and took our order for drinks. Matt and I opted for more water, I literally felt as though my clothes were sticking to me.

Matt and Gaél began to talk and I was lost, so I picked up the book Matt had been looking through. There was a photograph of three women, bare breasted, on a marble balcony; two brunettes each side of a platinum blonde. A Leopard skin was slung over the balcony in front of them. Their faces were beautiful with heavily painted lips, and I got the impression they were sharing a joke. Their lack of any modesty and sheer brazenness left me with the feeling that they were in charge, it rang out from the picture. The drinks arrived and Matt used the break in the conversation to tell me what Gaél had said.

'Gaél is part of the history preservation team with the government. They are working on a project for the World War Two commemorations in two thousand and nineteen. He's taken an interest in the Maison Closes because they were part of the German occupation. A lot went on in those places.'

'I'll bet,' I said, raising my eyebrows. Gaél found my expression very amusing and raised his glass to me.

'They were allowed to trade all through the conflict, but only with Germans and selected French officials. The houses were anonymous from the outside and lots of the French thought they were meeting rooms for the Nazis. The women inside were not allowed to go out, but the Nazis saw they had everything they could wish for – food, champagne, clothes, furniture. They were opulent and no expense was spared on their interiors. They were operated mainly by Madams, who had been former prostitutes themselves.'

'And does he know anything about the house in Rue Ercol?'

'He's coming to that,' said Matt and he began speaking French again with Gaél. A man and woman sat down in front of us. He was Chinese and his head was shaved except for a strip through the middle, which ended in a small plait. I was studying him intently as he talked to the woman next to him. His lips were pierced and the studs looked like little boils waiting to burst. I couldn't take my eyes off them.

'The house was one of twenty-two operating during the war. It was extremely opulent and smart with themed rooms and an exclusive German clientele. It was run by a very fierce woman known as Madame Odile, she selected the prostitutes and made everything run like clockwork. Some of the women in there could demand a week's salary from a German officer for just one session of how's your father.'

'How's your father?' I raised a quizzical eyebrow at Matt. 'That's very nineteen seventies.'

He stifled a smile and carried on. 'The downfall came when a high-ranking officer called Rechtstein found out he had been sleeping with a Jewess. This was nineteen forty-four. He murdered her and threw her body into the street. After that the place was run into the ground and sacked by the French at the end of the war. The prostitutes were hounded out by the Parisians and some of them were branded in the street. In those days they used to shave the heads of what they called Horizontal Collaborators.'

'Heavens,' I replied, thinking of Freddy and his poor mother. 'Does Gaél know anything about the maids?'

Matt duly asked him. 'No, he has no idea.'

'Has he heard of Madeléine March?'

Matt asked. 'Apparently not, but he knows someone who used to work there.'

'Can we meet her...or him?'

'Est'il possible de recontrer cette person?'

Gaél looked at his watch and pursed his lips, for a minute it occurred to me he might be after a payment for his services. I think it occurred to Matt too. At length he said; 'Oui, oui, certainement, avez –vous le temps de venir maintenant?'

'He's asking if we'd like to go now?'

'Yes, is it far?'

Gaél seemed to understand my question. He shook his head. 'Is near,' he said.

Gaél's idea of near, it transpired, was a bit further than my own idea of near. He threaded us through the streets of the Temple area, past crowds browsing in shops and sitting outside restaurants. Friends greeted each other with air kisses and there was a throb of excitement in the possibilities of a Saturday night. We felt business-like as we pressed through crowds of dawdling tourists, Matt turning every so often to see if I was keeping up. Our friend was very fast on his feet. 'I suspect it's because he's a Civil Servant,' Matt suggested. 'He sits all day so he makes up for it by running everywhere.'

After twenty minutes we reached a row of shops, one with a huge pencil portrait of a woman covering the entire window. I had to stop to take it in because it was so beautiful.

In between the next shop, a men's underwear shop and a boutique selling very expensive scarves, was an open archway, its huge medieval doors folded back against the walls. It opened into a small courtyard with a stone tiled floor and whitewashed walls. Numerous long grey planters, all empty or sprouting weeds, formed a funnel to guide people towards a fashion shop that had 'Solde, Solde, Solde' plastered across its windows. Inside I could see all kinds of cheap, glittery clothes, skyscraper heels and neon handbags. I couldn't, for a minute, work out why we were here.

Then I realized Gaél was knocking on the door of a small house, so small it looked like part of the archway. The grey door had chipped pots each side, one had a small dead tree in it, its branches long past budding. He must have heard a reply from inside, but the chatter of passing shoppers meant I heard nothing. He opened the door towards him and stepped inside, beckoning us to follow. I looked at Matt, unsure of how we were all going to fit inside.

The woman was sitting on a camp bed, her head wrapped in a scarf. Her widow's peak was grey. She had thin, wrinkled skin that puckered around her mouth because her teeth were all missing and her breasts sagged down to her waist. She was wearing a flowery blouse and skirt. The busy patterns jarred angrily against each other. The bed was low to the ground and had no sheets. There was an old blanket and a heavily stained pillow. Her eyes drew me in, a deep penetrating green, in spite of the cataracts that made them cloudy.

Gaél introduced us and Matt bent down to shake her hand, but she didn't move. There was nowhere else to sit, so we stood. A quick glance around the rest of the room and I saw that it had a small oven, a fold up table and a tap above a bucket. Everywhere was filthy, flies gathered on a plate of leftover food.

'This is Marie-Celeste, she used to work at the house in Rue Ercol,' Matt said. We both nodded. 'Marie-Celeste was one of the ladies.' I stared down in disbelief. The woman could not have been more different from the beautiful women on the balcony in the book, and I thought of Bette Davies who said that old age is not for sissies. She was right.

Gaél began talking very rapidly and I pretended to understand, to be polite, nodding along. Matt turned to me after what seemed a very long time. 'Marie-Celeste worked for Madam Odile from forty-two to forty-four. She was at Le Chabanais for two years before that. When Madame Odile walked out she came back for Marie-Celeste. She says she was head-hunted.' Marie-Celeste began to talk, waving her hands to illustrate her story. Matt listened, but he found it hard to understand her French. Gaél translated and Matt passed it on to me.

'Marie-Celeste was a favourite. She charged a lot of money because she was very beautiful.' Matt smiled at her kindly. 'When the war ended they took her out and paraded her in the streets naked, then they branded her. The other women who didn't escape were all treated the same. One of them committed suicide and another was beaten up in the street.'

Marie Celeste opened the top of her blouse and there were the rough edges of a scar on the left of her chest, exactly like the taxi driver's tribal scars, but on softer, wrinkled skin.

'It's a P for Putain, prostitute,' said Matt translating

271

Gaél's words. 'It's just a scar now.' Marie-Celeste closed her blouse, muttering to herself. There was no need to translate, she had bad, bad memories.

'Ask her if she knew anyone called Madeléine March.' I said. Gaél worked out what I was asking and he put it to Marie-Celeste. She shook her head. 'Ask her about the maids.' Matt did so. She told us that there were three maids, a cook and a handyman. She hated one member of staff in particular, a maid called Françoise Favelle. She was the sister of the handyman, a really nasty piece of work. She had burnt Marie-Celeste's foot in the bath once for no reason at all.

I looked down at the old lady; her small frame was so bent and crooked, her skin papery and marked all over with age spots. The air was putrid in her little hovel, unwashed clothing, urine, layer upon layer of dirt. She had nothing. I felt terribly sorry for her, for what she had been to where she had come to now. What an awful life.

Marie-Celeste began talking again, angrier, her voice rising in pitch. Matt was following her better now. 'She says we should know that she was once very beautiful, her hair was the colour used by Titian. She was once the most expensive woman in the place, Madame Odile's favourite. Then they took it all away and it was never the same. She says she used to be paid hundreds of francs a week for one man a night, but after the war she was sleeping with hundreds of men for a few francs.'

Her eyes began to mist over, there were tears waiting to fall. I knelt down and took her hands. 'I'm sorry,' I said as kindly as I could. Matt put a hand on my shoulder whilst Gaél watched with pity. The woman gazed at me, her hands tightening around mine.

'Ils étaient mes jours de gloire,' she said, her head shaking with emotion from side to side. 'Je suis fier.'

'They were her glory days, she's still proud of them,' Matt translated.

'Please ask her if there was anyone else in the house.'

Matt spoke softly and Marie-Celeste replied that yes, there was a boy. A baby called Daniel, he had been kept hidden from sight. One of the maids had rescued him because his mother was a druggie. It was the one she didn't like, Françoise Favelle. The irony was that it turned out she was with the Resistance, but they didn't know that until after everything was over. Favelle had worked for the notorious Black Jack Cell; they worked with Communists. She didn't tell them, it became known afterwards. It was the one that included a young doctor, Gabin, who was killed by the Nazis. People talked about it for a long time.'

'How did they find out she was with the Resistance?' I asked

Matt translated, asking her. 'She doesn't remember,' he said.

'Did she know where they went?' Matt asked, but I knew by the shake of the head that Marie-Celeste had no idea. She started speaking again, her small fingers clutching my arm as she looked at me. She was trembling and Gaél stepped forward, worried that she might be getting overwrought. Matt continued to translate. 'She was bedding a German, all along, none of us knew. An evil man, he was in charge at the end.'

'What was his name?' Matt asked.

She spat the name out like it tasted foul on her tongue. 'Fritz Keber, evil!' She said "evil" in English it made for

273

greater emphasis. I stepped back, the threads had come together and I could feel that Matt was thinking the same thing.

'We must go now,' said Gaél, pulling gently at my elbow. I reached into my bag and fished out a bunch of notes from my purse. I pressed them into Marie-Celeste's hands. 'Pour vous, Madam.' She wiped away a tear and said thank you. Then she held up the money close to her eyes and started to count it.

Chapter Forty Two

'I've just found out about the boy,' Claudette stood in the kitchen looking at Madame F, Jacques, Perrine and Marie. 'And now I've been made a nanny.' They all looked at her, each wondering what to say. 'So thank you for letting me in on that little secret.'

'Madame Odile wanted it that way,' said Perrine. 'She only tells people she trusts.'

'Like everyone in the house else except me?'

'Well, if the cap fits,' Perrine replied. All eyes returned to Claudette, like spectators at a tennis match. She walked over to the cabinet and began collecting together a tray of food for the boy and a drink for Agnès.

'What are you doing?' asked Madame F with indignance.

'I'm doing my job. That poor child has had no-one to give him love and I intend to change that, it's criminal.'

'No, what is criminal is shagging a Boche,' shouted Perrine, her voice bitter and hard. 'That is criminal!'

'What Boche?' asked Madame F; she beat Jacques to the question by a second.

'Keber, she's bedding Keber!' Perrine spat the words at Claudette whose hands were shaking as she cut the bread.

'No, she hasn't!' Jacques exclaimed. 'Don't tell such lies, Perrine.'

'Ask your little sister, Jacques, why don't you ask her, she's there?'

'Is it true?' asked Madame F, wiping her hands on her apron and moving across the kitchen to Claudette. She took hold of the girl's upper arm and shook it. Claudette dropped the knife and spun around to face them.

'Yes, it's true, I fell in love, that's all, but it's over. I didn't know about the boy.'

'Well, that's a fine mess,' said Madame F. 'I knew this was all going to end in tears. You stupid girl! What do you think, Jacques, she's your sister – has she put us more at risk?'

'It depends on what my sister does now,' he said coldly, emphasising the word sister. His expression had completely hardened against Claudette. 'If you give him up you'll make him mad and no doubt he'll take it out on all of us. If you keep him, the ladies upstairs will revolt, I'm bound to think. So, what are you going to do, for certain, I need to know?'

'I'm going to tell him it's over. He has a child that he should be taking care of now that the poor thing's mother is a lost cause.' Claudette reached for the milk jug and poured a small glass for Daniel.

'Then you will be condemning us to his whim,' Jacques stood up. He moved nearer to Claudette as Madame F stood back.

'The girl has no sense and she is not a good Catholic girl to be doing it with anyone before she's married. I've said it before but I'm bound to say it again, it will end in tears one way or another.' After her pronouncement Madame F bustled back to the table and the dough she was making. 'I'm ashamed on your behalf, Françoise.'

'She has no shame,' Perrine added as she put on her apron. 'And she has no thought for our poor soldiers in the camps in Germany. Or for that poor girl lying outside our door.'

Claudette took the tray upstairs biting her lip instead of replying. And what would she have said if she had spoken? She was in love with a man who was totally unsuitable for her in every way, a man they called evil and she was now looking after his love child.

Weeks passed and the house changed. Suddenly flour was unavailable, then sugar, then there was no fuel. The soldiers arriving at the house started turning up day and night. The women were expected to be on call at all times even when the Germans were raucous, or violent, or drunk. Soon enough, each woman became morose, frightened or lethargic, depending on how she had been treated. There was a sentry on the front door day and night.

Claudette picked up Keber's notes from under the lamp in reception and threw them away. She hid from him when she heard he was in the house and she made sure she was not in Daniel's room when he was around. Madame Odile saw him in and left him with the boy.

The night the car arrived she was in the Salon, tidying the mess left by a party of officers who were being moved out of Paris. It was their final taste of a bordello and they were acting like it. They had spilled wine, one of them had knocked over an expensive glass vase that had smashed into tiny fragments on the floor. One of the cushions had been slashed with a knife.

'Françoise,' Perrine's face was ashen, 'there is a soldier here with a car, his orders are to take you to the Hotel Meurice.' Claudette put down the cushion she was plumping. Her eyes darted to the clock, it was a little after seven. She knew it was the hotel used by the SS. 'Should I get Jacques?'

'No, he'll only get hurt, I'll go.'

'I'll get your handbag, you'll need money to get home,' said Perrine, reverting to her practical self before she hurried away. Claudette stepped through the door and found herself facing a young officer. His face gave nothing away.

'Are you Miss Favelle?' he asked. His French accent was perfect.

'Yes,' she replied.

'I have orders to take you to the Hotel Meurice for questioning.'

Perrine reappeared with Claudette's handbag. 'Do you have enough money to get home?' she asked with concern, in spite of herself. Claudette nodded. There was a frisson of fear spiking her backbone, but she tried to remain calm. The soldier indicated to her to open her bag and he put a hand in to feel for a weapon, then he handed it back, all without a change of expression.

Notre Dame looked broody and inky black against the gathering clouds above it. Under the dull sky Paris looked devoid of colour. The people were just as drawn and grey. The soldiers were businesslike, no longer sitting in cafés or standing about laughing; instead they were stopping people randomly on the streets and checking papers. Something was afoot, talk was of the Resistance growing in strength. Everyone was looking at everyone else and wondering.

When the car pulled up outside the Hotel Meurice, the soldier jumped out, walked round and opened her door. She stepped out, wondering what would happen if she just ran now, broke free and disappeared into the crowd. He would shoot her, that is what would happen. Instead, she took a deep breath and walked through the revolving doors.

She had never seen anything like it. Around her, huge gilt-edged mirrors reflected the cool onyx and marble of a place so opulent it could have been Versailles itself. Gold painted salon chairs and large lamps were set beneath a ceiling with magnificent trompe l'oeil ribbons and sashes painted on it.

German officers sat in groups dotted around the great lounge. They were talking with solemnity, no laughing or gesturing. She was told to follow an administrator, a small man with a slick of hair across his forehead, who walked in front of her.

'Where are we going?' she asked him, but he ignored her and marched onwards up the wide staircase and along corridors of endless doors. Françoise tried to memorise the layout. They took a lift to the third floor. Her heart was pulsing, the adrenalin rising in her body made everything sharper, more colourful. She could smell stale food on the man's breath. The administrator opened the door of room fifteen and let her in. 'Wait here,' he told her. She stood holding her handbag in front of her and looked around the room. Unlike the Rue Ercol, this room, even in one of the best hotels in the city, seemed faded and worn.

The pattern on the carpet was bleached out. It had been a beautiful room, but now it was uncared for, used as an office dominated by a large incongruent desk.

The double doors opened, there was a man standing in front of her with a woman in uniform at his side.

It was Rechtstein.

Chapter Forty Three

Coming out of Marie-Celeste's hovel into bright sunshine was a shock. I wanted to round on Gaél and ask him how the government he worked for could let someone live in those conditions. I was seething with anger. Matt's hand slipped into mine, he was reading my thoughts. He thanked Gaél, who didn't seem to think the old woman's plight was such a big problem. Gaél told Matt he was glad to be of service and handed over his business card as if some deal had been done.

'I can't believe it,' I said as he left us. 'I cannot believe an old lady can live in those conditions in the twenty first century.'

'Then I'll take you to Waterloo Bridge in London on a Saturday night,' Matt touched my cheek and pushed a strand of my hair behind my ear. 'It's the same all over the world. And, it's wrong.'

We found a café in a quiet backstreet, four tables lined up outside with crisp white linen and green glass tea-light holders twinkling brightly. 'Sit down here and rest your bones.' Matt pulled out a chair for me. I still felt dirty from Marie-Celeste's place. 'Dinner's on me.' I took a look at the menu; snails, not good, but then there was lobster ravioli and roast lamb, for me that was perfect. The waitress came out with a magnum-sized bottle.

'No need for choosing drink, we have wine special for you.' With a beaming smile, she proceeded to pour us both a white wine; it was crisp, light and delicious. 'See no need for aperitif, and it is for our restaurant,' she said proudly. Matt thanked her, complimenting her and saying her English was very good. She was very pleased with that and sashayed back inside.

We were waiting for our entrées when I said, 'Well, did we get anywhere with this whole Freddy thing?' I tore off some of the homemade walnut bread from the basket in front of me. It was divine.

'I'm very puzzled,' said Matt, taking a sip of the wine. He closed his eyes and let the flavour of it hit his tongue. 'This is beautiful wine, heaven knows what we're paying for it, though.'

An old man passed by, his tilted his Panama hat at us and gave us a kindly smile.

'We know that Freddy and Daniel's mothers worked in a house of ill repute.' Matt's old-fashioned expressions did make me laugh. 'And we know that they both had the same name, which is really weird, but not if they were in hiding or something. I don't know, it sounds strange.'

I looked down at the address Daniel had written down for me at the end of our visit, his father's address in Interlaken. 'They both are linked to Fredrik Keber. Freddy seemed convinced and he's named after him too, but why didn't Keber write back and acknowledge him?'

'I really wish I had talked to Freddy about his past. Poor man, losing your mum in that way and never having contact with a father he so dearly wanted to know. It makes your heart bleed.' I was staring into the middle distance.

'The Cell, the one the maid Favelle belonged to,' said Matt suddenly, 'Google it, see which one. I remember there was a list in one of my history books at school. God, where did that come from? I'd forgotten about it. When we did the Second World War there was a list of Cells of the Resistance. I remember thinking how strange it was they knew information about what was a secret organisation.'

I tried, but there was no reception, Matt had nothing too. Our starters arrived and reluctantly we put the subject to one side while we talked about other things.

When we were back in the hotel I tried Googling on my ipad. I typed in Black Jack Cell and there they were, lists of all the cells and their members, though not in alphabetical order. I ran my eyes over them until they rested on the words Black Jack. I clicked on the blue type and a list of members came up, including Gabin, Vincent Gabin, the doctor. The cell was mainly communist and operated out of a small town in Normandy called Vacily, and there was one female member, Claudette Bourvil.

'That's her, the only woman in the Cell,' said Matt, 'she was in the Resistance using Françoise Favelle as a pseudonym.'

'Are you sure?'

'Yes, it's a simple deductive leap. Think about it, according to Marie-Claire, Françoise Favelle saved Daniel's life after his mother died. She was with the Resistance, and we're pretty certain she was there in the house in Rue Ercol. '

Finally, we had got somewhere, but had we really found Freddy's mother?

Chapter Forty Four

Rechtstein leaned against the front of the writing desk. His breeches splayed out, giving him a strange shape. The boots were highly polished. She thought about the rows of shoes she and Perrine worked their way through on a Thursday morning every week. How she would love to be back there now, she would have happily cleaned a thousand pairs of shoes to not be here in this room.

Rechstein was short, about five seven, his face round and skin freckled. He had dark auburn hair, almost red, cut close to his scalp, and cold grey eyes. He was wearing a wedding ring. She looked straight at him, face to face, keeping herself as calm as possible. Behind her left shoulder was his secretary, her large bosom covered in the grey-green of her jacket, her face stern, unkind.

'So, Miss Favelle,' said Rechtstein slowly, 'do you have any idea why you might be here?'

'No,' she replied, trying to keep her voice neutral. Yves had taught her to say as little as possible and to remain calm. In the small compartment of her handbag there was a lipstick and inside the tube was her cyanide pill.

'You are a maid at Madam Odile's house?' His French was very good, but not impeccable like Keber's.

'Yes, I am.' Claudette could hear the scratching sound of the woman's pen as she wrote notes.

'And your duties include cleaning, some food preparation and looking after the…shall we call them… ladies, am I correct?'

'Yes, that's right.' Claudette felt a knot forming in her throat. She tried to swallow it down. She concentrated hard on Rechstein's face, looking at his lips when he spoke, wondering if anyone kissed them lovingly, trying to conjure up what his wife might look like.

'And, you have come from a farm near Vacily?'

'I have.'

'And Jacques Favelle?'

'He is my brother.'

'And you are very close?'

'No, not really. We have never had a close relationship, he is much older than me.' Suddenly she couldn't remember his birthday. Dates washed through her mind, fading in and out. March 8th, June 20th, May 11th. A spike of nerves rose up through her. She tried not to react, to stand perfectly still.

'Cigarette?'

'No, thank you.'

He lit one for himself, shaking the match so that the flame was extinguished, then he threw it into the waste paper basket. Everything he did was measured, deliberate. The plume of smoke rose up between them as he first inhaled then breathed out. He stood up straight.

'You see,' he said. 'I have a problem, Miss Favelle.' She closed her fingers around the handle of her bag. He took three steps until he was alongside her and leaned in towards her ear. 'Would you like to know what my problem is?' She refused to react, to give him any quarter.

'I shall tell you, shall I? The problem I have is that we can't find a farm in the vicinity of Vacily that has been inhabited by a Family Favelle, not currently, nor, in fact, going back a hundred years.'

Claudette swallowed hard as he walked behind her, the trail of cigarette smoke following him. Her mouth was dry, she needed a glass of water.

'Do you know what we do with people we can't reconcile to our satisfaction, Miss Favelle?'

'No, no, I don't.' Her throat was catching on the words. The smoke and the dryness of her mouth, as she became more and more nervous, were working against her.

'Well, let me tell you that our interrogation procedures are very thorough and gain excellent results, very quickly.'

'I don't understand. I come from a small farm two miles from Vacily, on the road to Fourgieres.' She tried hard to recall the road, the lake to the side of it, the forest, and then there was the smaller dusty lane running up to a farm, the abandoned farm with the old pink stucco barn and an orchard run wild. There used to be a black horse in the meadow.

'The name of the farm?'

'It is known as the Farm Favelle, it has never had another name.'

He withdrew from her and went back to his desk and leaned against it, his eyes resting on her. 'Tell me, Miss Favelle, do you think I am stupid?'

'No. I am telling you the truth.'

'Sadly, I don't believe you. You see, we come across this a great deal, Miss Favelle, people here in Paris who tell us they are something they are not.'

'I am a maid, I work at twelve Rue Ercol, I have nothing more to tell you.'

'Really?'

She tightened the grip on the handle of her bag.

'Put your bag down.'

Claudette lowered it to the floor and stood up, her legs starting to shake. The woman watched, her notepad perched on her lap, pen waiting for more words.

'Perhaps I should explain,' he said, 'people who tell us lies have terrible things done to them, things that would set your teeth on edge. So you can imagine I'm sure that telling us the truth is by far the best option for you.'

She nodded.

'So, shall we start with your name?' She was silent. 'Your real name?' Claudette was looking at the curtains, the roses that someone, very far away from this room, had woven into the fabric.

The cigarette burn was such a shock that she fell away sideways. The pain so sharp and intense that at first she didn't register what he'd done. She put her hand to the side of her neck; the pain was horrendous. She expected the woman to react, to find some water, hand her a wet cloth, but she sat expressionless, her hand poised over the pad.

'Please stand back here,' said Rechtstein, pointing to where Claudette had been standing. He was acting as if nothing had happened. 'Let's start again, shall we?'

She felt a tremble in her body that she couldn't control. 'I come from a small farm near Vacily, on the road to Fourgieres. There is a road out from the village past the lake and through the forest. On the right, after a stone cross, there is a small lane running up to a farm, it has a pink barn.'

'Really? We have your brother in the Rue des Saussaies, do you know what we do there?' Claudette shook her head, she didn't know the road at all. 'We interrogate people to find out what they know. There are meat hooks in the ceilings for our convenience. Actually, your brother is there right now, do you think he is describing the same place?' Claudette felt her breathing quicken. She had no idea how long she could hold out, an hour maybe, certainly no more. Right then it seemed like a very long time. Rechtstein took another drag of the cigarette. He let the smoke out slowly between his teeth then he stepped towards her, his eyes level with hers, and placed a finger on her throat. 'You have a very pretty neck,' he said in a low voice. 'It would be such a shame to mark it.'

The door flew open as if it had been rammed by something heavy. The air in the room changed and the cigarette smoke blew back into Rechtstein's face. He was absolutely taken aback and the secretary leapt up from her chair, spinning round in almost the same movement. The figure in the doorway was tall, his peaked cap and jacket with its red slash of ribbon familiar.

Fritz Keber marched into the room and looked down at Claudette, then up at his colleague. He was very angry. The exchange was in German and Claudette understood none of it. She could only read the expressions on their faces and when Keber turned to the secretary and shouted 'Raus, hier, jetzt bewegen!' she scuttled off, beetle like, into the hallway. Claudette picked up her handbag and wrapped her arms around it protectively.

The exchange was vicious, both men yelling at each other, voices raw. In the end Keber won, and Rechtstein took refuge behind his desk, making it a barrier between them. Keber brought a fist down on it and the small desk lamp crashed to the floor. He turned around, took Claudette by the arm and marched her out. She struggled against it, perceiving that it was the right thing to do. He pushed her through a pair of frosted glass doors and out into another long corridor. Then, without saying anything, he took her up a flight of stairs and unlocked the door to a room at the top.

When he pulled her inside, he kissed her, saying over and over: 'My baby, I'm so sorry, I'm so sorry.' He looked at her wound and kissed her forehead softly. 'My poor girl, you must have been terrified.' He took her to the bathroom and found a facecloth. He ran it under cold water and pressed it against the burn. 'I am so sorry, I can't believe he did that. I can't believe I didn't see it coming.'

He poured some water for her and she gulped it down, she was so grateful. Everything suddenly overcame her and she began to shake, all the time telling herself she could not submit to Fritz Keber, her mind full of warnings, Madam Odile's injuries, the face of the baby boy and the slumped body of Lilia. All of it down to him.

He led her to the bed and sat her down, his arm around her. Under his breath he was speaking German and still mentally arguing with Rechtstein. 'I am so sorry, I should have done something to stop him, he's looking for revenge. I told him I would deal with everything, all the investigations. It is very dangerous for you now. You must leave Paris, preferably tonight.'

'No.'

'I mean it.'

'He's got Jacques,' she said. 'He's being interrogated.'

'No, he hasn't, I told him I was in charge of the house. That was the deal we made, but he is still licking his wounds. He's angry as hell. I am livid, I could kill him myself.'

'What did you say to him in there?' she asked. 'How did you get me out?'

'I'm questioning you now,' he told her, kissing the top of her head and touching the tip of her chin with his forefinger. 'I told him I am in sole charge of the Ercol.'

'I have questions for you,' she said bitterly. Pulling away and still pressing the facecloth to her neck because the pain was intense, she asked; 'How am I supposed to have anything to do with you when you are capable of doing what you did to Madame Odile?'

'What did I do?'

'She came back bruised and bleeding. How can you pretend you do not know?'

'I slapped her face when she spat at me, but she deserved that, she's like a cat when she's angry, unpredictable. I kept her here for a few hours then sent her home, I didn't even question her.'

'You –'

'Bruised and bleeding?'

'Yes.'

'She must have gone somewhere else. Let's face it, she knows the right people to inflict pain on her, I have no doubt of that.'

'You think she got someone to do that to her? She had wounds on her chest.'

'She no doubt enjoyed every minute.' He was watching her expression and he was rewarded with a look of blank horror.

Claudette didn't understand. 'Why would she do that?'

'Because she hates me.'

'I know all about Daniel, I know you have a son. You can't tell me you're not responsible for him and for what you did to Lilia.'

He stood up, walked over to the window and lit a cigarette. He looked out across the Tuileries. The acres of budding trees and early blossoms fell away into the spring sunshine. 'I am responsible,' he said, emphasising the word am. 'I do everything I can for him.'

'Really,' said Claudette flatly. 'Because it doesn't look like it from what I've seen.'

'You can't see the money I am putting away for him, or the endless favours I do for your boss and her lost soul of a sister.'

'You are responsible for Lilia too, you have driven her to drugs!' Claudette was indignant, tired of the lies she was hearing from everyone.

'No, I haven't, she was already on them when I met her.'

'Most whores are, or so I'm told,' said Claudette.

'She wasn't a prostitute then. I met her when I was a student in Paris. I used to go to a restaurant which was quite risqué. I met Madam Odile there and fell in love with her. She didn't return my affection, shall we say, until I moved on to her little sister to make her jealous. And it worked, she couldn't bear it, she made our lives hell and she tried endlessly to wreck our relationship.'

291

'And Lilia?'

'She was a very willing pawn. She hated her sister, loved what it did to her to see us together. Madam Odile is a very spiteful woman. I fell in love with a harpy and a jealous woman for whom revenge is a way of life. I made a stupid student error. My days of freedom and adventure in Paris turned into a nightmare.'

'And Daniel?'

'Lilia made sure she got pregnant, the ultimate way of taunting her sister. I was horrified and yes, I tried to make her get rid of it. You see, by then I knew I felt nothing for either of them.'

'She's so much older than you, what were you doing?'

'Being infatuated. I was young and stupid, I had no experience of women.'

'So, you're telling me none of this was your fault?'

'Of course it was, is, my fault. I've created a mess. That's why I've tried so hard to make amends. I love that little boy, but can you imagine what would happen if people found out he was the son of a Nazi and a prostitute? In Paris, in the middle of this total fuck up of a war?' He turned to her, fixing his eyes on her. 'He'd be dead.'

'So, instead he's in a dark room with a drug addict mother and a silent old lady who stays with him whilst his mother sleeps with a parade of ghastly men.'

'That is how she has it. She is terrified of her clients finding out. What's the attraction of a whore who has your child. How do you explain that to your family and friends when the war's over?'

'You're both protecting your own reputations,' said Claudette bitterly. 'That's what it boils down to.'

'No, Françoise, I'm not. I have no reputation to protect, but she is shielding her business, I understand that.' He returned and sat next to her on the bed. 'Is it still hurting?' he asked.

'It's not so bad.' She lifted the facecloth for him to see. He leaned forward and kissed her on the cheek. 'I'm not sure who to believe about all this,' she said.

'Trust the one who loves you,' he whispered.

'I dare not trust anyone.' She leant away from him. 'I have never been so frightened in my life, everyone is telling me different things.'

'Make love to me,' he said, simply, with no air of authority. She leaned back into him, and placed her hand on his cheek.

'What have they done to you? And what have you done, as a soldier?'

'Terrible things.'

'Like?'

'No soldier will tell you that. We live with it if we can and we'll die with it, too. You'll say what I've done is horrendous, but it's only what others have done too. We have been following orders. It will be with my nightmares that I pay the price.'

'Have you been involved with the exportations?'

'In a way, but not directly. I have been involved in strategy but not implementation. But that doesn't mean I haven't carried out dreadful acts. Killing anyone is evil and I've done that, many times, but I no longer believe any of this is right. At the beginning we all did, you wouldn't have found a single person in our country who spoke out against Hitler. He took Germany from the gutter to glory,

Austria with it. You have to imagine how that feels, to have a chance at a new magnificent future, to feel as a nation that you have some self-respect at last.'

'But you were forced into it,' said Claudette

'I was, I didn't want to fight. I was an engineer, a planner, a person who builds futures. The last thing I wanted was to fight, but there was no choice.' He put his hand over hers. She looked at the hairs on the back of it, the strength in his fingers. She turned her hand over and clutched his.

'I think I understand. We're none of us who we were.'

'The impetus to follow Hitler has consumed us all and I'll never understand the inertia of our church in all of this. It has stood by and let it happen, they only had to say no, they could have stopped it from the very beginning. Catholics should have had the freedom to follow their conscience, but they do what their priests tell them to and those priests have been weak and cowardly.'

'And hundreds of priests are fighting with us, working against the Nazis' said Claudette, feeling bruised by his comment.

'But not the Pope, and I am sure when the war is over, whichever way the world is afterwards, the Pope will bend with the wind. That is why I am so tired, so ready for it all to end. Where is the opposition, the force against evil? How do we not learn from the likes of Burke? Where are the good men?'

'They're coming, the Allies are gaining strength.' Claudette lay back on the bed, her body relieved to be lying down. The burn on her neck was throbbing. He lay next to her leaning on one elbow.

'Can I make love to you now?'

She nodded and he kissed her, pressing his mouth on top of hers. He undid his jacket and pulled it off. It slid to the floor where nothing it represented meant anything, as she took off her black blouse. They were both naked, her body lithe, his muscular. She arched up to him giving herself to him completely. He kissed her over and over, tasting her as if she were a rare delicacy. He pressed down on her, the weight of him anchoring her to the bed as she held his face in her hands. Claudette stared into his eyes and she saw what she had sought her whole life in them. She stretched out her arms, feeling the edges of the bed, the silk of the stitches in the eiderdown under her palms. He reached out a hand and took hold of hers and they gripped together tightly.

'I love you, Françoise,' he whispered in her ear.

'I love you, Fritz, so very much.'

He entered her and she felt the urgency of him, the physical need for her. She closed her legs around his back and grasped his neck, knowing that soon she would have to let him go, that a future was impossible, that they were only in the now.

They lay together, arms around each other for an hour.

'I am not Françoise, I am called Claudette, Claudette Bourvil.'

He raised his head from the pillow as if he were looking at her for the first time. 'You are wanted by the Gestapo, I have a list with your name on it!' His eyes were wide; 'I had no idea who you were and they have no idea where you are, and the last place they will think of is a Bordello. Stay there, keep a really low profile and I'll make sure you're safe. For me, promise me you will stay safe.'

'I have been charged with looking after Daniel. I will be in his room with him from now on.'

A broad smile lit up his face. 'Thank you, thank you so much.' He looked down on her, eyes loving and warm. 'When this shit is over I will take you both away, make a new life for us. We will go to Switzerland and I will love you for the rest of my life. Uncomplicated lives for us, that's what I dream of.' Her heart swam with a pleasure she had never felt before in her life, a feeling of promise. She kissed him and he rolled onto her, his skin pressed against hers. 'And any child we have together will be Daniel's brother or sister.'

They made love again and then they lay together in his bed. She wrapped her leg around his, her head against his upper arm.

'I should get you back, they'll be worried about you.'

He dressed and became the Nazi she couldn't reconcile him with, the other side of him. While she dressed he watched her, taking in everything about her, then he walked to the desk and pulled open a drawer. He lifted out a manila folder and flipped it open. There were two typewritten sheets on the top. He picked them up and folded them carefully, making the edges match each other. 'Put these in your bag, and give them to your contact.' She glanced at them, they were duplicate sheets of a typewritten page, the wording was German. 'And do not tell them where you got them, not even which part of Paris. Promise me, my love.' She nodded and slipped the papers inside her bag.

He walked her through the hotel. No one looked as

she passed men and women busy with plots and plans, their work in crushing the French unceasing. His driver was waiting, reliable discretion on his face. Keber helped her into the car and she was driven away. He showed no expression as he turned back to the hotel door. Two soldiers walking towards him saluted him with 'Heil Hitler' and the outstretched arms of a Nazi salute.

Chapter Forty Five

We were sitting outside a café in a small village perché called Giréte. It skirted the steep side of a lone hill, a zigzag of roads leading up to it. It was the only high ground for miles around. I was looking away from it at the vast rolling fields of softly undulating land punctuated only by clumps of trees here and there. Matt had been drawn in by the photographer's need to get "amazing shots" and the old chateau on the top was beautiful, sitting on an outcrop of the cliff, a sheer drop from its western side.

The croissant I had just eaten was the softest and most beautiful I had tasted in my life. The lady was sweet too. She had strong forearms, broad hips and a round red face. She told me she had made the croissants herself as her mother had done before her.

Matt left me sitting at the table drinking fresh coffee in the sunshine while he walked further up to the chateau and began sizing up shots. I pulled out my phone and tapped Hat's name in my contacts. 'Hi Hat, it's me, Connie, in France.'

'Are you okay?' her voice was concerned. 'Shouldn't you be back by now, Mr C's going to start panicking!'

'Yes, I'm fine, tell Mr C I'll be home tonight. I just wanted to tell you that we might be on to Freddy's mum. We think she was with the Resistance, can you believe it?' I was suddenly brimming over with excitement. 'We're going to her home town now, we found out she worked for a secret cell in Paris.'

'Really?'

'And she was involved with a German, Fritz Keber, Fredrik. He was Daniel's father and Freddy must have believed that he was his son too. That's who he was writing to, but he never heard back. Poor Freddy.'

'And how did you find all this out?'

'It sort of all fell together in a weird way,' I replied. 'We started looking and the answers just cropped up – it's been amazing, really. Matt worked it out in the end. I'll tell you more when we get home, we're going to a place called Vacily now.'

'Good luck,' she said. 'Be good…oh, and talking of which, how are things with Matt?'

'Very good, Hat, very good.' I looked up to see him walking down the road towards me with a bounce in his step and a broad grin on his face. 'I'll see you later, take care.'

'I've worked it out,' he said brightly. 'Daniel said Fritz was madly in love with his mother, which is obviously true, because they had him. However, I think he was also having an affair with Freddy's mother, Claudette. She was working under cover under an assumed name for the Resistance, possibly as a prostitute.'

'Really, a prostitute and not a maid?'

'Either, or, but they were both there in the whorehouse. Two Madeléines.' Matt was putting his camera back in his bag.

'What about if Daniel's mum was the madam?' I suggested.

'No, that was another name, Odette, Odile. Odile.'

'But something here is ringing true, right?'

'It is,' said Matt. 'It's only that neither of us is with the CID.'

We drove to Vacily through the open plains of Normandy. Having missed the right turn because we were laughing so much, we took the next one down a long straight road, which took us through a forest. The sun was beating down on us and the road ahead was alternating stripes of light then shadow as we drove along it.

We passed a lake and then a left turn as the countryside receded. Then began the industrial park and a row of modern bungalows, cream walls and brown roofs. The town was quite modern with a massive SuperU supermarket and car wash, the car park half full. We pulled into a long layby, behind a Peugeot, to get our bearings.

'I can't see any older buildings at all.' Matt was peering round the car in front, 'there's a church at the end, though.'

'Try there first,' I said. 'The church will be in the oldest part of town.'

We pulled out and drove slowly along the long main street, only one or two cars passed us going the other way. The church was very pretty, it had a pink tower just visible above the yew tree hedge around it.

The old gate creaked as I opened it. The graveyard fell away from us and a line of white wooden crosses arranged along the far wall were visible between the gravestones. Inside we could hear the sound of people; a pushchair was folded and leaning against the door. Across the road was a small market square dominated by a tall fountain, water sprayed from three sides of it. The plaque on the side facing us was glinting in the sun. There was a list of eight names and Claudette Bourvil was at the bottom.

'It says "In memory of those in The Resistance from Vacily who fought for a free France", said Matt. 'We've found her.'

It seemed the right thing to do to stay quiet for a minute. I would have liked to lay some flowers for Freddy, but there were no shops, only a small café on the corner. There was no one under the awning outside, but the tables were all laid with peach coloured napkins on white plates as if customers were expected. I reached out and squeezed Matt's hand.

'Lunch?' he asked and I nodded. I felt very solemn and quiet as we walked across the square and sat at a small corner table. It was the oldest part of the village, a couple of the houses had the familiar and quite lovely organic shapes of buildings that had morphed over time. The other side of the square was a modern building, the Mairie.

The proprietor had a warm smile, he shook our hands and asked if we'd like to eat. The menus were in old French and an ornate typeface, so Matt went through them for me. We chose chicken in a white wine and mushroom sauce.

'What an amazing thing if we have found Freddy's mum with a bit of detective work, it's…well…amazing,' said Matt as he sipped his drink. I loved the way he sank deep into his quiet moments, the way he absorbed everything around him. He would fit in anywhere.

'But we haven't worked it all out, do you think we ever will?'

'No, but what a story. Freddy's mum worked for the Resistance. She was a heroine.'

'A murdered heroine.' We both sat, sipping an iced tea as a flock of doves landed on the fountain, seven white and one pied. They tipped their tails up as they drank. 'I wonder if there is anything in the village about the Resistance, a library or museum.'

'I doubt it,' said Matt. 'It feels a very empty non-touristy place.'

When the proprietor returned with our lunch Matt asked him, but there wasn't anything, but he said there was another, similar plaque in the church.

Our meal was beautiful, delicate flavours danced on my tongue. As we finished, the congregation began to filter out of the church and onto the square, a handful walked towards us and took seats alongside, nodding and smiling as they did so. The others broke into smaller groups and then ones and twos and disappeared along the street.

We went halves on lunch and Matt took my hand as we walked back to the church. There was an old-fashioned Fiat parked by the gate, a sun-bleached reddy orange colour. The coolness of the church interior was wonderful after sitting in the sun. It was small, the wooden pews each side of the aisle would take four people at a squeeze, and were charmingly rustic. The interior walls were whitewashed, the windows leaded with plain glass. At the front was an altar with a mural behind it of the village and the various residents, like the blacksmith, the butcher and the priest, walking along the winding path to the church. It was naïve in style and had once been colourful, but the hues and shades of paint had mellowed over time, giving it an ethereal quality. In some places the plaster had cracked and fallen away to reveal patches of stone.

On the wall opposite the small pulpit was a stone plaque with the same list of names, including Claudette's at the bottom. In a scroll over the top, the words "La Résistance Française de la Seconde Guerre Mondiale" were inscribed. 'There's Vincent Gabin,' said Matt, pointing to the name halfway down, 'the young doctor who was killed by the Nazis.'

'May I help you?' The priest took us completely by surprise and he was speaking English.

'Oh yes, sorry,' I said, as if we were doing something wrong and had been caught out. 'We're just looking for a particular person, Claudette Bourvil. She was a member of the Resistance and came from Vacily.'

'Yes, that's right,' said the priest. He was probably a bit older than us, with curly brown hair and brown eyes, his face earnest, openly willing to be helpful. 'She was instrumental in the rise of the Resistance in Paris in the latter stages of the war. She passed on important documents from the German High Command, risking her life in the process.'

'She worked in a house of ill repute and spied on the Germans,' said Matt, using another colloquial phrase that made my stomach turn a little loop of joy.

'Really, I didn't know that?' said the priest, looking the tiniest bit uncomfortable, I thought.

'Yes, we've been told she was a maid, though it seems she wasn't very popular in the house itself.' Matt added.

'And if she is the person we are looking for, we've found out she was murdered, but we have no idea where or how or by whom,' I told him.

'Well, I know she was murdered here,' he said, 'just

behind what was the washhouse. There's a small copse of trees – she was shot there. The village was profoundly upset by it all. You see, they had originally thought she was a collaborator, and she had not been here to put her side of the story. I think I'm right in saying she didn't come back here after the war, instead she went to England. That had fuelled their suspicions, the truth was only established years later.'

'So did she come back here?'

'Yes, she was looking for someone. I don't know who and of course the town had been razed to the ground during the Normandy Landings, so lots of people had died, including her parents. The Germans fled, but they made sure that they wrecked the village before they went. They detonated explosives everywhere, the only places they left standing were this church and a couple of buildings over the road. They had orders to leave a scorched earth behind them, as it's called these days. Of course, famously, Hitler had ordered Paris to be obliterated. He said; "The city must not fall into the enemy's hand except lying in complete debris." And it is said that his General von Choltitz disobeyed this order because he realised it was all over and Hitler was insane. In truth, it was the Parisians that made sure it didn't happen. Von Choltitz had laid waste to Sebastopol and Rotterdam and he had sent millions of Jewish people to their deaths, so he was no saint.'

'How do you speak such amazing English?' I asked him. There was barely a trace of a French accent. He smiled and seemed really grateful for the compliment.

'Thank you, that's kind. I went to Cambridge to study for my degree and then I answered my calling to become a priest. I am what you call a rarity, but my father was an academic and I was expected to follow in his footsteps.'

'And was the murderer ever found?' I asked.

'No, he or she got away with it as far as I know, but I'm not the person to ask, it was a very long time ago. You need to talk to my good friend Samuel, he will be able to fill you in much more than I can. His mother knew Claudette Bourvil.'

'Is he likely to be around today? We're travelling home this evening from Calais.'

'Oh yes, in fact you probably just walked past him. He's been in church this morning and he'll be at the café across the road having lunch with his family. I'll take you across to meet him.' With that, he bowed his head to the altar then turned and walked down the aisle, placing the pile of books he was holding on a table by the door.

'I'm Father Patrice, by the way.' He shook us both by the hand. 'How lovely to think someone remembers Claudette Bourvil. So many of those amazing people died under torture or were executed, it befalls us all to remember their bravery.'

'I knew her son, Freddy. Fredrik March.' I told him

'The playwright?'

'Yes, that's him.'

'I studied his work at university, a marvellous talent.'

'He was, and not mainstream, it's interesting that you knew of him,' I said. 'What were you studying?'

'English and Theology,' he replied. 'His plays are very widely regarded in both spheres, as you can imagine. I wrote my thesis on "The Final Solution"' replied Father Mathieu, 'but I had no idea Fredrik March was Claudette

Bourvil's son. That really has surprised me, I wonder if Samuel knows anything about that?'

We crossed the main street and walked back towards the café, which was now busy and full of locals enjoying a long Sunday lunch. A few of them broke off conversations as we approached, but then carried on chatting. Children and seniors alike were sitting side-by-side, lots of them eating the chicken dish we'd enjoyed.

'Samuel,' said Father Patrice, resting his hand on the back of an elderly gentleman with a shock of white hair. 'Ces personnes sont de l'Angleterre, ils savaient le fils de Claudette Bourvil, ça vous dérange de leur parler une minute?'

Samuel stood up, pulling his napkin out of his collar, and shook both our hands. His wife smiled up at us, she had the prettiest face with bobbed hair and green eyes. 'Hello,' he said, waving a hand at two empty chairs at the table. 'Asseyez-vous s'il vous plaît.' He introduced us to his wife, Sylvie, and she shook our hands.

We sat down and Father Patrice said something in French to Samuel and then turning to us, he said; 'I hope you find your answers, it was lovely to meet you.' He walked away and climbed into the small Fiat by the church gates.

Matt began talking and Samuel was listening intently, I couldn't follow it. My mind wandered and I found myself looking at the fountain and the plaque with Freddy's mum's name on it and I wondered if he knew about her activities in France. Somehow I doubted it and that I found very sad.

Chapter Forty Six

'Lilia is dead.' Jacques stood in the kitchen, his back to the stairs. 'She has killed herself.' There was silence. Madam F. stood with her mouth open, Marie placed a thin hand to her mouth and Perrine's eyes were wide with shock. It was Claudette, making lunch for Daniel, who asked how she had done it. 'She's in the bath, she slashed her wrists. An ambulance has been sent for and then I am to swill it all down like it's a slaughterhouse at closing time. There is blood everywhere.' He looked sick to the stomach.

'It's been a long time coming,' said Madam F. with a sigh as she turned to sit down at the table. 'Poor lost soul.'

'Someone will have to tell Keber,' said Perrine. All eyes turned to Claudette, but it was Jacques who spoke. 'Madam Odile is sending him a message now.'

Claudette took the tray of lunch up to the fifth floor. The other ladies were huddled together in the bar, talking in hushed whispers. They were shadows of their former selves. They didn't even acknowledge Claudette as she passed by.

Daniel was awake in his cot. His eyes, big and brown, expanded with joy when he saw her. As she picked him up he hugged her and she felt him fit against her body in the now familiar way. 'Hello, beautiful,' she said, kissing his face. 'I'm afraid there is not very much for lunch and no apple. The kitchen's not as fully stocked as it once was, so it's boring food today.' She changed his nappy and sang to him, exactly as her mother had done to her baby brother all those years ago.

She spoon fed him and told him he was beautiful again, and that his mummy, wherever she was now, was free of her pain and would be looking after him from heaven. He giggled, waving his arm at her and said, 'Mama.'

'That's right, your Mama,' she said. 'She's gone away, but she will always love you.' Out of the blue a tear pricked her eye. She blinked it back, refusing to cry in front of the child. Her mind was fixed on Lilia and the first time they'd met, the beauty and unselfconsciousness of her naked body. Last summer the house had been terrifying, the prospect of working amongst prostitutes equally so. Now it was work-a-day, seeing them in their fine lingerie or completely naked moving between rooms, watching them entertaining the soldiers. She, just like Perrine, had become immune.

Nowadays it was different. The officers were being moved out of the city, the soldiers remaining were fewer in number. Barricades had been erected on every street. There was debris and rubbish everywhere. Last week a horse had collapsed between the shafts outside the house and before it was properly dead, hoards of people descended on it, tearing it apart, until every part of it was gone. That evening they had eaten it too, because Jacques had been out there with a meat cleaver.

That evening Madame Odile came upstairs to see Daniel. Her face was drawn and white, she looked very much older. She took the little boy in her arms, but he leaned away and looked for Claudette who pressed the tips of her fingers against his to reassure him.

'You have done well with little Daniel,' said Madam Odile. 'I am very grateful. I am sure Lilia knew he was being well looked after, even at the end.' It was clear she had been crying, her eyes were red and puffy. 'I would like you to take him down to her room and keep him in there. I will have Jacques put a private sign on the door, barring entry. Use her clothes and shoes if you want to, you are the same size, you even look similar with your hair that colour.'

Claudette nodded. 'I'll take his cot down and his things tomorrow,' she said. 'I think it's good that he will be amongst her belongings.' Madam Odile pressed her face against Daniel's and stood silently for a long while. Claudette gathered up some toys and put them away in the white box she had taken from Eva's room.

'I tried very hard to do what was right,' said Madam Odile, swaying to and fro. 'Some might say I got it wrong, but I did my best.'

'I know,' said Claudette.

'I think it will soon be over now,' she said. 'I am travelling to Reims tomorrow to take care of a family matter. I will be back next week. Do you have your papers?'

'Yes,'

'Then make sure they are safe.' Claudette looked at her, puzzled. 'In the next few weeks I think everything will fall apart, make sure you can be identified at all costs.' Claudette nodded and with that Madam Odile kissed Daniel and handed her back the baby. 'Take care of him for me.'

Claudette awoke in Lilia's bed, beside her Daniel was asleep in his cot, a small grey rabbit tucked under his arm. The ladies had all been to see him and brought him things. Nannette sat him on her knee and handed him the little rabbit. 'It was mine, little one, when I was a small girl, smaller than you.' He took it and sucked its tiny ear.

'The Allies are almost here.' Claudette told her. 'It was on the radio this morning, we have only a few weeks until we are all free.'

'The clients are few and far between now,' said Nanette. 'Have you seen Keber recently?'

'No, Madame called to tell him about Lilia and they said he had left Paris,' said Claudette. 'But he will come back.'

'You love him, don't you?' said Nannette. She was stroking the top of Daniel's head. 'And his little boy.'

'I do.'

'Lilia would be pleased, I just know it, she used to talk to me about it. She hated him, you know, he only had eyes for her sister.'

'You knew all about it?'

'Yes, she used to confide in me. She told me that he was in love with her sister and she was madly jealous of them. Madam Odile could have had him like that.' She flicked her fingers making Daniel jump reflexively. 'But she wanted better and more powerful men to make true her ambitions.'

'Which is strange, because he's been in charge of her precious house for nearly four months,' said Claudette.

'Don't tell anyone, but Bella and Sophie are leaving tomorrow. One of Bella's clients has got her two German passports and she has been teaching Sophie German for months. They are scared that there will be retributions against us.'

'What do you think?'

'I think we'll be safe behind these walls and when it's over the important Frenchmen, our old clients, will drift back again and it will all be forgotten.' Claudette felt a grip of tension in her body. She was thinking of Keber; where had he gone and when would he be back for her?

He had visited less and less frequently, each time making love to her and each time he visited he looked less certain, less sure of himself. On his last visit he sat on the end of the bed. His uniform, once so neat and clean, was tired and creased, his socks had holes in the toes. He had his head in his hands. 'This is going badly. General von Stoltitz is in charge, he has been told by Hitler to leave Paris a ruin. There are plans to detonate charges all over the city when we withdraw. The Resistance is strong, they mowed down a unit of my men in the Champs Elysees last week.'

'What will happen to you?'

'If I'm not killed I'll make it back to Germany, then on to Interlaken. My family has a small house there, we used it for holidays when I was a boy. I will make it there and then I will contact you. Stay here, keep Daniel safe for me. No one will bother with a bordello, the fight will be taken to the streets, arm-to-arm combat, if necessary. Wait for me to get in touch, I will contact you as soon as I can. I will send for you, but don't leave Paris, promise me.'

'Promise me you'll send for me?'

'I promise.' He pulled on his boots and held each side of her face with his hands. 'I love you.'

Claudette looked at Daniel as he began to wake up, she could see Keber's face in his. He greeted her with a big smile and said, 'Mama.'

Chapter Forty Seven

Matt seemed to listen for some time to what Samuel said before translating for me, which was irritating. Samuel's wife smiled at me sweetly as we both listened. Eventually, Matt turned to me and said, 'Samuel's parents knew Claudette, they were at school together and his father led the network. He was called Yves and she was Giselle. The Cell operated out of Vacily, but some of them went to Paris, including Claudette. She didn't come back straight after the war, it was seven years later, she was looking for Yves. She wrote to her friend in the village asking to be told when he returned.'

'Where had he gone?' I asked. Matt relayed my question.

The answer was that he had gone looking for his wife. 'She was pregnant with Samuel and as the wife of a wanted Resistance Fighter she was in real danger of arrest. She was trying to reach her parent's house in the Auvergne, they had a farm high in the hills and her mother was a nurse. She never arrived and Yves went to find out what had happened to her. The Vichy Police had arrested her and used her as bait. Yves unwittingly walked right into the trap, they imprisoned and tortured him. The Resistance rescued him when he was being transferred to a prison camp and he was able to get Giselle and Samuel's brother, Louis, to the Auvergne.'

'So why did Claudette come back to Vacily?' I asked.

'She wanted to see Yves, to connect with him again. Samuel says they were very close and also she needed to visit her parents' graves. They were killed when the Allies invaded. She never saw them again after she left for Paris.' Matt translated again for me.

'When did they come back, Samuel's family?'

'Five years after the war finished. Samuel's father was very seriously injured during the war when he was tortured, and it had made him very nervy and unsettled for a long time.'

'What happened to Claudette?'

Samuel must have guessed what I was asking, his eyes dipped and his wife stopped smiling. 'She was shot by a tramp. No one knew anything about it, she was found in the land behind the washhouse. It was very upsetting for the village and doubly so because of course, after all, she was a war heroine, a terrible end.'

'So no-one was brought to account?'

'Seems not,' said Matt. Samuel and his wife looked very upset and he kept apologising. Matt asked a question and they both shook their heads. The murder had not been in the national media. There had been a lot of lawlessness after the war, people tried to hide as much as they could. The tramp was never found, though he was seen around the town from time to time for years after the war.

'No wonder Freddy couldn't get over what had happened to her,' I said. 'What a dreadful thing, poor thing.' I felt desperately sad for them both, Claudette and Freddy. 'Does he know why she used the name Madeléine March?'

314

Matt asked the question but Samuel shook his head.

'I suspect that's all there is to know,' said Matt. 'She died here and Freddy was orphaned, so he tried desperately to connect with his Dad. Poor lad. Samuel began talking, waving his hands excitedly. Matt cocked his head to one side like a dog trying to understand as the French was coming thick and fast. 'It seems that Samuel's brother, Louis, lives in London and he has something he's been holding onto for Freddy. He didn't know how to get in touch with him but, naturally, he's been looking for Claudette Bourvil's son.'

'Does he have any idea what it is?'

'Some personal effects, I think, and a letter, she had given it to Yves.'

'We need to get hold of whatever they are,' I told Matt with urgency, 'I need to bring this all together for Freddy.' Matt was already typing Louis' address and phone number into his phone.

Chapter Forty Eight

There was a barricade at the end of the road. When Claudette stepped out to look she realised the German guard posted outside had gone. Eva's body had been removed weeks before, but the piece of red and gold cloth still lay against the kerbside black with street dirt, a fading memory of her.

Bella and Sophie had been picked up the day before by a German car, their hats perched on the backs of their heads, gloved hands waving goodbye. Claudette watched them go from Lilia's bedroom; it was the last time she saw a German come near the house.

She took Daniel down to the kitchen and sat him on the rag rug in front of the fire. Jacques was sitting reading a notice from the Collaboration. 'Shits, all of them,' he was saying, shaking his head. 'Even now they are trying to convince us to fight with the Germans.'

'I can't believe it,' said Claudette.

'The Resistance is gathering strength and about to be boosted by the French Forces. The problem is we have no arms, but there are still going to be huge repercussions. We have the Boches on the back foot, where we want them running scared.'

'Madame Odile is not back,' said Claudette, 'Do you think she'd desert us?'

'No, I trust her and I know she has her life invested in

this place. I can tell you with certainty that she'll be back. But she has to be back soon because the train workers are going on strike. I can't see her hitching a ride from Reims on the back of a donkey cart.'

'I'd be surprised if there was a donkey still alive in Northern France. Everything has been eaten.'

'Talking of which, Madam F. has gone out looking for food, there is hardly anything left to eat.' Jacques lit a cigarette, 'And my stomach thinks my throat is cut.'

'And Perrine?'

'I haven't seen her since yesterday. I have my doubts she'll return, everyone is being called on to build barricades.'

'Is Marie around?'

Jacques raised his eyes towards the ceiling. 'She's in bed, not well. I suspect she's hungry too.'

'You once told me not to trust her, why?' Claudette asked.

'Her father has been working with the Vichy Government all this time. I doubt that if she spies for him, but you never know.'

'The papers I gave you, the ones Keber passed to me, did you hear anything?'

'They were the minutes of a meeting outlining plans to destroy Paris on Hitler's orders. The new general in charge has been tasked with obliterating the city if the Boches have to capitulate. Now, it's down to us to protect her and to try to convince him otherwise.'

'And is it going well?'

'Too early to say, but the Allies are within striking distance.'

There was a sound of the door slamming upstairs and they both looked up. The footsteps were familiar, it was Madame Odile. She looked tired. Her hair was done in a simple plait as if she had had no time to do anything to it, her lipstick had worn off, leaving a red rim around her lips.

'It is like a living hell out there, debris and barricades everywhere, people fighting each other, one Parisian pitted against another. The Germans have executed Resistance members in the street, now they plan to starve us to death.'

'Would you like some tea?' asked Claudette. 'We have a bit left.'

'Thank you, Françoise, I am exhausted. Are there any clients in?'

'We have had no one for days, not since you left,' said Claudette. She passed Daniel the last biscuit. He sat sucking on it, looking up at Madame Odile. She took a seat and rested her hand against his cheek. 'And, something else, Bella and Sophie have left.' Madame Odile shrugged her shoulders, she was resigned to hearing such news.

'The sentry has gone, that's good news' said Jacques quickly.

'Does that mean Keber has gone too?' said Madame Odile, fixing her eyes on Claudette.

'I think so,' she said, handing the tea to her boss.

'I can't keep you here, either of you,' she said flatly. 'And I can't pay you, that's the truth. I can keep you safe behind these walls, I think, but I won't make promises I can't keep.'

'I have to stay,' said Claudette. 'This is where Fritz can find me afterwards.'

'You don't have to stay, I can pass any messages to you,' Madame Odile suggested, but one look into her eyes assured Claudette that no messages would find her.

'I'll stay, and look after Daniel for you,' she said, picking up the little boy.

'I'll stay too,' said Jacques. 'But I might need to go at any minute, it depends on what is happening.'

'Well, not me!' exclaimed Madame F, who had appeared without anyone noticing. She held up a brace of ragged and bloody pigeons. 'This is all I could get in the whole of the city, people are eating rats.' She laid the birds on the table. Daniel stretched out to touch them, nearly unbalancing Claudette. 'And I bought them from a little boy. I'm sorry everyone, Madame, but I cannot stay here any longer.'

'What do we do now?' asked Jacques as Madam F bustled away to pack her bags. She was talking to herself about how everyone would starve to death before the Allies reached the city.

'I have no idea,' said Madame Odile. 'I really have no idea.'

Chapter Forty Nine

Hat was sitting beside me on the window seat, her hands wrapped around a mug of tea. The house had been sold to a builder who had bought it to convert into flats. The furniture had all gone, and we were waiting for the estate agent to arrive so that we could sign over the key.

'I am so happy about you and Matt, at least something good has come from all this, and the story is intriguing too, but Freddy's poor mum – no wonder he couldn't think about it, he had nightmares about her right until the end, you know. I often had to go to him in the night. It must have been a random act, someone just killed her in an opportune moment, is that what you think now?'

I nodded. 'Looks like it.'

'Have you contacted Louis?'

'I've left a message and written to him but he hasn't come back to us, I've told him everything I know.'

'And what now?' said Hat. 'Have you got work?'

'I'm doing bits and bobs for Matt, and a company in Oxford wants a website, so I'm alright.' I felt downbeat, something felt wrong, but nothing I could verbalise.

'Thanks for everything,' She reached across and squeezed my hand. 'I simply couldn't have managed without you, or Matt, for that matter, you've both been brilliant.'

'When are you off?' I asked. Losing her to Brighton was so hard.

'At three. Jon and I are having lunch with some friends from Banbury, in Elwell, and then I'm off.'

'So this is goodbye?'

'I'm afraid, finally, it is.'

I felt the emotion gushing up inside me, it was uncontrollable. I began to cry. Hat leapt up and pulled me to her. 'Oh honey, don't cry, you can come and visit, please don't, you'll set me off.' She hugged me tightly. 'I promise everything will work out, you and Matt, your work, it's just you've become too involved with Freddy's story.'

'I feel like I've met his mother, seen what she went through, only to hear that she died like that, and so young.' I sniffed.

'Most of those poor people died a horrible death, my love, there's nothing we can do for them now except appreciate and remember what they did.' Hat kissed the top of my head. 'Come on, cheer up.'

'I'm not sure about Matt,' I blurted, completely out of the blue. 'I can't tell you what it is but I don't feel right.'

Hat's eyes widened with surprise, just when she thought it was all going so well for me. I felt I'd let her down when she said, 'Tell me your kidding.' She even sounded a little irritated.

'The thing is I met this lovely man, Theo, in France. I can't get him out of my mind. His flat, his books, his gentleness, I want someone like him and yet Matt is so lovely.'

'Do you know what?' she said, pouring us both another cup of tea from Freddy's old chipped teapot. 'I think you haven't had time to get to know each other, and you come with built in reservations, don't forget. You've been so wrapped up in Claudette and what has gone before, you need to start again, date in the conventional way. Take it from there.'

'I'll miss you, Hat,' I said. 'And your wise words.'

'Well, do come and see me soon.' I understood finally that she was ready to go, she wanted to move on.

The doorbell whirred in its usual staccato way and the sound echoed through Freddy's house for the last time.

Chapter Fifty

Claudette was sleeping with Daniel, he had tucked himself between her body and her arm. A strip of grey light filtered through the gap between the curtains, cutting a slice across the bedroom. She slid out of bed and went to wash her face, but the water puttered from the tap and died. They had all been worrying about this and now it had happened. There was a low growl in her stomach; it was hunger, she hadn't eaten for twenty-four hours straight, and now there was no water being fed to the house.

There was a knock on the door, she pulled on a silk robe and opened it. 'The Allies have arrived, they have marched on Paris,' said Jacques excitedly. 'De Gaulle is about to march down the Champs Élysées, come and see!'

'No, I can't leave Daniel alone and it would be too much for him to go out.' She turned to look at the little boy who was awake and watching them both.

'Fair enough,' said Jacques. 'But it's a day we'll all remember. When I'm out I'm going to try to get us some food.'

'I would eat a rat,' she told him. 'I've never been so hungry in my life.'

She put on the blue dress Nannette had given her and dressed Daniel in a little sailor suit Madam Odile had bought him in Reims. The ladies were in the salon, they were complaining about being hungry, and how were they supposed to make any money now? Babette held out her hands to Daniel and he toddled towards her. 'Look who's walking! Bless him, he's looking really happy at last.' She swept him up into her arms. Claudette watched her, Babette looked happy too amid all the chaos, the hunger and the uncertainty.

'Are you leaving?' Freya asked.

'No, I'm looking after Daniel, for Lilia,' Claudette replied.

'And of course no doubt you're waiting for the return of your Boche.' Pollo was sitting on the sofa, her hair thin and unwashed, the chestnut colour now almost all a dusty pink. Hair dye had not been available for weeks. Claudette didn't acknowledge her. 'He won't come back,' Pollo said. 'He will be in Berlin by now, shagging German whores.'

Claudette bit her lip. 'He won't,' she said. 'He'll come back for me.'

'Yes darling, you keep telling yourself that,' Pollo scoffed. 'They'll all come back and marry us and we'll all have lovely blue eyed babies called Herman and Gelda.' They all laughed.

'I bet Bella's pregnant already,' laughed Freya. 'By two different men, as well!' They roared laughing and Claudette couldn't help but join in with them, because where Bella was concerned anything was possible.

'When will we get food?' asked Monique. 'I'm going to die if we don't get fed soon.'

'Jacques has gone to find something. He says de Gaulle is marching down the Champs Élysées right now, the Germans are gone.'

'Really?' said Babette. 'Shouldn't we go and watch?'

'It wouldn't be safe,' said Claudette.

'It's over now though, isn't it?' said Monique. 'I mean the Boches are gone, we can go back to how it was before, can't we?'

'In your dreams, honey,' said Pollo. 'We're called Horizontal Collaborators, we have a lot to fear out there.' There was a long silence, Babette chewed on her lip, they all looked frightened. 'Madame Odile will know what to do, we just have to wait, she has all the right contacts. It'll be all right.'

Daniel waddled towards Claudette and held out his arms to be picked up. She hugged him, he was lighter and much thinner, she had run out of food for him too.

Jacques was back later that day brimming over with excitement. 'It's over, the Americans are here and the French army is with them, marching in the same uniforms, can you believe it? They have brought food too.' He held up a bag of tins. 'Hot Dogs and Bully Beef, and coffee!'

'We need to tell the ladies, they are all starving.' Claudette looked through the cans thinking how unappetising everything looked in spite of her being so hungry.

'Feed Daniel first, make sure he's all right, and then we'll share it out.' Jacques patted the little boy on the head. 'Poor little sod.'

It was days later, just after Madame Odile had left the house to meet with a friend, that they came. The hammering on the door could be heard from Lilia's room. Claudette was lying on the floor with Daniel, they were playing with

Indian ornaments from the shelves. She leapt up and looked out of the window. There were people in the street looking up at her. They were chanting 'Whores, whores, whores.'

Below, the window in Eva's room opened and Jacques leaned out with his rifle pointing down at the door. 'Away, all of you, or I will shoot!'

'Shoot your own?' One of the men in a grey cap shouted up to him. 'Traitor!' and he started to barge the front door with his shoulder. Claudette grabbed a bag from Lilia's wardrobe and stuffed Daniel's toys and napkins inside. She wasn't even thinking what she needed, she grabbed anything and everything.

'Quickly!' Pollo was at the door. 'Upstairs with him.' They both fled up the flight of stairs to floor five and ran along the corridor, Pollo was carrying the bag. Claudette was tightly holding the boy, her heart was thumping, he was white with fear. The first door was open and the key was in the lock. They shut and locked it behind them and then continued through the second door. The room smelt foul. It was dark, drear and abandoned.

'What do we do?' asked Claudette, realising she was with the one person she disliked most in the world. 'What will they do?'

'If we stay here as quiet as we can they might not find us.' Pollo was looking for any break in the walls, an indication there was space behind them, but there was nothing. There was the sound, very far off, of shattering glass and then the blast of a shotgun. Claudette felt her heart lurch, she tightened her grip on Daniel without realising. He squirmed and tried to break free from her.

'Sush now, baby,' she said, placing him on the floor. He stood up and wobbled over to Pollo who had sat on the bed. He laid his tiny fingers on her arm.

'Look at you in your little sailor suit, you gorgeous little man,' said Pollo and Claudette watched, fascinated, as they interacted for the first time. Pollo leant down and picked up a ball that was wedged under the bed. She rolled it across the floor and Daniel, half walking, half crawling followed it like a dog to fetch it.

There was a sudden sound of screaming, shrill and clear, from the floor below and then banging sounds. 'Babette,' said Pollo, 'I think that's Babette. They've got her!' There was a long silence, well over half an hour, Pollo crept to the door listening. 'I think they've gone.' Claudette, who was sitting on the floor with Daniel, stood up and came to listen. Everything was still. Pollo put her hand on the door and stepped outside into the small room, tiptoeing across the floorboards. Daniel let out a little shriek, so Claudette ran back and picked him up. Still there was silence.

Pollo turned the handle of the outer door, it clicked open, the corridor outside was empty. There was an eery silence.

Just at that moment Daniel decided to howl.

Chapter Fifty One

The package had arrived, it was on my desk in front of the window. It was an old-fashioned brown paper parcel tied up with string, I had to find my kitchen scissors to open it. The rain had been incessant all day and now rivulets of water were running down the glass making the whole room shimmer.

I pulled open the paper and saw that there was a handwritten note in English on top, it was folded neatly in two. Under it were three pages typed on foolscap paper, all in French and beneath them was a small box with a ribbon tied round it.

I opened the note, it was from Louis.

Connie,

How lovely to hear from you and please forgive my tardy reply. I am literally between flights. I work for Médicins sans Frontiéres and I have to leave for West Africa in four hours. I was in Syria only yesterday! I would have very much liked to meet you. Samuel explained in an email that you had been uncovering information about Claudette Bourvil and, as I'm sure he told you, I have been trying to trace her son or daughter for a long time. She came to Vacily to see my father but he was working in the Dordogne and they missed each other. The tragedy of what happened to her upset him very much, he thought the world of her. She wrote this letter to him whilst she was in Vacily, (her parents had been killed in the war) she wanted him to know that although she was treated like a collaborator she had never done it intentionally.

Alas, in life, the circle is not often squared, as you Brits say, how lovely it would have been for them to meet, especially as my mother died the following year, Claudette could have been a great comfort to him.

I was sad to hear that Freddy died recently, but pleased that Daniel is still with us too. It would make a good novel, such interweaving of life stories.

If I can be of further help please do not hesitate to ask. In the meantime, I feel I have returned Claudette's letter and, I know you will look after it or do with it what you think fit.

With all good wishes

Louis

I read it over again. Claudette was in love with Yves, that's why she had gone back to see him and to clear her name. I wished she had seen him. And then there was poor Giselle who died so soon afterwards.

I opened the box. Inside it was a tortoiseshell hair comb. The wavering light of the water shadows caught it and for a moment it gleamed topaz, gold and brown. The letter was in the old typography of the typewriter so unfamiliar these days. The letters sat next to each other unevenly, depending on the key, it looked so strange when you are used to a computer. I remembered Freddy's keys on his typewriter stuck in mid air, A and S.

I would need Matt to translate and he would want to see it. I tapped his name on my phone and it was ringing. A woman answered.

'Matt's in bed at the moment, can he call you back?'

Chapter Fifty Two

'Stop him, for God's sake,' snapped Pollo, pushing the door closed. 'Get back in the other room, stop him!' Claudette backed away and, pulling the door closed, she sang to Daniel and bobbed him up and down on her hip.

'Sush Baby, sush, please sush.' But Daniel was screaming, his face red, mucus oozing out of his nose. He would not be stopped. Suddenly there was the sound of wood smashing and then Pollo swearing.

'Take her!' shouted a man, his voice deep and brusque. 'I'll look in the next room.' He barged in. Claudette gripped Daniel to her as hard as she could, he was bawling, his anxious, terrified screams only equalled by Pollo. Claudette could see her scratching at the face of the man who had his arms around her thin waist.

'Bastard!' she screamed. 'Let me go, damn you!' but he had the better of her. He flung her against the wall and slapped her hard. She looked completely dazed, the welt of red was visible immediately, her mouth started to bleed and her head drooped. He hit her again, punching her under the chin, making her reel back against the wall.

Claudette watched, frozen to the spot. Two other people arrived, an old woman and a young man, his face was half melted like molten wax. He looked at Pollo and then at Claudette. 'See what your Boches did to me?' he was pointing at his face. 'Now it's time to get even.'

Daniel stopped crying, as if he was scared into silence by the sight of the face. 'Please no, I have to look after this little boy.'

'The whore's boy.' The woman spat out the words.

'His mother is dead, she died not long ago.'

'Good, one less whore in the world is a good thing,' said the man who was holding up a dazed and bloody Pollo.

'She is a maid, just a maid,' said Pollo, though her eyes were closed, blood running down her silk blouse.

'Well, we have it on good authority that she's a collaborator,' said the woman, 'And they all have to pay for what they've done.'

'I'm with the Resistance,' said Claudette, 'Ask Jacques.' Pollo opened her eyes in total surprise and then she smiled to herself.

'He's dead,' snapped the woman. 'He got in the way.' Claudette felt a shock of pain inside her. Jacques was with the Resistance, he'd been working for these people.

The big man took her by the arm and led her out onto the landing, then forced her roughly downstairs. She couldn't see her feet on the treads. Daniel was clinging to her, his little fingers digging into her neck.

'Please,' she pleaded. 'Don't hurt him.'

'We make no allowances for the children of Germans and whores.' There was spittle forming on the side of the man's mouth.

The house was silent, no sound of anyone else. 'Where are they?' Pollo was being pulled along behind, she was talking as if her jaw was injured. 'What have you done with them?'

'You'll soon find out!' the woman was shouting as she followed them all down the steps. 'No more than you dirty lying whores deserve.'

Jacques' body was lying in the hall, his back to Claudette. Daniel pointed at him. 'He's only asleep,' said Claudette, biting back tears. 'Night, night Jacques.' The man shoved her through the front door and down the steps, not caring if she fell or not, not thinking at all about the child.

There were crowds outside, they cheered as Claudette appeared and cheered more loudly when Pollo was dragged out, her face bloody and hair bedraggled. The day was grey, overcast, everything was the colour of stone. They were marched along the street. Claudette searched wildly for Madam Odile, surely she could stop this, but she was nowhere to be seen. The man holding her arm shoved her forward and she nearly fell, which made Daniel cry again. His howls were deafening her, the crowd were baying relentlessly like a pack of animals. 'Whore, whore, whore,' they chanted in unison.

It was as if the mob were carrying her as they pushed along the street, she could get no purchase on the ground. They were pinching her and spitting on her, one hand grasped her breast and another plunged between her legs. A trail of saliva landed on Daniel's arm. There was nothing she could do, she pressed her lips to his cheeks. 'I love you, baby, don't be scared.' She was willing him to stop crying but he was too distressed. At the end of Rue Ercol they turned left into a narrow street. Half way along there were some double gates, grey metal with a Fleur de Lys handle standing proud half way down each one.

'This whore says she isn't a collaborator,' shouted the man, his words echoing off the walls of the houses opposite. 'Where's the girl who told us about these women?'

The crowd bunched as they turned their heads and then stepped aside to let someone through. It was Perrine. Her hair was pulled back into a chignon she looked pinched and mean. 'You, you girl, you told us. Is this one of them?' Perrine stepped forward until she was standing face to face with Claudette. Claudette's chin began to quiver, she could feel the tears burning behind her eyes. She had the strange feeling she was being physically pulled down towards the ground.

'It's not true.' Claudette was almost hoarse with nerves. 'He gave away their plans, he told me what they were doing. I passed them on.'

'Rubbish,' said Perrine, her eyes burning with fury. 'He is as responsible as the next Boche. They all must be punished and the whores that had them in their beds must pay for it now.' She turned and walked away. They pushed Claudette into the courtyard where a flight of steps rose up to a galleried landing where there were people looking down on her. She glanced up to see if any one of them could help her before she was forced inside a small run-down shop on her right. Pollo was being thrown inside the one next door.

The man had heaved Daniel out of her arms before she had time to think. The baby disappeared into the crowd, his little blond head bobbing between one person after another until his crying stopped.

Inside there were piles of rubbish, old boxes and newspapers, a shop counter pushed against the wall and a single chair. The man flung her down onto the boxes and undid his belt. His eyes were bulging with anticipation and sweat was running down his face. 'Now it's time to make up for your Boche fucking.' He kneeled down and grabbed at her knickers, pulling them off. She tried to squirm away but he pulled her back. Then he rammed his hand between her legs. When she tried to fight him he brought his hand down on top of her left breast, pinning her to the floor, the pain was unbearable.

'I should make you suck this first,' he said with a lascivious smirk. He unbuttoned his trousers so she could see he was hard, ready for her. She turned her head away, trying not to look, her face pressed against the hard edges of the boxes. He rammed into her. 'Take that, whore!' he shouted. There was a cheer from outside. Claudette realised they could probably hear what was going on, or maybe it was something they were doing to Pollo. She reached out and scraped the baked earth of the floor under her nails, trying to create pain to stop her feeling him inside. He thrust himself into her again and again and on until he was hurting her. Then he released himself and there was a sticky mess between her legs and he was panting as he stood up. She looked at him, the greasy black hair, the dirty skin, a factory worker or street cleaner, or even a tramp. He was dishevelled, much older than her and he was triumphant.

He staggered out and there was another cheer, the same as a few minutes before. It had been for Pollo, they had done the same to her. Claudette pulled up her pants and looked around for a weapon. If he was coming back she would kill him, or anyone else who was coming, there might be more men, ten, twenty more.

There was nothing, then the sound of a man's voice, a shout of laughter and the women filed inside. They stood looking at her, one held out a pair of heavy black scissors. 'Time to pay the price, whore.'

Chapter Fifty Three

I had put the phone down and stepped back from the desk. The woman was his mother, or sister, or cleaner, that was it. Why was he in bed? Why was he in bed in the middle of the afternoon? Why did she answer his mobile? I felt sick. I went to the kitchen and poured myself a glass of water. I sipped it, looking at my small patch of a back garden and the hollyhocks growing against the back wall, tinged with rust. Even at the end of their season they were beautiful and even in the driving rain they could cheer me up, but as I stared at them, the pink flowers began swimming before my eyes and suddenly there were tears rolling freely down my cheeks. Hat would have told me what to do but she was no longer here. I felt the bitter pain of being completely alone.

My phone buzzed, it was him. I was in two minds, part of me said answer it but the other part of me was too scared. I felt my stomach churn so I grabbed my coat and went for a walk. The rain was heavy by then, sheeting across the hillside. I took myself down to the water meadows, past the station and over the bridge where my heart yearned for it all to be as it once was, before Freddy died.

I walked on to the forest where I used to ride. It was beautiful in there, the rain was struggling to break through the canopy of trees and I saw two Roe deer leaping through the undergrowth. Then I was walking back up the hill towards my cottage, my legs heavy, my body aching.

He was standing there, his hands deep in the pockets of his Barbour. I felt like turning and running away, back to the trees and the silence of the forest paths.

'I've been here for ages,' he said. His hair was wet because he had no hat or hood.

'Where's your car?'

'M.O.T. I was dropped off,' he said, his teeth were beginning to chatter.

'Who was she?'

'Can I explain inside?' I looked at him, so the answer wasn't simple, it was going to be bad news. I pushed my key into the lock and opened the door. He followed me in like a lost dog. I took off my coat and hat and he unzipped his. He didn't sit down and I didn't offer him coffee.

'She's my ex-fiancé. She dropped by out of the blue and we went out for a meal last night for old times and stuff. I imagined we could get on like good friends but she had other plans. It's no excuse, but I was drunk.' I just looked at him, dumbfounded, my cheeks set solid, making any attempt to speak impossible. 'It was a huge mistake and when she answered the phone she was being a bitch.'

I couldn't fathom it out, how did he think any of this was worth relating? I was out of my depth and worse, every fear I had in being in a relationship was rising inside me. 'Please go, Matt,' I said quietly. I stood still, in the middle of my small lounge, the shimmering effect on the window was playing with the shadows on the wall, it felt like everything was moving around me in this awful, stationary moment. He looked forlorn, with hair dripping water onto his face.

338

'It was a stupid, idiotic mistake, a one night stand that should never have happened,' he said. I just stared at him, thinking of all the things we'd done during our short sorry little affair.

'Please go,' I said again and eventually he turned away and the next thing I knew the door had closed behind him and I was dialling Hat's mobile number.

'Oh, my darling, I wish I was there for you.' Hat was mortified for me. 'What a terrible, terrible thing to happen, especially for you.'

'I should have explained more about my trust issues thing,' I replied. 'I never told him everything, it all happened too fast.'

'My love, he shouldn't have done it at all, being faithful is part of the package, unless you agree otherwise. If you need to come and see me down here, I'll cheer you up.' I thanked her, saying I missed her very much, and then to change the subject I told her about the package I'd received from Louis. 'Wow! How fascinating to have something that you know was hers. Which means the comb we found in the shed was probably a matching one. I wonder what the story is behind those?'

The letter was still there looking at me on my desk. 'I have no idea and I can't very well ask Matt to translate. I don't understand a word.' I was feeling grumpy as well as hurt, or maybe grumpy because I was hurt.

'Haven't you techy people got a translation thingy on your computers?'

'No,' I said miserably. 'I don't fancy typing it all into a translation programme, there are three pages... in written French.' Then a thought occurred to me, I could scan it and download a programme to read and convert it. 'Hat, my brain's just clicked into gear, I can do it, and I can translate it.'

Half an hour later, with a free trial of some translation software, the words were appearing on my screen, slowly, but all in English. When it was done I printed it out and suddenly I was holding Claudette's words and my eyes couldn't take it in fast enough.

Vacily 19 June 1952

Dear Yves,

I am so upset that I didn't see you. I must have missed you by only a few hours. Giselle told me you had to go sooner than you had thought. I was glad that she was safe and well and I met your lovely boys.

I have a boy of my own, my beautiful Freddy. He and I have met a wonderful couple that have taken us to their hearts, they are called Elwyn and Catherine Benedict. I work for Elwyn as a translator, he is an entrepreneur, a superb businessman, I marvel at his abilities. I had to learn English very quickly and Elwyn tells me I speak it with a Welsh accent!

I worked for Madame Odile in twelve Rue Ercol as a maid. I did everything I could to pass information on to the Resistance, I was told by a person I trusted that what I did made a difference. Only one person found out about me and he said nothing. It was a Bordello, as you know, and I found it very hard at first. In the end, those women

340

were amazing because they were survivors. Six of them were marched through the streets of Paris after the war finished. I was too. We had our heads shaved and they branded us.

I escaped France with a little boy called Daniel, I was hoping I could give him a new life, a fresh start because his mother had killed herself. But that chance was taken away from me.

I wanted to see you Yves because I never saw you again in Paris, I wanted to see how you were because Annalise said you were badly tortured during the war. I was very worried to hear this and I wanted to make sure you were better. It took me a long time to get over what they did to me and, even worse, they were the people I had helped in my work with the Resistance. Catherine is a psychiatrist and she has helped me overcome the nightmares and helped me to be strong again.

I fell in love in Paris, Yves, deeply in love with a German Officer, he left the city just before the end of the war, I pray that he made it home safely. That is wrong, I don't pray, I lost all faith in a God that can stand by and let all those innocent people die in the camps. There never was a greater evil than the Nazis and I regret that I was ever involved with them at all. Only after the war did it all become clear to me how depraved they were and what they had done, none of us knew.

Our town capitulated so quickly and everything seemed so normal until Vincent was killed. I still grieve for him because he would have gone on to be a great doctor. It is a true blight on all humanity what has been done and a sadness that will never leave us.

I have a broken heart, but I never tried to mend it by finding Fritz Keber, my lover. I needed him to stay in my past, along with the death of my friends, and the stain Nazi Germany left on our country, which will take decades to heal.

Freddy asks me all the time about his father and I tell him about the man I loved and not the soldier he was, I heard that he had done terrible things much later on, as the true story of our occupation became clear. In the end I did what I did for France and for any betrayal I may have subjected my country to, I paid for it.

When I get home to England I will telephone you and I will tell you more, in the meantime, I send you my love, the one man I met in my life for whom I truly have undying respect and admiration. You made us fight and you were cruelly dealt with. I hope one day they all realise the sacrifices we made, but that we must leave to history.

I enclose one of my written exercises that Catherine made me do. I am not looking for compassion or forgiveness, I would like this passed to a museum or a historian in France or maybe an author who might write about the Horizontal Collaborators; their page in history is as valid as any others.

I leave you with my love and best wishes,
Your friend.
Claudette Bourvil.

The old woman's shrew face tightened above mean, thin lips. She was so close I could feel her hot, sour breath on my face. She held up a pair of heavy black scissors and wrapped a twist of my hair around her fingers. Then she pulled the strands towards her and the blades took hold, the softness trapped in the sharpened metal. She chopped and spliced until my hair fell in defeated heaps around me.

A razor was dragged across my scalp, it nicked at the skin, slices of pain. If I raised my head even slightly I could see leering faces, four of them, so I kept my eyes fixed on the cracked tiles beneath me. When it was done I was trembling.

'Get her up, make her stand.' It was easy enough, I was thin and sapped of strength. Their eyes bulged, eager with excitement and anticipation. The words were hissed in my ear; 'Strip her!' I saw only her flat, dirty shoes. They didn't stop to undo buttons but ripped and pulled apart my dress. Then, with a single slice of a blade, my bra was cut off so that my breasts were naked.

'Go on!' It was the oldest woman, the one in the widow's weeds, her eyes glazed blue with cataracts. 'Do it.' They pulled off my knickers. The thin fabric tore away easily.

A fifth one, in the shadows behind me, grasped at my buttocks, her dirty nails scratching the skin, the others howled with laughter. 'Give her the child. Fetch him!'

I snapped out of my trance, the whole room was suddenly loud and real and they reeked of old, rotted things.

'No, not him!' I cried. 'Do what you will with me, but please not him.'

343

'Whore, whore, whore…' they chanted, ignoring my pleas. The door opened and I saw his little face grubby with the tell tale marks of tears on his sweet cheeks.

The old man who carried him in sneered at my nudity, taking in the swell of my breasts with a lecherous grin. Yes, I thought, for all that I am a whore you too would have me right now, right here. He shoved the boy into my arms with a crude roughness, just as he might have treated a sack of kittens to be drowned. The child smelt foul, of dirt and grease and other people's sweat. He had passed the stage of crying. Spent of tears, he sought me for comfort and nestled his face into my neck, his thin arms clinging on for all he was worth. I clung to him too, covering his face with my hand, as if it were possible in some way to shield him from what was to come. What hope was there of that?

They opened the door and the noise from outside swelled. It was a dull late summer's day, the branches of the plane trees stretched towards a colourless sky. Perhaps if I kept looking up towards the sky I would not see what was coming. Perhaps, I thought, even now God would look on me and take pity, but He wasn't there for me, I knew it.

The crowd mocked as the women pushed me forward into the street, their screeching exciting more animal noises from the mob. Someone was braying like a donkey and the man, his face melted from eye to chin, spat on me, a globule of green phlegm landed on my shoulder. I felt the blow of a missile as it hit the small of my back and trickled red down the inside of my legs. The remains landed between my feet, a blackened tomato. Then something else struck me on the forehead and I saw a rotten windfall

344

apple on the road, the brown, dead skin oozing a slash of rotten flesh.

We were both shivering with fear; I could hear a low animal moan running through him. I pressed his face to mine; his thin shirt and shorts were all that was between him and my cold flesh.

I set my eyes forward as I took cold, hesitant steps along the wet road. I had no way of protecting myself from the things they hurled at me and there were hundreds of them lining the way. They were catcalling, howling and calling me a whore over and over again, until the sound was a wall around me.

I desperately searched the crowd for his face, just one glimpse, just to know he had found out, that had tried to do something to save me, but he was not there.

Then I saw Pollo. Her hair was gone, her body was covered in red welts so, like me, she was pathetic. A large man hauled up her limp body, her head was lolling to one side, her once beautiful face distorted. Another man, his sleeves rolled back, turned towards her holding a long piece of metal, steam rising from the end of it. There was a smell of fire, burning metal and a glow of bright red.

Someone in the crowd barged me, making me stumble so that I lost sight of her for a moment, then the mob roared and when I saw her again I realised what they had done. The smell of burning flesh seared through the wet air.

They had branded her.

Why didn't she react? Why didn't she scream? I couldn't see. There were people crowding round her, spitting on her, but I could do nothing except offer a prayer to God that she was already dead. I asked if he would take me too, kill me here on this cold, sodden street in Paris, but spare an innocent child who should live without blemish, despite all that I have done.

Spare him, I cried from the depths of my heart. Please God spare him!

Chapter Fifty Four

They left Claudette in a doorway with the boy lying next to her. People passed by, she saw the shapes and muted colours of their clothes. She could hear the distant hum of a city wounded and unknown even to itself. There was a thrum of pain in her ear and the blood on her chest was running freely down her breasts. Daniel was asleep, his little body pressed into the curves and crevices of hers. His clothing was ripped and he smelt of urine and rotted food.

She pushed herself up on one elbow. Instead of her hair hanging to each side of her face, there was nothing, a brightness flickering in her peripheral vision. Her eyes felt too tired to cope with the daylight. It was a man who stopped, a man in an ochre coloured uniform. He stooped down, laying his hand gently on her shoulder. When he spoke she realised he was an American. She didn't understand what he was saying. His mouth was moving but his voice wasn't clear, it had to compete against the noise in her head. Then, he was lifting her, his strength being all she could rely on, her legs were like jelly.

Daniel woke up and began to cry, his eyes were dry and crusted, there were no tears. The American was speaking again. He slid his jacket off and slipped it around her shoulders, buttoning it up. It was huge on her.

He bent down to pick up Daniel and then looked

frantically around for help. He shouted 'Parlez vous Anglais?' in terrible French to passers-by, but they ignored him. Half carrying her and still holding Daniel he managed to get her to an old broken armchair, which had been used as part of a barricade across the street. The fabric felt rough against the back of her thighs. He had a metal canteen and he gave her some water, making her take small sips. Her lips were bruised and her jaw stiff.

There were people gathering around now, looking at her and the boy as if they were part of a freak show. 'Parlez vous Anglais?' the soldier implored, begging one of them to speak to him. Claudette saw the shadows of people, the sounds of laughter mingled with the American's voice.

'Moi, je fais.' It was a young man, the first signs of stubble on his chin, answering the American's plea. He came forward, his lip curled with the horror of the sight he saw in front of him. Claudette heard an exchange between them, then the young man was asking for her address. She could only mutter the words, they would not form properly in her mind.

She felt a pain in her ribs as they lifted her up, the soldier one side, the young man the other. She couldn't see Daniel, but the soldier said something and an elderly woman turned to pick him up.

The door to the house was locked. The soldier asked if Claudette knew where there was a key and the young man asked in French. She shook her head. They knocked and she felt the despair of being barred from the place she lived, she had nowhere else to go.

Suddenly there was sound behind the door and it opened. Marie was there and she cried out as she saw the mess that was Claudette. Moving to one side, she let everyone in, then Claudette's world went black.

When she awoke she was in Eva's room. There was no furniture. The mirror on the wall had been cracked from side to side, it reflected a multitude of images in the shattered glass. It felt like morning, the strange pre-dawn greyness was lifting and a new day was beginning. The curtains were missing, the pelmet ragged.

She tried to sit up, but the pain in her chest felt like her skin was ripping apart. She looked around for Daniel, but he wasn't there. Instead, on the rug, covered in a single blanket, was Marie sound asleep and softly snoring.

Claudette lay in the quietness of the room, her mind was full of flashing images, the man's greasy hair, the feeling of him inside her, the foul smells, the women and the man with the melted face. Her body juddered involuntarily, the muscles waking up and bristling with stiffness.

'You are all right, Françoise, you're going to get better.' It was Marie, her thin fingers rested on Claudette's forehead.

'Daniel?' her voice was little more than a croak. Marie pulled the sheets up around Claudette and folded them back, neatening them out.

'He's fine, Madame Odile has him. He's very shaken but he'll be fine, he's very young.'

'It was terrible,' Claudette felt the tears rise in her, she felt totally vulnerable. 'They raped me.'

'We know, so were all the others,' Marie's face darkened, she had grown up, she had her own demons. Her father would be facing his own conscience now somewhere in

349

Vichy. 'They are all here, and Jacques is laid out in the salon. But you need to rest now, it's only six o'clock, go back to sleep.'

Claudette slept again until twelve when the door opened and Daniel toddled in. He ran to her, throwing his little arms around her as she pulled him, painfully, into bed with her. Madam Odile followed, her hair hung around her shoulders, she was in an old housecoat and looked very worn and tired.

'He didn't sleep last night,' she said. 'He kept waking up and crying, I couldn't do anything for him. He kept saying Mama, Mama.'

'How is everyone?' Claudette asked, her mouth still painful when she talked.

'About the same as you, they have all been branded, all raped and all beaten. Nanette is the worst, for some reason they took it out on her, I can't believe it.' She looked desolate. 'I thought it would be bad, but not this bad. I'm to blame for everything, everything.'

Claudette reached out and put her hand into Madam Odile's. 'You couldn't have seen this coming.' Madam Odile was looking down at her chest, as if she was gathering the strength to speak.

'Françoise, before Jacques was killed he was going to have to tell you something, something very bad indeed. It's about your parents. The Germans put up a fight in the area surrounding Vacily. They held the town for two days and then, when they left, they detonated lots of explosives. The Allied bombings and the Germans between them virtually razed the town to the ground. Your parents were killed, I am so sorry.' Claudette felt the tight constriction in her throat as she wrestled back a scream. It was the end of everything, for nothing was how it should be any more.

Eventually she summoned up one word. 'How?' The images of Vincent Gabin were racing through her mind.

'I don't know, Jacques was terribly upset, he was waiting for the right moment. He thought the world of you, you know, you have lost your whole family and the brother who looked out for you.' Madam Odile sat silently whilst their thoughts passed between them, unspoken, there was a feeling of loss so great neither of them could react any more. For a split second Claudette thought Madam Odile should know the truth of her identity, but something made her hold her tongue.

'I have to go out and try to find food, I'll leave Daniel with Marie. She has been a rock to us all, I never could have coped with all this without her.'

'What if they come back?' Claudette felt a panic, a fear that it wasn't over.

'They won't. They have ransacked the house, everything is gone. They've smashed mirrors, thrown the paintings out of the windows onto the streets, the furniture is either slashed or stolen. Monique and Babette are in the same bed, all the others have been broken or taken, if they didn't take it they smeared it with faeces. There was only one room untouched. They didn't get into my office thank goodness because it was double-locked, but they have taken apart my apartment and I have nothing left.'

'And Lilia's room?'

'They wrecked it, some things are left but everything of value is gone, except this.' Madam Odile held out her hand and dropped the silver pendant into Claudette's palm. 'Your rosary and your valise have gone but I found this on the stairs, they must have dropped it. Do you have your papers safe?'

Claudette shook her head. She wrapped her fingers around the pendant. For a moment she could see Keber's face, his beautiful eyes and the lips she had kissed so many times. Then he was gone, drifting away from her, faint as a ghost. 'What will happen now?' she asked.

'I have a plan, I need to give the other ladies their papers and see that they will be all right. Luckily, they were in the safe in my office. Then I will concentrate on you, me and Daniel.' As she left the room, and Marie came in to take Daniel away, Claudette realised she hadn't asked where Madam Odile had been for the last twenty-four hours.

Chapter Fifty Five

I sat staring into space, I had read and re-read what Claudette had written. It was worse each time. She had risked everything at huge cost to herself. I wanted to reach across the years and put my arm around her shoulder to tell her I understood, that I knew her story. I also wanted to tell Matt, to bring everything to a conclusion for him. But that was the thing, it wasn't concluded. Daniel didn't even know who his mother was or what she did and he had presumed Fritz Keber had been in love with her.

Did I leave him with that understanding, or did I tell him what I knew? Would I want to know if I were in his shoes? I decided to leave it as it was, then instantly changed my mind. Didn't he have a right to know who rescued him and saved his life?'

And Freddy, just what had he known of his mother? Did she tell him anything or had he found out later, or was it her murder that had torn him apart? I weighed it up in my mind, all the pieces of the puzzle where racing around in my head. I searched through Google abstractly trying to pull things together, but my eyes were heavy, I had to sleep on it.

At six the next morning I woke up wringing wet with my nightie clinging to my skin. I clutched at my head, relieved to find I wasn't bald. It had thankfully all been a nightmare. I had been looking at images on the Internet of women having their heads shaved and being paraded through the streets. They called them Tondues and all over France women were treated the same and were desperately humiliated.

I went back to my desk in the living room and read Claudette's letter and enclosure again. I made a coffee and paced the floor then I made a decision, a big one. I unplugged my laptop from where it had been charging and began typing an email.

Chapter Fifty Six

One by one the women came in to see Claudette and Daniel. Monique's hair was shaved so unevenly there were ugly tufts all over her head and Freya, once so stunning with her platinum blonde hair, was wearing a turban. Her eyes were black, her nose blue. She kissed first Daniel and then Claudette.

'We are leaving in a hour,' she said blankly. Monique stood agitatedly by the door clutching her elbows with nervy fingers and saying nothing. 'We're both sorry it happened, you got caught up in our world, it should never have been like that.' She handed a small package to Claudette. 'Take that and please accept it as a gift from all of us.'

Claudette stood up unsteadily and hugged them. They were both trembling. 'Where are you going?' she asked.

'We came from Bergerac, my sister lives there, she will take us in if she is still alive. I haven't heard from her for six months.'

'And if she isn't?'

'We'll find something,' said Monique. 'We're survivors, aren't we Freya?' Freya nodded, her arms were folded protectively to her body again, she was nothing of her former self. Monique bent down and gave Daniel a hug. 'You look after yourself too, young man, don't let this part of your life damage the rest.' Freya kissed her finger and placed it on Daniel's little cheek. Then they were gone.

Claudette sighed heavily and sat down next to Daniel. 'Let's look at this, baby.' She opened the box, inside was a pair of tortoiseshell hair combs and a note, 'For when it grows back, don't go back to mousy! With love from all of us.'

There was a knock on the door, it was Babette, there were tears welling up in her eyes. 'I hate goodbyes,' she said, sitting down next to Claudette. 'They've stolen everything from my room, I don't even have a bed.' Her scalp was blue, the same colour as Claudette's. In the cracked mirror across the room their reflections were repeated like a mosaic; they both looked thin and pitiful. 'I'm leaving tonight, I'm taking my chances and looking for work in Paris. The Americans will want to fuck as much as the next man, they all do.'

'Where will you go?' asked Claudette. 'Will you be safe?'

'I'll live on the streets if I have to, but there will be other whore houses in other parts of the city. I just need to find clients who don't mind spiky hair. Look, it's already growing back.' She pulled at a tiny tuft of hair behind her ears and smiled. 'Until then I will wear a silk headscarf wrapped around my head and start a new trend.'

The next morning Claudette stepped out of her room for the first time, her legs feeling weak, her stomach so past the stage of hunger it had turned into a solid mass beneath her skin. She balanced Daniel on her hip, he was like a limpet, stuck fast to her. The house was worse than she could have imagined. The purple carpet had been urinated on, the word 'whore' painted on every landing where the beautiful pictures of the women had been. Downstairs, all the bottles in the bar had been smashed on the floor, the mirrors and lights shattered. The stools were broken and the tables turned over.

Claudette looked through the small gaps in the pattern of the frosted glass in the salon door. She could see Jacques lying on the floor, a trail of blood behind his body where it had been dragged. Where the blood had been in the entrance hall, the dirt and debris of destruction had taken its place.

Downstairs, in the kitchen, Marie was washing some clothes with the last fragment of a bar of soap. A broth was cooking on the stove, it smelt foul. 'Don't ask.' she said, 'You don't want to know what it is. There is an apple purée for Daniel, I found an apple in the street this morning.'

'Thank you, Marie, and thank you for nursing me.' Claudette placed Daniel on a kitchen chair. He grabbed a spoon and started banging it on the table. 'Where will you go now?'

'Madame F has found me a job, I'll be working with her, I miss the old trout,' she said ruefully, 'but I'll be more grown up than when she last saw me, and I've said I want more money.'

'Good for you,' said Claudette. 'I hope it all works out for you. Where is Nanette?'

'She hasn't woken up yet. Madam Odile has sent for an ambulance and she has written to her parents, they are coming for her.'

'Her parents know she is here and what she did?'

'No, but they are about to find out. Madam Odile

found their details in Nanette's passport and she wrote to them.' Claudette felt a pang of sadness because Nanette was the kindest and sweetest of them all.

'And Apollonia?'

'She walked out yesterday and hasn't come back. She said nothing to any of us, she's been in a daze.'

Madam Odile was in her room when Claudette knocked. She and Daniel were called in. 'I've heard about everybody leaving and I wondered what I should do, I want to stay.'

'Why?' Claudette chewed on her lip, Madam Odile still unnerved her a little. 'Is it because you are waiting for him?'

'Yes,'

'Then you will wait for ever, he won't come back.'

'He said he would, he promised me.'

'Fritz Keber doesn't honour promises, my dear, he breaks them. Trust me, you are better off without him. Leave him behind in the past and move on.' Claudette's hopes sank, but she knew in her heart that Madam Odile was right. She would never see him again, it was about facing the truth and moving on. 'I have an idea, I think it makes a lot of sense,' Madame Odile continued. 'I have these.' She opened her drawer and lifted out four passports – two were British, two French. She handed one to Claudette.

The picture was of Lilia. She was serious looking, her eyes clear, her hair neat and pinned back into a roll. She was much younger, nearer Claudette's age, wearing a white blouse and a simple scarf. It stated that she was the wife of Laurence George March. Underneath were Daniel's details, he was entered as her son, born 18th November 1942.

'That's Lilia's passport.'

'She had a British passport?'

'And a French one,' said Madame Odile. 'That is why I went to Reims, to have Daniel added. I didn't have a birth certificate for him so I had to pull some strings. I had one of each done, I had to cover all eventualities and I too have one of each, under my real name, Camille du Pré.' She struck a match and lit up a cigarette, the brand was American. 'It is my idea that we leave for England at the end of the week. You will travel as Lilia. You are so thin and bony, we both are, we look nothing like our photographs. That way we can escape this wretched country and I will get work in England.'

'How?'

'I have contacts there. I have many contacts everywhere. You make a lot of friends in this game. I will offer my services as a translator or similar and I will teach you English. You can look after Daniel for me and I will provide for you until you too can work.'

'You speak English?' asked Claudette.

'Enough, certainly enough to get by.'

'And have you been to England before?'

'No, but the English have always come to me,' she raised an eyebrow. 'Diplomats, actors, royals, I've had dealings with them all.' Madame Odile moved forward and ran a finger down Daniel's soft cheek, but he turned away. 'But I never made a friend of you, did I Daniel?' she said. 'That's why I need you, Françoise.'

'But what if we're stopped?'

'I have a letter from a very important French official that says I have free passage, and my recently widowed sister does too.'

'Was Lilia's real name Madeléine March and was she married?'

'No, she was Danielle du Pré, daughter of a French car worker and a woman who cleaned people's houses, as of course was I.'

'What will happen to this house?'

'It is leased. The owners will come and find me gone, there is not a stick of furniture or a stitch of fabric worth saving. By rights I should burn it down, purge it.'

'You have lost everything,' said Claudette.

'Except my spirit,' said Madam Odile, 'And that can never be vanquished or I should cease to be.'

Chapter Fifty Seven

Conniew57@aol.com

Dear Daniel,

I am writing to update you on what I found out about Freddy's mum. It's all quite tragic. I have really struggled with telling you, but I think you deserve to hear it. She was with the French Resistance working in Paris. She had a job as a maid in Rue Ercol and became involved with your father.

She fell in love with him. Your mother had died and when the war ended Madeléine, AKA Claudette Bourvil, left France to go and live with you and your Aunt in England. This was early September 1945, according to her passport. She travelled under a false identity as Madeléine March, I can only presume she had a French and an English passport at the same time.

What I wanted you to know was that Freddy's mum must have adored you because she and your aunt brought you up. They both took you to England. At some point she met Elwyn Benedict and he maybe fell in love with her, or saw her as a daughter by proxy. Anyway, he made Freddy his ward.

In 1952, Claudette travelled back to France to see a man she had known all her life. Her good friend Yves had led the cell she was part of in the Resistance. She missed seeing him by hours and she wrote the attached letter to him, copy enclosed. She had a horrific experience as you can see from the piece she has written. The boy was you, Daniel, you had a very bad start in life. I hope you understand why I think you should know about her. I think we owe her some recognition for her bravery and sacrifice. Personally, I am intrigued by her and the other women who were punished as horizontal collaborators. I plan to find out more, if I can. Freddy has left me some money and I will be coming to Paris for a month to carry out my research. I want to try to write a book about her and tell their story.

I hope you understand why I have written to you. If you want to leave the past behind don't read the attachments, I would understand. All I know is, she loved you very much and you should know that.

With best wishes,

Connie Webber

As I hit Send my mobile went off, making me start. I dreaded that it might be Matt and I was ready to hit decline, but the number was an 0033 code, French.

'Bonjour, Connie?' The soft accented voice was familiar, but I couldn't place it.

'Yes, this is Connie, can I help you?'

'It is Theo, Theo Arnold. We met some weeks ago, in Paris.'

'Theo, what a lovely surprise. How are you?'

'I am well, thank you.' He left an uncertain pause.

'How can I help you?' I said.

'I am coming into London next week to an auction of books,' he cleared his throat, 'and I wondered if you would meet me for dinner, I feel that I would like to meet you again.'

'I would love to, really love to,' I replied. There was a flutter inside my stomach and a sudden lifting of my deadened spirits.

'Me too. I would like to know more about what you found out from Gáel...and more about you. I'll be in touch. Is that fine with you?'

'Yes, it would be great,' I said.

'Au revoir. See you then.'

'Au revoir, Theo.'

Chapter Fifty Eight

The man was looking at Madame Madeléine March. He looked at her passport and then back at her. 'Is it a business trip or for pleasure, Madame?'

'A bit of both, I am visiting Paris, I used to live there, and then I am travelling to a little town I stayed in a long time ago, Vacily.'

The immigration officer looked at the passport again and said; 'I'm sorry to see you have been widowed, Madame, did you lose your husband in the war?'

'Yes,' she said slowly. 'I did.'

'I am very sorry for your loss, Madame, I hope you have an enjoyable trip.'

She nodded, and thanked him as he handed back her passport.

It felt strange because it was the first time she had left Freddy behind, but he was with Elwyn and Catherine, what could happen to him in their house in Ledbury? It was so beautiful and out in the countryside he was perfectly safe from harm.

In Paris she stayed at a small hotel in the Latin Quarter, a simple place with a glass front door and the name 'Hotel de Delacroix' etched into it. Her room was neat and small, a plain green counterpane covered the bed and small sprays of forget-me-nots dotted the wallpaper. Across the road was a little square with small trees at each corner of it. The house where the artist had lived was to the right, a very old building. It was June and the spring had turned to summer, there was a light breeze and she left her window open, letting the fresh air fill the small room.

The next morning, after breakfast, she walked along the Rue Ercol and found number twelve. It was now a private house. The front door had been replaced with a new one, the doorknocker was a carved head of a lion, its mouth open in a roar. The street was neat and quiet, no significant damage.

She stood next to the spot where Eva's body had lain and where months later the paintings, pulled down from the walls of the staircase, lay smashed and broken all over the road. She walked through the Luxembourg Gardens and stood by the boat pond watching the children push the little galleons across the water. She moved out of the way for one little boy who was eager to reach the one just in front of her. He was blonde, with brown eyes. She stared after him, he looked so much like Daniel. She felt the flutter of sorrow in her stomach, after all these years she still felt the pain of losing him.

It had suited Camille very much to have her as a nanny, caring for the little boy, feeding him, mopping his tears, picking him up when he fell over and kissing a wounded knee better. The pay off was that Claudette had learned English very quickly and there had been a roof over her head and food on the table.

She had given birth to Freddy in April 1945. She knew he was not Fritz Keber's child. He had dark hair and brown eyes of the Gallic. She loved him in spite of everything, he was beautiful and he had charmed her boss Elwyn from the minute they met. Freddy and Daniel were like brothers and she loved them both equally.

Claudette walked on through the gates and down the street and past the church of Saint-Germain-des-Prés. It was a long time since she had entered a church and those days were in the past, as lost to her as the rosary they took when they ransacked the house. If she thought it might have helped she would have prayed for Daniel, that he was all right and that Camille was looking after him and not thinking only of herself. She even wondered if he was with his father, in Interlaken. She suspected Camille had taken him to see his father. It would be like her to rub salt into the wounds and tap into an income that she didn't even need. She had met a Swiss Financier and within weeks she had vanished. She left without a word, and Daniel was there one minute and gone from Claudette's life the next.

She walked to the Seine and took a deep breath, letting the warm air fill her lungs. She could feel the heat of the sun on her back as she opened her handbag and felt inside it. It was there, tucked safely into the inside pocket and when she held it up to look at it, the bright light glinted off it. It was the pendant of a swan flying in front of the moon. She kissed it and for a short moment closed her eyes, taking a minute to remember the colours, the smells, the feelings, all spent in the distant haze of the past. There was a church clock striking ten as she held it at the tip of her fingers, watching it sway a little in the breeze. It made barely a sound or a splash as it hit the water. For a second she could see it floating, then it was sucked down deeper by the current and she imagined it sinking down and landing in soft silt at the bottom of the river.

Chapter Fifty Nine

Harriet sat with me on a round bench in front of the coffee kiosk at the station, the minute hand defiantly slow as it clicked around the face of the clock. She held my hand. 'I hope this is going to work for you,' she said. 'Matt was such a huge hope for you and it all ended so badly.'

'I'm over it, Hat,' I told her honestly. 'I'm looking forward now, it could have been such a huge mistake.' The minute hand clicked onto the twelve just as the light changed and a crisscrossing of shadows fell across the concourse from the glass roof. The train was quietly pulling into the station, the disturbance in the air making us stand up and check automatically that I had left nothing behind. The clipped announcement told us that this was the ten o'clock to London Victoria via East Croydon and Clapham Junction, which would be arriving at ten fifty three. From there I was going to make my way to St. Pancras and then on Eurostar to Paris.

'Thank you for having Mr C to stay.' I hugged Hat goodbye and she held me tightly.

'I'll take care of him, take as long as you need.' She gave me a big reassuring smile as I heaved my case onto the train and waved to her from my seat, but I saw her turn away and wipe a tear. There was a lump in my throat as it pulled out of the station, the stone chippings flashed before my eyes as it picked up speed. For a moment I found myself thinking of Freddy and a strange feeling came over me. It was an intense feeling of loss but, at the same time, a gratefulness that he had opened up so many experiences to me. Thanks to him I was on this train.

'Thank you, Freddy,' I said softly under my breath.

On the Eurostar itself I leaned my head against the window frame and watched the familiar fields of Normandy pass by the window, the endless chequer board acres; the rise and fall of buildings and great plane trees lining purple roads. Eventually, I opened my notebook; on the inside of the cover I had written Theo's number and underlined it, he was collecting me from the Gare du Nord.

I leafed through my notes about Claudette Bourvil. I was going to start with the Musée de la Resistance and then see where it took me and what I could find out about the women who fought for a free France.

Chapter Sixty

Claudette was sitting with Giselle taking afternoon tea. The china was delicate, an old pattern similar to one she remembered from her grandmother's glass-fronted cabinet. She didn't admit it to Giselle, but she was heartbroken to have missed Yves. He'd had to go, she realised that, he was travelling with his business partner and they had decided they needed extra time to get to their destination. Giselle had explained that Yves could not drive. His arm muscles had been damaged during the torture and he lived in considerable pain. Claudette knew in her heart that she was also a form of torture to him because seeing her was to revisit old memories he didn't need to think about.

Giselle was still the very gentle person she had always been and her soft voice was calm and reassuring. Their small house was on the outskirts of town. It had suffered damage to the kitchen during the war, but Yves had had it rebuilt and it was now light and airy, looking over a vegetable garden that was yielding all manner of produce.

'Yves will be so sad to have missed you,' Giselle passed a tray of delicate pastries to Claudette. 'To be honest, though, I think you may have been shocked, he is a very different man. He went through so much, the Nazi who tortured him didn't hold back. He has nightmares even now, it breaks my heart.' Claudette felt the twist of her guts as she thought about him, how beautiful he had been, how he looked when he was planning and leading them into action.

'It changed us all,' she said. 'No-one came out of it unscathed.'

'It changed your name!' said Giselle with a lightness in her voice that transformed, in an instant, the reflective mood. 'You are Madeléine now, aren't you?'

'I will always be Claudette in my heart,' she said. 'I haven't left her behind, I just try to forget what happened to her. It is all best left in the past; the only person I wanted to explain anything to is Yves. Do you think I might write it down for him? I'd like to entrust my story into his care.'

'Yes, of course, I have paper and a pen. You can sit in the bedroom, Yves' desk is there and it looks out towards the forest, perfect for thinking.'

'Thank you. That is perfect.'

When she left the house, she hugged Giselle and the boys. 'Thank you for coming, Claudette,' said Giselle warmly. 'It was lovely to see you again.' The boys had been out playing and their faces were streaked with dirt, their hair unkempt. Louis, the oldest, looked like a small version of Yves.

She walked up the street to the church. There was a pair of collared doves rooting around in the brush by the back wall. They fluttered away as she walked towards them, but were soon back ready to carry on picking at small red berries that had fallen onto the path, after she had passed by.

Beneath the shelter of a hedge she found a row of small

white crosses and on one were her parents' names. There were no dates or epitaphs because she hadn't been there to write something. She touched the cross and stayed like that, resting her hand on it for a few moments. Then she moved on and through the little gate at the back of the graveyard, down the path to the old washhouse.

There was a man there, in a flat cap. His clothes were shabby, his hair and beard thick, both black, but streaked with white. She saw him in profile because the sunlight was behind him. She followed the path down towards him and, as she drew level, she nodded politely but instead of letting her pass he straightened up and stepped in front of her, blocking her way. His dirty face was familiar but she couldn't place it.

'Claudette Bourvil,' he said, his voice even, without tone.

'Yes,' she answered guardedly, stopping and preparing if necessary to retrace her steps. He looked at her, his thick eyebrows linked together in a scowl. The eyes were sinister above pock-marked cheeks and all of a sudden she knew exactly who it was.

'I've come here every year. Spring, summer, autumn. Time after time, nothing, but now you're here.' His eyes were empty, they were reflecting his soul.

The gun had a silencer, a German issue. It made no sound, nothing to alert anyone in the village. She fell to her knees, her eyes staring up at him; the blackness overtook her before she hit the ground.

Two doves flapped their wings and rose up to the sky and then there was silence.

Epilogue

Lucy phoned me to tell me that Bertie had died. She'd passed away in her sleep peacefully and at the grand old age of ninety-four. 'I thought you'd like to know,' she told me. 'I've just come off the phone with Harriet.'

'I'm sorry, Lucy, I really am, I liked Bertie a lot. I wish I'd known her longer, she was quite a character.'

'Yes, she was that, I will miss her. I've been with her for eighteen years, you know.' There was a little gap, she was taking a breath before continuing. 'I found something in the hatbox when I was trying to sort out her papers. It's a press cutting, in French, I thought it might be of interest to you, shall I read it?'

'Yes please,' I said. I felt my heartbeat quicken.

'It says that a man called Maurice Joubert was committed to an asylum in Paris following his conviction for the murder of several people since the war. Psychiatric assessments will be ongoing. Joubert, whose wife and children were killed during the First World War by a rogue group of German soldiers, is likely to face incarceration for life.'

I felt a strange sense of relief. It was closure, no more doors to open, no secrets left to unlock. 'Thank you for that, Lucy, I think I know exactly why that cutting is important.' I said goodbye and pressed the end call button. Bertie had

had the answer all along. I was lost in my thoughts when Theo came into the Salon with a cup of green tea for me.

'Are you all right, ma Cherie?' I love the way he says that, he mixes sentences between English and French all the time.

'Yes, thank you,' I replied. I took the tea from him and gave him a smile. 'I think the final piece of the puzzle just fell into place, it's taken four months, but it's finally all over.'

Theo laid a gentle, reassuring hand on my shoulder. 'And now you can start writing that book of yours, you have a huge amount of material and the time and space.'

'Thanks to you,' I said, turning my head to kiss his hand. 'I do love you.'

'And I you, my darling.' He ran the back of his finger over my cheek, gentle as a butterfly. 'Now I'm going to unpack those boxes of books you brought with you and find a place for them all, though only heaven knows where they will all go. Then I will feed Mr C and see if I can make friends with him. If not, I will threaten him with the home for the cats.'

I felt a warmth rising through me, the feeling was like no other I'd experienced in my life. I watched Theo's face as he opened the first box of my books. He stroked every spine as if he was welcoming each one to his home, our home.

This book is dedicated to The Women of the Chabanais

Acknowledgments

Without the constant support of my husband, Paul, there would be no novel called The Seven Letters. I am indebted to him for his energy, commitment and proof-reading skills, both in English and French.

Arabella McIntyre-Brown began the whole adventure with a simple writing workshop and talk of possibilities. Meg Harper, Janet Gover, Alison May and numerous other kind hearted authors taught me well. I am very grateful to the authors and agents who generously shared their experience and expertise at The ChipLitFest where I learned so much.

I owe my first readers for their honest feedback and kind comments. Sarah Fitzgerald, Paul Nelson, Annette Rainbow, Max Harvey and Judy Hand. I am grateful to Richard Weiss for checking the German. Then there was the lovely French gentleman Yves Cornillon, who came to my Art Exhibition in 2014, and who answered all my questions about life in his country thereafter with great patience.

During my research in Paris, I was given a tour of the Hotel Meurice by the lovely Sophie who stood by and let me marvel at each room. Deborah, at the Musee de l'Erotisme in Montmatre, provided no end of useful, and eye-opening, information. That was an afternoon I will never forget!

I am indebted to Morgan Bailey for the initial guidance; Fiction Feedback for the positive critique and to Joanne Edmonds for the proof-reading.

The image of the Ladies of the Chabanais was supplied for me by Alexandre Dupouy, at Les Archives d'Éros, it was the image that began the whole story. I also owe Michael Neiberg for kindly taking the time to write The Blood of Free Men, which shored up all my research and became my go to source on The French Resistance.

I received huge value for money from Bryony Hall, Contracts Advisor at The Society of Authors, a highly professional lady.

And finally, everyone at Troubador for publishing this book. It's taken four years hard work, but what an adventure it has been.

Thank you.

Jan Harvey

About the Author

Jan Harvey is an artist and author based in the Oxfordshire Cotswolds. She is a tutor in creative writing, drawing and painting.

In her spare time Jan loves to relax listening to jazz or watching old black and white movies, particularly when they star Cary Grant.

Jan is married to Paul. She has one son, Max and a large extended family. She owns a rather badly behaved Flatcoated Retriever called Byron.

Picture by: Haddon Davies

Jan would love to hear comments and feedback from readers on her facebook page, Jan Harvey Author.

www.janharveyauthor.com